D1006870

Avalon Bay

A Jewelry Hunter Thriller

Ronald von Freymann

authorHOUSE®

AuthorHouse™
1663 Liberty Drive
Bloomington, IN 47403
www.authorhouse.com
Phone: 1-800-839-8640

© 2012 by Ronald von Freymann. All rights reserved.

No part of this book may be reproduced, stored in a retrieval system, or transmitted by any means without the written permission of the author.

Published by AuthorHouse   08/06/2012

ISBN: 978-1-4772-2019-1 (sc)
ISBN: 978-1-4772-2021-4 (hc)
ISBN: 978-1-4772-2020-7 (e)

Library of Congress Control Number: 2012910541

Any people depicted in stock imagery provided by Thinkstock are models, and such images are being used for illustrative purposes only.
Certain stock imagery © Thinkstock.

This book is printed on acid-free paper.

Because of the dynamic nature of the Internet, any web addresses or links contained in this book may have changed since publication and may no longer be valid. The views expressed in this work are solely those of the author and do not necessarily reflect the views of the publisher, and the publisher hereby disclaims any responsibility for them.

ACKNOWLEDGMENTS

I could not have written this novel without the understanding and support of my wife, Janet. Janet's reading, analyzing, and editing of the manuscript at each phase of its development were indispensable. Her insistence in including captivating description wherever possible was crucial to the refinement of the final product.

The patience of my editor, Dr. Dania Sheldon, to my shortcomings in writing and her prompt and thorough responses to repeated requests for additional edits of my work on short notice cannot be overstated.

The reading of various drafts by my wife, Janet, my daughter, Amy, who bought her years of experience in theater and television script writing to my drafts, Bob Heflin, Steve Perryman, Ted Tabor, Bill and Carol Correia, Rance Farrell, and Holly Ward were instrumental in steering my thinking in the correct direction to complete the novel.

A special thanks to Larry Strickland who had to interpret my meandering thoughts concerning what I wanted for the cover design.

The silent but consistent companionship of our pups, Schatzi and Misty and twenty-year old cat Bob made the hours of solitary writing bearable.

Finally, the professionalism, focus, and attention to detail of the AuthorHouse professionals completed the final touches to the project.

CHAPTER ONE

6:52 PM Friday, August 13, 2010
Top Level of the Parking Facility at Catalina Landing
Long Beach, California

Damn how did I get so far behind?

If Jenn missed the 7:00 PM express boat, the next boat was at 6:15 AM, tomorrow.

Everything had gone wrong for her today. She slammed shut the hatchback to her Subaru then raced to the elevator. Since the lower levels of the parking garage were full, she had to park at the top level. More delay and every second counted in the race to the 7:00 PM express boat. *Damn, the elevator is broken—again!* Now she had to run down three levels of step stairs to the street—no easy feat in three-inch sling back heels lugging a suitcase, laptop, and an oversized briefcase crammed with weekend work.

Usually, getting to the Catalina Landing on Fridays was a piece of cake. Jenn normally had time to change from business clothes to casual wear. Often she had time to take a judo class and still make the express boat. But today had been trouble since 6:47 AM when she had arrived at Raytheon. There was the typical end-of-the-week bullshit; the tedious routine of approving time cards followed by the weekly meeting with her boss and peers. The meeting had run long, much longer than it usually did. Then she met with her employees to share the crap disseminated at the prior meeting. That didn't go smoothly and also ran long. The weekly conference call with the Department of the Army was a disaster. With all the coordinating, communicating and updating, Jenn wondered how she got any work done. Then there was Lt. Colonel Harold Hughes, her primary liaison with the Department of the Army, a perpetual pain in the ass and professional time sucker. Today had been one of her worst days with him. *Thank god, he's on the short list to colonel—a promotion would likely lead to a reassignment, and that would make my job infinitely easier. He needs to get a life away from me.* Then she read the latest battlefield report—a task that always depressed her.

The entire day had been a nightmare.

She ran through the Catalina Landing express boat terminal building toward the wharf taking care not to slip on the highly polished concrete floor. She considered taking off her heels but that would take time and her arms were full anyway. She was pleased that she had gotten her commuter book pre-stamped. Express boat reservationists did not allow additional bookings within fifteen minutes of the boat's departure and some dumb regulation prohibited passengers from boarding an express boat within five minutes of departure. It would be tight. She glanced at her watch . . . 6:56 PM. *Oh my god!* She sprinted to the gate. The ticket taker was already placing a chain across the ramp to the mooring. *My kingdom for a tight blouse exposing cleavage and a short skirt—what am I thinking, I would never wear clothes like that. I'll have to settle for the poor-me flirtation bullshit and fat chance that will work. Express boat employees are chiseled from ice.*

She yelled as she approached the gate. "I'm sorry. There was traffic. I got off work late. My husband will meet me when this boat gets to Avalon and I have no way to contact him. I have a meeting tomorrow at 7:00 AM with the Island Company. I have to get on this boat."

Have I covered all the reasons? She thought. *After all, I only missed by a minute.*

The ticket taker recognized Jenn and then glanced at the ship's captain standing near the stern of the express boat. The captain was preparing to board the ship after having scrutinized each passenger as he or she boarded the ship. Jenn didn't know whether it was company policy for the captain to watch each passenger board the ship, or some kind of convoluted overkill dictated by the Patriot Act. If it was the latter, she was doomed.

She flashed an alluring smile.

"Hurry. You need to get to the gangway before the captain boards the ship," said the ticket taker furiously ripping the coupon from Jenn's commuter book.

7:01 PM Friday, August 13, 2010
Main Cabin of an Island Express Catamaran Express Boat
Long Beach Harbor, Long Beach, California

She made it.

Catching her breath, Jenn dropped into a window seat. The express boat was already pulling away from the dock. She had made it without having to sell her soul to the express boat company. When composed, she took inventory to insure she had remembered to bring everything with her and hadn't left anything in her car or the office in her mad rush to the boat . . . not that she could do much about it now if she had. At her side was a small suitcase—she did not need very much in the way of clothes or personal items, as she and her husband, Bill, had a condominium on-island with a full complement of those kinds of things. She had her laptop. She had her briefcase with the actuators sent by Afghanistan along with an extensive report of how and where they had been found. During the weekend, she planned to evaluate the electronics of the units and circumstances surrounding their discovery in Kandahar. Also in her briefcase were the last seven editions of the *LA Times* and the latest battlefield report, describing an improvised explosive device incident. Her heart sank at the thought of the IED incident. She stared at the report. Teeth clenched and face grimaced, she mumbled, "Damn it, Charley Alpha 5, why didn't you follow the standard operating procedures?"

Battlefield reports routinely found their way to Jenn's desk, as Raytheon's Director of Military Response to Insurgent Tactics.

Self-discipline, attention to detail, a degree in applied engineering from Carnegie Mellon and an MBA from the Tepper School of Business imminently qualified her for her job—a job she loathed. She could reel off from memory the horrible details of hundreds of such battlefield reports, each describing an instance surrounding the combat death of at least one American soldier. The reports infuriated her. She set this one aside but could not get the details out of her mind so she picked it up again and reread the transcript for at least the hundredth time:

Lieutenant James: *Charley Alpha 6 this is Charley Alpha 5. Over.*
Private Higgins: *Damn Sir, that's the largest IED I've ever seen.*
Lieutenant James: *Charley Alpha 6 this is Charley Alpha 5. Over.*
Private Higgins: *Our CO's in the middle of that smoke and debris.*
Lieutenant James: *I know—we have to help him.*
Private Higgins: *Sir, the SOP what about the SOP?*
Lieutenant James: *Screw the SOP. That's our CO. Radio Battalion and report the situation.*
Private Higgins: *Yes sir.*
Lieutenant James: *Charley Alpha 6 this is Charley Alpha 5. Over. Damn. Let's go, Higgins.*
Private Higgins: *Sir, Battalion says not to go there.*
Lieutenant James: *You heard wrong Higgins. The message was garbled.*
Private Higgins: *Sir, I understood it.*
Lieutenant James: *Charley Alpha 6 thi . . .*

It was a fucking mess and there seems to be no way out, thought Jenn. *The Muslim fundamentalist extremists' single-minded resolve to impose their beliefs on the rest of the world is nothing but bullshit. The free world stands by while moderate Muslims, heeding commandments decreed by the Qur'an, turn their back on the venomous behavior of their brethren. Unfortunately, the buck stops with our soldiers who are blown to bits by IEDs, lose body parts, come home brain damaged, or wind up with a sniper bullet in their head. Lieutenant James you should have known better—four dead and two wounded became eight dead because of your well-intentioned, but imprudent rescue attempt. Every IED has a twin with the first responder's name on it. You know that the Muslims extremists exploit our compassion for life. They know that a U.S. soldier will always go to the aid of a fallen comrade.*

Trembling, Jenn set the report on the seat next to her then sorted through a stack of unread *LA Times*. Locating the previous Sunday's edition, she opened it to the obituary section that reported military deaths in Iraq and Afghanistan. Obituaries had become her self-imposed gauge of success. She read, *"Omar Townsend, 33, of Rockland, Idaho. Sergeant Townsend . . ."*

Her margarita remained untouched during the sixty-five minute trip to Catalina Island. Jenn needed to unravel and longed for the time when she could quit her job, join her husband full time on Catalina, and pursue her passion. She smiled. She knew Bill would have made dinner reservations at the Portofino. He always took care of her.

CHAPTER TWO

(Three Years Earlier) 9:17 AM Wednesday, June 6, 2007,
Watson Financial Services, Metropole Avenue
Avalon, Santa Catalina Island, California

I must spend a fortune on post-it notes. Every scrap of paper in every file has at least one attached to it.

Getting his files in order had proven more challenging to Bill and a hell of a lot less stimulating than creating diversified portfolios. He sighed at the mess and hoped he had not been premature in opening an Avalon office. Two business locations separated by twenty-six miles of ocean were going to be work.

Lost in thought, he didn't notice the woman standing in the doorway.

"Hello, Mr. Watson. Do you always sit in the middle of the floor when you work?"

Bill turned his head toward the woman. She was over-dressed for a Catalina Island resident looking more like an employee at a New York auditing firm.

"Hi, I'm Tiffany Castilingo."

Bill nodded a greeting, got to his feet, and, extended his hand, "Hi . . . Bill Watson."

"Pleased to meet you, Mr. Watson."

"Please call me Bill. Come in. Floor sitting is part of opening a branch office and relocating files, not running a financial services company. It's good to meet you. It is Tiffany, isn't it?"

"Yes." She gave a brief smile. "I watched you build your office. You have done a great job. Can I help with your floor filing?"

"Thank you, no. I created the mess so I'll clean it up. Please, have a seat."

Bill pointed to a chair in front of his desk.

Bill's "office" was a storefront on Metropole Avenue. Since he planned to work without employees for at least a year or two, his desk was in the front of the store so he could greet his clients as they walked in. He had chosen this arrangement to create a sense of intimacy. Maybe later, when his practice had grown and he had employees, he would move his desk to the rear of the store for more privacy.

Tiffany stepped over and around the jumble of papers, files, and god knows what else to reach the chair. Once there, she had to look for another one.

"Oh, I'm sorry, let me help. These can go on the floor with the rest of the filing . . . there, that's better."

Tiffany sat down. Bill slid into a chair behind his desk, scrutinizing her. She had long dark hair and was tall and slim with perfect posture.

"I've been doing business in Avalon for a while but I don't think I know you."

"We've never formally met, however, in a town of thirty-seven hundred people eventually everyone gets to know or know about everyone. My husband is Tom Castilingo. When we married several years ago, I moved to the island."

"I apologize. I didn't make the name connection. How can I help you?"

"I want to work for you."

Bill was taken aback by her directness. "I'm flattered . . . this is a small company and I'm just getting started here. I have about twenty or thirty clients on the island and another hundred-fifty or so over-town."

"That's a great base. You should be proud."

"Thank you, I am. I haven't given much thought to hiring an employee. I'm just getting established on island—maybe when the business gets going—perhaps in a year."

"Your business is already going. Don't allow yourself to fall behind or your business will be going, going . . . *gone!*" chided Tiffany.

"I can appreciate tha . . ."

"I know your business is new but I want to work for you. I can make you more productive by me freeing you up to do marketing. You would more than make up in new business what you paid me. I was a senior marketing assistant to Jim Goosen at Merrill in Century City before I married Tom."

"Sounds like a big job."

"It was a great job, I loved it. I have two degrees from the University of Pennsylvania, one in marketing and one in finance, and extensive experience in financial services, but I haven't found an opportunity to use my skills in Avalon."

"It *is* a small town and opportunities for a person with your background and credentials are limited. My wife and I face similar issues. She works over-town but when I get this business established she'll move here."

"I can help that happen!" said Tiffany, immediately seizing the unexpected opening.

Bill instantly comprehended Tiffany's gambit.

"I worked for Jim for over five years. I'm Series 7, Series 66, Life, Health, and Property Casualty licensed."

Bill saw a way out of his perceived predicament. "I'm not licensed in Property and Casualty."

"That's okay. It's easy to get licensed. Then I can also work for you in that capacity. I'll do all the legwork. I'll sign up clients. I'll administer accounts. I'll handle the claims. We'll have another line of business. See, I've already figured out how to make you money."

Bill gazed thoughtfully at this persistent young woman. Her dark gray business suit, skirt just above the knee, patterned hose, and black sling-back heels accented her build. She looked out of place in Avalon. She knew the financial services business and had the designations that would make her an immediate asset, and her demeanor was excellent. Nevertheless, he was convinced that he could in no way afford her.

"Could you share with me what your duties were at Merrill?" asked Bill.

"I was Jim's assistant. I did all the inside work. I processed applications, set up the files, kept his calendar, and worked with the clients after the business was on the books. When he was out of the office or with clients, I executed trading orders. We were like a team." Reaching into her purse for a slip of paper, she continued, "Please take this. It has Jim's direct telephone number. Call him and he'll tell you about me."

Tiffany paused a moment and leaned closer to Bill. Her intense dark brown eyes stared directly into Bill's sky blue eyes. "Bill, I really, really, really want this position. I don't need the money but I miss working. I want to do things that interest and challenge me every day. Everything I've tried on this island has been just a job—a boring job. I can start today."

"My business is new, just getting started, maybe when the business gets larger—a few more clients."

"That's great but remember every client deserves the best, the best service, the best attention. I can do that while you grow the business. We're small but we'll grow. We don't have any competition on island."

We thought Bill. *She is talking as if she already works for me.*

Tiffany stood up and walked toward the back room. At the door, she looked into the room and then turned to Bill. Pointing at a desk in the room, she said, "This could be my desk. We can get another computer terminal and telephone line and we're in business."

She sat down at what apparently was now her desk and began to arrange the papers and files strewn across the desk.

"These are a mess they need to be categorized by account type."

She pointed to the files on the desk and then to three file cabinets along the rear wall of the room. "Are these for those?"

Apparently, this was now her office.

(Several Weeks Later) 7:47 AM Thursday, July 5, 2007
Watson Financial Services, Metropole Avenue
Avalon, Santa Catalina Island, California

"Good morning, Tiffany," said Bill cheerfully, walking into the office. "How's the day shaping up?"

"It should be an easy one. Stuff for you to sign is on your desk, and you have a few calls to return. The numbers and names are on your desk. And then there's Robbins."

"Robbins?" Bill looked puzzled.

"Yeah, she's called several times. She says her friends are making thousands and thousands in the market and she isn't. I tried to explain her account to her . . . she wants to hear it from you."

Bill looked at Tiffany. "It's hard to make thousands and thousands if you have only $1,500 invested."

Tiffany nodded, "I would think so unless you hit it lucky in the lotto. She doesn't get it. She said we must have been doing something wrong. Good luck. She'll be at home after nine."

"She's never has gotten it," Bill added. "Has Ken been here?"

"Come and gone."

"Thank god."

"He was gloomy. He told me that before I started here, you came in earlier. He misses you."

"I can't say the same about him," said Bill. "Thanks for putting up with him."

"He's a pain in the ass but harmless. He doesn't like to talk with me so he leaves quickly. It's harder to get him out of the office when you're here."

CHAPTER THREE

(A Year Later) 10:41 AM Tuesday, August 12, 2008
Watson Financial Services, Metropole Avenue
Avalon, Santa Catalina Island, California

"Is this where I apply to rent the condo?"

Startled, Bill looked up. He returned the Jackson file to the in-basket. A woman with straggly, dark-brownish hair stood in the doorway. She wore a dress, which desperately needed an iron, and contrasted sharply with Tiffany's sleek appearance and demeanor.

"Oh hi, I'm sorry. I didn't see you. The condo—ah yes, the condo . . . it's available. Please come in . . . have a seat."

The woman sat down in a chair in front of Bill's desk.

"I'm a little surprised. The ad runs in *The Islander* on Friday. How did you learn about the condo?"

"Someone at the bar told me."

"Bar?"

"I work at the Avalon Bay Bar."

"I see . . . I'm Bill Watson." Bill held out his hand, which she shook lightly after a brief hesitation. "It's a pleasure to meet you. It's my condo."

"I'm Laura Mulholland. Do you have an application?"

"It's right here . . . it's here . . . somewhere on my desk. Sorry, I'm a little unprepared. I expected applicants to start coming on Friday or the weekend. Ah yes, here it is. Do you need a pen?"

"I have one."

No small talk, no pleasantries. Bill thought it was better than the alternative—visions of Ken and his endless small talk came to mind. Laura looked about forty. Her nails were not manicured, her hands were calloused and dry, and she wore no makeup. Bill wondered whether she did landscaping or some type of manual labor. She seemed slim but you couldn't tell as her plain gray granny-style dress covered her body from neck to ankle. Bill found her detached demeanor somewhat unnerving.

"Any questions?"

"No," she said, without looking up.

Within minutes, she slid the application across the desk to Bill.

"I can pay now and move in today."

"Don't you want to see it?"

"That won't be necessary."

"Okay," said Bill matter-of-factly. "We can discuss move-in in a moment, but first things first. I need to review the application then we can talk."

Bill rapidly scanned her application.

"So . . . you've been on the island four months."

"Yes."

"And you live on Clarissa."

"Yes."

"You work as a bartender at the Avalon Bay Bar . . ."

"Yes."

". . . and as a tour guide with the Conservancy during the day."

"Yes."

"Are you full-time at the Conservancy and part-time at the bar?

"Both are part-time."

How do you like working two jobs?"

Bill waited for her answer but none came. Communicating with this woman was like talking to an answer machine. He continued, "How do you like working at the Conservancy?"

"It's fine."

So much for openness, he thought.

"The rent is $1,800 per month. Will you be able to pay that?"

"Yes, I have first, last, and security."

Bill rubbed his head in thought. "Well, I'm not sure."

"My mom can co-sign the lease. She lives in New York."

"I'm not sure . . . you're the first to apply and . . ."

"I can pay now and move in today."

Laura rummaged through her purse and pulled out a crumpled yellow nine-by-twelve envelope.

"That's $5,400 . . . correct?"

She started counting hundred-dollar bills before Bill could answer.

"One, two, three . . ."

"That isn't necessary right now."

Ignoring his comment, she continued to count.

"That's it—$5,400."

Laura shoved fifty-four hundred-dollar bills across the desk.

"My mom's name and telephone number are on this paper."

"Well, I guess so . . . err . . . no roommates, no subletting. You'll have to sign a lease."

"Of course. Besides my mom, you can speak with my bosses at the bar and the Conservancy. I'll move in today."

"Come back at one o'clock. If everything checks out, we'll drive out to Hamilton and you can look at the unit. Is that okay?"

"That's fine. Keep the money."

"See you then," said Bill as he scooped up the pile of bills. "Do you need a receipt?"

There was no response—Laura was gone.

"Tiffany?"

Tiffany's head popped around the doorframe.

"Not a clue, boss. I don't know of her and I've never seen her before. But then I've never been at the Avalon Bay Bar."

Typical Tiffany. At times, she was blunt—Bill usually appreciated her brevity, but in this case, her response was not much help.

So what am I going to do about Laura he wondered. *She's odd for sure, all business, few words . . . what the hell, I might as well rent to her. Fifty-four hundred cash in hand is a strong motivator.*

With that thought, he decided she would be okay, and if she didn't work out, he knew there'd be others lined up behind her.

CHAPTER FOUR

(Several Months Later) 11:49 AM Saturday, November 8, 2008
Building 18, Unit 42 (18-42), Hamilton Cove
Avalon, Santa Catalina Island, California

"Isn't it beautiful!" said Jenn, admiring a gold art pin in the likeness of Claude Monet's *Woman with a Parasol.*

"They all are, but you can't wear each piece—remember, you bought them for your business," said Bill. Gazing at her fondly, he mused, *what a contrast.*

Jenn dealt with the savagery, senselessness, and sorrow of the human aspect of the wars in Afghanistan and Iraq during her workday at Raytheon. To offset the sadness inherent in her job and bring a sense of balance to her life, Jenn had developed an Internet jewelry business she called The Jewelry Hunter. Jenn's passion was jewelry. Her first business line had been a collection of large gold pins. Each depicted an image from the painting of a famous nineteenth-century *plein air* artist. She longed for the time when she could dedicate herself fulltime to the jewelry business. For now, she worked at it on weekends on Catalina.

"I'm in the jewelry business; what better way to promote my merchandise than to wear it?"

"You sell on the Internet. Your customers can't see you."

"I know, but wearing the jewelry is psychological not just visual. It's a mindset thing . . . think positive."

Jenn had a knack of stretching reality to her benefit.

"I'm not denying you enjoying your business, you deserve that. However, you might want to consider tempering your fun with a little reality. Wearing jewelry you intend to sell is like working in a candy factory and eating the inventory."

"I know . . . but they're so beautiful it's hard to resist. I can't wait until I can be here with you full time and give more attention to my baby business. It's not as if my job at Raytheon isn't important or challenging, it is, but it's so frustrating. My effort all too often goes ignored. Jewelry is a hell of a lot more personally satisfying and certainly more fun than banging my head against the wall with the Department of the Army."

"I know, honey . . . the time will come. Tiffany is working out very well. She's exceeded my wildest expectations. It's as if she's been with my business forever. She knows the clients as well as I do, and in more than a few instances, better. Her vision when I hired her was right on the mark—she's made me money from the day she started."

Jenn glanced toward Bill and said, "She seems like an okay person too."

"She is. She's loyal and knows not only the ins and outs of the island but also the nuts and bolts of the financial services business. She's a perfect fit and she's good with clients. However, some of the things she says and does in her private life are a bit over the top."

"Is that so? I like the way she dresses."

"That can also be over the top."

CHAPTER FIVE

(Six Months Later) 2:17 PM Thursday, May 14, 2009
The Runway at the Airport-in-the-Sky
The Interior, Santa Catalina Island, California

Adventurous recreational flyers brave enough to negotiate the Airport-in-the-Sky's treacherous runway, and commercial carriers flying venerable DC-3s bringing fresh produce to the island are virtually the airport's exclusive users. The art deco architecture of the control tower and airport terminal building coupled with DC-3s taxiing on the runway in the background, recall a 1940s movie set. Operating under visual flight rules, the air traffic controller is more concerned with bookkeeping and the collection of landing and tie down fees than with controlling aircraft.

"What are you doing? And who is that man that ran into the sagebrush?" bellowed Marilyn, pointing at the manzanita underbrush. "Why were you unloading that plane? Where *is* this stuff going? What *is* this stuff? I want answers, young lady, and I want them now."

"This is for friends," said Laura pointing at the jeep and concocting a story as she spoke.

"Friends, what friends? You have no friends!"

"My friends, the ones down the road."

"Follow me, you brazen thief."

Laura's mind raced. Did Marilyn have information that could expose the Avalon Jihad? Why had the stupid evildoer followed her in the first place? Although Laura knew what had to be done, she continued to evaluate her options as she followed Marilyn. Laura had borrowed Conservancy jeeps many times under the pretense of becoming a better tour guide. So why did Marilyn follow her today? This was serious. Questions and consequences flashed through Laura's mind. Had Marilyn found out she was a terrorist? If so, had she told anyone? This could be a disaster . . . this could expose everyone . . . undo everything.

Aaliyah stepped close behind Marilyn, reached forward, and cupped her left hand over her mouth. Simultaneously, her right hand grasped the back of her head and jerked it counterclockwise while she hissed into Marilyn's ear, "Die . . . the torture is your reward. Inhabit the fire." The sound of the crack of vertebrae, followed by relaxation of Marilyn's struggle, assured Aaliyah that Marilyn's neck was broken. Marilyn's eyes swirled, her throat emitted a muted gurgle, her body quivered, and then it fell limp. Her lifeless form slumped into her killer's arms. Aaliyah stared at Marilyn. She had killed her first unbeliever—an evildoer! Allah would reward her. She would inhabit the garden.

Abu Tarek returned to help Aaliyah drag Marilyn's body toward the hanger. Just before they hauled the corpse behind the hanger, Aaliyah glanced back at the airport café and control tower. She didn't see anyone and concluded she would be able to cover up the murder.

Aaliyah glanced at Abu Tarek and asked, "Have you seen anything, anybody, any aircraft?"

"Only our plane . . . there hasn't been a tour bus since before noon."

"Good. The only witnesses would've been in the tower or at the café, and I haven't seen anyone in either place."

They slid Marilyn's body into the front passenger seat of her jeep and secured it with a seat belt. Aaliyah looked into Marilyn's dilated fixed eyes and spat, "You caused your own death, you stupid unbeliever! An agonizing torment awaits you." Then she mouthed a sura from the Qur'an, Women 4:49: "If they neither withdraw, nor offer you peace, nor restrain themselves from fighting you, seize and kill them wherever you encounter them. We give you clear authority against such people."

Aaliyah quickly changed from reciting the Qur'an and said to Abu Tarek, "I'll drive Marilyn's jeep; I've driven that one before, so evidence of me in it won't be a problem. You drive the other jeep. We'll dispose of her body at the compound, and then return to Avalon. It'll be after work when we get there so we won't we be noticed. The infidels will have already begun their frivolous nighttime gratifications. We'll park Marilyn's jeep near her home and return the other jeep to the Conservancy. I'll falsify the logbook. Reporting this to Khalid will be the worst part of our day."

2:29 PM Thursday, May 14, 2009
Escondido Road
The Interior, Santa Catalina Island, California

Escondido Road was deserted.

Islanders often drove the semi-improved road between Avalon and the Airport-in-the-Sky but only the adventurous ventured beyond. Escondido Road was dusty, potholed, and mostly rock-strewn compacted dirt. The Catalina Island Conservancy has the responsibility for regulating and maintaining the Interior but lacks sufficient capability to do so. A long, hot walk back to civilization awaited a person whose car broke down beyond the airport.

Aaliyah and Abu Tarek turned off Escondido Road onto a narrow, deeply rutted path overgrown with withered vegetation clinging to dusty, dry dirt. The path led to a narrow canyon that concealed the jihadists' compound, a cluster of old, low-slung, dry-rotted wood buildings. The faded brownish color of the buildings blended into the surrounding brownish landscape. Khalid had rented the compound over a year ago and the homegrown jihadists had taken up residence two months later.

The crisp snaps from the release of the safeties of the terrorists' antiquated Kalashnikovs echoed through the otherwise silent canyon. Five jihadists locked their eyes on the approaching jeeps.

Familiar with the approach of a single jeep, the jihadists were alarmed to see two approaching the compound. They braced for the worst. Short of the buildings, Abu Tarek stopped, got out, and waved his arms overhead as he walked cautiously toward his comrades. The jihadists recognized him. Relieved, they reverted to stand-down.

"Peace be with you and the blessings and mercy of Allah, Abu Tarek," said Mohamed.

"And upon you be the peace and Allah's blessings," responded Abu Tarek.

"Why two jeeps? Who's in the other one?"

"Aaliyah . . . We have trouble. An unbeliever confronted us at the airport. Aaliyah killed her."

"What can we do?"

"Dig a shallow trench for her body. Her evil soul awaits the fire."

Mohamed shook his head in disbelief while mumbling, "Evildoers never heed the message." Then pointing, he said more loudly, "Take her body to that patch of dirt and rock beyond the buildings."

"That will work," said Abu Tarek.

He motioned Aaliyah to drive the jeep beyond the buildings and follow Fikriyya, Saleem-Ali, Mohamed, and Abdel el-Shinawy.

Aaliyah stopped her jeep short of the gravesite and waved off the advance of two of the jihadists. "This is the body of an evildoer. Don't touch the jeep or her body while it's in the jeep. We don't want evidence that could link her to us."

Aaliyah kicked Marilyn's body out of the jeep. "Be quick, don't waste time with this. God, `azza wa jall*, commanded her death. Her soul will inhabit the fire." Motioning to the location of the gravesite, she added, "That's just to hide her body."

* * *

Aaliyah and Abu Tarek drove from the compound, waving silently to their comrades. Aaliyah dreaded telling Khalid about the day's unexpected turn. Aaliyah organized her thoughts while she drove, rehearsing in her mind various ways to tell Khalid of Marilyn's death. She knew none would placate him. The meeting would not go well.

Khalid would think poorly of the American jihadists—especially of her. As it was, he never had an encouraging or pleasant word for anyone except Mohamed and Abdel el-Shinawy. Somehow, she had to present Marilyn's murder in a positive manner.

She grimaced. *Fat chance.*

CHAPTER SIX

6:49 PM Thursday, May 14, 2009
East Whittley Avenue
Avalon, Santa Catalina Island, California

Aaliyah parked the jeep on East Whittley, noted the mileage, and dropped the keys into a side pocket of her purse. "After I speak with Khalid, I'll chuck these keys into the ocean."

Abu Tarek nodded.

To help placate Abu Tarek's anxiety, she added quickly, "This is working out as we planned. No one has seen us."

Several minutes later, Aaliyah backed the other jeep into the parking lot adjacent to the Conservancy.

"The lazy infidels don't work late, so no one will be inside," she said to Abu Tarek. "I have to alter the vehicle log. Wait for me in the alley behind the bar. If I'm not there in twenty minutes, you must tell Khalid what's happened so he can make plans. If I'm discovered in Marilyn's office, all of us may have to flee the island."

"I will tell him . . . he'll be angry," mumbled Abu Tarek barely inaudible.

This was all wrong, thought Abu Tarek. *I should be telling Aaliyah what to do. Why does she always take charge? She doesn't know her place. She is a woman.*

"I know. He'll be upset . . . he has to know. I will tell him if I'm there, you must if I'm not. If I'm discovered and detained, you have to tell him—you must tell him. Go, I will meet you, if Allah wills, Mighty and Majestic is He. And upon you be the peace and Allah's mercy and blessings."

Abu Tarek hesitantly responded by rote.

Aaliyah unlocked a side door to the Conservancy building and entered. She walked quickly but quietly along the hallway to Marilyn's office. Despite the dry heat, the air in the hallway smelled like a mildewed basement. She wondered whether there were buildings that smelled of mildew in Islamic countries. Immediately she chastised herself for such a frivolous thought and regained her focus. She thought about Marilyn's work patterns. If Marilyn followed her usual routine when she left her office during the day, she would return to her office before going home. Her office should be unlocked. Aaliyah turned the handle to the door of Marilyn's office. It opened. She breathed a sigh of relief.

Once inside, she saw an open book lying on the middle of Marilyn's desk—the vehicle logbook. She frowned and moved to the other side of the desk to look at it more closely. It was open to a page that showed pencil marks on several days that Aaliyah had borrowed a jeep. Things were beginning to make sense. Marilyn had marked each of the entries and circled the mileage. Aaliyah's hand flew to her mouth. She gasped, caught her breath, and thought, *what a fool I've been! This book is damning.* But she could not remove the book. A missing logbook would be a red flag in an investigation into Marilyn's disappearance.

Marilyn's marks were in pencil, whereas the actual postings were in ink. Aaliyah stared at the pages. If she made additional pencil entries and then lightly erased all the marks, no one would be able to connect the dots, and certainly not to her, at least. Being careful not to touch the book's pages in a way that would leave finger prints, Aaliyah made additional pencil marks of circles, checkmarks, and underlines on the pages already marked by Marilyn. She made similar marks on several pages before and after the pages, Marilyn had marked. Then she lightly erased all the penciling so only faint traces remained. It looked as if Marilyn had done a routine analysis of the log and erased her work. Then Aaliyah turned to the page for the activity of May 14th. She falsified the times and miles she had driven and initialed the entries. Then she forged Marilyn's initials, signifying approval for Aaliyah's use of the jeep. She made a partial entry that indicated Marilyn had taken a jeep at 2:47 PM, and had yet to return it. Aaliyah left the book open, as she had found it. A smile curled across her face—done.

Aaliyah left the building, being sure to lock the side door behind her, and unenthusiastically walked the half block to the alley behind the Avalon Bay Bar. Abu Tarek was pacing. His haggard face and furrowed brow showed concern, fear, or both. Walking, he sidestepped slimy, decaying garbage that had spilled from unemptied trashcans, and aged rubbish that had lain on the ground for weeks. The alley smelled like a combination of spoiled castor oil and damp, mildewed laundry that had been left a couple of days in a washing machine.

When Aaliyah appeared, Abu Tarek sighed in relief. "Thank God, Mighty and Majestic is He, you're safe. I couldn't think of how to tell Khalid what had happened. You'll have to do that." Abu Tarek's facial expression reflected what Aaliyah was feeling—today could be the end of the Avalon Jihad.

"I will. Don't worry jihad, is safe," she said with more confidence than she felt. "Despite Khalid's rage, we'll go forward. We have done a good job in covering up Marilyn's murder. There is no evidence and no witnesses. No one will know Marilyn's fate or link her to us until long after we've completed our work for Allah and probably not even then."

They entered the bar through the alley door.

"Remain here. I will go upstairs and speak with Khalid," said Aaliyah.

She wanted to hug Abu Tarek to help calm him, but quickly thought better of it. *Why did it occur to me to do such a thing?* she thought. *He would be uncomfortable if I touched him.*

Aaliyah walked up the ill-lit stairway, gingerly placing her feet on the narrow, unstable steps. At the top of the stairway, she stepped onto a worn, soiled, and fetid carpet running the length of a short, shadowy hallway to the second-floor prayer room. As she entered the prayer room, one of two remaining operational light bulbs in the hallway sputtered and went out, further darkening the shadows. She shook her head in disbelief.

She had expected Khalid to be in the prayer room, as she had called earlier to tell him that she had found the keys (the code for she had important information to share). Jihadists never discussed specifics on the telephone. If they had to call, they attempted to use public phones and interleaved their brief, nondescript messages with alternative-meaning words.

"Where is he?" mumbled Aaliyah, gritting her teeth and shaking her head.

She crossed the hall to Khalid's room, knocked on his door, and waited for permission to enter. A few moments passed. Then, at last, a response.

Aaliyah incanted, *"As-salaamu `alaykum."* She slipped into the room, being mindful to remain in the shadows and out of Khalid's direct sight.

Khalid responded indifferently, "And peace be upon you."

He did not know what she wanted. His tone expressed annoyance at the disruption. *Women always whined,* he thought. They were unreliable, uncommitted, and easily distracted. He believed the Avalon Jihad would be a piece of cake without the women. Women made lousy jihadists—jihad was the work of men.

"What prompted your earlier call?" His voice was curt. He looked at her with dark disapproving, cold eyes.

"Marilyn . . . my boss at the Conservancy."

"Yes, go on. What about this Marilyn?" said Khalid apathetically.

"She followed me to the airport and there she confronted and accused me of inappropriately using Conservancy vehicles. She was furious."

"So you told her that this was a one-time thing or something like that?"

"Not really. Abu Tarek was with me. She had watched us unload the plane before she confronted me. She said I hadn't been following established tour routes. She wanted to know what was in the jeep. I told her I was helping friends that live near Middle Ranch. She saw that one of the boxes contained electronics and another had the word 'dangerous' stenciled on it in large red letters. She called me a thief and said she would get to the bottom of what I was up to."

"What do you think she knows?"

"It's irrelevant. She's dead."

"You killed her!" shouted Khalid, bolting upright in his chair.

"I did. Abu Tarek and I took her body to the compound and buried it."

"Where exactly?"

"A few hundred feet beyond the buildings. No one will find her, at least not until long after we're done, and then it won't matter."

"Aaliyah, how could you be so stupid . . . how could you let this happen? You've compromised all of us and also jihad . . ."

Aaliyah already knew that.

". . . Discipline, Aaliyah, discipline, discipline, discipline . . . jihad demands total discipline. You have been irresponsible. You have an obligation to protect jihad, to protect your fellow jihadists. We are God's workers, `azza wa jall*. We are obligated to absolute secrecy and the precise execution of our plan. We've been over this many times. Why you and the others don't understand is a mystery to me. Where's your commitment to God, `azza wa jall*, Mighty and Majestic is He. Your actions are inexcusable. We cannot fail Allah, `azza wa jall*. It was your responsibility to insure that no one followed you. Sloppiness causes operations to fail, destroys confidence, destroys morale, and ultimately destroys jihad. Your sloppiness could get us killed. It could lead the police to us. Jihad is not a game."

"I know, I know . . . but we weren't discovered. No one will know what happened. It will look as if she took a jeep, left it at her home, and disappeared. It happens all the time on Catalina . . . in Avalon. One day a person is here, then poof, the next day they're gone. They get on an express boat and leave the island. No one hears from them again."

"You don't know that. You don't know if she told someone. They may be looking for her as we speak. They may know she followed you. They may be looking for you—for all of us." Khalid paused a moment. "Don't use a jeep until I determine the impact of what you have done. We may have to abandon the Avalon Jihad and leave the island."

"I know that. What do you want me to do?"

Khalid paused, his eyes again dark, cold, and cruel and he glared at Aaliyah. He thought women were the worst. They did not think, they could not think. He was disgusted that he had been forced to work with her and the other American converts, but he needed her skills. She was not expendable.

Finally, he snarled, "Presume everything is normal. When they tell you Marilyn is missing, act surprised and concerned, but continue to behave as if nothing out of the ordinary has happened. Do you understand?"

"I do."

Khalid continued to brood and frown and then repeated, "Don't use a jeep until I say it's okay." He thought for a moment. "I'll make arrangements for the pick-ups at the airport or I'll postpone the flights."

"Anything else?" said Aaliyah in despair. "`Annaa `aasif `u *dh ran*, I'm sorry I apologize."

Khalid frowned again.

In disbelief, and with anger in his voice, he said, "Sorry isn't part of jihad! I need to think on this. Brooklyn will not be pleased, Afghanistan will not be pleased, and surely, God *is* not pleased. He knows all, He hears all, He sees all, the record is written. You will get your record on the Day."

Khalid's statement implied things would not go well for Aaliyah on Judgment Day. When a Muslim meets Allah on that day, his earthly record is presented to him. If it is given to his right hand, he goes to paradise; if it is given to his left hand, he burns in the fire.

"Go and relieve that airhead, who substitutes for you at the bar, and remember, act as if nothing has happened. Keep your eyes and ears open. If you learn that we're coming under suspicion or the police are getting close, tell me. Now leave."

"*As-salaamu `alaykum*," said Aaliyah.

"*Wa `alaykum as-salaam*," mumbled Khalid.

Aaliyah slipped out of the room.

*   *   *

The jihadists disgust me at times more so than the infidels do, thought Khalid. *This is not like the World Trade Center bombing. Those jihadists may have been naïve, but at least they were committed to jihad, to Allah. They understood jihad was the will of God and never allowed anything to interfere with accomplishing it.*

Khalid had to think through this turn of events before telling Brooklyn. Undoubtedly Brooklyn would be incensed. Brooklyn did not like problems. Wisely, chosen words would be crucial when he communicated the incident.

CHAPTER SEVEN

(Several Weeks Later) 6:34 PM Tuesday, June 16, 2009
Escondido Road
The Interior, Santa Catalina Island, California

Enraged, Khalid drove to the compound.

I work with idiots and I work for idiots he thought. *The American homegrown jihadists are a sorry lot. They are committed to a vision of Islam that exists only in their naïve minds. They don't understand what real Muslims have endured. Our lands have been exploited, our cities have been stripped of their identity, and our natural resources have been confiscated. The homegrown jihadists at times disdain Islam and demonize the sacred Qur'an. They corrupt God's will to convert the world to Islam. I will do more than my part to make happen, what God wants. The American converts have not suffered as true believers have. They are not committed. They do not know what a commitment to God means. Their shallow belief make them untrustworthy—not steadfast. They aren't tested and they'll crumble at the critical moment. True jihadists are ordained to make the future the present. The American converts don't have that conviction.*

As he drove, his rage intensified.

Brooklyn and Afghanistan don't understand. Why wasn't I able to convince them of the lunacy of their misguided notion to include women in jihad? Their decision dooms the Avalon Jihad to failure unless I modify their errant plan. As always, I have to fix it.

Khalid shook his head angrily. He did not feel the bone jarring potholes, blistering heat, or blinding dust as he drove.

Al-Qaeda mistakenly attributes the abysmal record of terrorism since 9/11 to profiling. They're fools . . . they don't understand. They search for excuses instead of making things happen. I certainly would do better—and will when it is my turn.

His rage lifted as a smile crossed his face.

Al-Qaeda had come to believe that the physical appearance of Middle Eastern men prohibited their blending with American culture and therefore made them unsuitable for terrorist operations in America so Al-Qaeda directed Brooklyn to choose another course of action. Since Americans suspect anything remotely Islamic, Brooklyn mandated the use of Americans who had converted to Islam. In addition, Brooklyn specifically required that Caucasian American women be included in the Avalon Jihad.

Khalid believed the Avalon Jihad mandate was to test al-Qaeda's misguided notion about profiling but in doing so it put the Avalon Jihad in a position to fail.

Someone has to be the fall guy if al-Qaeda is wrong. The problem isn't profiling, thought Khalid, *it's the jihadists' lack of understanding and their ineptitude. Leaders chose poor operatives and didn't plan or execute well. Jihadists must be Islamic fundamentalists' first, mujahedeen second. Without interference from al-Qaeda, I could have been on and off this god-forsaken island in weeks—months at the outside—the others martyred. I would have recruited experienced Islamic terrorists whose motivation was martyrdom. Their eyes on the garden with constantly flowing streams of cool water and graced with beautiful companions. They would be driven, they would be easy to guide.*

Khalid detested al-Qaeda's directive. As far as he was concerned, it violated the Qur'an and the traditions. Brooklyn countered that the traditions permitted compromise, *halal*, in the pursuit of jihad. Exceptions to Islamic rules were allowed, even encouraged, in achieving an end that served God. Lying and misdirection were acceptable. In Khalid's opinion, the Avalon Jihad had become one messy compromise in *bid`ah* or innovation. Jihadists fought against *bid'ah,* not for it. He felt Brooklyn was wrong thinking and their edict relegated the Avalon Jihad to a senseless flawed experiment unless he saved the day.

Begrudgingly, Brooklyn had allowed Mohamed Aliz and Abdel el-Shinawy to remain with the Avalon Jihad, but insisted that all other members of the Avalon Jihad be homegrown American Islamic converts who spoke fluent English—this was blasphemy as far as Khalid was concerned. Worse than that, the Avalon Jihad *had* to include Caucasian American women. But Khalid had relented, as the alternative terrified him. He'd recruited Laura Mulholland who took the Arabic name "Aaliyah," Christine Olson ("Fikriyya"), Jeffery Tebbins ("Abu Tarek"), Wanda Peabody ("Faiza"), and Boris Massouli ("Saleem-Ali"). All were the best of the worst. Al-Hussein (Khalid's real name, unknown to the other Avalon Jihadists) knew that his troubles were just beginning.

Al-Hussein's thoughts drifted to a meeting in a Brooklyn mosque several years ago. His Imam, Abdul Humaid, had told him that Afghanistan had approved his concept for an attack against the Catalina Island tourist industry. The Catalina attack would be part of a larger, countrywide, coordinated plot designed to strike fear into the hearts and souls of ordinary Americans everywhere. The torrent of attacks would break the collective will of American's commitment to its evil *"war on terror"*—a war against God. When he was told this, a false wide grin hid Al-Hussein's disdain and skepticism.

Abdul Humaid told him al-Qaeda believed the attacks would draw millions of Americans to the sanctity of the Islamic faith, rather than face certain torture and torment from God and be doomed to taste the fire. Al-Hussein knew better. The Americans, although misguided to be sure and often fractious, were nonetheless a strong-willed people. The al-Qaeda attacks would unite them (perhaps for only a short time, as after 9/11) in intensified resolve.

What did that Japanese admiral say after Pearl Harbor? Al-Hussein knew the answer to his rhetorical question, "I fear all we've accomplished is to awaken a sleeping giant." Only outright total war was the solution. Al-Qaeda had not thought through its misguided strategy to a logical conclusion. The terrorist acts might be singularly successful in local areas, but the Americans would not roll over easily. Local Islamic terrorist groups would have to deal with the fallout. Al-Hussein thought al-Qaeda's leadership foolhardy.

As he turned onto the uneven dirt trail of the road that led to the terrorist's compound, the truck skidded in the dusty soil. The lurching was enough to return him to the present. When the truck drew nearer to the buildings and his jihadist recruits, he was Khalid again.

7:04 PM Tuesday, June 16, 2009
The Men's Prayer Room, the Terrorist Compound
The Interior, Santa Catalina Island, California

"I wonder what will happen to jihad. That must be why Khalid called this meeting," said Abu Tarek. I hope that God, `*azza wa jall*, has directed we go forward."

"It has to be something like that. He never comes here unless it's to berate us or lead *jum`ah*." said Faiza.

The dry-rotted one-by-eight vertical planks of the exterior walls of the buildings also functioned as interior walls. The mere sight of the buildings, constructed perhaps fifty, sixty, or over seventy years ago, brought to mind images of their imminent collapse. Scraps of crumpled cardboard crammed into the spaces between the ill-fitting planks prevented light from escaping to the outside. Similarly, thick blankets covered the door and window openings so that at night the structures blended into the darkness. The air inside the buildings smelled like partially dry sweat soaked gym clothes.

The men's prayer room was the largest room in the largest building of the dilapidated complex. Carpets and blankets littered the floor. The unkempt, austere room epitomized Islamic fundamentalists' perception of earthly life. Khalid, the Avalon Jihad's self-appointed Imam, conducted Friday prayers, *jum'ah,* in the men's prayer room. Women jihadists strained to hear the sermons while packed into a windowless room smaller than a walk-in closet located next to the men's prayer room. Aaliyah referred to it as a pantry. She experienced claustrophobia whenever she entered it.

Bombs were to be constructed in a smaller building at the south end of the compound. It was empty now except for three wooden tables, a chair, a table lamp, several unopened crates of useless equipment and material, and a few partially completed bomb parts. The jihadists awaited shipment of the remaining bomb-construction material: detonators, actuators, and Semtex. The remaining buildings in the compound served as living quarters and a mess hall.

"*As-salaamu `alaykum*, the Avalon Jihad is a go," announced Khalid as he strode into the room. "Brooklyn and Afghanistan have determined Aaliyah's indiscretions have not impacted our goals. However, there will be minor changes."

Aaliyah fumed inside. *What does Brooklyn know? They're unable to send us suitable equipment and materials, so how in the world could they assess the impact of Marilyn's murder? Brooklyn doesn't have a clue.*

"Brooklyn has authorized the use of the Conservancy's jeeps on a reduced basis so as not to create concern with the evildoers. Brooklyn is confident that Aaliyah's boss acted alone and did not share her concerns with anyone before Aaliyah killed her. The Conservancy and the police believe Marilyn left the island unexpectedly without telling anyone. They have lost all interest in the incident. According to the sheriff, it happens all the time."

Annoyed at Khalid's words, Aaliyah shook her head. She had told Khalid exactly the same thing right after she had killed Marilyn. *He never takes a women's opinion seriously. He prefers to rely on al-Qaeda associates insulated from reality three thousand miles away in Brooklyn.*

"This will slow down our preparation because equipment and supplies will be sent to us less frequently," continued Khalid. "The timeframe for our jihad has been extended a year so we'll be able to strike during the peak of the tourist season the summer after this one."

Aaliyah's murder of Marilyn *had not* been the reason for the delay. There was no delay. The timeframe had always been two summers distant in order to coordinate with the other attacks around the United States. Khalid had used Marilyn's murder to disclose to the jihadists for the first time, the actual timeframe.

"Why extend jihad?" yelled Abu Tarek. "Our exposure to the police will be drawn-out."

"So we will not be pressured to strike at an inappropriate time," cautioned Khalid. He ticked off the remaining tasks on his fingers. "We still have to obtain material to build the bombs, complete our training, and practice. Jihad against the West and their puppets during the last twenty years consistently failed due to inadequate planning, poor training, and sloppy execution. The Cole wasn't the intended target in Yemen. The first attempt to attack a U.S. ship in Yemen failed when a small boat overloaded with explosives sank moments after its launch."

Terrific, thought Aaliyah, *at least they had* explosives. *Al-Qaeda gave explosives to idiots in Yemen twice, but only gives us crap. Al-Qaeda created the delay with the Avalon Jihad, we didn't.*

"And in London, jihadists tried to explode a pair of car bombs. When that failed, they moved to an unsuccessful suicide bombing. One jihadist died of burns but no infidel died . . . no infidel tasted fire. Well-meaning but ill-prepared jihadists botched those attempts. It makes jihadists look inept . . . incompetent. *We* will not fail this time, infidels *will* die, evildoers *will* experience the torment, and unbelievers *will* taste the fire. Plan, plan, plan, practice, practice, practice and execute flawlessly," snarled Khalid, the volume of his voice rising as he spoke. "Remember 9/11, a near-perfect operation from start to finish. That's our goal—perfection."

"We're ready," hissed Saleem-Ali. "We're ready to go. All we need are explosives."

"We are *not* ready. We are not trained," retorted Khalid. "We need more detonators, explosives, and actuators. We need more training to be prepared physically to maneuver the bombs. Remember, each bomb weighs more than two hundred pounds."

"Jihad . . . martyrdom . . . we must get on with it!" yelled Saleem-Ali.

The others echoed his call.

Fikriyya screeched, "We're ready. We can make the bombs from local material, that's easy. We learned how to do that in Hamburg."

"We're ready," added Abu Tarek.

"*You—are—not—ready*. Brooklyn knows you are not ready. Afghanistan knows you are not ready. God commands, *`azza wa jall*."

"Brooklyn knows shit!" muttered Aaliyah, and then she silently chastised herself for inappropriate language.

"There'll be no further discussion. This matter is decided, this meeting's over." As he left the room, Khalid exclaimed over his shoulder, "*As-salaam `alaykum*."

CHAPTER EIGHT

10:33 AM Tuesday, December 8, 2009
The Bomb-Making Facility, the Terrorist Compound
The Interior, Santa Catalina Island, California

"How am I supposed to assemble bombs in this pitiful light? I can barely see the chips," mumbled Aaliyah.

Sweat poured from her temples and forehead. She rubbed a forearm across her brow and wiped her eyelids and face with a dirty rag. She looked at the materials assembled on the wobbly table and mumbled, "The solder is so old, and the contacts so small, it'll be a miracle if the joints hold up. The friggin' dust-filled air doesn't help matters. Brooklyn never sends what I need when I need it."

Aaliyah had become convinced that Brooklyn focused only on an outcome of haphazard mayhem without considering the logistics, resources, or materials to achieve that goal. Brooklyn just did not get it.

"*As-salaamu `alaykum.*"

"*Wa `alakum as-salaam,*" responded Aaliyah by rote without looking up.

"How are the bombs we build for Allah coming?"

Startled by the question, Aaliyah looked up. It was Khalid.

What's he doing here? She wondered. *Other than leading jum'ah, he never comes to the compound and he's never been in this building before. What does he want? Probably to give me crap.*

"As well as can be expected," said Aaliyah seizing the opportunity to say her mind, however inappropriately. "Material and parts just dribble in, and more often than not they aren't what I expected or need. When Brooklyn sends what I don't need, I have to make do. I've got more than a dozen subassemblies in various stages of completion." Aaliyah pointed to dust-covered parts of bombs scattered on the two narrow tables along the far wall. "A schedule of materials and when I can expect them would be helpful."

Khalid looked at the mess strewn around the room. "It looks like you are making good progress."

"How would you know? You've never been here before."

He ignored her comment.

"When do we need the bombs?" she asked.

"Remember what the Prophet told us: 'Islam is the religion of the sword.' Brooklyn confirmed jihad would be this summer. We'll have everything by next month."

"They tell us that every month."

"Aaliyah, you must show respect."

"Respect . . . what does that have to do with making bombs? The copper wires that I have personally stripped out of the walls of this dilapidated hellhole have to be more than seventy years old. You would think Brooklyn would send new wire so I wouldn't be concerned about using this junk to make bombs. Poor-quality bombs could compromise jihad. You would think *they* would show respect for *us*. I have four unrelated responsibilities in the Avalon Jihad and I do the work of six. If the bombs don't work, everything else is down the toilet—*that's what's important and no one seems to care.* The focus should be on the bombs . . ."

Khalid recalled the incident of al-Qaeda failing to consider the proper size of the boat used to carry explosives to destroy the Cole. Aaliyah's observations could be correct. Quickly reconsidering, he promptly dismissed his incongruous inference.

". . . How to books to construct sophisticated bombs that fit into scuba tanks don't exist. I get no help, no support, no encouragement, and certainly *no* respect—only criticism."

"Aaliyah, when you're in God's employ, `azza wa jall*, you do his bidding without questioning—Allah knows best. The Qur'an says, 'You may dislike something although it is good for you. He has promised all believers a good reward. Those that strive are favored with a tremendous reward above those that stay at home.' Your work will be rewarded."

"Respect." Aaliyah spat out the word, not heeding Khalid's preaching. "We've been here almost two years and have little or nothing to show for it. We're lucky the police haven't discovered us and marched us off to Guantanamo Bay. All I have to show for my work are large modified duffel bags with wheels, a mismatched collection of partially completed bomb parts, and minuscule amounts of expensive potentially unstable explosives decaying in scuba tanks. When will the rest of the Semtex . . ."

"Aaliyah, enough, *Allaahu a `lam*, God knows best. We serve God, `*azza wa jall*."

"I know all that . . . when will the rest of the Semtex get here? The small amount I have received is pressed into scuba tanks. Who knows how long it will maintain its strength in that environment? I certainly don't. The detonator and actuator subassemblies are in worse shape. I've had to redesign and retool each subassembly every time a shipment of incorrect or substandard components arrives. If Brooklyn had our level of commitment, the Avalon Jihad would already have been evening news. American unbelievers would wonder how it had happened again and I'd have my ultimate reward—to die a martyr, if God wills, `*azza wa jall*."

"The explosives will be here soon."

"When is soon? I need results, not promises."

"Brooklyn knows what God tells them, `*azza wa jall*. When do you expect to finish your work?"

"What! Haven't you listened? Without knowing when I'll get proper materials, how can I possibly answer your foolish question? Ask Brooklyn."

Khalid frowned, his dark eyes showing concern.

Aaliyah continued. "If I'm forced to complete my work using unproven, substandard materials that may not work as we expect, I won't be responsible for the senseless slaughter of my brothers and sisters; that'll be on your ticket or, more likely, Brooklyn's."

Aaliyah realized she had gone over the top—way over the top. The Qur'an and the traditions forbade Muslim females speaking to a male as she just had. *I have to get a grip on myself.*

Khalid said nothing but thought. *Why did I come here to be belittled by a woman? She doesn't know her place.* He stomped out of the building.

Aaliyah grimaced with dislike. *What a jerk.*

*   *   *

Outwardly calm, Khalid fumed inside as he walked from the building. Aaliyah's attitude disgusted him, as did the presence of women in the Avalon Jihad.

Muslim men do not behave as Aaliyah just did, he thought, *and she shouldn't either. Fortunately, for her, this is not Saudi Arabia. Brooklyn and Afghanistan don't know what a horrible mistake they've made. Brooklyn is ignorant of the sayings and traditions of the Prophet. Women have their place as allowed by the Qur'an. Jihad is not that place. Aaliyah is a perfect example but unfortunately, she is not expendable.*

Khalid shook his head as he recalled the Marilyn incident. Aaliyah almost single-handedly botched the Avalon Jihad.

She is a fool.

CHAPTER NINE

Before First Light, Friday, January 15, 2010
The Canyon beyond the Jihadist Compound
The Interior, Santa Catalina Island, California

Faiza stumbled for the third, fourth, or fifth time—she had lost count, not that it mattered.

Bone-chilling mid-winter cold in Southern California Catalina is always unexpected, always seems out of place, but the weather was not the cause of Faiza's precarious situation. She cursed her stupidity. Her thoughtless positioning of rocks in her backpack unbalanced her stride so she could not keep up. When would she learn?

Equipment adjustments are not permitted after a conditioning run begins. Jihadists suffer if their equipment and clothing are improperly adjusted. The resultant hardship was intended to send the message that poor planning, poor preparation, and poor attention to detail inevitably led to poor execution, and poor execution inevitably led to failure. Khalid and Mohamed drilled precise planning, selfless conditioning, and flawless execution at every opportunity. Faiza's predicament was her own fault.

"Keep up. Faiza, you are falling behind! If you can't keep up on a simple run, how do you expect to succeed on jihad?" barked Mohamed.

"All I need to do is adjust my pack; it'll only take a few moments," she panted.

"No. Next time you will do it right. Don't fall behind, don't fail God, `azza wa jall*, don't fail us and don't fail yourself. You must condition yourself to be mentally nimble as well as physically tough."

Mohamed, a Saudi Wahhabi of single-minded fury, despised anything associated with Western culture—although he made exceptions now and again, like when he wore Levis and a polo shirt over his sinewy tall frame and driving a Corvette. A consummate Islamic fundamentalist, he was cruel, tough, hardened, and angry. Mohamed had modeled the Avalon Jihad's training and conditioning program after Taliban and al-Qaeda training camps in Afghanistan. He accepted no excuses for failure. As he watched and listened to Faiza, he knew she was expendable and had to go.

Mohamed is right, thought Faiza, *but he's a man*.

Mohamed ran with a heavier backpack than did everyone else. He also draped a twenty-seven-pound scuba weight belt around his shoulders as a self-imposed badge of superiority.

Where is Khalid? thought Faiza. She frowned.

Khalid never participated in runs or, for that matter, any physical conditioning. Although he was also on jihad, except for *jum'ah*, he never involved himself in day-to-day training. What did he do in Avalon holed up in the prayer room above the bar?

Faiza was completely committed to jihad and to God. She knew she would prove herself when the time came. On Judgment Day, she would earn the reward and live forever in the garden laced with streams. Allah would place her record into her right hand. For now, though, the run was another test and the most difficult parts lay ahead. She would do better. Silently she mouthed, "*Laa hawla walla quwwata illaa billaah*, there is neither power nor strength save by Allah," and staggered on.

Eleven Minutes after Sunrise, Friday, January 15, 2010
The Terrorist Compound
The Interior, Santa Catalina Island, California

Faiza sighed with relief when the compound came into view.

The others had been there for more than fifteen minutes. Her dismal performance compounded her grief and anxiety. She had missed the prescribed time for *salat* and hoped God would understand. Inwardly she cringed. In her mind, she could hear Mohamed's anger for the second time in as many hours. He would portray her as undisciplined, unfit, and soft—a liability to jihad. If only she could switch responsibilities with Fikriyya. Faiza was sure Fikriyya's schedule was easier. As cook, Fikriyya seldom left the compound. Faiza knew she could do Fikriyya's job.

"Hurry, Faiza," urged Aaliyah. "We have calisthenics before breakfast."

Aaliyah and Faiza lived in Avalon, their jobs with the Conservancy and the Island Company giving legitimacy to their identities. Their in-town cover permitted them to monitor gossip and rumor, and complete errands, such as grocery shopping and buying equipment and supplies, without attracting suspicion. They were American-born, but more importantly, looked American-born. They were the eyes and ears of the Avalon Jihad. Faiza and Aaliyah envied Fikriyya. They believed her schedule allowed her time to learn more about her adopted faith and become more familiar with all aspects of the Avalon Jihad. They were sure Fikriyya had more time to rest and recharge. She did not have to split her time between town and the compound—she did not have to be on her game 24/7. Aaliyah and Faiza thought their duties and responsibilities more demanding than Fikriyya's, yet their efforts were not as appreciated.

Faiza decided that after *jum'ah* she would speak with Khalid. He was rigid in his ways and at times appeared detached from the objectives of the Avalon Jihad, but she knew she could make a case for lightening her burden.

7:26 AM *Friday, January 15, 2010*
The Terrorist Compound
The Interior, Santa Catalina Island, California

"Where is Faiza?" yelled Mohamed.

The calisthenics program required an equal number of men and women. Designed to optimize conditioning, strength, and hand-eye coordination, it placed men and women in situations abhorrent to Muslims. The Qur'an dictated that unrelated Muslim men and women not speak with one another and not even look at one another. Al-Qaeda's homegrown mandate forced men and women to work in close physical proximity. The arrangement, contrary to their faith, created enormous, abnormal personal and cultural stress.

"Where is Faiza?" repeated Mohamed, his voice elevated.

"Performing *salat*, she finished the run after us," said Abdel el-Shinawy.

"We're aware she failed us. She's undisciplined and her behavior is unacceptable."

Mohamed singled out each of the jihadists with a purposeful glare as he demeaned Faiza.

"Let's do an exercise that doesn't require a partner," proposed Abu Tarek.

"That's a good idea," added Saleem-Ali.

"I agree," chimed in Aaliyah.

"That's not a good idea . . . it's a terrible idea," snapped Mohamed. "This isn't a democracy. Democracy is not the way of God, `*azza wa jall*. Where's your dedication, discipline, and alignment with God, `*azza wa jall*, and dammit, where's Faiza?"

That's inappropriate language, thought Aaliyah. *That's not the way of God.*

"I'm coming, I'm coming. My backpack made me late, I'm sorry . . . I'm ready."

"It wasn't your backpack that made you late. It was the incompetent way you packed your backpack that made you late," shouted Mohamed.

"You're correct. I am sorry, `*anna `aasif `u dh ran*."

Faiza partnered with Abdel el-Shinawy.

To deflect Mohamed's attention from Faiza, the others partnered and prepared for exercise.

"Enough," said Mohamed. "Assume the attack position."

Each jihadist faced his make believe adversary . . . feet shoulder width apart and hands and arms at the ready. Instead of giving the expected command to attack, Mohamed froze them in place.

"You're all undisciplined. You perform poorly, without enthusiasm, and make excuses," he ranted. "Your behavior must change. We are on jihad. We do the bidding of God, `azza wa jall`. If any of you fail, we all fail. You must discipline your minds and bodies so as not to compromise jihad.

"According to Women 4:95, 'although He has promised all believers a good reward, those that strive are favored over those that stay at home. Persecution is worse than killing. They will not stop fighting until you reverse your faith.'" He continued in his own words, "We don't negotiate, we don't make excuses, we don't make alliances, and we don't indulge in idle talk. We act. We act without remorse, without hesitation, and without a need for justification. We do not need justification to honor God's will, `azza wa jall`. We do not need reasons for our acts other than His reasons. If you cannot accept that, you are a burden—you flirt with *takfir*, becoming apostate. Americans are unbelievers—infidels. They are gullible and do not follow the straight path. God, `azza wa jall`, does not guide those that don't follow the straight path. They do not deserve His mercy and guidance unless they become believers.

"The Bee 16:17 tells us, 'Those who reject God after believing in Him and open their hearts to disbelief will have the wrath of God upon them and a grievous punishment awaiting them. This is because they love this world more than the one to come and God does not guide those who reject Him.' Our jihad, our destiny, is to revive the widespread terror of 9/11 and deliver a civilization of unbelievers to Islam. We must force the American unbelievers to take the path guided by God, `azza wa jall`. We will strike terror into those who do not believe, those who turn the other cheek, and those not on the straight path. God, `azza wa jall`, is the answer. We deliver his message. He is the Mighty, the All Knowing. Jihad has always returned misguided civilizations to the obedient, moral, and ethical mandate of God, `azza wa jall`."

Mohamed paused and with his cold, dark eyes looked in turn into the pain-stricken eyes of each jihadist. His cruelty knew no depth and he exulted in their unspoken plea to liberate their burning muscles. He knew *they* knew that they had brought this on themselves.

"Attack!"

CHAPTER TEN

Noon, Friday January 15, 2010
The Men's Prayer Room at the Terrorist Compound
The Interior, Santa Catalina Island, California

"America is foul and empty. The Qur'an tells us to, 'read in the name of your lord, obey, and worship God. Anyone who opposes jihad is an enemy of God. An agonizing torment awaits those who insult God's messenger,'" preached Khalid.

Khalid was the Avalon Jihad's self-appointed prayer leader, its Imam for all practical purpose. However, Khalid avoided all other involvement in the Avalon Jihad's day-to-day training and seldom visited the compound except to lead *jum'ah* each Friday. *Salat* is the daily prayer routine of devout Muslims, a precise worship performed individually five times a day every day. *Jum'ah* is communal prayer. It substitutes for the Friday noon *salat* and is led by an Imam.

"Jihadists loathe America's support for Israel, as well as America's decadent and intolerant culture," continued Khalid. "America and Israel are committed to the destruction of Islam. The Qur'an tells us, 'not to take the Jews and Christians as allies. They are allies only to each other. Anyone who takes them as allies becomes one of them. Those who reject God after believing in Him and open their hearts to disbelief will have the wrath of God upon them and a grievous punishment awaiting them. This is because they love this world more than the one to come and God does not guide those who reject Him.' Driven toward the reverence of martyrdom, Jihadists embrace the wonders of the All Mighty, 'Their eyes are on the garden graced with constantly flowing streams of cool water and populated with beautiful companions like hidden pearls, a reward for what they used to do. They will hear no idle or sinful talk, only clean and wholesome speech. They will dwell with incomparable companions. We have specially created virginal houris, loving, and of matching age. Jihadists are comfortably seated on couches arranged in rows and we pair them with beautiful wide-eyed maidens.' Islamic jihad is the noblest of human endeavors to please the All Mighty, the All Knowing, the All Seeing."

Khalid looked out at his captive congregation. His eyes flashed obvious contempt at the American homegrown converts to Islam as he continued in his own words. "America is the great Satan, a fountain of evildoers, a place where infidels live. We must destroy America as He has destroyed past civilizations of unbelievers. Christians and Jews who oppose Muslims are nothing more than allies of each other, pathetic unbelievers, and the spawn of Satan. To kill those that oppose Islam is a legitimate and appropriate response. It is the obligation of jihadists. *Just kill them, kill them all! It is okay to kill them!* 'If they turn on you then seize them and kill them wherever you encounter them.' Never forget Mohammad's proclamation: 'Islam is the religion of the sword.'

"The Qur'an tells us, 'If you live in my property and you don't pay rent, you get out. Jihad is to get you out. The world is the property of God. God owns everything. He is all-seeing He is all-hearing He is all-knowing. If you don't worship Him, you get out. How do we get unbelievers out? We kill them. If anyone alters God's blessing after he has received it, God is stern in punishment. Do not hate evil because it could be God's gift to you.'

"Heed the example of nineteen brave observant mujahedeen, the 9/11hijackers. It only took a few brave, steadfast believers to bring *hiraba,* terrorism, to America. We will not only emulate their success, we will exceed it. *Hiraba* brings people to their knees. *Hiraba* changes everything. *Hiraba* serves God, `azza wa jall*. Now is a satanic time. Pathetic American infidels define the right way and the wrong way different from God's way, `azza wa jall`, and different from the Qur'an. The unbelievers are not steadfast; they do not follow the straight path. God, `azza wa jall`, does not guide those that do not follow the straight path. Innovation is the gravest of sins against Islam, against God, `azza wa jall`. Innovators and unbelievers are *takfir*. They must die. It is the only punishment. 'If anyone seeks a religion other than Islam, the complete surrender and devotion to God, it will not be accepted. He will be one of the losers in the hereafter. It is the only torture. He will inhabit the fire. He will reside in Hell, a horrible punishment.'"

Khalid continued for another hour.

"God is great! God is great! God is great!" cried the jihadists at the end of Khalid's sermon.

Khalid returned to his chair physically exhausted but mentally exhilarated by his sermon of condemnation. He loved this part of jihad. He imagined how Muhammad had felt when he preached to the Khazradites and Koreishites. From his chair, Khalid exclaimed, "The power to change the world, God so wills, `azza wa jall`, 'I witness none deserves worship except God, I witness that Muhammad is the messenger of God.' Peace be upon you, and the blessings and mercy of Allah." Khalid had finished his sermon. He acknowledged the exuberance of the male jihadists with a wry smile and announced, "*Jum'ah* is over—go about your day."

*　　*　　*

"Khalid . . . Khalid . . ." called Faiza. "I need to speak with you."

"Faiza, what do you want now?" said Khalid with irrefutable revulsion.

Faiza peeked around the door to Khalid's room then slipped inside, her eyes cast downward.

"I am not doing well. My schedule exhausts me. Every day I travel from Avalon to the compound and then, if I have to conduct a tour, back to Avalon. I'm physically and mentally drained."

"So, what do you want from me?" Khalid had not anticipated Faiza's plea, although he knew she was not up to her tasks. "Fighting is ordained for you, though you dislike it. 'You may dislike something although it is good for you or you may like something although it is bad for you.' What matters is that you choose the straight path."

Whenever possible, Khalid sought to legitimize his rambling pronouncements by quoting the Qur'an.

"I don't know for sure . . . an adjustment in duties, perhaps a swap with Fikriyya."

"Why? We're all engaged in jihad. We're in this together. 'Although He has promised all believers a good reward, those that strive are favored with a tremendous reward above those that stay at home.' Learn from the Qur'an, it illustrates the straight path. You need to be disciplined and subservient. *Allaahu a`lam.*"

"But . . ."

Khalid scowled at Faiza. "Enough . . . there is no but. The subject is closed. Since you do not have to go Avalon today join one of the other teams and better prepare yourself for jihad. Rehearse your role," he concluded coldly. "*As-salaamu `alaykum.*"

"*Wa `alaykum as—salaam,*" responded Faiza meekly.

Khalid continued to glower at her as Faiza left his room. *American women,* he thought, as he shook his head. *American women don't know their place.*

CHAPTER ELEVEN

10:34 PM Thursday, February 25, 2010
The Prayer Room above the Avalon Bay Bar
Avalon, Santa Catalina Island, California

Aaliyah flipped a scarf-encased cable over Faiza's head, tightened the garrote-like death loop around her neck, thrust a knee into the small of her back, and dragged her backwards.

"God commands me," said Aaliyah. "'If anyone alters God's blessings after he has received them, God is stern in punishment.' Faiza, why did you take up with a drug dealer?"

Faiza flailed her arms as if to say, "What are you talking about?" She gasped for air . . . her heart beat wildly. She fought the assault but to no avail; it was an uneven contest. She desperately exhausted her full repertoire of defensive techniques. But Aaliyah was superior in technique, physically stronger, and most importantly, had the advantage of surprise.

Faiza and Aaliyah had trained together, helping one another become proficient in the roles of attacker and defender now playing out in a real life-and-death struggle. Aaliyah neutralized each of Faiza's defensive movements. Aaliyah's arms ached, her arm muscles twitched, her back muscles burned. Surprising to her, actual killing was physically exhausting and mentally draining. Faiza died slowly, her death throes lasting a full three minutes. When Aaliyah was able to relax her muscles, she released her death grip. Faiza slumped to the floor. Dispassionately, Aaliyah fumbled for Faiza's carotid artery and waited several seconds. No heartbeat. She was definitely dead. Aaliyah's execution had been flawless.

Now came the difficult part of the strategy. She and Mohamed had to dispose of the body. In anticipation of Aaliyah's successful completion of her gruesome assignment, Khalid and Mohamed reentered the room. Khalid verified that Faiza was dead. He didn't trust Aaliyah's judgment—Khalid trusted no woman's judgment. "She's dead," announced Khalid. "Take her body to the dump, but first both of you insure the bar is clear."

After Aaliyah and Mohamed left to check out the bar, Khalid stuffed several small bags of heroin, a used hypodermic needle, and four hundred dollars in small-denominated, mostly counterfeit bills into Faiza's purse. Then he opened a mini-bottle of scotch and splashed a small amount of the liquid on her blouse and lifeless face. It would look like a drug deal gone badly or the tragic end to a violent disagreement between lovers. He grimaced in disgust. Then a ghastly smile glimmered across his gaunt face.

Downstairs, Fikriyya had already run off customers who had come to the bar on this bone-chilling evening.

Aaliyah and Mohamed entered the bar and looked around.

"Are all the customers gone? Are any in the rest-rooms?" questioned Aaliyah.

"They all left over half an hour ago," said Fikriyya. "The Marlin and the Locker Room are open; no one will be back."

"Good. We'll be down in a few minutes."

Aaliyah and Mohamed returned to the prayer room.

"The customers are gone. My cart is on Descanso."

Khalid watched as Aaliyah and Mohamed dragged Faiza's body to the stairwell. Tossing Faiza's purse to Aaliyah, he said emphatically, "Don't forget to leave her purse with her."

Aaliyah looped the purse around Faiza arm.

At the bottom of the steep, narrow stairwell, Aaliyah said, "Mohamed, make one last check before we drag her through the bar."

The dimly lit bar was eerily quiet. Fikriyya stood by the front door to ward off any customers that might approach. When Mohamed poked his head into the bar from the stairwell, Fikriyya announced, "All clear."

Aaliyah and Mohamed walked Faiza's body through the bar. Aaliyah supported her under her left arm, Mohamed under her right. Then they walked the corpse out the door of the bar. "*Masaa' ul khayr*, goodbye, Fikriyya," whispered Aaliyah over her shoulder as she and Mohamed left the bar. Outside, they turned left, walked to Aaliyah's cart, and fastened Faiza's body in the passenger seat with the seat belt.

10:57 PM Thursday, February 25, 2010
Pebbly Beach Road
Avalon, Santa Catalina Island, California

Late-night traffic in Avalon was unpredictable. While Aaliyah expected there to be little traffic, people and golf carts might still be on the streets. She drove to Crescent Avenue and then south on Pebbly Beach Road. Pebbly Beach Road wound through the service-support area of Avalon: the freight line office and warehouse, the Island Company's vehicle maintenance facility, the heliport, the boatyard, the Edison plant, and terminated at the dump.

"Mohamed, see those people?" said Aaliyah, nodding at the Edison plant. "It's a shift change. Do not look at them. Look straight ahead or at me. Pretend we're in conversation, ignore them."

Aaliyah and Mohamed faked indifference.

Several workers watched the cart as it passed the plant. One worker commented to the group that it was odd that people would be on the road this late at night. Another observed that there were residences further down the road and probably they're headed there.

Aaliyah drove the cart without changing speed or direction or looking at the Edison employees. She made a mental note to allow sufficient time to pass before returning to insure the shift change was completed. Even better, a different route back to town would insure they weren't observed. Near the dump, she turned off the headlights. Aaliyah had checked out the dump earlier in the day, memorized the location of the piles, noted the composition of each pile, and had tentatively chosen the pile to receive Faiza's body.

Khalid would be proud of me she thought.

Quickly, she realized her foolishness. Khalid would not be proud of her. To Khalid, women were worthless except as baby machines. He would never tell any woman, especially Aaliyah, she had done a good job. In Khalid's opinion, only men had the capacity to do good jobs.

Aaliyah stopped the cart on the pavement about ten yards from the dump. She did not want cart tracks in the soft dirt, those could come back to haunt her during the investigation that she knew would follow. She pointed to the far side of the dump. "We'll dump Faiza behind that trash pile. We'll have to carry her."

Mohamed jumped off the rear seat to assist Aaliyah. With him supporting Faiza's shoulders, and Aaliyah holding her legs, they carried her body through the dump.

"We'll put her in the pile to the left of the shed."

The stench of rotting fish and vegetables, mingled with the odor of rancid grease hung in the air and infiltrated their nostrils as they neared the pile. Most of the trash in the pile had come from restaurants.

"Perfect," said Aaliyah, smiling. "The putrid odor will mask Faiza's decaying body.

Aaliyah and Mohamed dropped Faiza's body onto the slimy ash-matted muddy ground, the result of years of burning decaying trash and garbage and then hosing it with salt water. They hollowed out a depression about a third of the way up the rear side of the pile and tossed Faiza's body into it, then covered her with less decomposed trash from another part of the pile.

"With any luck, no one will discover her body for days . . . maybe not until Monday. By the time they find her, dozens of trucks will have obliterated our footprints. Good job, Mohamed."

He nodded.

Satisfied they had properly disposed of Faiza's corpse, Aaliyah and Mohamed drove back toward the Edison plant and Avalon.

Although the Edison workers were gone, Aaliyah insured she and Mohamed would go unnoticed by driving the golf cart left onto Wrigley Road and over the step hill down into Avalon.

12:21 AM Thursday, February 26, 2010
Wrigley Road
Avalon, Santa Catalina Island, California

While Aaliyah drove, she concluded the curious Edison plant workers were of no concern. She felt elated their mission was a success. "We did good . . . no one will know who killed Faiza or who brought her to the dump," she said to Mohamed.

"Maybe the police will connect her to the drug dealer and then he'll be gone too," he said.

"That would be great; we can only hope."

She mused, that Faiza's situation called to mind Cow 31:6. "But there is the sort of person who pays for distracting tales, intending, without any knowledge, to lead others from God's way, and to hold it up to ridicule. There will be humiliating torment for him." Aaliyah felt confident that the nonbeliever drug addict who had taken advantage of her former friend, would also taste the fire. Surely, both Faiza and the drug dealer would inhabit hell.

Aaliyah had known Faiza since their days at Berkeley. She'd liked Faiza—they had a similar outlook on life, and together they had embraced Islam. She and Faiza, along with Fikriyya had performed shahadah, the declaration of faith. The three then drifted deeper and deeper into radical Islam. They became committed to jihad because it made them feel whole. They looked forward to martyrdom and believed it was their fate as the date for the Avalon Jihad drew close. Then Khalid called the meeting—angrily, she reflected on that black day.

Not everyone had attended the meeting. Usually, meetings of the Avalon Jihad included all its members, but this time Abu Tarek, Saleem-Ali, and Faiza were absent. The meeting was about Faiza. Khalid told the group that he had evidence Faiza had strayed from jihad, and indeed, from Islam. He believed she had abandoned the faith, an act that itself demanded her death, according to the Qur'an. The facts of the situation were irrefutable and created concern beyond Faiza's personal fate. She had put the Avalon Jihad at risk. He reminded the group of Cow 2:211. "If anyone alters God's blessing after he has received them, God is stern in punishment." She had to die.

When asked what Faiza had done to warrant such punishment, Khalid said that Faiza had fallen in with a *kafir*, an infidel, but worse, the unbeliever was a drug dealer. The evidence indicated that she had assisted the dealer in his immoral trade and had herself become an addict. Her behavior was inexcusable. It violated the basic tenets of Islamic faith. He lied.

She had to die. Even if she repudiated and repented her actions by pleading *tub lil-la* and was permitted to live, she could not be trusted to fulfill her assignment with the Avalon Jihad—her role was too important. Khalid determined that Allah precluded him from offering her the opportunity to confess and repent. She had chosen the path to the fire and her fate was inevitable.

Khalid decided how Faiza would be killed. Aaliyah, Fikriyya, and Mohamed would be the execution team. The strategy was simple: secrecy and surprise. Khalid would lure Faiza to the prayer room above the Avalon Bay Bar, a location she considered safe and where surprise would be the sole province of the executioner. Aaliyah would kill her. Then, Aaliyah and Mohamed would take her body to the dump and bury her in a trash pile. Faiza could not just disappear. A second woman going missing so soon after the disappearance of Marilyn Hastings might call undue attention to the situation and raise suspicion potentially triggering renewed questions of Marilyn's disappearance.

Khalid contrived a pretense for the meeting—the redistribution of the Avalon Jihad's female assets. Faiza would believe it was in response to her request for reassignment. Faiza would be caught off guard in anticipation of a change for the better. In attendance would be Fikriyya, Aaliyah, Mohamed, and Khalid. The female attendees would receive a written proposal for the reassignment of their duties, whereupon Khalid and Mohamed would excuse themselves to allow the women to read the proposal in private. Fikriyya would leave the prayer room to read the proposal in the bar downstairs. As there were no chairs in the prayer room except for at Friday prayers, Aaliyah and Faiza would have to read the proposal standing. Aaliyah would attack Faiza from behind. Faiza's fate was sealed.

CHAPTER TWELVE

(A Month Later) 11:45 Sunday, March 29, 2010
Watson Financial Services, Metropole Avenue
Avalon, Santa Catalina Island, California

"Not bad for a week. Business is picking up," Tiffany said positively.

Jenn and Tiffany confirmed the cliché that opposites attract. Jenn was deliberate, precise, and thoughtful. She applied knowledge, experience, and common sense to her life, although she could easily make instantaneous, seemingly illogical decisions when the situation demanded it. Jenn was conservative in dress and action with an intense desire to be in control of her life. She was inquisitive and adventurous and attracted to ill-defined situations that required investigation and resolution, even when she did not own the situation.

Common sense or lack of substantiated fact *never* inhibited Tiffany—she had no second thoughts about winging it. Surprisingly, her decisions were more often than not right on, despite the human wreckage she created along the way. She too wished to be in control of her life. She loved her husband, Tom, the Chief Executive Officer of the Santa Catalina Island Company, but hated living on Catalina. To her, the island was boring, boring, and more boring. She jumped at any opportunity that hinted at adventure. Her thrill genes were more numerous and more intense than Jenn's. While she dressed and behaved conservatively in her professional life, she pushed the envelope in her personal life where her behavior and dress was boisterous, outgoing, and flamboyant. Propriety was a nebulous concept to Tiffany—what came into her head generally came out of her mouth—and usually not at an appropriate time or place. Nonetheless, most everyone loved her freshness.

Jenn and Tiffany had first met when Bill hired Tiffany as his assistant. Their relationship rapidly grew into friendship, and in a short time, they were best friends. Both were fitness freaks. Although Jenn preferred to work out in gyms, with an occasional run, Tiffany was a fanatical jogger. On weekends, they made it a point to run together. Often they jogged from Hamilton Cove down past the Casino, through the town of Avalon, up Old Stage Road to Hogs Back Gate, around Chimes Tower Road, back down through Avalon, and back up to Hamilton Cove—a round trip of more than eight miles that included multiple elevation gains of over six hundred feet.

Jenn had incorporated Tiffany into her Internet jewelry business. Tiffany maintained the inventory on island while Jenn did marketing and sales. On weekends, they reviewed the week's orders and packaged the jewelry for shipment—allowing them ample time to gossip.

"Yeah not bad, seven pins and fourteen pendants with chains," agreed Jenn proudly. "The business is growing, but it has to get a lot bigger before I can quit my day job."

"It'll happen," assured Tiffany, conceding to what was a familiar discussion.

Jenn's business plan was to sell, over the Internet, jewelry that was not available in malls. Ultimately, though, she also wanted to open a shop on Catalina. To do this required that Bill expand his financial services business so Jenn could leave Raytheon and move to the island. She loved the concept but knew the reality of her objective was in the distance.

"Did you hear about that woman they found dead at the dump?" asked Jenn.

"For sure . . . it's the talk of the town. They found her body Monday," said Tiffany.

"Who was she . . . did you know her?"

"I didn't. Her name was Wanda. She worked for the Island Company as a tour bus driver and that's about all I know about her, except what I read in the newspapers and what Tom has told me—which isn't much," said Tiffany with a disgusted look on her face.

"Really, I thought you knew almost everyone on-island, especially if they worked for the Island Company."

"Hardly," said Tiffany sheepishly. "Tom said she was a good employee and doesn't believe the drug connection."

"Drug connection?" asked Jenn.

"Yeah, *The Islander* says the sheriff found drugs and drug paraphernalia on her body and in her apartment. Tom doesn't believe it for a second."

"Really. Are there any leads?"

"None, according to *The Islande*r

CHAPTER THIRTEEN

4:59 PM Friday, April 16, 2010
The Bomb-Making Facility, the Terrorist Compound
The Interior, Santa Catalina Island, California

"He's late," said Saleem-Ali.

"He's always late. That's unless he's called the meeting," said Aaliyah.

Aaliyah had requested the meeting to discuss bomb construction issues.

"Yeah, and then he's usually late anyway," grinned Saleem-Ali.

"This is important. I've had to build bombs different from our plan. The crap materials Brooklyn's sent me might work or it might not work. I've had to jerry-rig everything. The bombs could just be junk."

"They'll work, I know they'll work," said Fikriyya.

"You know no such thing. Only God knows, `azza wa jall,*" said Saleem-Ali. "We need to test the bombs because there's no second chance. If they don't work, we wind up in Guantanamo, if not dead."

"Dead's okay . . . then we're martyred," chirped Fikriyya. "We're martyred whether we're successful or not. It's the effort and commitment that God rewards, `*azza wa jall,* not the results. He is all-hearing, He is all-seeing, He is all-knowing."

"I've been thinking about that. Does that make any sense?" asked Aaliyah.

"Are you serious? Of course it makes sense," gasped Fikriyya. "How could you question God? `*azza wa jall.*"

"*Anaa `aasif `u dh ran, Allaahu a `lam.* I'm sorry. I apologize, Allah knows best," said Aaliyah hurriedly wondering why she had let such words slip. To redirect the conversation, she reiterated hastily, "Where's Khalid?"

"He'll be here soon," said Fikriyya. "He's been talking with Brooklyn and is anxious."

"I bet he is. Brooklyn probably wants to know why this has taken so long even though *they* are the problem. More uncertainty, more delay, more changes, I can just see it coming. We should've been done with this a year ago," griped Aaliyah.

"*As-salaamu `alaykum,*" said Khalid as he strode confidently into the bomb building.

"*Wa `alakumus salaam,*" responded the three in unison but unenthusiastically.

"Why did you make me drive all the way out here? This better be important."

"The bombs are completed," said Aaliyah.

"Excellent—it's about time. But someone could have told me that in town; I didn't have to drive out here just to hear that."

"There's more," said Saleem-Ali. "We need to test the bombs."

"Why? If they're done, they're done."

Aaliyah tried to keep her face from showing emotion, but this was incredible. Khalid had pounded *plan, plan, plan, practice, practice, practice* into their minds day in and day out, but he did not seem to understand that the same concept applied to bomb construction—even more so as bomb construction was the critical element in the plan. No bombs, no Avalon Jihad.

"We don't know whether the bombs will work," said Aaliyah evenly. "They're complicated and we didn't get the materials we'd expected so I had to improvise. Brooklyn sent us Radio Shack parts, which I had to reconfigure. We've bench-tested the components but we're not sure the complete system will work."

"You're not sure—*you're not sure*? What is the matter with you? This is simple stuff. You know how to do this, don't you? However, alas, I've forgotten all of you are substandard. This disgusts me. *You all* disgust me," said Khalid, looking directly at Aaliyah.

"Nothing's the matter with us. We were forced to work in development mode," said Saleem-Ali quietly. "Testing is the norm in development mode. We don't want to test a full-sized bomb. We want to test the circuits, the actuators, and the detonators to insure they will work as a system. We'll detonate a small bomb. No one will hear it."

"I'd expect such nonsense from Aaliyah, but not from you Saleem-Ali, so there must be something to what you say. I don't know. I'll have to ask Brooklyn."

"Ask Brooklyn? Why? We aren't stupid." Aaliyah knew she should shut up but kept going. "They sent us to do a job; they should let us complete it. They are the ones responsible for the delay. Their indifference caused our predicament. They didn't do their job and that prevented us from doing ours."

"Aaliyah, how many times do I have to warn you to watch your mouth and show respect? Brooklyn knows, Afghanistan knows, God knows, *`azza wa jall*. He is all-hearing all-seeing all-knowing. You don't know of these things. You must stop challenging our leaders. God guides all believers, *`azza wa jall*. You must maintain your place, know your role." Khalid folded his arms across his chest. "I'll let you know. The next time you have trivial issues such as this, come to town, I don't need to come out here."

If it is so trivial, thought Aaliyah, *why do we need Brooklyn's input?*

Without uttering pleasantries dictated by the Qur'an, Khalid left the building.

Outside, he gathered his composure. *I cannot let a worthless American woman get to me.*

(Five Days Later) 6:15 PM Wednesday, April 21, 2010
The Bomb-Making Facility, the Terrorist Compound
The Interior, Santa Catalina Island, California

Khalid said, "I told Aaliyah yesterday that Brooklyn has granted limited testing of a small bomb. I hope you've set up your test. I do not appreciate coming here a second time to compensate for your pitiful shortfalls. If you knew what you were doing, all this would be unnecessary."

"We're ready," said Saleem-Ali. "The site is half a mile from here. No one will hear the explosion."

Aaliyah, Abu Tarek, Mohamed, and Saleem-Ali led Khalid up a low hill and then into a deep canyon.

"We've placed a small amount of Semtex in small metal containers to simulate the bombs. They're much smaller than the actual scuba tank bombs." Aaliyah pointed, "The containers are about an eighth of a mile up the ravine. They are approximately thirty feet apart. We've attached detonation devices to the bombs and covered them with heavy layers of cloth to create a configuration similar to what we expect on the express boats. We've synchronized the frequencies of the actuators and detonators. We will . . ."

"Synchronized?" interrupted Khalid. "Can the frequency be changed? Is there any chance the frequency can inadvertently change—say if the bombs are bumped or dropped?"

That's a strange question, thought Aaliyah. *Could he be testing me?*

"Not by dropping or bumping. The frequency is set on a dial and then the dial is locked," said Aaliyah. She held an actuator in her hand to show Khalid how the frequency worked. "This dial and a similar dial on the detonator are synchronized to the same frequency. If you release the lock on the detonator, you can change its frequency. The frequency displayed on the face of the actuator is then irrelevant and won't explode the bomb. It's simple but I think it will work."

"Good. I understand," said Khalid smiling.

"The detonators on the test bombs each have a different frequency, just as do the real bombs."

"Why?" asked Khalid.

"Each bomber's actuator is set to a different frequency. Only a unique frequency from the actuator will activate the detonator for a specific bomb. That's why we test two bombs, each bomb's detonator responds to a unique frequency. We will explode only one bomb. The primary purpose of the test is to ensure the actuator and detonator work together. A secondary purpose is to insure there's no cross-over of frequencies."

To Khalid this all sounded like so much crap. The bomb would explode or it would not. Why did American women make things so complicated? If the idiots knew what they were doing, this wouldn't be necessary. They had not divested themselves of their sick western mentality. Yet he needed to understand better how the system worked and only Aaliyah could help him with that.

"Khalid, do you want to be the bomber?"

"I do," he said with a wide grin. "How do I do this?"

"Press the button on the actuator twice within a second and the bomb explodes. That feature protects against an inadvertent detonation. Try it. Press the button once and release it . . . see? No explosion."

"I understand."

"Everyone get behind these boulders and scoot down. There isn't much chance of shrapnel or rock fragments reaching us, but just in case, the boulders will provide protection," said Aaliyah.

"Why are you concerned, Aaliyah? God will protect us `azza wa jall," said Khalid.

"Just a precaution. Is everyone ready? Now get down . . . Okay, Khalid, detonate the bomb."

Khalid despised Aaliyah's lack of faith. Arrogantly, he stepped from behind the boulders and depressed the button twice. A single explosion occurred two hundred yards up the ravine.

"See, apostates, I'm under God's protection, `azza wa jall. However, the explosion was too loud. You said no one would hear it."

"It *was* louder than I'd expected," said Aaliyah. "I've never detonated Semtex before. Don't worry, though, no one heard it, and if someone did, they'll think it was hunters."

"You'd better hope so."

"Now that everything's in place, when will we execute our plan?" asked Mohamed.

"I must confer with Brooklyn," said Khalid.

CHAPTER FOURTEEN

9:23 PM Friday, August 13, 2010
Ristorante Villa Portofino
Avalon, Santa Catalina Island, California

"Hi, good to see you guys again," said Irene.

"Hi," smiled Jenn.

"You look great . . . very professional, I must say. Did you just come from over town?"

"I didn't have time to change. I went straight to the boat from work. I even had to skip judo practice."

"I've reserved your favorite table," said Irene, pointing at the window in the front of the restaurant.

Irene led Bill and Jenn to a small table tucked into an intimate corner of the restaurant next to an open window that had an unobstructed view of the bay. Balmy, sea-scented air wafted through the window. Irene placed menus on the table.

"When I saw you folks, I ordered daiquiris. Joan will bring them to you. Have a great meal."

"Living in a small town with unique tourist destination amenities is really great," said Bill, holding Jenn's chair for her.

"It is. I can't wait until I live here full time," said Jenn.

"How was the crossing?"

"It was smooth. She pisses me off."

"Who—Irene?"

"Yes."

"Irene was as nice as she could be."

"Irene is lovely . . . a wonderful person, a sweetheart, I love her, but she pisses me off."

"Somehow I know I'll regret asking, but why?"

"Look at her. She has a great figure, great tan, great boobs. Her sheath looks like it's taped to her body . . . not a wrinkle anywhere. When she walks, she floats, only her hair moves. Her ass doesn't jiggle and her boobs don't bounce. I bet she doesn't own a bra. She pisses me off."

"Honey, Irene's in her early twenties, she's allowed to look like that."

"No she isn't. I didn't look like that when I was in my twenties."

"You looked great in your twenties . . . you look great now. She's in her twenties; you're a research engineer in your thirties."

"I hate that too."

"That you're in your thirties?"

"That I'm a research engineer."

"Why?"

"I'd rather be a bench engineer."

"Your job is important. If you didn't get the grunts on the right track, there wouldn't be solutions and you get involved with all the projects not just one or two. You do great."

"Thanks . . . did my ass and boobs bounce when I was in my twenties?"

"I don't remember."

"What! Why don't you remember?"

"I wonder what the specials are for tonight. What do you think about the cold teriyaki scallop appetizer?"

"Screw the scallops. Why don't you remember?"

"Jenn, give it up, you've had a bad week."

Jenn grimaced. "Iraq and Afghanistan are hard for me. They're hard for our troops and hard for their families. They're hard for America. They're particularly hard for my group. Our boys are getting the shit kicked out of them by those lunatics. My group thought we had the IED problem beat when we found an easy way to intercept and scramble cellphone signals. In a few days, the assholes came up with another way to detonate the IEDs. Now they use sophisticated actuators . . . every one of them encoded differently and they have a slew of makes. Baghdad found a cache of over fifty and sent them to us to evaluate. I have some of them with me this weekend. We can't stay ahead of the bastards. They have better support than we give our troops. We aren't holding up our end of the bargain with our soldiers and that troubles me. It seems as if the insurgents shit 155-millimeter artillery shells. Actually, Baghdad believes Iran sends the shells to the insurgents. It is a mess. My group is bummed. I'm bummed. We need to pound those assholes into the sand."

"You didn't bounce when you were in your twenties."

"Thanks . . . I really have to wind out."

"Yes you do."

Jenn sighed.

"Here're your daiquiris. Good to see both of you again." Joan set two large martini glasses on the table.

"Thanks," said Bill.

Jenn merely smiled.

"Will it be Nobilo with dinner?" asked Joan.

"What do you think love . . . Nobilo?"

"Sounds good."

*   *   *

For a while, they talked about other things—the financial markets, the latest news from friends but Jenn remained restless.

"How's your halibut, love?"

"Excellent. And your lamb? I don't know how you eat that stuff." Jenn wrinkled her nose.

"They've got the best lamb here. From what you said earlier, it sounds like work is getting worse."

"It's okay," she said unconvincingly. She set down her cutlery and reached for her wine.

"My group works on ugly stuff. I'm organizing two new projects."

Her voice, already low, dropped lower.

"One is to develop a chemical detection system to locate IEDs—kind of like sophisticated bomb-sniffing equipment. The other is a form of electronic surveillance. Those assholes could keep my group employed for years, maybe decades, if our government lets them. No one understands how they stay ahead of us. We develop a counter to one of their horrific tactics, and in weeks, they're using a new tactic. The bastards aren't independent groups of radicals, they're organized. New tactics appear simultaneously throughout Iraq or Afghanistan. A larger, well-backed organization has to be running the show. It's depressing. I can't wait until I can resign my job, I'm here with you all of the time, and I can focus on the Jewelry Hunter business."

"I miss having you here babe," said Bill. "It'll happen. You'll be here full time. We're close, within a year or two, maybe sooner. Business is building nicely. Tiffany's been a godsend. She frees me up to spend time marketing and growing the business."

"Everything okay here?" asked Joan, gliding elegantly to the table.

"Everything is great, the meal's really good," said Bill.

"Jenn, have you heard any good blonde jokes lately?" asked Joan, herself a honey-blonde.

"What did the blonde do when she heard that ninety percent of all accidents occur in the home?"

"I don't know," said Joan.

"She moved."

Joan laughed noisily. "Room for dessert?" she spluttered while laughing. "Sorry, but I'm required to ask. I know you folks never take dessert. What about coffee?"

"Thanks, but no to both, we'll pass," smiled Jenn. "We're full and it's late, maybe next time."

"I'll be back with your check."

Joan could be heard chuckling as she made her way to the till.

"What's up next week?" asked Bill.

"Same old stuff and I've got those new projects to set up."

CHAPTER FIFTEEN

10:25 PM Friday, August 13, 2010
The Prayer Room above the Avalon Bay Bar
Avalon, Santa Catalina Island, California

Khalid was annoyed as he looked up from his frayed Qur'an.

"What is it Aaliyah, what do you want?"

What Aaliyah wanted was peace of mind. She felt martyrdom slipping from her grasp. She was a believer, a devout believer, but recently things were not computing. Khalid was at times thoughtless, always callous, often ruthless, and routinely unfocused. He irreversibly lacked respect for women; she understood that. But he was the leader, the Shaykh. She had deliberated whether to talk with Khalid, however, there was little alternative. She had to confide in him.

"Jihad troubles me, I'm ambivalent," mumbled Aaliyah struggling with the words.

She sat at a table leaning forward, her forehead in one-hand, and tears creeping down her cheeks.

"Ambivalent . . . what does that mean?" asked Khalid, while thinking. *Damn, more whining.*

"I don't know I'm uncertain. I feel uneasy."

"About what? Why?"

"It just doesn't seem right to kill, it seems senseless. The infidels haven't done anything wrong . . . they just don't know."

"Unbelievers do nothing right! They haven't chosen the straight path, they aren't steadfast," counted Khalid sharply.

"They're uninformed, all they need to be is educated," sobbed Aaliyah. "We should be able to accomplish our goal in a more compassionate way. They don't know that they are infidels. Why can't we do what needs to be done in ways that doesn't kill clueless people? To kill is wrong. The Qur'an, the traditions, and Sharia all tell us it's wrong to kill."

"Anything is wrong if it doesn't please God, and anything is right if it pleases God, `azza wa jall. Your thoughts are illogical. The Qur'an tells us so," said Khalid, holding the sacred book above his head. "'Let those of you who are willing to trade the life of this world for the life to come fight in God's way; to anyone who fights in God's way, whether killed or victorious, we shall give great reward.' Islam expects the use of force in the furtherance of God's will, `azza wa jall. Remember, what the Prophet said, Islam is the religion of the sword. Jihad is a tool. It honors the glory of God, `azza wa jall."

Khalid paused and drew a deep breath. "Remember 9/11. Three thousand pathetic uninformed unbelievers were rightly killed. Killing them got the attention of the entire non-Muslim world. That is the purpose of jihad. We kill unbelievers to get the attention of those that remain so they will change their misguided ways and accept Allah, the one God, `azza wa jall. The unbelievers have already forgotten 9/11. They didn't change . . ."

Aaliyah thought Khalid's statements and his beliefs inconsistent. 9/11 proved killing did not achieve jihadist's goals and exposed inconsistencies between the traditions and Qur'an. On one hand, Muhammad extols Islam as the religion of the sword, and on the other killing as immoral.

". . . The destruction of their god-forsaken, irreverent edifices to evil, death, and darkness are a distant blur. We killed over three thousand people, yet those remaining scarcely remember. If that didn't work, talking is an exercise in futility. Until the entire world is Muslim, jihadists have an obligation—there is no middle ground. *Allaahu akbar*, God is greater."

Khalid's not consistent thought Aaliyah, *he's not making sense.*

Khalid's facial expression and body language revealed his repugnance for Aaliyah. In his mind, she was a hypocrite. She no longer accepted her commitment to God, had lost sight of God's wishes, and had reverted to contaminated Western thinking. She was no longer steadfast and had abandoned the straight path . . . she was no longer useful. *Women. They are only springs of sexual enticement, sources of evil, and creators of divisiveness . . . mere baby machines.*

"It's one thing to kill a morally corrupt drug dealer," lamented Aaliyah, "but it's quite another to kill hundreds, maybe thousands of people, whose only sin is that they don't know any better." Troubled, Aaliyah momentarily relived the moment when she had felt the life drain from Faiza. She cried out involuntarily, "Damn it, Faiza, why did you take up with that druggie? How could you abandon your faith for a sick unbeliever?"

Khalid glared at her.

"Forget about informing the infidels—forget Faiza! She wasn't committed. She was impure. Jihad, Aaliyah, the Avalon Jihad, that is what is important. We're obligated to God. God knows best, `azza wa jall*. We are duty-bound to send his message . . . we're not duty-bound to guide unbelievers. God, `azza wa jall*, doesn't guide such people, so why should we? Unbelievers have no excuse . . . they have no place to hide. They have been warned. We teach with the sword. They change or they die.

"Remember what the Prophet said: 'Different prophets have been sent by God to illustrate different attributes. Moses preached clemency. Christ preached righteousness, omniscience, and power: his righteousness by purity of conduct, his omniscience by the knowledge he displayed of the secrets of all hearts, and his power by the miracles he wrought. However, none of these attributes was sufficient to sustain conviction. Even the miracles of Moses and Jesus have been treated with disbelief. Therefore, I, the last and greatest prophet, come *with the sword*. Let those who promulgate my faith enter into no argument or discussion but slay all who refuse obedience to the law. Whoever fights for the true faith, whether he falls or conquers, will assuredly receive a glorious reward. The sword is the key to paradise . . . and to the fire. All who draw it in the cause of the faith are rewarded with temporal advantages. Every drop of their blood and every peril and hardship endured by them will be registered on high as more meritorious than even fasting and praying. If they fall in battle, their sins will at once be blotted out and they will be transported to paradise, there to revel in the pleasures of dark-eyed houris.'"

Khalid immediately regretted he had shared the entire passage. Aaliyah would not be interested in the dark-eyed houris, nor did it matter. Paradise was for men not women. Aaliyah's expectations are elusive—elusive propaganda spread unknowingly by so called moderate Muslims. Women ascended to paradise if their husband did and even then, they shared their husbands with his other wives and seventy-two houris.

"I know! I know! I am sorry. I apologize," sobbed Aaliyah. "But what about the Prophet's bloodless return to Mecca? When some of his most vicious, deadly, and uncompromising adversaries were marched before him, he forgave them, even when some of them falsely converted. Did that not demonstrate forgiveness and love?"

She wiped her sleeve across her eyes and sighed. "I cherish martyrdom, but feel I won't achieve it."

Khalid stared at Aaliyah and pondered how to respond. Her comments worried him. He recalled the madrassah, his memorization of the Qur'an, and his studies of the Sunna and Hadith. Privately, then as now, he was perplexed. Why were there scandalous discrepancies between the Qur'an and the sayings? Even more troubling were contradictions within the Qur'an itself. The explanation that passages appearing later in the Qur'an trumped contradictory passages appearing earlier makes little sense since the Qur'an *is* the word of God. The logic is baseless rationalization. Why wouldn't God get it right the first time—He knows all, He sees all, He hears all? Why had the Prophet declared Islam the religion of the sword only to behave differently when the sword was the obvious response? Khalid could not share his confusion with his teachers at the time—his reprisal would have been horrific. Moreover, he could not share his confusion now, as it would compromise his rhetoric with Aaliyah.

Finally, Khalid replied, "Aaliyah, previous exploits of the sword foreshadowed the Prophet's conquering of Mecca. The infidels fell before the Prophet, fearing the sword, and converted. The Prophet knew that those who had lied would fall before the sword in due time."

Pausing, he looked at her gravely. "Do not forget the Prophet's pronouncement: 'We fight for the faith—paradise is our reward.' On to victory and martyrdom, Aaliyah, your reward awaits."

She remained silent, her head bowed.

Khalid hoped Aaliyah would accept his explanation at least for now.

Finally, he added, "Aaliyah, sleep on it and we'll talk tomorrow. You'll feel better."

"That's a good idea. I'll do that."

"May the blessings of Allah be upon you," said Khalid.

"And upon you be the peace and Allah's mercy and blessing."

She rose slowly and walked the dimly lit hallway to the staircase, down the stairs to the bar, and exited to the alley.

It was clear to Khalid that Aaliyah had outlived her usefulness. She had broken with the faith and reverted to being an infidel. Khalid rationalized the decision was Allah's, not his. Khalid believed she was unreliable. Her concerns about paradise were without merit, she would never see paradise. Nevertheless, his conversation with Aaliyah troubled him. It bothered him that his personal needs, not God's, drove the passions of his life. He reasoned his ambitions were his ultimate commitment to the faith . . . and to Allah. He strained to substantiate his position, but could not reconcile the agonizing ambiguities that went back to his days as a youth studying in the madrassah. Then, he recalled the words of one of the Prophet's companions, Omar. "To convince stubborn unbelievers, there is no argument like the sword." *I am like Omar*, thought Khalid. Immediately, he felt comforted. He rationalized that his behavior *was* due to his commitment to the faith . . . his commitment to Allah. *There are no issues to cloud my conscience . . . my hands are clean.*

10:37 PM Friday, August 13, 2010
The Alley behind the Avalon Bay Bar
Avalon, Santa Catalina Island, California

Aaliyah walked through the alley to Third Street. There, she slid into her cart.

It was midway through the summer tourist season and Avalon was booming with electrifying excitement. Tourists and residents, including small gang-like groups of pumped up anti-tourist local male teenagers, filled the streets. Aaliyah drove through town and stopped at the intersection of Metropole and Crescent. Oblivious to the traffic, pedestrians crossed the street nonchalantly in front of her cart. She sat impatiently while her senses welled up with frustration as she watched the mindless mass of humanity. *Infidels don't obey their own laws*, she thought. *Americans are undisciplined. They couldn't be Muslim, if they wanted to be.* When there was a break in the parade of people through the intersection, she promptly applied pressure to the accelerator. The golf cart jerked forward and through the intersection. She turned left and drove out of town, past the Casino, on to potholed riddled Descanso Way.

The distraction and confusion of Avalon behind her, she considered her plight. She did not drink, smoke, or use drugs, and detested America's decrepit, misaligned, and corrupt ways. Americans had no sense of reality or morality. Why didn't they understand? As her cart bounced from pothole to pothole, she could feel tendrils of doubt wrapping around her. Islam had filled her life with meaning, why at this point did she feel uncertain about jihad? Descanso Way paralleled the shoreline, so as she drove, she contemplated the sailboats, luxury motor yachts, and catamarans moored in the bay . . . *worthless materialistic toys,* she thought. She drove skillfully through the sharp left turn at Descanso Beach but had to slow to negotiate the immediate tight S-turn before the steep ascent to Hamilton Cove.

CHAPTER SIXTEEN

10:44 PM Friday, August 13, 2010
Back Room of the Avalon Bay Bar
Avalon, Santa Catalina Island, California

Khalid waited a few moments then silently followed Aaliyah through the squalid alley as far as the dry-rotted board gate hanging from rusting hinges.

Concealed behind the gate, he watched Aaliyah drive away. Satisfied she was gone, he returned to the bar, climbed the stairs to the poorly lit hallway, entered the prayer room, and changed his clothes. Donning trousers, a wool hoodie, a watch cap, socks, and running shoes—all black. He stuffed a flashlight, a change of socks and shoes, and a 9mm Glock 17, with an Evolution 9 silencer into a small backpack. He waited an additional fifteen minutes to insure Aaliyah did not return to the bar or prayer room.

While he waited, he reflected again on the discussion he had just had with her. He rationalized that she had alienated herself from the faith. Then a smile crossed his face. He thought himself clever that to advance his goal, he had deceived her into sharing her knowledge about the detailed electronic workings of actuators, detonators, and bombs.

"That foolish woman sealed her own fate," he laughed to himself. "She allowed herself to become unneeded—an unneeded liability."

He chose an indirect route to the green pier to avoid the late evening locals and tourists who either lingered on the streets or made their way to homes or hotels. At Crescent Avenue, he glanced left and then right. The people remaining on the streets were engaged in conversation or fixed on the performers in an open-air karaoke bar. Calm and confident, he strode across Crescent, scrambled over the low seawall, and dropped onto standing seawater and wet sand that smelled of rotting marine life. The sea wall concealed him as he made his way toward the green pier. Once beneath it, he ascended unsteady stairs to the top of the pier. He walked halfway to the end of the wooden pier and then descended the gangway onto the dingy dock. He pulled on sturdy surgical gloves before locating the twelve-foot West Marine Zodiac owned by a resident who was off-island, on vacation. A single quick pull on the starter cable and the Yamaha twenty-five horsepower outboard sprung to life.

He backed the commandeered boat away from the dock. Keeping its speed under the legal five knots per hour, he steered between the rows of moored boats, toward the Casino side of the Bay. He frowned as he approached the Casino. In his opinion, the Casino was as much a statement of western decadence as was the World Trade Center. There, he steered right and pointed the Zodiac at the Pacific Ocean and the row of buoy floats that superficially partitioned the waters of the Catalina Island dive park from the waters of the San Pedro Channel. Once past the dive park, he increased speed. Four hundred yards into the Channel, he drove the boat north, parallel to the shoreline, into wind-generated three-foot swells. A moonless, clear blue-black sky and the swell intermittently obscured his view of the shore.

Khalid was mindful of other boats. Although he was unlikely at this time of night to encounter another boat, the wake from a larger craft could easily swamp his small skiff. Khalid could not swim and the boat's owner had stowed the life preservers off boat. His speed caused his boat's hull to smash rhythmically into the forward face of the swell so he slowed to lessen the noise and avoid attracting attention. Even at reduced speed, the bow sent sheets of stinging cold Arctic Current salt water into his face. His outer clothes were drenched but inside he was warm and dry. Approximately three hundred yards from Hamilton Cove, Khalid killed the motor and rowed the remaining distance to the dock.

CHAPTER SEVENTEEN

11:27 PM Friday, August 13, 2010
Descanso Canyon Road, Hamilton Cove
Avalon, Santa Catalina Island, California

Steep rocky hills covered with impenetrable vegetation on three sides and the ocean on the fourth shelter Hamilton Cove from unwanted intrusion. The gated Mediterranean-style condominium community is built into the hillside; each unit overlooks the ocean. Access to the community is at the sole discretion of the on-duty guard at the single gate. Security cameras record ingress and egress, as well as movement along interior roads.

The guard recognized the "1/19" decal on the front of Aaliyah's golf cart and immediately raised the manually operated gate and waved her into the community. Aaliyah and the guard exchanged cursory customary hand waves and smiles. Aaliyah wondered why she bothered. She knew the infidel did not care about her. Still, these trivialities were expected, and failure to display them would make her stand out.

Aaliyah proceeded to Building 1, parked in her designated space, and walked down the twenty-one steps to her unit. It was a relief to be home, but it felt like home only in a strange way. *How had it come to this*? she wondered. *Why am I feeling so unsure?* She was a devout believer, so why her inner conflict? Aaliyah shook her head slowly for at least the hundredth time in recent weeks, trying to reconcile her belief in Islam with the conflict that confused her. She hoped that after a night's rest she would feel better and less uncertain when she talked with Khalid.

Her condominium unit was small, but its design and orientation took optimal advantage of ocean views and balmy winds. The wall that separated the bedroom from the living room had been modified with a large, window-like opening, partitioned by shutters. Standing in the bedroom, she opened the shutters and looked through the living room to the balcony that overlooked the ocean. The moonless night sky faded into ocean to form a single dark expanse. On nights when the moon was full and the skies clear, the channel sparkled like millions of diamonds dancing on the water, but not tonight. Tonight the sky was blue-black save for starlight and tiny points of light from Long Beach twenty-six miles away that twinkled like dim yellow-orange stars on the horizon.

Her thoughts turned to the spectacular sunrises she experienced almost every morning. She walked to the French doors, opened them, and stepped onto the balcony. The cool air coming off the sea caressed her. All was natural—God's creation. There were no innovations, no modifications, just naturalness. "There's no power or strength save by Allah," she sighed.

She closed the French doors and walked back to the bedroom, turning off all the lights in the unit except for a single recessed lamp in the ceiling over her bed. Although exhausted from the emotional rigors of the long day, her self-imposed discipline demanded she read from the Qur'an. She silently mouthed the words as she read. In time, she had planned to memorize the Qur'an and not have to read to know.

She read from the sura, Battle Gains 8:33: "Nor would He punish them if they sought forgiveness." The reading made her feel better, stronger. Tomorrow she would tell Khalid that she had repented and returned to God, *tub lil-la*. The Qur'an required devout believers to accept repentance from others of the faith without question. She had done nothing wrong to betray her faith, as had Faiza. Khalid had denied Faiza the opportunity to seek repentance because she had deliberately violated crucial aspects of the faith. She had become a drug addict and helped a drug dealer. Faiza's situation was very different from hers.

Sleep began to win the battle over reading so she returned her Qur'an to the nightstand and switched off the ceiling reading light. She knew sleep would clear the cobwebs of confusion; her outlook would be better in the morning. Aaliyah slipped into a deep sleep.

CHAPTER EIGHTEEN

12:37 AM Saturday, August 14, 2010
San Pedro Channel, Offshore from Hamilton Cove
Avalon, Santa Catalina Island, California

Khalid rowed to the south side of the Hamilton Cove dock, where the surveillance system's effectiveness was limited at night. He could avoid detection tonight; however, the surveillance system might record shadowy images. If something went wrong—and something *would go terribly wrong*, images, even blurred images, could be his undoing. He lifted himself slowly to the dock and cautiously moved up the walkway. To avoid the surveillance system as best he could, he faced away from the rigid camera, feinting being cold, and casually covering his face with his hoodie.

Khalid made his way up a hillside clogged by patches of coastal scrub and manzanita to a road that led to the bottom of Building 1. He walked slowly to minimize the squishing and sloshing sound from his drenched shoes and socks. He was now well beyond the range of the surveillance cameras. There he changed into dry socks, running shoes, and put the wet articles into his backpack. He took the Glock, with the attached silencer, and the flashlight from his backpack. He put the flashlight in his denim pants pocket and ceremonially pointed the Glock forty-five degrees up the stairway that separated Building

1 from a slope of near impenetrable underbrush. Khalid then put the Glock in his waistband, sighed quietly, and commenced the nearly vertical seven-story climb to Aaliyah's unit.

Out of breath and his legs burning from what seemed like thousands of steps he neared the top of the Building. There he surveyed the four units that occupied her level. All, except for Aaliyah's, appeared to be either unoccupied or the unbelievers were downtown, hoping to get lucky. During the summer months, many Hamilton Cove owners rented out their units as vacation rentals. It was midsummer and partying at the Cove was at fever pitch.

The lights in Aaliyah's unit were on, presumably, she was awake. Khalid hoped she had not fallen asleep. Finally, her unit went dark. He waited another twenty minutes to be sure she would be asleep. The long stairway that he'd just climbed hugged the side of the building and opened onto a series of shorter stairways that led to the balcony of each level of the building. Khalid located the stairs to the balcony of Aaliyah's unit and walked up them to the balcony that fronted her unit. He silently edged along the in wall of the balcony to the French door of her unit and peered through the glass into her unit—all was dark and quiet. Khalid gently pulled the French door—it opened easily. He did not need his lock picking tools.

In Khalid's mind, the unlocked French door reinforced his judgment. Aaliyah had become sloppy and no longer exercised the revered discipline of a terrorist—assume nothing, leave nothing to chance, trust no one, expect the unexpected. Probably she had not locked the front door either, or searched her unit before turning in for that matter. She was no longer willing to abide by the unwavering discipline, unerring execution, and unselfish dedication required of a terrorist. She had become a liability and expendable. He had known it would come to this. God commanded the solution. She was a woman, nothing more than a sexual distraction and a source of evil and discord.

Khalid slipped through the balcony door into the living room and walked slowly, silently, and stealthily through the living room to Aaliyah's open bedroom door. He smiled faintly; bringing a change of shoes and socks was a stroke of genius, as Aaliyah's unit was tiled not carpeted. He moved to the side of her bed, observed her deep rhythmic, breathing for a brief moment, and then drew the Glock and pointed it at her head. As if to justify his actions he silently mouthed the words of Bee 16:17: "Those who reject God after believing in Him and open their hearts to disbelief will have the wrath of God upon them and a grievous punishment awaiting them." Scornfully, he murmured, "I condemn you to everlasting torment, you spawn of the devil."

He pulled the trigger.

The single hollow-nosed slug shattered as it entered Aaliyah's head. The shredded shards tore through her skull. An eruption of blood and brains covered the pillow, headboard, and wall behind the bed. Khalid looked at the mess impassively. She deserved worse. He would rather have beheaded her or inflicted a more tortuous, painful, traditional penalty dictated by the Qur'an. Any of those methods of death, though, would have raised unneeded questions.

He left the bedroom and checked the front door, which to his surprise was dead bolted. He returned to the living room. From his pocket he withdrew small plastic bags of crack cocaine and counterfeit bills. He scattered the packets and some of the bills on top of the coffee table in front of the couch. Then he placed additional bills in the drawer of the coffee table and sprinkled minute traces of the white powder on the couch and on the red tiled floor beneath the coffee table. Returning to the balcony, he looked left and right and seeing no one, slipped through the French doors. He closed and locked the doors behind him and backtracked to the dock and his boat.

Khalid rowed the Zodiac past the boats moored off the narrow rock strewn beach fronting Hamilton Cove and out into the open channel before he started the motor. A quarter mile from shore, he tossed the Glock and silencer into four hundred feet of cold black water. The now following swell aided his progress and significantly reduced rhythmic cavitation. He would be back to Avalon in no time.

Khalid powered the Zodiac into Avalon Bay at reduced speed to avoid the watchful eyes of the harbor patrol. He tied up the boat at its initial location, climbed the steps to the green pier, and strode triumphantly into town. The Avalon Jihad was once again secure.

Brooklyn and Afghanistan would be pleased.

CHAPTER NINETEEN

7:07 AM Saturday, August 14, 2010
Building 18-42, Hamilton Cove
Avalon, Santa Catalina Island, California

Jenn bolted upright.

"What the hell? Who could that be, it's 7:00 AM, for god's sake . . ."

A sharp knock, followed by another harsh ring, infuriated her.

". . . and they're impatient!"

"I'll get it, babe," said Bill, wiping the sleep from his eyes.

"I'm up now anyway," said Jenn. "I'll put on coffee. Make them go away. I hate disruption. I get disruption all week. I don't want to speak with anyone."

The image of a carved bas-relief of a Mayan chieftain on the outside of the thick teak front door would be in the face of the unwanted visitors. Hamilton Cove was a conglomeration of Mexican, Spanish, and Mediterranean French architecture. Bill could not recall which Mayan chieftain adorned his door. Maybe he had never known but he was sure the chief would not have tolerated uninvited visitors first thing Saturday morning. Bill opened the door without looking through the peephole, a needless feature in Avalon homes. Avalon was safe, the Cove more so. Islanders took pride in leaving their front doors unlocked and keys in the ignition of their golf cart when parked in town, with purchases on the front seat. Seldom was anything stolen.

The disruption was two uniformed police officers.

"Good morning," said Bill. He was surprised to see Lieutenant David Morales, the commanding officer of the Avalon Sheriff's Station, accompanied by one of his deputies.

"What brings twenty percent of Avalon's finest to my door at the crack of dawn? Have I missed a court date for a parking ticket?"

The Avalon Sheriff's Station was infamous for quirky anecdotal law enforcement. Minimally staffed during the winter, the department swelled with over-town rent-a-cops during the tourist season. Islanders considered the summer augmentation nothing more than "deputies do vacation on Catalina." The station had a reputation for ignoring the hard stuff and micro managing the small stuff. They focused on drunk and disorderly offences, parking violations, and minor infractions of the fabled, convoluted Avalon City Municipal Code. Compounding consistent law enforcement was that everyone in Avalon either knew or knew of everyone else.

"Can we come in?" asked Morales, ignoring Bill's feeble effort at levity.

"Sure. Jenn just put coffee on, it'll be ready soon."

Bill looked toward the kitchen to see Jenn slipping into the kitchen, tightening her robe and waving him off.

The two men trundled through the doorway. Morales stepped into the hallway and brushed dust from his perfectly spit-shined shoes. His highly polished, silver-plated brass badge gleamed to distraction. He stood when others sat because he did not want to wrinkle his impeccably creased trousers. His performance as chief was commendable, considering the quality of his staff. Deputy Jimenez was a case in point.

"So, what can I do for you guys? Are you here to repatriate an overdue library book?"

"We're not here about parking fines or overdue books. Laura's been murdered," snapped Morales uncharacteristically.

Morales's curt retort caught Bill by surprise. Bill stared blankly, trying to make a connection, "You mean Laura Mulholland?"

"That's right, Laura Mulholland."

"My god, when did that happen?"

"Late last night or early this morning; we found her body about two hours ago."

Bill's mind wandered to another murder several months ago, Wanda something or other. He had not heard anything recently about that one.

"Where?"

"In your condo. Shot in the head while she was asleep."

"What? A Shooting at Hamilton Cove! No way, that can't be. If someone sneezes in Building 1 someone in Building 10 says, 'God bless you.' If there was a shot, everyone would have heard it."

"Maybe the killer used a silencer," offered Deputy Jimenez.

Morales glanced at Jimenez in disbelief. "We don't know anything like that, Deputy."

"Maybe she was killed elsewhere and dumped in the condo," said Bill. He immediately reflected how lame that sounded. "Let's talk on the balcony."

Bill felt curiously detached. He had heard that homes where someone died of questionable causes became near impossible to sell or rent—hexed, as it were. His brow wrinkled.

"Coffee's almost ready," said Jenn, joining the group on the balcony. "Hi, Dave. You guys want coffee?" Jenn noticed three serious faces and quickly added, "So, what's up?"

"Laura's been murdered," said Bill, evenly.

"Laura?" asked Jenn, her face a blank.

"Laura Mulholland, our tenant," said Bill.

"Oh my god, the poor thing!"

Standing on the balcony the collective eyes wandered to Building 1. Bill and Jenn's unit 42 in Building 18 had an unobstructed view of unit 19 in Building 1, two hundred yards and twelve multiunit buildings away. Deck furniture and barbeques crowded the balconies of most of the intervening units. While they watched the activity around Building 1, ever-present seagulls soared among the buildings, keeping an eye for a handout. A bald eagle perched on a eucalyptus tree branch just beyond building 1, scrutinized the water, anticipating a meal. The scent of eucalyptus mixed with ocean spray permeated the air.

"Any clues?" asked Bill.

"No, we're just getting started," said Morales.

"Any suspects?"

"None."

Morales's tone did not strike Bill that Morales was in sharing mode.

"Other than that Laura rented from us, how can we help?"

"I thought you might have background information on her . . . help us fill in the blanks."

"Yeah, sort of fill in the blanks," repeated Jimenez.

Jimenez's unsolicited, unnecessary comment earned him another glance of incredulity from Morales accompanied by a slow shake of his head. Morales' attention quickly returned to Bill.

"We don't know much about Laura," said Bill. "She seems . . . err . . . seemed like a nice person. She rented from us for almost two years. I believe before that she'd been on island only a few months. She worked as a bartender at the Avalon Bay Bar. When I told her that the rent might be a little high for a one-bedroom, $1,800 a month, she told me she could do that. I was a little concerned but agreed to rent to her. She said her mom in New Jersey would co-sign the lease but I never contacted her mom. Laura paid her rent on time and she was never a problem . . . that's about it."

"That's all you know? Laura rented from you for almost two years and that's all you know?" Morales's eyes narrowed.

"Yes. She paid on time and she wasn't a problem. What else does a landlord need to know?"

"What about visitors, boyfriends, parties?"

"I don't know. As I said, she paid her rent on time and she wasn't a problem. I never got a complaint about her."

Bill struggled to keep from sounding annoyed.

"Any credit issues? Did you ask her for credit references before she rented?"

"Not that I can recall. I probably should have but I was new at the landlord thing."

"Is there anything else you can tell us?"

Bill considered telling him to fuck off but decided against it. Under the circumstances, he felt it was not wise to share. Lips pursed, he shook his head no.

"Okay. If you think of anything else, let me know. For now, stay out of Laura's condo."

"How long do I have to stay out of my own property?"

"I'll let you know. Oh, did you keep that information on Laura's mother? You know, in case Laura didn't pay rent or there was an emergency?"

"An emergency, like to tell her that her daughter has been murdered?"

"Well, yeah." Morales gave Bill a strange look.

"I may have it."

"Can you get it for me?"

"If I have it, it'll be with her application. Hang on, I'll check."

"I'll have that coffee now," said Morales, turning to Jenn.

"Me too," chimed in Jimenez.

Bill walked to the den, wondering whether he should give Morales the information—it could be a privacy issue, but this was a murder investigation. He considered telling Morales that he had not kept her address and phone number but decided that was not a good idea. After he found Laura's file he took a moment to review its contents. The coffee pot was full and he was sure Morales would not notice the short delay. Bill read from the file. Laura's previous address had been on Clarissa but she had not written down a street number—he should have gotten that. Before the Clarissa address, she lived in San Francisco. She had not provided an address, only that she had worked there. Bill began to feel embarrassed by his lackadaisical screening. She had listed several jobs in San Francisco, all her work was for chemical companies. No local number, just her mother's phone number—a number he had never called. Her mother lived on Long Island, not in New Jersey. In addition to the bartender job, she was a part-time tour guide with the Conservancy—Bill had forgotten that. Her earnings were $2,000 per month. *How could anyone afford $1,800 in rent on earnings of $2,000? I should have been more diligent,* he thought in disgust. Bill wrote down Laura's mother's name and telephone number and returned the file to his desk.

Dave and Deputy Jimenez had settled in and Jenn had refilled their cups. They were groaning about a long, frantic weekend with no prospect of fishing.

"Here's what I got on Laura's mom," said Bill handing the scribbled note to Morales.

"Did you check local references on Laura?"

"What would've been the purpose? This is a small town, everyone knows everyone's business, and no one badmouths anyone. Besides, I knew where she worked and, bottom line, year-round rentals are at a premium. If Laura hadn't worked out, there would be others."

Morales and Jimenez downed their coffee, made a bit more small talk, and then thanked Jenn. Bill escorted them to the door.

"We'll be in touch," said Morales.

"We'll be in touch," echoed Jimenez.

Another glance of disdain from Morales and again it did not register with Jimenez.

Bill closed the door and turned to Jenn. "I don't like this."

"Don't worry, everything will be okay. What should we do for breakfast?"

"I'll start with a daiquiri."

CHAPTER TWENTY

9:32 AM Saturday, August 14, 2010
Building 18-42, Hamilton Cove
Avalon, Santa Catalina Island, California

Bill leaned away from the breakfast table. "I hope we don't hear from those guys again."

"Amen. I don't need the hassle, work's enough hassle."

"Our connection to Laura will make it tough to stay under the radar. Do you think Morales believed Laura was just our tenant and that we didn't have any other relationship with her? She would've been killed wherever she lived, if someone had it in for her . . . sorry about breakfast."

"That's okay. I do like to eat healthier, though. You don't eat like this all week, do you?" asked Jenn separating bacon from eggs on her plate. She did not intend to finish her meal. "I'll need extra hours of exercise to work this off."

"I know; supper will be better," said Bill, washing down yolk-saturated, buttered white toast with his third latte, that he had sweetened with two packets of white sugar.

"Morales will go away when he finds genuine suspects. Everything will be okay."

"I'm sure it will, but I still don't feel good about this. We were just Laura's landlords. Why the hell did Morales press so hard?"

"He's just starting and not sure where to go . . . so we're it. She was our tenant, killed in our condo. He hoped we could jump-start his investigation, and we were convenient. I'd be surprised if he's not on his way to the bar or the Conservancy to talk with more likely suspects."

"It's Saturday morning neither of those places are open."

"He'll get to them." Jenn paused a moment and reflected on the situation. "I wonder if our condo was damaged? The place could be ransacked. Morales never mentioned anything like that."

"Not to worry," said Bill, although he was worried. "I'll take care of everything. We'll have it rented by September. I'll call the cleaning service."

"Remember that murder about six months ago?" said Jenn, reconsidering. Her questioning eyes focused on Bill. She pressed her lips together as she tried to recall the details. "Wanda, um . . . Wanda Peabody, wasn't it? Do you think there could be a connection? I mean, murders just don't happen around here."

"Detective work isn't in our job descriptions, honey."

Bill hoped that Jenn had not become captivated by Laura's murder. Jenn's energy, inquisitiveness, and craving for adventure; combined with her proclivity to try to solve problems that aren't hers had gotten her in trouble before.

"The police haven't solved Wanda's murder and now they have this one on their hands," she continued, either not hearing or, more likely, disregarding Bill's comment. "I wonder how that works."

"We don't need to know how the sheriff department works—that is, unless Morales turns the investigation over to Jimenez," Bill said, his face expressionless.

"What, are you nuts?"

"A joke, honey, it's just a joke."

"This murder is right under our noses. She was murdered in our condo. We should keep an eye," counseled Jenn.

"She lived there. Where else would she be that late at night? This isn't our job, forget it."

11:37 AM Saturday, August 14, 2010
Building 18-42, Hamilton Cove
Avalon, Santa Catalina Island, California

"You've been blankly staring forever. What's up?" asked Jenn.
"Nothing."

Bill knew he was not convincing. Jenn's raised eyebrow confirmed his thought.

Bill sighed, then began to talk. "Laura was murdered in a town that prides itself on safety. People just don't get murdered around here. We don't know why she was murdered—it almost seems like an assassination. Moreover, who the hell carries a gun in this town? Why didn't someone who purportedly heard the shots report them sooner?" He paused and reconsidered his thoughts. "I'm sorry, honey. I should let this go—put it out of my mind. Let's go in to town and buy some fish for dinner. What do you think?"

Jenn looked at him and said with a smile, "I'll drive."

That's not a surprise, thought Bill. "Okay by me, honey."

*   *   *

Jenn backed the golf cart onto Playa Azul and drove toward the Hamilton Cove entrance gate. The scent of eucalyptus filled the air. Coastal sage, tinted a chocolate brown from intense summer heat, grew in the patches of rocky, dry, soil between boulders that bordered the road. The sage clung as tenaciously to the uphill side of the road as the condominium buildings clung to the downhill side.

"My god," said Jenn. "Look at that craziness . . ."

Throngs of people forced Jenn to slow the cart as she approached Building 1.

"Where the hell did all these people come from? The sheriff's done a terrible job of securing the crime scene," she added.

"Drive careful, hon . . . drive slowly. We don't want to hit someone."

Yellow crime-scene tape garlanded Building 1 as if it were a Christmas tree.

"What a mess. The curiosity seekers are in control," said Jenn, chuckling.

Uniformed and plainclothes police seemed everywhere, ID badges hung from necks, clipped to belts or shirt pockets or attached to purse straps. The curiosity seekers looked dumbfounded. The law enforcement professionals looked annoyed. A uniformed officer, whom neither Bill nor Jenn recognized, motioned Jenn past the building. When she failed to comply, he snapped in an elevated voice, "Move it, lady."

Bill noticed one group of curiosity seekers slip past the guard gate and into the complex while the guard was occupied on the telephone. The group attracted the attention of several police officers, who raced up the road screaming incoherent instructions on bullhorns in an attempt to force them out, to unreceptive people intent on remaining in.

Another group of curiosity seekers descended the stairs to the right of Building 1, attracting other officers who likewise bellowed through bullhorns, "This area is for residents of this building only!"

"I *am* a resident!" shouted one rather belligerent man.

"Pull over, honey. I'm going to see if I can find out what's going on," said Bill.

Jenn nodded and edged the cart to the uphill side of the road. She parked and turned off the ignition. Bill hopped out and walked toward the stairwell to the left of Building 1. Police, preoccupied with crowd control near the main gate and at the other side of Building 1, did not notice him. He walked confidently down the stairs toward the unit. Several groups of two or three officers stood on the large balcony in front of Laura's unit. Engrossed in focused conversation, they did not notice Bill. He purposefully walked past them and continued further down the stairs. Then he turned and walked casually back up the stairs to the balcony of Laura's unit. Bill blended in; the police didn't realize he wasn't one of them.

". . . They were locked from the inside, just like the front door," reported an overweight, balding police officer, pointing at the balcony doors. A policewoman recorded his statement in a dog-eared, yellow cardboard-covered, Staples two and a half-by-three and a half-inch spiral notepad.

"Has anyone checked the windows in the dining room?" asked another officer.

"Yeah, there're two but they're so small a midget, couldn't squeeze through them. Anyway, they have a mechanism with a handle that opens and closes them. The handle would catch the crotch of anyone who tried to crawl through."

The policewoman considered this information important enough to include in her notepad.

Bill chuckled inwardly and wondered whether she was writing down the midget or the crotch analogy, or both. If either statement got out, some activist group would sue the county for sure. Bill smirked and edged closer to the balcony's French doors, mindful not to touch anything. Morales would come down on him like a ton of bricks if he found Bill's fingerprints on anything associated with the unit. Bill nudged the balcony door open with his elbow and peered into the condominium. Surprisingly, it looked the same as when Laura had first rented it—almost as if no one lived there. Everything was in order. *Jenn will appreciate that the unit wasn't ransacked,* thought Bill.

Small plastic bags containing white powder were scattered on the table. Bill wondered about that. He looked through the large, window-like opening between the living room and the bedroom,. *Was Laura's body still in the bedroom?* Morales said she had been shot while in her bed. Blood splattered the rear wall. *God, what a mess,* thought Bill.

Several officers stared at the bed making observations while one officer entered notes in his spiral note pad.

11:58 AM Saturday, August 14, 2010
Playa Azul Road, Hamilton Cove
Avalon, Santa Catalina Island, California

"You can't park here, lady. Move it!" said the same officer that had admonished her earlier.

"I live here."

"Your cart says Building 18; this is Building 1, so move it!"

Jenn wondered whether the officer's vocabulary was limited to various versions of, "move it."

"I *own* 1-19."

The young officer froze and then yelled over his shoulder, "Lieutenant Morales, Lieutenant Morales!"

There was no response from Morales. The officer cocked his head toward the microphone affixed to his chest harness and keyed his radio. "Lieutenant Morales, this is Soubert up on the road. There's a woman here who claims she owns unit 1-19."

Still no response. Soubert's frustration intensified. He shouted into the microphone as if that would help.

"Lieutenant Morales! Lieutenant Mor . . ."

"I'm right behind you, son," said Morales, strolling up to the now frantic officer.

"Good afternoon Jenn, what can I do for you?"

"Sorry, Lieutenant," said Soubert.

"I'll handle this, Soubert. Now, Jenn, how can I help?"

"We were headed to town when we saw the crowd so we stopped. Bill and I . . ."

"*Bill?* Is Bill here?" sputtered Morales, looking around.

"Bill got out of the cart before *he* showed up," said Jenn, pointing an accusing finger at Soubert. "I don't know where Bill is now."

"Jenn, please remain parked and stay in the cart."

"I'll find Bill and be back," said Morales.

Morales spoke briefly with Soubert and then headed down the stairs.

12:09 PM Saturday, August 14, 2010
Balcony of Unit 1-19, Hamilton Cove
Avalon, Santa Catalina Island, California

"Hey, you!" shouted an officer.

The scam was up.

"Who are you?" the officer bellowed, hand creeping toward his sidearm.

Bill pretended not to hear.

"Don't move!"

Other officers looked toward the voice, then at Bill.

"Don't move! Who are you?" yelled another voice.

"Hi guys, I own this place," said Bill, with a ludicrous disingenuous smile.

One of the officers got within two feet of Bill and glared. "Your identification, sir . . . slowly, and I want to see your hands at all times."

"What the hell are you talking about? I own this place." Bill flailed his arms gesturing as if he owned all of Hamilton Cove.

Morales walked up behind the officer who was in Bill's face. "Good afternoon, Bill. What brings you here?"

"Jenn and I saw the crowd and wondered what was going on."

Morales displayed impatience and irritation. "There's been a murder, remember?"

"I know. It was in my unit, *remember?* said Bill mocking Morales. "We're concerned. There must be ten to fifteen police rummaging through our condo."

"I appreciate your concern. We're treating your place with tender loving care."

Bill ignored the sarcasm in Morales's voice. "When can I get my unit back?"

"We'll let you know; maybe in a few days."

"A few days! It's my unit. I own it for Christ's sake."

"This is a crime scene. For now, *I* own it and you are interfering with my investigation. You wouldn't want to destroy evidence, would you? You do want this crime solved, don't you?"

"Of course, but it's my unit. All I wanted to do was check it out."

Part of Bill knew he was being unreasonable, yet part of him wanted to push the envelope. He frowned. All he wanted to do was check out his unit yet Morales was stonewalling him.

"I appreciate your concern. We'll be careful with your unit, but you need to leave so we can complete our investigation."

Morales walked deliberately to the stairs that led up to the road, presuming Bill would follow.

12:21 PM AM Saturday, August 14, 2010
Playa Azul Road, Hamilton Cove
Avalon, Santa Catalina Island, California

Jenn released her grip on the steering wheel when she saw Bill and Morales.

"Hi, Jenn, I found Bill," announced Morales.

"Hey babe, things are under control. We can continue into town. Thanks Dave, we'll talk."

Morales gave a feint-knowing smile.

Bill slid into the passenger seat and motioned toward the main gate. "Let's go, honey."

Jenn maneuvered the cart through the throng of people. At the gate, the guard smiled, raised the gate and waved her through. Jenn did not return the courtesy.

"This must be a tough day for the guards," said Bill dispassionately.

"Screw the guards. Why the abrupt departure? I thought you wanted to know what was going on. Isn't that why we stopped?"

"Enough with the questions. Did you go to sheriff school? Morales is only doing his job. He did tell us to stay out of the unit."

"Did you get close enough to see anything?"

"I got a brief look inside. The balcony doors were partially open. There were ten to fifteen people inside. The place was in pretty good shape except for the bedroom. The coffee table was covered with small plastic bags."

"Plastic bags?"

"Yeah, the police were collecting stuff."

"What kind of stuff?"

"Don't know—things related to the murder, I guess," chuckled Bill.

"Not funny, this isn't a joke," Jenn frowned. "Speaking of jokes, that jerk Soubert—I've never seen him before, have you? He is really a joke. The way he treated me, I felt like I was a suspect."

"Welcome to the group. He's just doing his job."

"Right, everybody's just doing their job . . . that's *the* prevailing joke for today." Jenn fell silent, and then asked, "Do you think there's something more to this than just murder?"

"There's always more to a murder than *just* murder. That is, unless it's a serial murder. Even then, there's probably more to it."

"A serial murder . . . what about that woman they found in the dump?"

"What about her?" asked Bill.

"Maybe Laura is the second of more murders to come. Or maybe there have been others."

"Perhaps, but I don't think so. Serial killings are similar. Wanda was strangled and left at the dump. Laura was shot in her bed." Bill's head was starting to throb—it was tough getting his arms around the situation. "Oh, I did hear something interesting. All the doors were locked."

"The killer locked all the doors? That's odd."

"What do we want in town?" asked Bill.

"Fish for supper, remember? We also need something to go with it and how about lunch? I'm getting hungry. We can get sandwiches at Chris' for lunch."

"Sounds good."

Bill was unsure what kind of sandwiches Jenn would buy as Chris was widely referred to as the fanatical health food nutcase. She could concoct the weirdest food. "We'll divide and conquer." Bill thought Chris was a little over the top, so he was quick to segregate the duties to avoid her. Bill jokingly referred to Chris as a recovering hippie. Chris loved hearing herself talk. With a murder to speculate on, it would likely take longer to get away from her than usual.

"I'll get the groceries and fish, you take on Chris. We'll meet back here."

"That's not nice. Chris has a heart of gold," said Jenn with a frown that showed the conversation was a familiar one.

"She does, but she's trapped in the sixties. Drop me here. I'll walk. See you in about twenty—that's minutes not hours," said Bill, laughing. "Good luck."

Jenn drove off wearing a scowl.

CHAPTER TWENTY-ONE

12:47 PM Saturday, August 14, 2010
Vons Supermarket
Avalon, Santa Catalina Island, California

Apart from the Vons Supermarket, the nearest full-line grocery store serving Avalon is twenty-six miles away—by boat. *Vons* is Avalon's grocery store, general store, convenience store, and gigantic coffee klatch. More merchandise, produce, meat, dry goods, wine, and liquor are crammed into the store than seems possible. A quarter of the merchandise requires a ladder to retrieve it. One wonders, at times, how long the merchandise had been up there. Miniaturized grocery carts are unable to pass each other in the narrow aisles so shopping is a one-way tour through the store—there is no turning back, no retreat, no U-turns, no options. If you miss something, you start over.

Bill shivered as he stood in the checkout line. Open meat, produce, and refrigerated display cases cooled the temperature in the cramped store to that of a walk-in refrigerator. Often customers lightheartedly commented that they wouldn't be surprised to see frost-damaged fruit and vegetables in the cases. Today, the coffee klatch buzz was definitely intense.

"Must have been drugs. It's always drugs."

"Did she have a boyfriend?"

"I think she was married. She was married, wasn't she?"

"I don't know, I can't place her. What did she look like?"

"I don't know."

"Bet she picked up some guy at the bar. She worked at a bar, didn't she?"

"No, she drove a tour bus."

"No she didn't, she drove a jeep.

"A jeep . . . she drove a jeep?"

"Yeah, the jeep for the Eco-Tour . . . I think."

"How could she afford Hamilton Cove?"

"She was murdered at Hamilton, wasn't she?"

"I think so."

Bill shook his head . . . he had to get out of the store as soon as he could. In Avalon, everyone either actually knew everyone else's business or pretended they did. Fact was not a precondition to sharing at the Vons's coffee klatch. Separating fact from rumor and rumor from fiction was a learned survival skill in Avalon. Bill had hurried to complete his shopping, hoping to avoid a discussion about Laura. He'd almost made it when he heard, "Hey Coach!"

It must be Henry Gonzales. He always calls me his financial Coach, thought Bill.

"Hank, how are you?"

"Fine and you?"

"I'm good, I'm okay."

"You live out at Hamilton, don't you? What's going on with that Laura murder?"

"I don't know, I wish I did. She was murdered in the condo she rented from me. Did you know her?"

"Your place. Wow! I knew her a little but she never said much. She'd say hello, and that was about it. She seemed like an okay person, but distant."

"Did you ever have a conversation with her?"

"Occasionally . . . once she criticized me when she saw a case of beer in my cart. She told me God says alcohol is wrong."

"Really . . . anything else?"

"Not much. She was very quiet and always seemed distracted."

"I gotta run, Hank. Jenn's waiting for me. Let me know if you think of anything else."

Gonzales opened his mouth to speak but Bill was out the door.

1:05 PM Saturday, August 14, 2010
Armstrong's Fish Market and Seafood Restaurant
Avalon, Santa Catalina Island, California

Armstrong's Fish Market and Seafood Restaurant is at the end of a walkway that leads from Crescent Avenue to a rectangular wharf that extends about forty feet over Avalon Bay. The restaurant is flanked by two other restaurants, the Busy Bee and Antonio's. Customers enjoy an unforgettable view of the bay from the patio of Armstrong's. Superb ultra-modern motor yachts, sailboats with bright red, white, or blue sails, seagulls, pelicans, pigeons, and an occasional sea lion entertain customers while they await their meals.

It was nearing mid-afternoon and the lunch business was winding down. Cynthia spotted Bill, grabbed two menus, and hustled up to him. "Hi, good-looking—outside or inside?"

"No lunch today, babe. I'm here for fresh fish. What's good?"

Cynthia looked confused. "Where's Jenn? Did she come over this weekend?"

"She's at Chris's, getting sandwiches. What do you recommend?"

Cynthia slipped behind the fresh fish case and pointed. "Halibut's always good, the salmon just got here, and the swordfish is locally caught, it was in the water yesterday . . . and not on the menu, we have petrale sole."

Why petrale sole was never on the menu but was always available seemed odd, thought Bill.

Cynthia did not continue through the eight or more other selections, as she knew Bill would choose one of the four she described—he always did. Bill ordered half-pound portions of halibut and swordfish as that was the only portion size available.

While Cynthia wrapped the fish, Bill nonchalantly commented, "Laura Mulholland was murdered last night."

Cynthia's face was matter-of-fact. "The woman at Hamilton?"

"Yes."

"I didn't know her. Who was she?"

"She worked at the Avalon Bay Bar as a bartender. You tend bar, don't you?"

"Yeah and it's been a busy, busy summer, and, as usual, the employment pool is pretty much empty. It's great extra money, and the tips don't hurt."

Bill knew that if a person wanted to, it was easy to get work in Avalon for eighty or ninety hours a week during the summer months—that is if you had housing.

Bill asked, "Have you worked at the Avalon Bay Bar?"

"I can't find the owner to make an application. No one seems to know how to get to him. The same people are there all the time and *they are useless.* It's not popular with the locals—tourists hang out there. Locals use the Marlin Club or the Locker Room, and locals tip better so, in a way, I'm lucky I haven't been hired. What does this Laura look like? I can't place her."

"Dark complexion, straggly brownish black hair, tallish, maybe 130, pounds, about forty."

"Cute?"

Typical Cynthia thought Bill. "Not very. She rented my condo and was murdered there."

"Bummer! That's got to be trouble." Cynthia was silent for moment, and then a quizzical expression crossed her face. "How could she afford your place? Am I missing a good deal? What's the rent?"

"$1,800 . . . but I have no idea when I can rent it again. Morales says it's his until the investigation is over."

"Morales is a jerk . . . $1,800 a month. That's over twenty grand a year. What the hell else did she do? Sell dope or her body?"

"She had a second job as an Eco-Tour guide."

Cynthia gave Bill his change, but held the package while she talked. "Part-time bartender and jeep jockey and she lived at Hamilton. Boy, what am I doing wrong?"

"Is my fish ready?"

"It is . . . sorry," said Cynthia, handing the package to Bill. "Keep me in mind if you can't get the $1,800. I'm sure we can work something out. I'd love to live at the Cove. We could be neighbors."

Over my dead body, thought Bill. Cynthia would be a nightmare tenant and a worse neighbor.

"I'll keep you in mind," Bill lied. "Take care, see you later."

"Stop by at the Marlin Club for a drink . . . I get off about nine," said Cynthia. Bill smiled briefly, avoided answering her, and ducked out the door.

He didn't expect to see Jenn for a while, but was pleasantly surprised to see her driving toward him. She almost collided with another golf cart and then nearly hit a pedestrian. Bill retreated to a section of the sidewalk, protected from the street by a high curb, and waited for Jenn to come to a complete stop before stepping off the curb and slipping into the passenger seat of the cart. "Hi, love, how was Chris?"

"Damn pedestrians. That jackass stepped into the crosswalk without looking. Either that or he was challenging me," griped Jenn. "Chris is Chris." Jenn goosed the accelerator. The cart shot north on Crescent Avenue toward the Casino.

"Sorry to hear that. Did she have anything to say about Laura?" asked Bill.

Chris believed she knew everything about everybody in Avalon. Lack of facts or knowledge on a topic never deterred her from offering an opinion. She would take an irreversible position on anything and then defend it with her life, even if her position was categorically incorrect, which often it was. It made for interesting discussion, if you could afford the time.

"She said it was drugs. Chris thinks everything's about drugs."

"Did she know Laura?" asked Bill.

"She didn't and that's odd. She prides herself on knowing everyone in town and everything about everyone in town."

"I'm beginning to wonder whether Laura existed," lamented Bill.

"How can you say that? She's dead in our condo."

"I know, but we haven't found anyone who *really* knew her or even knew *about* her. She's lived in Avalon almost two years and no one can place her or describe her. She's like a ghost."

Once past the Casino, Jenn accelerated the cart north on the worst maintained road in Avalon taking aim at the Descanso Beach Club. Bill braced himself, preparing for disaster. Jenn approached the sharp left-hand turn just before the Descanso Beach Club. Bill hoped Jenn would slow down otherwise they might wind up on top of the Descanso's outdoor bar, which was situated just below road level. Jenn sped through the turn with ease then careened through the tight S-turn that followed, and rocketed up the hill toward Hamilton Cove.

Bill pondered whether it might be wise to install a regulator on the cart as had many residents done.

CHAPTER TWENTY-TWO

4:32 PM Saturday, August 14, 2010
Unit 18-42, Hamilton Cove
Avalon, Santa Catalina Island, California

"What kind of fish are we having for supper?"

"Two large, lean, but well-marbled New York steaks," said Bill matter-of-factly.

"What! We had meat for breakfast. You said we'd have fish for supper."

"Right. Then for lunch, we had dry gravelly organic peanut butter gook on stale multigrain bread. So, to keep to a balanced diet that experts recommend, I thought it would be appropriate if I bought us two large steaks," said Bill smugly.

"You said we'd have fish . . . and that wasn't peanut butter . . . you said fish . . . I'm eating out. Do you want to join me or will you eat both steaks?" Continuing to rant, Jenn dialed and put the telephone to her ear.

"Halibut and swordfish . . . we'll grill them and dip them in ponzu sauce," laughed Bill.

"Not funny," said Jenn, frowning but satisfied supper was fish. "How're those daiquiris coming?"

"Just about done, it's your favorite . . . extra tart. I wonder how Morales is doing. Better than we did I hope?"

"From what you said, the police were conducting a meticulous search of our condo."

"No dust ball will go unturned," said Bill, "but to solve this mess he'll need to find out a hell of a lot more about Laura than we did."

"There doesn't seem to be a whole lot to find out."

"One thing for sure—she doesn't have the personality of a bartender."

"So now you're an expert on bartenders."

"Bartenders are outgoing—gregarious. They engage people in conversation, which encourages customers to hang out and drink more. Speaking of which, here's your daiquiri."

"Thanks." Jenn sipped her drink. "Mmm, excellent. I'm curious, why would someone kill her?"

"This whole thing doesn't make sense."

"It doesn't. She's not suited to tend bar, yet she worked at a bar almost two years. She could have gotten another job. The unemployment rate in Avalon is negative if you count second jobs. How did she make rent? This could become a problem for us. We should stay close," said Jenn.

"As I said before hon, that's not in our job description."

"But we're already involved, thanks to you," grimaced Jenn in mock annoyance.

Bill smiled faintly then grew serious again. "I wonder who the police will question."

"Her employers. Beyond that, I haven't a clue. She didn't seem to know many people."

"And even those who did know her don't have a lot to say about her." Bill shook his head.

"And now the bozo cops have a second murder on their hands. Two murders on Catalina in six months can you believe that? That's not a good trend for a town without any murders for years, decades, or god knows how long . . . and what about that missing woman? They never really figured that one out. They concluded that she had just left the island . . . disappeared."

"That's bullshit. She had a good job, as I recall, with the Island Company or Edison or some other big company. Why would she leave?" asked Bill pointedly.

"I can't remember where she worked either, but you're correct, there could be a connection. Did you get to see Laura's body?"

"It was in the bedroom I think . . . actually, I didn't see it. There was blood splattered on the wall behind the bed. The gendarmes picked up on me about then."

"Do you think she was murdered in her sleep?" Jenn's shoulders hunched as she contemplated this possibility.

"I don't know. If she were, that would be important. It means the murderer probably entered the condo with the sole purpose to kill her."

"That figures. Just as you said it looks more like an assassination. Are there more daiquiris?"

"You bet." Bill turned toward the front door as someone knocked. "Who the hell could that be?"

"I'll get it," said Jenn.

Drinks in hand, Bill, arrived at the balcony about the same time as Jenn, Morales, and a man Bill did not recognize.

"Hello again Lieutenant. Having trouble finding your way out of the Cove? How about a daiquiri?"

Morales wasn't smiling. "No thanks, I'm on duty."

Bill glanced at Jenn, whose face had turned inquisitive.

"Bill, this is Detective Marv Blessinggame from the LA Sheriff's Department. He'll be the investigator on the Laura case."

"Welcome to Avalon, detective, this is my wife, Jenn."

"I've already met your wife, Mr. Watson, she answered the door."

Okay . . . thought Bill, recognizing that an impersonal stake had just been slammed into the ground. "Please, call me Bill." Bill gestured for the men to sit down, but they remained standing.

Reading from a small spiral notebook, Blessinggame reported flatly, "Sheriff Morales has told me that you and your wife own the condominium where Laura Mulholland was murdered. Is that correct?" Blessinggame's eyes flashed at Bill . . . "Is that correct Mr. Watson?" repeated Blessinggame, with an elevated voice, before Bill could answer.

Morales was a barrel of laughs compared to Blessinggame. An image of an Easter Island stone monolith zipped through Bill's mind.

"Yes, we own the condo. Please, call me Bill," suspecting his first request had fallen on unreceptive ears.

"Mr. Watson, how did you first learn of Laura?"

"Learn of Laura? Like, when did I first meet her?"

"Yes, when did you first meet her?"

"When she rented our condo."

"You didn't know her before then?"

"I didn't know her at all before then. I've told all this to Dave."

"So you didn't know her, but rented to her."

"Correct-a-mondo," said Bill, a satisfied expression on his face. "Landlords do that all the time. They seldom know who will show up to rent. Actually, it's very common."

"Very funny . . . so why did you rent to her?"

"Why?" asked Bill, perplexed by the question.

"Yes. Why?"

"Well . . . she completed an application, paid me first, last, and security, and seemed like a nice person."

"So Mr. Watson, since Laura seemed like a nice person, you rented to her?"

Bill glanced at Morales who avoided eye contact his eyes focusing on the mahogany railing bordering the balcony. Bill looked back to Blessinggame. "Detective Blessinggame, this is a small town on a small island in the middle of a large ocean. I rented to her because she completed an application, had a job, and came prepared to pay rent. Rentals, especially year-round rentals, are at a premium on Catalina. If she didn't work out, there would be ten others lined up behind her. People pay their rent on Catalina or they are on the street with nowhere to go except to the waiting line for the next express boat. I told all of this to Dave. He lives here so he understands the housing situation."

Bill glanced at Morales, whose eyes remained riveted on the railing.

"Did you check references?" asked Blessinggame.

"No. Laura offered to have her mom co-sign the lease."

"She did?"

"Dave knows that."

"Did you ever speak with Laura's mom?"

"After Laura gave me the telephone number, I figured why bother? Her mom lived three thousand miles away. Realistically, she wouldn't be a backup for rent and what mom would badmouth her daughter . . . not likely, so I didn't call her."

"So Laura was behind on her rent. How often did that happen?"

"I didn't say she was behind on her rent. She always paid on time and was never a problem. I told all this to Dave. Don't you police guys talk with one another?"

"Give me her mother's telephone number. What's her mom's name?"

"I believe its Lucy . . . I don't remember."

"Mr. Watson, I want a copy of Laura's lease and her mom's name and telephone number."

Bill looked at Morales and in mock exasperation asked, "Dave, are you withholding evidence again?"

Dave was not amused and scarcely looking away from the balcony railing said, "Bill, Detective Blessinggame is trying to solve a crime."

"He can get the number from you," said Bill.

"I can get a warrant, if you'd prefer. Mr. Watson," said Blessinggame authoritatively.

"A warrant . . . are you nuts?"

"The lease, telephone number, and name Mr. Watson."

"Honey, I'll get it," said Jenn. The expression on her face said it all. *Back off, this guy is a real jerk; he could cause us a lot of trouble.*

"No babe, I'll get it. I know where it is. I did the fetch-and-return gig this morning. I've got the routine down."

Within less than a minute, Bill returned with papers in hand. "Here's what you wanted," handing a scrap of paper and the lease to Blessinggame.

"So what did her mom say when you called?" asked Blessinggame, after glancing at the scribbled note.

"What! Are you deaf or just plain stupid? I never called her, I've never spoken with her, I just told you that, and I told Dave the same thing this morning."

"Is there anything else, gentlemen?" Jenn's voice had taken on an edge.

"There is," said Blessinggame. "Why were you at your condominium today?"

"We own it—duh! We're concerned . . . actually, we're worried about damage and cash flow—we have mortgages to pay. Nobody's told us anything about the condo's condition."

"That's all? One of my people said you were poking around in areas where you shouldn't have an interest. Maybe you were trying to cover up evidence."

My people, I hate terms like that. It had to be that idiot Soubert, thought Bill. "*Your people* are wrong. Police are supposed to be fact finders, not speculators. Which of *your people* told you this?"

"Another of my people said you looked inside the condominium. Did you?"

"What law prevents me from looking inside my property?"

"I know the law Mr. Watson."

"I told you I was concerned about our property. I wasn't hunting for evidence or anything like that. How do you know there weren't other people there who had a real reason to mess with the crime scene?"

"There weren't other people, just you and your wife."

"You don't know that, and apparently *your people* weren't paying attention. Many other people besides Jenn and me were there. Oh, by the way, how's the Wanda case going?"

Jenn briefly closed her eyes, gritted her teeth, and mentally shook her head. She willed Bill to give it up.

"Wanda? Wanda who?" stammered Blessinggame, looking quizzically at Bill and then to Morales.

"Wanda Peabody," said Morales. "She was murdered about six months ago. We found her body at the dump. The case isn't solved and there aren't many leads."

"Ah yes, now I remember hearing about that. What do you know about Wanda's murder Mr. Watson?"

"Nothing, I was just curious about how you were doing."

"None of your business," said Blessinggame in a belligerent tone. "You have no need to know how well the Sheriff's Department is doing. Why are you interested in Wanda's murder?"

"I'm not. Well, I guess that's about it," said Bill, folding his arms. "You guys need anything else? If not, I'm busy. Have a great day. I'll show you out."

"Not yet. There is something else, Mr. Watson—keys. Who has keys to the condominium?"

"You mean our condo?"

"Yes, *your* condominium . . . don't try me."

"I'm sure Laura had keys. I have no idea if she changed the locks or gave duplicate keys to anyone. We have keys. In case you've forgotten, we own it . . . Oh, the Association has keys."

"What Association? Who has keys there?"

"I don't know who has the keys at the association. This is a condominium complex. Problems can and do occur that require access to a unit. Most of the units at Hamilton Cove are second homes and not occupied year-round."

"Who has the keys at the Association? Give me their phone number."

"I just told you I don't know who has keys and I don't care. As for the telephone number of the Association, try the yellow pages. I have no reason to memorize the Association's telephone number. I don't know it"

"Mr. Watson, I expect straight answers. You try me. I don't like that."

"And I deserve responsible questions. I don't like your questions . . . we're even."

"The phone number," growled Blessinggame.

"I don't know it."

"Do you and Mrs. Watson live here?"

"This is our home, yes."

"So you live on the island or is this a second home?"

"I live here. Jenn splits her time between here and over-town."

"Over-town? Where is that?

Bill thought, *this man's a blithering idiot.*

"Over-town, it's an island colloquialism. It means the mainland. I'm sure Dave can fill you in on the language spoken here. Oh, but wait, I forgot, you and Dave don't exchange information."

"Mr. Watson, I've told you not to try me. I have a murder to solve. Do you go to the mainland often?"

"If you mean over-town, I go there about three or four times a month. I have clients there."

"Don't leave the island unless you let me know," said Blessinggame, abruptly.

Sounds like inquisition time is over, thought Bill. "Why, am I a suspect?"

"Just let me know before you leave the island, do you understand?"

"I do . . . it'll be my pleasure. Now I trust we're done. May I show you to the door?"

"We're done. Here's my card."

Blessinggame and Morales marched toward the door. Bill caught Morales's eye and gave him an exaggerated shrug with partially raised arms and hands pointed toward Blessinggame.

Morales ignored him.

"Good day, gentlemen," said Bill.

"Good day," said Morales.

Blessinggame was mute.

Bill slammed the door.

"Good job, sweetie," scolded Jenn. "In fifteen minutes you went from a person with relatively unimportant information, to a person of interest, to suspect, to prime suspect, and now you're under house arrest. I doubt anyone could have done as well in such a short period. We have a problem."

"Jenn, I'm innocent, you're innocent. We're not going to jail."

"Tell that to the three-point-two percent of the people on death row who are innocent."

Jenn remembers every fact she's either read or heard thought Bill. He waved a hand dismissively. "We'll be fine, this'll blow over. These guys don't impress me as able to fight their way out of a telephone booth much less solve murder cases. Wanda's murder is a case in point."

"Whatever," Jenn sighed. "For now, let's deal with the matter at hand: supper. We have to chill out—relax. After all, this is our time."

6:57 PM Saturday, August 14, 2010
Unit 18-42, Hamilton Cove
Avalon, Santa Catalina Island, California

Bill sat back contentedly. Baked fish and Ponzu, Brea Bakery baguettes, Brussels sprouts, and Crossings Sauvignon Blanc . . . The meal had restored his mood.

"This meal was great and the evening is glorious."

"So, my almost-convicted-felon husband, how do we deal with the Laura thing?"

"I don't know . . . but it shouldn't be difficult. If nothing else we keep our eyes open and ears to the ground."

"I wonder if there are *other* suspects," said Jenn sarcastically.

"Very funny."

"I mean it. You *are* a suspect. Blessinggame will construe anything we do or say as an attempt to cover up our involvement."

Bill took this in. "So what do we know?" he asked.

"Our tenant is dead, murdered in her bed, and her condo was locked from the inside . . ."

". . . she worked at a bar and was a part-time tour guide. She was an ideal tenant, paid her rent on time, and never caused us trouble . . . and Tweedle Dee and Tweedle Dumb are on the case."

"Very funny," said Jenn. "The police are batting 0 for 1, maybe 0 for 2."

"0 for 2?" asked Bill.

"The missing woman."

"That's a good point. There could be a connection. Laura lived in Avalon for almost two years but she seems to be virtually unknown . . . anything else?" asked Bill.

"Probably, but that's good for now. So what's next?"

"I'm not sure. I don't have a clue what to do about the bar, but Melinda at the Conservancy might be able to shed some light on the situation."

"Melinda, who's Melinda?" asked Jenn.

"Melinda Offen—something or other; she works at the Conservancy. She and Tiffany are friends. Melinda comes by the office regularly to share gossip. I don't know what she does at the Conservancy. Who knows what they do there. It seems every program they come up with involves killing . . . either animals or plants or both."

Jenn thought for a moment, "I'll do a search on Laura and the bar. What's the bar's name?"

"The Avalon Bay Bar. It's on Catalina Street."

"Anything else?"

"What about Laura's mom?"

"I'll do a search on her," Jenn smiled, hiding her concern. She savored a large sip of wine.

CHAPTER TWENTY-THREE

4:20 PM Sunday, August 15, 2010
Unit 18-42, Hamilton Cove
Avalon, Santa Catalina Island, California

"Have we forgotten anything, honey?" asked Bill. "What do we need from over-town?"

"We're good to go," said Jenn.

"I'll count the seconds until Friday. Is there a chance of you working from home this week?"

"Probably not . . . Wednesday or Thursday has potential. It depends on the outcome of tomorrow's project meeting. Wish me luck."

The doorbell rang.

"Oh shit, what now?" groaned Jenn.

"I'll get it. I hope it's not our new friend. I thought we'd get through Sunday without him."

Bill looked through the peephole. He'd never done that before. "Oh shit, it is Blessinggame."

Jenn shook her head in frustration.

"Welcome back," said Bill sourly, opening the door open. "We hadn't missed you."

"Can I come in?" asked Blessinggame.

"Sure, why not, you're already halfway there. What brings you here to ruin an otherwise beautiful Sunday afternoon? Is this a seek-and-destroy mission?"

"Laura, actually, Laura's mom," said Blessinggame.

"What about Laura's mom?"

"I don't think she's real."

"Sorry to hear that," said Bill caustically.

Blessinggame glared. "The number you gave me is disconnected. It belonged to a chemical company in Brooklyn. They told me they had the number disconnected a year ago and didn't know why they had it in the first place. They also told me that they had never heard of Lucy Cutler. Are you sure the information you gave me is correct?"

"No."

"What? You gave me incorrect information?" shouted Blessinggame. His veins created a network of raised, thin red lines along his neck and temples. "This isn't a game, Watson. I've warned you before don't toy with me. You have gone too far this time. I should arrest you for obstruction of justice in a murder case."

"I don't understand," said Bill, with a faked quizzical expression, enjoying Blessinggame's fit of anger.

"You give me incorrect information and you don't understand why I'm upset? What's the matter with you Watson?"

"I did no such thing."

"You told me the telephone number was correct. You lied to me."

"I didn't lie. I told you that I never called Laura's mom so how could I know if the number was correct or incorrect?"

Blessinggame stared blankly then in intense anger, said, "Stop toying with me."

"I don't toy with people. I answered your question. You have wasted a lot of my time the last two days. You have asked questions that have little or no basis with respect to the case and absolutely no merit. I answered many of the same questions several times."

Blessinggame scowled at Bill.

"So why did you come all the way out here to tell us that you dialed a disconnected number? Unless you have more questions, we're through."

"How was Laura able to pay her rent?"

"How would I know? It wasn't my concern. She never missed her rent. I didn't care where the money came from."

"Never once missed it?"

"Never once."

"This is the high-rent district." Blessinggame waved both his chunky arms over his head and motioned to all of Hamilton Cove. "Didn't you wonder how she was able to pay for this on her income?"

"No."

Bill lied. On occasion, he had wondered where Laura got her money . . . maybe from her mom he had concluded.

"Did you make copies of her checks?"

"No."

"Why not?"

"There weren't any—she paid in cash."

"She paid in cash?" asked Blessinggame, growing angrier by the moment.

"Yes, cash. Eighteen one hundred dollar bills every month."

"Why would she pay in cash?"

"Detective, that's not my concern and I don't read minds. She was a bartender. Bartenders get cash tips. I don't know."

"Or maybe she was involved in drugs or prostitution. Are you aware of anything like that?"

"I hardly knew the woman, for god's sake."

"Any chance you have any of those hundred dollar bills?"

"No, we deposited them . . . we have mortgages to pay. Are we done? I have to get Jenn to the boat."

Blessinggame pondered a moment and finally said in disgust, "We're done for now."

"Great, there's the door, have a wonderful evening."

Not to be cheated out of the last word Blessinggame shouted over his shoulder, "Don't leave the island without telling me."

"Don't worry, Daddy, I won't," Bill responded.

Bill slammed the door. "Sorry about the door. I've had it with him. I'm fed up with this whole damn affair."

"Terrific. I thought we'd discussed not agitating him," said Jenn in disbelief.

"We did, but come on . . . after this latest onslaught? I think the incompetent jackass actually believes I'm his prime suspect . . . maybe in Wanda's murder also. We may have to get involved before I become his solution. For now, though, we need to get you to the boat."

"I'll get my things." Then her face, which had been a mask of worry, brightened. "It'll be exciting solving a murder."

Bill winced.

CHAPTER TWENTY-FOUR

6:25 AM Monday, August 16, 2010
Watson Financial Services, Metropole Avenue
Avalon, Santa Catalina Island, California

"XSTY announced, in after-trading hours, reduced guidance," droned David Faber. Then the chatter between CNBC's Faber and Joe Kernan turned to golf.

"What the hell has golf got to do with the stock market?" mumbled Bill sitting at his desk.

"So, did you kill her? Did you kill her because she didn't pay her rent?" laughed Ken Westerly, standing in the doorway from Metropole Avenue.

Startled, Bill looked away from the television. He was in his office to get an early start on organizing the day around fact-finding on Laura. He had forgotten about Westerly. Tiffany usually arrived at the office before 6:30 AM. Bill avoided Westerly by getting to work after eight. Ken Westerly arrived daily before seven with a new batch of unrelated questions about finance and investments. Paying for the advice was not a consideration for Westerly. When he was not squeezing Bill for pro bono professional advice, he rambled on about most any topic that entered his head. Westerly had told Bill that he had retired early from Northrop Grumman—four years ago.

Unfortunately for Bill, Westerly chose Avalon for his retirement home. Westerly acted as if he was financially secure but Bill had no idea as to his uninvited visitor's financial situation, since Westerly had resisted Bill's efforts to convert him from distraction to client. Bill had known Westerly for two years and still did not know where he actually lived.

Gaunt and dark-skinned, Westerly had a perpetual five o'clock shadow, along with an unruly bushy mustache. He could have been the poster boy for Avalon's unofficial male uniform: loose-fitting khaki cargo shorts, floral-print collared shirt, well-worn leather boating loafers, and, of course, no socks. Bill often wondered, sarcastically, why there seemed to be an acute shortage of men's socks in Avalon. Knowledgeable residents avoided men wearing this uniform. The men were thoughtless, condescending, and convinced they knew everything about anything. In short, they believed they were god's gift to Avalon. Tiffany absorbed the brunt of Westerly's daily antics.

What a pain in the ass, he's already hassling me about Laura, thought Bill. He stifled a sigh and forced, "Good morning Ken."

Westerly seized the TV remote from Bill's desk and increased the volume. Maria Bartiromo had replaced Faber and Kernan. Today she was grilling some unfortunate mortgage company CEO under indictment for his involvement in the sub-prime mortgage lending scandal.

"Look at that, she's got the little squirrel backed into a corner," howled Ken. "The SOB deserves it. Screw him to the wall, Maria. Bury the lousy capitalist."

"Ken, it's a proven fact that people on TV can't hear the viewers," said Bill laughing.

Ken Westerly acted strangely at times. Actually, he acted strangely most of the time. Although somewhat knowledgeable about financial issues, he scorned any obvious manifestation of capitalism.

"And for the record, I didn't murder Laura."

"What do you think about the sub-prime folderol?" asked Westerly.

At least that was a tolerable subject.

"It was bound to happen. Lenders lent to individuals who lied about their income, had no funds for a down payment, no experience with home ownership or real estate, and lousy credit. It'll get worse before it gets better."

Immediately, Bill inwardly cursed himself. He had repeatedly resolved not to let Westerly draw him into debate.

"So the corporate mortgage pukes screwed the little people."

"I'm not sure that's entirely correct; lenders and borrowers share ownership," said Bill.

"But the brokers made a lot of money."

"Lenders aren't debt counselors. Borrowers have obligations, too. They can't hide behind claims that they lack sophistication. Many borrowers caught up in the mess were opportunists, basically speculators and some were very sophisticated."

"Is the coffee ready?" asked Westerly.

Westerly never responded to a direct question or commented on opinion. When conversation got involved or required a thoughtful, fact-based response, Westerly opted for a new subject.

"You know, there is a coffee shop across the street," yelled Tiffany from her office, obviously annoyed by Westerly's behavior.

Tiffany's multi-tasking ability, to eavesdrop while engrossed in work, including detailed number crunching, was remarkable. She could absorb, process, and make informed opinions on the spot and not skip a beat with her work. Bill appreciated her skill. Clients never realized that a human tape recorder inhabited the back office.

Westerly ignored Tiffany's comments and stayed immersed in CNBC. "Maria looks great today."

"You think Maria looks great every day. It's her job to look great," said Bill.

"So what's looking good in the market?"

"Ken we've had this conversation a thousand times. I don't care what's happening in the market today."

"You're no fun. I can't believe you make money at what you do . . . What do you do again?"

"I'm a financial planner," said Bill with a sigh.

"Okay, so what about Laura? Did you murder her because she didn't pay her rent?"

"Give it up. I didn't murder Laura. I've had to deal with questions about Laura all weekend."

Bill found it annoying that Westerly, as well as most everyone in Avalon, now knew of Bill and Jenn's connection to the murdered woman.

"Morales and Blessinggame have been all over my ass the past two days. They're determined to elevate me to suspect one." Bill then added quickly, "Only kidding, Ken . . . only kidding."

"You think she was murdered for drugs? I do."

"What makes you say that?"

"Or maybe she had a boyfriend. Yeah . . . and it wasn't working out so he killed her."

"What is your preoccupation with Laura? Did *you* kill her?"

Ken laughed. "Maybe it was robbery."

"That would be burglary not robbery," corrected Bill.

"You agree then, it was burglary?"

"I don't know why she was murdered. Give it up!"

"What did the sheriff say? Does he have an idea who murdered her?"

"The sheriff didn't share his thoughts with me. He and Blessinggame asked questions . . . a lot of stupid questions. They didn't offer opinion."

"What questions?"

"Ken, give me a break," said Bill, exasperated. Since Saturday morning, I have dealt with the police every couple of hours. I believe they haven't a clue what happened."

"Bill, can you please get the phone? I'm on the other line," called Tiffany from her office.

"Excuse me, Ken, I have to take this. "Hello, Watson Financial Services, this is Bill."

"Bill, it's me," whispered Tiffany. "Tell the jerk you have to deal with an emergency and that it'll take a while . . . exaggerate."

Bill was thankful for Tiffany's cleverness and immediately played to the ruse. "Hello Nan . . . yes, I see. I can explain that. Can you hold a second? Thanks." Bill covered the mouthpiece of the phone with one hand. "Ken I have to deal with this in private, could you please leav . . ."

". . . sure okay, no problem, see you later. I'll just get my coffee and go."

"Thanks." Bill took his hand from the receiver. "Okay Nan, take me through the details?"

Westerly wandered out of the office, with a mug of coffee in hand.

"Try to remember to bring the cup back," yelled Tiffany.

Westerly gone, Bill stuck his head into Tiffany's office. "Maybe he'll forget to return."

"We can only hope. I ordered the CDs for Sisterne, Nanette, and Hernandez. I placed the order for a thousand shares of Microsoft for Beery, and Henry Gonzales left a message. He wants to talk to you about Laura. He mentioned a conversation he had with you on Saturday."

"Thanks babe. I never know how to get rid of Ken. Anything else I need to do?"

"No, you're good to go. Tough weekend, eh?"

"Horrible. It's bad enough Laura was murdered, but the follow-on questioning by Blessinggame was draining."

"Blessinggame? Who's he?"

"An over-town detective responsible for the case . . . he's a nut-case. He's uninformed, belligerent, self-centered, and driven to get a quick resolution regardless of the facts. Jenn believes I'm his prime suspect. I can't leave the island unless I tell him beforehand."

"God that sounds terrible—house arrest. Why you?"

"Long story. Bottom line, Jenn says I was a smart-ass and hassled him."

Tiffany pursed her lips and nodded knowingly. "Anything I can do?"

"Not really. Jenn and I are going to dig around on our own, so I may be out of the office more than usual over the next few weeks."

"No problem. I'm available to help. This sounds exciting."

Unbeknownst to Bill, Tiffany's passion for adventure trumped most other aspects of her life. Her thrill genes put Jenn's thrill genes to shame.

After a pause, Bill added, "Actually, there is something. Melinda, your friend at the Conservancy. Do you think she would know anything about Laura? Laura was an Eco-Tour guide."

"She might. If she doesn't, she'd know who would. I'll call."

"That'd be great. I'd like to meet with her today, if possible."

"I'll see what I can do."

"Okay good. Thanks. I'll call Henry."

Bill tried to recall his exact conversation with Henry on Saturday while looking up Henry's telephone number.

*   *   *

"Hi Hank, this is Bill Watson. How are you? . . . Great. And Margie? . . . I'm glad to hear that. Tiffany said you called."

Henry was silent and then said, "Remember Saturday . . . in Vons?"

"I do," said Bill, although his recollection of the details of the conversation was hazy.

"Well . . . we didn't get to talk as you were on your way." Henry paused. "It's about Laura."

Bill became expectant. "You know something about her murder?"

"I knew her a little, spoke with her in Vons a few times, but I'm sure I don't know anything about her murder."

Bill's excitement waned. "You seem to meet a lot of people in Vons."

"Don't we all. Well . . . lately, she seemed more distracted than normal. Laura's not social. Recently, though, it was as if she lived on another planet. About a week ago, she told me she was leaving the island."

"Really? Did she say where she was going?"

Laura had not given Bill notice, but then the landlord is always the last to know.

"No. All she said was that she sorry."

"Sorry? Sorry about what?"

"She didn't elaborate. She just said that she was sorry."

"That's it?"

"That's all. Do you think that could be connected with her murder?"

"I don't know. It could be . . . I can't put the two together right now. Did she share anything else?"

"Not that I can recall."

"She was a loner and had been here almost two years, yet most people can't place her. You're the first person to tell me they had a real conversation with her."

"I wouldn't call them real conversations. They were superficial. 'Hello, how are you,' yada yada, you know what I mean. Lately, she seemed sadder than usual—not that she ever seemed up. The only times she volunteered anything, it was as she was on a crusade." Henry paused. "You seemed stressed Saturday so I thought you might find this helpful. I don't know why, other than that it had to do with Laura. It's probably meaningless. Oh, there *is* something else. She always had a lot of stuff in her basket. Dried food, canned food, crackers, and bread—lots of white bread. Unhealthy stuff like that. She never had produce or perishables."

"Maybe it was for the bar. When was the last time you saw her?"

"Hmm . . . err . . . last Wednesday or Tuesday, I can't recall."

"Did she seem different?"

"Not really."

"Thanks, Hank. Thanks for the information. Is there anything I can do for you?"

"How's the market?" asked Henry, as if he needed to say something.

Bill shot a glance at the TV.

"Dow's up sixteen. We should meet to complete that plan update."

"I'll give you a call."

"If you remember anything else about Laura, let me know."

"I will."

"Take care."

Nothing earth shattering about that, thought Bill. *It's interesting that he called. Maybe he knows more and isn't prepared to share just yet.*

Bill decided to keep Hank on the radar. Tiffany came from her office and stood at Bill's desk. "Melinda isn't involved with the Eco-Tour department but she knows the person who's in charge of it. She said for you to drop by anytime today and she'll introduce you."

"Thanks."

Tiffany returned to her office and Bill contemplated his Laura to do list.

"You look anxious . . . a penny for your thoughts."

Bill looked up from his desk. Michelle Gooding's lithe form graced the doorway. She was the consummate entrepreneur and another non-client, but not in the mold of Westerly. Bill believed she would become an excellent client someday. Michelle stopped by nearly every day on the way to her dress shop. She was a network person and made it known that she was available to help with anything.

Bill smiled. "Hi babe."

Michelle yelled to the wall behind Bill knowing Tiffany was on the other side, "Hi, Tiff!"

Tiffany shouted to her side of the wall, "Hey."

"So Bill, what do you know about Laura? She rented from you, didn't she?"

"Not much other than she was murdered in my condo. The sheriff has drilled down on Jenn and me all weekend so I'm on empty. Did you know her?"

"No. I saw her in Vons a few times and we said our hellos. When I went to the Avalon Bay Bar, she was usually there. She wasn't a conversationalist."

"Isn't that odd for a bartender?"

"Very. That bar's dead anyway. She could've been part of the problem. She wasn't so hot on drinks. Other than beer and wine she was clueless. More than once, I heard her ask a customer how to mix a drink."

"You used to be a bartender, right?"

"Yeah and still am, when I need extra money. I don't know how she made a living or how that bar stays open. Most of its customers are bar-hopping tourists, looking to pick up someone."

"Interesting . . . What's up with you today?"

"For openers, I hope I missed Ken. He's been here and gone hasn't he?"

"We tricked him into leaving."

Westerly hit on Michelle, a woman half his age, whenever he had the opportunity.

"Today's cruise ship day, so I gotta open early. Pick a number between one and five ninety-three."

"Two forty-six . . . why?"

"Two forty-six is the lucky cabin number. If the occupants of cabin two forty-six come into my shop today, they get a gift."

"Good luck and good luck to Mr. and Mrs. Two forty-six."

Bill chuckled.

"Thanks. See you guys."

"See ya," shouted Tiffany from her side of the wall.

Bill waved as Michelle left, but she was already out the door and down the street. Michelle reinforced Cynthia's comments about Laura and the Avalon Bay Bar. How had Laura made rent? He had occasionally given that a thought, but since she always paid on time, that had been the end of it. If Blessinggame heard Michelle and Cynthia's comments, Bill would be in for a major grilling. Things were not adding up. He wondered if Jenn had learned anything.

He touched two on his cellphone.

"Hi, love," was the immediate response.

"Hi, honey. Sleep well last night?"

"Yes, and you?"

"Surprisingly well, considering . . . The mystery of Laura grows as we speak. Have you found out anything new?"

"What do you want to hear first?"

"Save the best for last."

"Okay, then Laura first. Before Avalon, Laura worked in San Francisco. She had a clerical job at a chemical company called Kilgore Chemical. Her boss was Ahmed Shah. And get this: she attended bartender school at night."

"Michelle said Laura was a terrible bartender."

"Michelle?"

"Michelle Goodings."

"Miss I'm-going-to-be-a-multi-millionaire-before-I'm-thirty Michelle?"

"Spot on," said Bill.

"Well, prior to San Francisco Laura worked in New York, actually Brooklyn, for another chemical company, Allied Solutions. Her boss was Nidal Ayyod. Allied may have two locations, one in Brooklyn and one in Jersey City. Ayyod has possible links to the group responsible for the first World Trade Center bombing. He owns another chemical company in Chicago called City Center. While in Brooklyn, she joined the Al Farouk Mosque and volunteered at the al-Kifah Refugee Services Center. While there she associated with someone named el-Gobrowny, also linked to the World Trade Center bombing."

"This is fascinating. There seems to be a lot on her if you dig a little. The telephone number that gave Blessinggame heartburn, did it belong to the Brooklyn company?"

"Yes. I double-checked that. They disconnected it just as Blessinggame said. Prior to Brooklyn, there are gaps. She grew up on Long Island, went to Berkeley, and graduated with dual majors: chemical engineering and political science. After graduation, she returned to Long Island, and then there's a gap. 'Laura Mulholland' is an alias. Her real name is Laura Cartwright."

"Berkeley—chemical engineering and political science. She was no dummy. Was she an activist? When did she change her name?"

"She wasn't an activist. Berkeley gets a bad rap on that sort of stuff. It's actually a very conservative school. I'm working on when she changed her name. She went by Mulholland while in Brooklyn, Cartwright while in college."

"This is amazing. I wouldn't have guessed any of this in a million years. Is she a terrorist?"

"She isn't referred to as a terrorist *per se.* I suspect she's lumped with the others since she belonged to the Al Farouk Mosque and knew Ayyod and el-Gobrowny."

"Geez, Laura had two lives."

"Want to know about Lucy Cutler?"

"Jenn, stop with the baiting, of course I do."

"I can't find anything on a Lucy Cutler."

"Really!"

Laura's middle name is Lucy. Laura's mom's name is Georgia Cartwright."

"Georgia Cartwright . . . where is she now?"

"I think she's dead but I've been unable to confirm that."

"So Laura Mulholland is actually Laura Lucy Cartwright?"

"I believe so."

"Do you think Blessinggame knows all this?"

"He should but I doubt it. He wouldn't access information of this sort under the circumstances as he sees them. I bet he's digging around in vanilla databases."

"Yeah, he's probably off in druggie and prostitution land, so why would he think about terrorists."

"Want more, the best for last?"

"What could be better than what you just told me?"

"The owner of the Avalon Bay Bar is Jim Barber."

"So . . . who's he?"

"Who *was* he . . . he's dead, killed in a one-car auto accident in Norwalk three years ago."

"Whoa. So who owns the bar now?"

"Jim Barber."

"You just said he was dead."

"Damn, you're quick. Although Barber is dead, the California Alcoholic Beverage Control Board, the Federal Department of Alcohol, Tobacco, Firearms and Explosives, and the City of Avalon have not quite caught up with the deceased Mr. Barber's status. Business reports are filed in Barber's name. All reports and fees are current, so, why should regulators be concerned? Taxes and fees are paid, everything's cool in regulation land. Why stir things up?"

"How can that be?"

"Stranger things happen."

"So who's in control of the bar?

"I don't know."

"Are we in over our heads?"

"We're in better shape than Blessinggame. We shouldn't share this with him."

"Why?"

"I'm on your side, remember? Blessinggame's a jerk. He would construe this as an attempt to get him off our . . . excuse me, off *your* case, Mr. Prime Suspect, or he'd dismiss it out of hand or he'd pursue it in a half ass-manner. Whatever he did, he'd screw it up."

"Should we tell anyone?"

"Not yet. Let's dig around and see what else we can find. We aren't the police so we're less threatening and could be more successful. When we have a more complete story we can tell Tweedles Dee and Dumb."

Bill could almost hear the excitement crackling in Jenn's voice.

"Is that it? Is there anything else?"

"Geez, what do you want, the name of the murderer?"

"Okay, okay, great job, but where do we go from here?"

"You visit the Conservancy to see if someone there can shed additional light on Laura."

"Tiffany gave me an introduction. I hope to see Melinda this afternoon. Good work, babe."

"I wish I were there. This is becoming exciting."

"Not yet. We may need to have you do more research," said Bill, struggling to be upbeat. He did not want Jenn on island—at least just yet. He was concerned she would drag them down a road they did not need to go.

"I can't get out of here anyway."

"I'll let you know what I find out at the Conservancy."

"Good. If I find anything more, I'll call you. Good-bye, love, I'm late for a meeting."

"Talk to you later—bye, love."

Bill hit the red button and thought, *Boy have we stumbled onto a doozy of a mess.*

CHAPTER TWENTY-FIVE

2:10 PM Monday, August 16, 2010
Catalina Island Conservancy
Avalon, Santa Catalina Island, California

Standing on the second-floor landing of the Conservancy, Bill wondered where Melinda's office was.

He peered beyond the chaotic landing area and down a hallway. Open packages of Green, goldenrod, pink, and even white paper in letter and legal sizes littered the soiled carpet of the second-floor landing of the 1930s-era bungalow. As he looked at the jumble of color and clutter, Bill realized the landing served a few purposes: landing, copier room, storage area, and employee lounge. The stale, pungent odor of hours old morning coffee in partially empty glass carafes sitting on a small wobbly card table in the corner wafted in the air. A coffee maker and a two-cubic-foot refrigerator emitting crackling noises that signaled its imminent demise, sat atop a narrow table that fit snug along one side of the landing wall. A bulky ancient Xerox copy machine abutted the table and stuck out into the walking area. Electrical cords from the refrigerator, coffee maker, and copy machine were a jumble. Like legs on an octopus, the cords attached to an extension cord that lay across the hallway and plugged into a single duplex receptacle on the opposite wall. *What a hazardous mess* Bill thought. These old buildings had their charm, but unless remodeled outside, and more importantly, inside, they created challenges for modern lifestyles. They certainly weren't meant to be office locations housing the electronic demands of twenty-first century technology.

Bill made his way down the hall while thinking it was only a matter of time before the overloaded circuit shorted and burnt the building to the ground. The potential fire hazard aside, this was a veritable obstacle course—a workers' comp claim waiting to happen. Bill stepped through the colorful paper clutter, past the appliances and copy machine, and over the electrical cords to better scrutinize the hallway. He walked past an open door and then leaned back to peer into a room. Two women sitting at desks glanced at him. He realized, to his dismay, that although Melinda visited Tiffany almost weekly, he could not quite remember what she looked like. He winged it.

"Hi, Melinda," he said to the woman at the left desk.

The young woman with wavy, brunette hair highlighted with magenta looked up. Her eyes, dark brown, doe-like and dewy, with long, curled black lashes, gave Bill the once-over. "No, sweetie, I'm not Melinda, she's two doors down to the right, but I'd love to help you."

Her smile was peculiarly friendly. Bill could not help noticing the contrast between the chaotic appearance of the Conservancy offices and hallway with their near-picture-perfect, flawlessly groomed occupants.

"Oh, no thank you. Melinda's expecting me. I've just gotten a bit disoriented."

"That's easy to do around here," said the other young woman, who was sitting at the desk to the right. A come-hither smile came over her full, pink, glossed lips as she winked at him.

"I'm sorry, please excuse me. Thank you. Thank you both."

With a faint smile on his face, he walked two doors down the hall and peered into another room that needed to be organized. Bill wondered if physical chaos was a Conservancy cultural thing.

Melinda, older than the first two young women, was talking on the telephone. Bill took her in so he would remember her next time. She twirled the ends of her almost blonde hair as she spoke into the phone. Not too tall, Melinda stood leaning over her desk, but looked up when she realized someone was in her doorway. Her white satin V-neck T-shirt hugged her frame and covered the top of a black-and-white polka-dot pencil skirt that wrinkled at her stomach and stuck to her hips. Bill thought she was somewhat cute. Melinda smiled, nodded at him, and motioned for him to come into her office. Bill walked through the door as she finished her conversation on the phone and hung up.

"Hi Melinda. I hope I haven't interrupted you. If I am, I can come back. Tiffany said it'd be okay to come by."

"It's so good to see you. Yeah, I spoke with Tiffany earlier. I'm glad you were able to make it. Please . . . sit down."

Melinda motioned toward a chair covered with piles of loose papers. "Oh, I'm sorry . . . last month's after-action reports on the volunteer program . . . Here, let me clear this mess so you can sit down."

She moved the stacks of dog-eared, dust-covered forms to the floor, next to larger stacks of similarly untidy papers.

"Thanks for seeing me on short notice," said Bill.

"No trouble, I'd love to help. Tiffany said you wanted to know if I knew Laura Mulholland. No . . . not really. She worked in the Eco-Tour group as a tour guide. Helen runs that department; she'll be delighted to help you."

"That's great. Is she in? Could I see her?"

"No problem, I'll take you to her."

Melinda smiled and winked as she stood up and moved to the door. The wink startled Bill. Actually, it was more the iridescent plum colored eye shadow that covered her eyelid that took him aback.

He quickly recovered and said, "I can't thank you enough." Bill was becoming uneasy with these Conservancy women.

Melinda walked into the hall. She looked back at him over her shoulder with lowered eyes that revealed more of her dark purple eyelids and said, "I'll show the way. Follow me."

Bill followed thinking his encounters with the three women had been bizarre. Melinda walked toward the office he had first visited. His stomach clenched. But she glided past the office. The tips of her black three-inch stiletto heels punched through several sheets of the brightly colored copy paper scattered on the carpet. She stopped and leaned on the copy machine to steady herself as she pulled a blue sheet of paper off her heel. She tossed the sheet back onto the carpet, ignoring an almost empty wastepaper container under the table, and continued to the stairwell. She sashayed down the steep narrow stairs. Pausing midway to the first floor, she peered over her shoulder again and said, "Tiffany told me your wife lives over-town."

"Well kinda. She's here several days a week, usually weekends. She has an over-town job."

"Must get lonely." Melinda's voice trailed off into suggestive silence as she continued down the stairs.

Bill got it, or at least he thought he did. Apparently, some Conservancy people spoke in riddles designed to create awkward situations. A direct response might lead to trouble, but a vague response might provide wriggle room. He resolved to stick with vague responses. "We work it out quite well." Bill felt distracted. He hoped Helen's office was not much farther and Melinda would pick up the pace . . . but not increase her rhythmic, seductive hip action.

"Helen's office is just ahead," purred Melinda, again looking back at Bill. "Let me know."

"Know what?"

Damn, I screwed up the vague plan, he thought. *I should've ignored that one.*

"The lonely thing . . . Here we are—Helen's office."

"Helen," said Melinda playfully. "This is Bill. He's a *very* dear friend . . . Treat him as I would."

Bill thought *I hardly know the woman. How did I become her very dear friend?*

Melinda turned, winked, and gave Bill a slow peck on his check. Her nipples, erect under her satin T, traced a line across his chest when she slithered past him to leave Helen's office.

"Let me know," she whispered, then smiled and walked slowly away.

Flushed, Bill turned toward Helen. Here was another young woman, younger than Melinda was for sure. As she stood up to extend her hand and introduce herself, he noticed her clothes draped a slender body and shoulder length brown hair framed delicate facial features.

"Hi," said Bill extending his hand. "Sorry for the interruption."

Helen's hand lingered when she took his. "No problem. Please excuse Melinda. She's being her usual self."

A faint, knowing smile across her lips acknowledged Melinda's impact on Bill. She found a tissue in her desk drawer and handed it to him.

"You have lipstick on your check . . . Now, how can I help you?"

Bill felt addled. "Err—thanks again for seeing me."

"You're quite welcome. It'll be my pleasure to help you in any way I can."

Bill plunged ahead awkwardly. "Laura Mulholland—Melinda told me Laura worked for you. Laura was murdered over the weekend in a condo that I rented to her."

"I know . . . poor Laura." Helen looked genuinely upset, shaking her head. Chagrined she said, "We'll miss her. She was a beautiful person and an excellent employee . . . always on time; impeccably dressed . . . guests loved her . . ."

Impeccably dressed . . . that's not the Laura I knew, thought Bill. *Helen thinks highly of her. So far, most others had no opinion of her . . . most couldn't even remember what she looked like.*

". . . I hope they find her murderer soon. We're all anxious here. You must be also."

"I am. Although she rented from me for two years, I hardly knew her. She was a model tenant, just like the employee you described."

"She worked part-time as one of our back-up tour guides," said Helen.

"You have more than one back-up?"

"We have several jeeps. None of our guides is full-time. Some are primary some are backup. We staff to insure we have a guide when we have a guest. We book a tour and then check our list to see who's available."

"Laura was on the list?"

"Yes, as a back-up, not as a primary."

"How did she get on the list?"

"According to Marilyn, she came to us from out of the blue and wanted to be a tour guide. Marilyn said Laura had a keen interest in the Conservancy and knew a lot about what we did here. She wanted to help."

"Marilyn?"

"Yes. Marilyn Hastings had this job before me. I was her backup at the time. We all have several responsibilities here."

"Does she still work here?"

"No, she's gone, disappeared. We believe she just upped and left the island. No one knows for sure why or what happened to her. It was odd. We were all sad about it."

"Disappeared?"

Could this be the mysterious missing Marilyn? Bill checked his impulse to learn more. Marilyn would have to wait.

"Yes, just gone. Sad, too. She was a great person. Everyone loved her. One day she was here, the next day, poof, gone. Marilyn told me that Laura wanted to become a better tour guide but she wasn't getting enough on-the-job-experience, as she was junior and a backup. She wanted to learn more so she borrowed a jeep whenever she could and drove the tour routes to rehearse the scripted narratives and learn the terrain. Marilyn hoped she would stay on and become a primary."

"Did she get paid for the time she spent expanding her knowledge?"

Why did I ask that dumb question? thought Bill.

Helen paused before answering. "Oh we couldn't do that, we're nonprofit. We couldn't afford to pay her."

"What about insurance? Did insurance cover her?"

Damn, another dumb question, thought Bill.

Bill sensed Helen thought her judgment had been questioned so he quickly added, "Just curious. I'm a finance guy, you know." *Like that made any sense.* He winced inwardly.

"Oh, I totally understand," said Helen softly, her former demeanor returning. "Our insurance is based on hours, and as long as a qualified driver operates the jeep, we're covered. Actually, the risks on a real tour are greater. Our guests are frequently in and out of the jeep, so there is more chance for injury. Even so, we've been fortunate. In all the years, we've only had a few accidents, mostly trip and fall type stuff. Want to see our records?"

For a moment, Bill had mixed feelings. Would he want to see the records? Then it dawned on him. The records might help him learn more about Laura. He paused and then said, "Oh, you're very busy,

Helen. And I've taken way too much of your time already." He then made as if to leave.

"Not at all, sweetie," whispered Helen as she stood and moved to a file cabinet in the corner of her office. Facing the file cabinet, she looked back over her shoulder at Bill, smiled, and winked. She pulled out the top drawer of the gun metal-gray four-drawer, scratched, dented, and rusting file cabinet. "Ah, here it is."

Bill recognized the book as one of those speckled black and white, stiff cardboard-bound notebooks from his grammar school days. He was surprised to see they were still made. Helen moved her chair to the front of her desk where Bill sat and leaned into him as she placed the book on the desk. Her perfume came over him like fumes in tear-gas training—unavoidable and overwhelming. However, in this case, it was a pleasant experience. Bill had not noticed the musky scent before now. When Helen opened the book, Bill saw vertical penciled lines that separated the pale blue-lined pages into columnar sections for date, time, driver, odometer-out, odometer-in, and comments.

"See, it's all here for the insurance company. They never ask to see it, though. We use the data to calculate mileage and hours, and then give the insurance company a summary."

"Complete, very complete, this is great work," Bill continued while silently evaluating the information. "This would survive an insurance audit or scrutiny by the IRS. It'd be excellent evidence in a court case. You should be proud. You have an admirable record keeping system."

Helen beamed.

Bill wanted the book.

"Look. Here's Laura on the twenty-second," exclaimed Helen. "The comment section indicates no customers."

"That would be borrowed, right?"

She nodded yes while keeping her eyes on the book.

Bill's eyes skipped to other entries that indicated borrowed use—all were Laura's. None of the other guides borrowed jeeps. He made a mental note of the mileage for each trip. Trips using the borrowed jeeps were in the twenty-five to thirty-five-mile range. Bill scrutinized other entries and then he casually turned a page.

"There," chirped Helen, "there—see that. That's when Laura was on tour."

The tour was at least seventy miles. Bill concluded he needed more time with this book.

"This is great. Is this the only book?"

"Yes, but it has a lot of pages."

"How far back does it go? When did Laura start?"

"It goes back to when we got the first jeep. That would be four or five years ago. Maybe longer. I can't recall I was in another department then. I believe Laura started a year and a half maybe two years ago. Let's see."

Helen thumbed through the pages too quickly for Bill to absorb information.

"Ah, here we are. This looks like when she started . . . in April. Here's her first tour and there, there's another one."

Bill made a mental calculation. Both were in excess of sixty or seventy miles. Helen continued to page through the book.

"And here she borrowed a jeep."

A thirty-three mile jaunt noted Bill silently.

"Here she borrowed a jeep, and again, and here again."

Helen was on a roll, moving through the book too fast for Bill to calculate mileage for each entry. It was clear, though, that the frequency of Laura borrowing jeeps trended higher over the months. Her combined jeep tours and borrowed jeep trips easily exceeded each of the other guides' use, even the primary ones. Several borrowing entries were back-to-back, groups of two and three, usually in the winter months. Then there was a gap. In May, at the end of her first year, she stopped borrowing jeeps but still toured. She resumed borrowing at reduced frequency a couple of months later.

"Great records, I'm fascinated. But I must let you get back to work," said Bill as he stood up.

While eager to see additional entries, he was losing focus. His mind began to wander to conclusions rather than cataloging information for analysis. He needed a break to think.

"Oh, I'm just fine and this is important," murmured Helen, as she moved closer to him. Only thin cloth separated them so he felt the warmth of her thigh against his.

"Thank you, Helen. You've helped me better understand Laura. I appreciate your invaluable assistance, but I must go and let you get back to work."

"This has been fun. You must come back. I have something else that may interest you."

Bill ignored her comment.

She stood up and leaned over the desk. Her thin silk blouse allowed the nipple of her left breast to be felt as it brushed along Bill's upper arm and stopped at his shoulder. Then she closed the book. Maintaining continual eye contact with Bill, she dragged her chair to her side of the desk, but her scent lingered.

"You live on-island, don't you? Maybe we'll see each other around town." With a playful wink and soft smile, she said slowly, "You have a wonderful afternoon and great evening. Evenings are so fun in Avalon, aren't they?"

"Err—yes—thanks again, this has been very informative. I can find my way out. See you around town." *Why did I say that?*

Bill walked out of Helen's office and left the building through the main lobby. Two receptionists lolling behind the visitors' information counter looked up and smiled. One of them said something like, I hope we've been helpful. Please return soon.

Bill was out the door. The air refreshed him as he walked briskly to his office. *Wait until I tell Tiffany about my experience,* he thought, and then he chuckled to himself. *Who am I kidding? She'll already know what happened by the time I got there.*

Bill had spent almost an hour in flirtation purgatory. It had been worthwhile, though. Laura's personality and behavior were coming into focus. Her tour guide job, the borrowing of Conservancy jeeps, and her dual persona all appeared to be deliberately created to create an image of a sincere woman wanting to do a good job for a worthy purpose on one hand and remaining below the radar on the other. Yet murky gaps and vague questions of her actual purpose remained unclear.

CHAPTER TWENTY-SIX

3:07 PM Monday, August 16, 2010
Watson Financial Services, Metropole Avenue
Avalon, Santa Catalina Island, California

"How'd it go?" asked Tiffany with the hint of a smirk.

"Fine, everything went fine."

At least Tiffany doesn't wink, thought Bill.

"And what did you learn from Melinda and Helen?"

"Both were fine . . . really helpful. They were both helpful."

"Fine . . . helpful—give me a break! Fine and helpful are copout words."

Bill presumed Tiffany was not searching for an update on the proposition box score. She probably already knew that. She wanted to know about Laura. What should he do? He trusted her . . . she would not compromise a confidence, he would bet money on that. If she did not like what was going down, she would resign, and not tell anyone the reason. He would need an on-island confidante, if for no other reason than as a cover for him, when he was out of the office.

"Tiffany, I have to share something with you . . . it's confidential. Are you okay with that?"

"Sure."

"Jenn and I think there's something bizarre about Laura's murder; actually, most things we've learned about her are bizarre."

"Really?"

"Jenn and I believe Laura was involved in something that may have dire consequences and it could be why she was murdered."

"Geez, this is exciting. What was she into?"

"Jenn's done the spade work, and based on my discussion with Helen, I believe Laura staged her position as tour guide. I'd bet her bar job was also a deception. Laura lied to me about her mother. She told me her mom was Lucy Cutler but Lucy Cutler doesn't exist. Laura's real mother was Georgia Cartwright. Laura Mulholland was an alias. *Most significant*, Laura associated with known Islamic terrorists. She's included as a bit player in terrorist databases."

"A terrorist . . . oh my god, Laura was a terrorist?"

"Borderline . . . we don't know for sure. Jenn doesn't know why Laura's in the database other than she associated with known terrorists. It gets murkier. The Avalon Bay Bar's owner has been dead for over two years and we have no idea who operates it now, but whoever does has stolen the owner's identity. On my visit to the Conservancy . . . oh by the way thanks for the heads up on Melinda and Helen . . ."

Tiffany shrugged her shoulders as if to say, you're an adult, deal with it.

". . . I learned Laura worked for a person named Marilyn before she worked for Helen. Laura used Conservancy jeeps allegedly to learn how to do her job better, but all her training trips were for distances about half of a typical tour."

"Marilyn . . . do you mean Marilyn Hastings?" asked Tiffany, wide eyed.

"Bingo babe," said Bill, pointing an index finger toward Tiffany.

Jenn would have drawn the same conclusion at least as fast, thought Bill. She and Tiffany were so alike in so many ways and so unalike in so many other ways.

"This is unbelievable. I'm sorry about Helen and Melinda, I should have warned you," said Tiffany apologetically. "I consider their game weird but harmless. They always chicken out and abandon he game, if it goes too far."

"Terrific, I'm sure Jenn will be thrilled to know all about that. Speaking of Jenn, I should call her. She may have learned more since we last spoke."

"Marilyn disappears, Wanda is murdered, Laura is murdered, and they were all involved with Interior tours. Do you think there's a connection?" posed Tiffany animatedly.

"Maybe. That'd be a good guess. Jenn might have an answer."

Bill started to punch Jenn's number on his speed dial but a glance at Tiffany revealed disappointment on her face.

"Want to join the call?"

"Now?"

"Now."

"You bet!"

"The speakerphone is out of the question. Lock the front door. We'll call from your office."

"Roger."

Bill wondered what he was getting into. First Jenn had gone gung-ho, over the top on this sleuthing stuff, and now Tiffany had fallen in lockstep. *What will be the greater challenge, trying to untangle this mystery or restraining them?*

Jenn's phone rang once. "Hello, this is . . ."

". . . Hi, babe," interrupted Bill.

"Why the land line? My phone's secure. I doubt yours is. Is your cellphone dead again?" said Jenn knowingly. "Our conversations are sensitive. We have to be careful."

"We're okay," said Bill cavalierly. "Tiffany's on the line with us."

"Isn't this is exciting," burst in Tiffany.

"You've brought Tiffany into the Laura thing?" asked Jenn.

Did Bill detect disapproval in her voice? "I did."

"That's great. Now you stand a chance of making it through this without going to jail or being killed. Welcome to the team, Tif."

"Excited to be on board. We're going to solve this, I know it!"

Bill brought Jenn up to speed on his findings at the Conservancy, leaving out his experience with the proposition competition. Of course, Tiffany felt compelled to jump in and fill Jenn in on the particulars of that part.

This was going to be tough, reflected Bill, two against one.

"Anything new?" He asked Jenn.

"Yes, Laura had a passport. I've e-mailed you a copy of her passport picture. I know her."

"You know Laura?"

"I do. Not as in, we were best friends. She worked out in the weight room at the Cove. She was buff with not an ounce of fat on her—pure muscle. She lifted weights and rode the stationary bike for what seemed like hours. She barely acknowledged I was in the room. She said hello sometimes, but usually ignored me. Oddly, if a man came into the room she immediately broke off in mid-exercise, put her sweats on, and left. Her response to a man's presence was always the same."

"Her passport . . . any idea where she's traveled, it might help with the gaps."

"Not yet. I'm working on it. People-oriented searches are tough—privacy crap and such. I can learn specifics on precedent-setting top-secret, military weapons within hours of their first tests, but where U.S. citizens have traveled is more closely held than the development of cold fusion . . ."

The frustration behind Jenn's comment on governmental vagaries of information sharing was familiar ground for Bill. She had vented about it on several occasions.

". . . Aside from inconsistent application of privacy rules, nothing had changed much since 9/11 with respect to interdepartmental sharing of information on terrorists. *Newsweek* was correct—the ownership mind-set had changed for a brief time when collaboration had become the *in* thing. However, sharing reverted to the old ways within a year, if not months. Information again became sacred. Agencies vied with each other to be *the one* to tip off the world about the next 9/11. After all, budget money is at stake," Jenn said sarcastically. "It's pathetic. I'm working through it though. Guess who attended Berkeley at about the same time as Laura?"

"Who?"

"Wanda Peabody."

"What! Wanda and Laura were friends before Avalon?"

"I knew it," shouted Tiffany. "Laura, Wanda, and Marilyn, they're connected—it's a conspiracy."

Bill cast a glare at Tiffany and thought. *Conspiracy. Give me a break.*

"Nothing indicates that they were friends . . . they could have been. I'm working on it."

"Is Wanda in the terrorist database?" asked Tiffany.

"No. Laura earned that distinction due to an alleged, but unproven, association with Mohammed Salameh or Kamal Ibrahim in the late nineties."

"Mohammed Salameh and Kamal Ibrahim, who are they? Their names sound Middle Eastern," said Bill.

"Actually, it's one person with two names and he *is* Middle Eastern, a Saudi National. He was involved with the first Trade Center bombing. From what I've been researching, there were shitloads of militants involved in, or claiming involvement in, that bombing. Most have dodged the Guantanamo bullet and retain status as practicing terrorists, that is, if they're still breathing."

Silence stopped the conversation. Bill spoke first.

"This is big and dangerous."

"So what's your point?" asked Tiffany.

"Yeah, what's your point, you're Ranger qualified," chimed in Jenn sarcastically.

"Fair enough, but *then* my MOS was infantry, *now* it's financial planner."

Bill knew he was doomed. There would be no turning back with these women allied.

"Where should we go from here?" asked Bill.

"We decided you would stop for a drink at the Avalon Bay. I think you might find something there. It may be a dead-end, but so far, nothing has been a dead-end. It turns out there is no lack of information about Laura. All you have to do is get past the obvious and scratch the surface a little and information bites you on the nose but it's still not clear what her real purpose was."

"I'd bet it wasn't good. I'll check out the bar tonight."

"Good," said Jenn.

"There's a new search criterion," said Tiffany. "We need to know more about Marilyn Hastings."

"Wasn't she the person who disappeared . . . left the island without a trace?"

"Yes, but when she *allegedly* left the island, she was Laura's boss! There could be more to her disappearance," added Bill.

"Oh my god, another link to Laura," said Jenn.

"They're all dead, I know it, and there could be others. If so, I know they're also dead or will be soon," said Tiffany confidently.

"Getting a little ahead on this aren't we Tif?" said Bill, his tone chagrined.

"I'll look into Marilyn and drill down on Laura and Wanda," said Jenn.

"What about me . . . the new partner?"

"We'll need a central control point for communication and coordination, which will be this office. For now, you're in charge of that," said Bill, hoping he had convinced her.

"I'm not a desk jockey! I'm operations—I do field operations."

Bill groaned and thought, *Field operations, my god a de facto military organization is forming before my eyes.*

"Tiff, we'll need extra eyes," continued Bill. "There's a lot of ground to cover and we don't even know where most of the ground is. It'll take all of us. We'll morph as the needs arise. Everyone will be involved—agreed?"

"Okay," said Tiffany, showing dejection.

"Done," said Bill.

"Done," said Jenn. "I'm really glad you're on board, sweetie. Let's get to it."

"Okay, done," agreed Tiffany, beginning to sound a little more excited again.

CHAPTER TWENTY-SEVEN

8:45 PM Monday, August 16, 2010
Avalon Bay Bar, Catalina Avenue
Avalon, Santa Catalina Island, California

Bill observed the bar from across the street.

Unreadable beyond fifteen feet, a small sign, swinging from a single rivet, identified the Avalon Bay Bar. The once bright red lettering had faded to an inconsistent light, almost blush pink. The lettering, partially obscured by bird excrement and street dust, looked like it had not been cleaned since the sign was mounted.

Mottled beams of pale amber light streamed through the dirt and dust coated windows. Through one of the windows, the beam flickered as though a bulb needed changing. To the left of the windows was the front door. Whoever had installed the door had left a half-inch gap between the door and frame, allowing faint light to show through around all sides of the dented, unpainted sheet metal door. Bill took all this in. He wondered how people were able to recognize the storefront as a bar and if they could, who would dare venture in. Contrasted with the other bars in Avalon, the Avalon Bay suggested a dreary, boring experience.

God forbid I run into a client.

Cynthia had told Bill locals did not frequent the bar. He hoped she was right. Bill crossed the street, grasped the rusted door handle, and pulled the door toward him. As he stood in the doorway for a moment to look inside, two couples walked briskly out and hurried down the street.

"Excuse me," he blurted. They continued down the street without acknowledging Bill. *That's not a good sign.*

The high-pitched, screech of metal on concrete that had accompanied the door's opening had disheartened Bill. He hesitated; maybe he should leave. However, he decided he had passed the point of no return. He would draw more attention to himself by leaving than staying. A rapid assessment of the inside allayed Bill's anxiety. He recognized no one. He breathed more easily as he had been worried that a resident would see him in the bar and make an offhand comment the next day at the Vons coffee klatch. Successive coffee klatch storytellers would elaborate on vague information . . . *Married respected local financial planner haunts tourist bar, seeking one-night stands.* In Avalon, embellishment always accompanied revelation.

Desensitized to the screeching sound of the door, no one looked at Bill. The woman who tended bar gave Bill a quick once-over. The interior ambiance of the bar, if it could be called ambiance, paralleled the exterior appearance—grubby. The bar stools were disorderly and each seat had at least one tear patched with duct tape. The venetian blinds were askew, dusty, and slightly open. The bottom of each blind draped unevenly on the sill. The once cream-colored pull cords were now gray black with grim and held together by a series of improvised knots. The bar counter itself was unoccupied, except for a man who sat at the far left. A few other customers were seated in mismatched chairs at small rickety tables sipping beer from bottles. Bill wondered if the beer was cold or warm.

Bill noticed the bar walls needed paint so badly that the pale yellow light bleeding from the underpowered ceiling lamps reflected unevenly off their surfaces. A fifties-era jukebox stood mute against the wall on the left side of the room. The play list of dated recordings served silent witness to an earlier demise of the machine. A ceiling fan, the surface of its blades laden with years of accumulated grimy, grease-encrusted dust and insect remains, whirled slowly struggling to compensate for two other inoperable ceiling fans.

Bill stood just inside the front door for a moment and surveyed the room. He speculated on the existence of a room directly behind the bar counter. A narrow curtain soiled from countless hands hung limp and concealed a passageway. A sedate, expressionless barkeep sat on a stool behind the bar counter blocking access to the curtained-off area. Bill wondered if it was worth ordering a drink. What could he possibly learn in this dump?

The bulky man who sat at the bar was slouched over a bottle of beer. His oily, disheveled hair plastered against his ears. He wore a wrinkled, soiled jacket and looked hostile, as if he had just gotten off a job he did not like. Although Bill didn't recognize the man, he was sure he had to be a local. Bill tagged him Mr. Scruffy. Bill eased onto the stool next to Mr. Scruffy.

Other than the initial cursory once-over, the barkeep had not acknowledged Bill. He could observe her better now. She did not wear jewelry or make-up. Her crumpled, loose-fitting dress concealed her body, with the exception of her head and hands. She sat motionless, unenergetic on a stool. Her demeanor indicated tending bar was not her idea of a fun way to spend an evening.

Bill heard a growl-like mumbling. "Tourist?"

Mr. Scruffy has a voice. It's a start, thought Bill, although he hardly knew what to do with it. He answered, "No, I have a place here but I live mostly over-town."

Certainly not entirely true, clearly unrehearsed, and undoubtedly poorly executed. Bill winced inwardly. "Are you a tourist?" Bill asked, believing he knew the answer, but somehow he had to fuel conversation . . . and at present, Mr. Scruffy was the only game in town. The barkeep still had not moved a muscle. *Had she known Laura?* wondered Bill.

"No, and don't insult me. I'm a local," said Mr. Scruffy.

Adopting Mr. Scruffy's point of view, Mr. Scruffy had just insulted Bill. He considered pointing that out but decided that would be counterproductive. "Sorry."

No answer from Mr. Scruffy.

"Is Miss Exuberance dead?" asked Bill with a nod toward the far end of the bar. *Damn, bar conversation can be tough.*

"She's new . . . hasn't quite figured it out. I give her the benefit of the doubt."

"What's to figure out?"

"Good point. Wave at her . . . let's see if she'll come over."

"Is she any better than the person she replaced?" asked Bill, as he raised a hand and waved in the barkeep's direction.

"God no. Laura could fog a mirror . . . not anymore, though. She's dead."

"Dead, like, as in not living?" faked Bill.

"Yeah, she was murdered over the weekend," said Mr. Scruffy matter-of-factly. "It's really bad publicity for the island, lousy chamber of commerce material." Mr. Scruffy took a long drink and then added, "Laura worked here every night."

At last—things might be going somewhere. "Bill's my name," said Bill extending his right hand. "Do you come here much?"

Mr. Scruffy stared at Bill's hand then haltingly responded with his own.

"Name's Joe, I come here a lot in the summer. The pickings are better here."

"The pickings . . . I don't understand."

"Locals hate this place, lousy service, no pool table, and the jukebox's busted. There's no camaraderie, the place sucks."

"So why are you here?" asked Bill looking around at the dilapidated room and its contents.

"Tourists . . . tourists come here. The poor fools don't know any better. My chances of picking up a bitch are better here than at other bars. The bitches here get bored. I encourage them to consider alternatives. I'm like a counselor and a tour guide rolled into one. I suggest choices and guide them through the ins and outs of Avalon. I suggest other bars, alternatives to bars, escort them to the Marlin or Locker Room, and get to know them better along the way. After we've had a few drinks, I suggest activities that are more exotic. You know, 'your hotel or my place?'" Joe grinned. "I have good success when I work from here, maybe one in ten. If I lose one, I come back and try again. I get two, maybe three shots on a busy night during the summer. I need a good-sized herd of quality bitches. Tonight the herd's lousy. The bitches are ugly and all are with men. We're only mid-way through the game day, though. I could score nearer midnight. Early or late are the best odds."

"Oh, I see." Bill concealed his disappointment. So far, all he had learned was a pathetic strategy for picking up women.

"Wave at Christine again," said Joe.

Bill waved. At first, Christine did not respond, and then a glimmer of hope—she moved.

"Here she comes," said Bill eagerly, with an elbow nudge to Joe, who muttered, "Christine's a poor excuse for a bartender. She's a lousy broad and has no life."

Bill felt sorry for the semi-comatose woman.

"Does anyone want a drink?"

"Yes, I would, thank you. What kind of wine do you have?"

She stared at Bill and said nothing.

I wonder if there is a trick to ordering a drink, he thought.

A few seconds passed and finally she said, "Red and white."

"What kind of white?"

Christine stared and then, after another longer pause, said, "White."

"Err . . . that's great, I'll have the white."

She slinked away. Bill was not optimistic. "What is with this place?" muttered Bill sideways.

"It's a mystery how this place stays in business. It's the shits," said Joe.

"What about Laura, did you know her?"

"Laura was like Christine, but smarter. If you asked for a beer, you got a beer. It might not be the beer you ordered but it was a beer. If you ordered a martini, you got a stare. If you ordered rum and Coke, you got Coke with a splash of rum or rum with a splash of Coke. The proportions were a crapshoot but at least she tried. Christine's a lost cause."

Christine returned with a water goblet filled to the brim with a pale yellowish liquid that resembled and smelled like turpentine. The glass was so full it spilled over the top and streamed down the sides onto the sticky bar counter. The rim of the glass was chipped and had two lipstick imprints. One imprint was of lips that had worn a pink gloss, the other imprint was coral colored.

Bill thought, *if the wine doesn't kill me, germs surely will.*

"Thanks. I'm Bill," said Bill, extending his hand.

Christine stared. Bill waited. Eventually she responded, "Christine." She did not offer her hand and Bill slowly withdrew his. Christine retreated to her stool.

"This place is unbelievable." *How in god's name had Laura made a living?* thought Bill. *She had a less than part-time job at the Conservancy and bartended in this dump. Nothing makes sense.* He turned to Joe. "So, Laura was a dead fish?"

"Yep, a dead fish. That's a good one. You're right, she was a dead fish."

"Did you ever speak with her while waiting for the herd to fatten up?"

"I tried to . . . it didn't work."

Joe's attention was wandering. Three middle-aged women had entered the bar.

"The herd's been upgraded," said Joe.

Bill watched a smile cross Joe's face; it was like a hyena eyeing a carcass. Not that Bill could distinguish between a hyena and a German Shepherd.

"The older blonde—the chubby one, she's mine. You pick from the others."

Suddenly Bill realized with a sickening lurch that Joe assumed he had come to the bar with the intent of scoring.

Joe straightened his back and prepared to get up, then said, "Shit," and sat down.

Three middle-aged men doing their loud obnoxious man thing entered the bar.

"They're attached to the women, damn. Maybe there will be an argument. Arguments can lead to rejection and rejected bitches are excellent targets. The odds improve to about one in eight. We'll wait and see. This could work for us. Keep tuned."

Bill did not want to keep tuned and certainly was not interested in how Joe calculated odds.

"What about Laura? You said you had no luck speaking with her. Did anyone?"

Bill took a sip of wine and nearly retched.

"Nah, she wasn't a talker. She hardly said anything. But she read a lot."

"You're kidding. What'd she read?"

"How the hell would I know? It's so dark in here an owl can't see. She'd sit on her stool and read with this little light clipped to her book. A customer would come in and she'd read, another customer would come in and she'd turn a page and read. Soon the customers left. That didn't bother her. She just kept reading."

"Probably Harlequin romances or something like that—right?"

"They was books with science stuff on the covers."

"Really, what kind of science stuff?"

"You know, science stuff, like chemistry, physics, and electricity. What the hell is physics?"

Bill took this to be a rhetorical question. "Maybe she took courses."

"Could be. She wrote in a book. She'd read and she'd write, all evening long, she'd read and write, read and write. On a slow evening, when there was a crappy herd and such, she'd read all fucking evening. She never talked to me or no one, she just fucking read and wrote. There's this one dude, though, he dressed in dark clothes like cat burglars in old movies. He blended perfectly into this joint. He'd come in and sit on the stool at the far end of the bar, right across from Laura like where Christine is now. He never ordered a drink and Laura always sat in front of him. She stared directly into his face, while they talked. She totally ignored everyone and everything while the dark guy was here. She didn't take drink orders while the dark dude was here."

"What did he look like?"

"Hard to say. He had darker skin but was nondescript, as they say. I never understood a word he said, he spoke so quiet, but Laura paid close attention to him, very close attention. She always answered him. She never spoke to anyone like she spoke to him."

"Was he Hispanic?"

"A wetback, yeah, he coulda been a wetback but he was different. He wasn't like the other wetbacks around here, though. Maybe he was one of them, I can't say for sure. Oh yeah, he had a bushy moustache. He was a strange dude, actually."

Women must be pretty far gone to settle for Joe, thought Bill, but he kept a bland face and carried on trying not to sound overly interested. "How often did he come in?"

"Dunno, maybe three or four times a month, probably less."

"Any special time?"

"Early. He always got here early. I like to get here about six to get a crack at the transition crowd, it's good hunting time," said Joe, waving his right hand around the room. "Often he'd be here by six or six-thirty."

Bill sighed inwardly.

"Did Laura ever say anything to you about him?"

"No—wait, yeah, once she referred to him as her boss. He's the owner, I guess."

"Humph. Wonder what his name is?" said Bill matter-of-factly.

"Kaylid."

"Kaylid?"

"Yeah, she called him Kaylid. What the hell kind of name is Kaylid?"

Bill looked up. Christine was back. What shitty timing.

"Everything okay?" she asked.

What an inappropriate time to commence a marketing campaign, thought Bill.

"The wine is fabulous," replied Bill, eliciting a glare of disbelief from Joe.

Bill hoped Christine would return to her vigil but instead she turned to Joe.

"You want another one, Joe?" prompting another look of disbelief from Joe.

"Yeah, I'll have another, a Bud."

A hint of a smile crossed his face as Christine headed down the bar.

"I'll be damned. The bitch actually acted polite. There's hope for her. She might make the list." Then Joe turned to Bill. "The wine is fabulous. Are you fucking shitting me? The wine is fabulous. Gimme a break, good try, but you're butting up against a brick wall. You'll never make it to first base with Miss Personality. She's just like Laura. There ain't no chance in hell you'll get into her panties. That's if she wears panties."

Bill opened his mouth to protest but Joe continued.

"There was a nigger she spoke with."

Wincing at Joe's word choice, Bill said, "She spoke with a black man?"

"Yeah, a nigger. Not a customer. He came out through the curtain behind where Miss Personality is sitting. I'd bet he was an employee."

"Not many black men live in Avalon. Have you seen him other than here?"

"Can't say I have and I only saw him here two or three times."

"Recently?"

"A month or two ago, maybe longer—hey, look at that."

A grin widened on Joe's face and he licked his lips.

Commotion had flared up at the new arrivals' table. One of the women, the heavier blonde, bolted for the door. Joe followed without as much as a goodbye.

A pro in action, thought Bill with a shake of his head. *Disgusting.*

Christine returned with the Bud, stood in front of Bill, and looked around. "Where's Joe?"

"Joe left, sweetheart. I'll pay for his beer."

Christine turned, without comment, and walked toward the other end of the bar. On the way, she tossed the newly opened bottle of Bud into the trash.

Bill exhaled. It was definitely time to go.

CHAPTER TWENTY-EIGHT

9:47 PM Monday, August 16, 2010
Outside the Avalon Bay Bar, Catalina Avenue
Avalon, Santa Catalina Island, California

Bill pushed the door to the bar open and stepped out into cool, still, night air.

Avalon faces east across the San Pedro Channel to mainland California, an orientation that exposes the town to early morning sun and searing midday rays. To the west, and behind Avalon, hills rise steeply to block the late afternoon sun as early as 3:00 PM and cast a cooling shadow over the town. The town's proximity to a southward flowing Arctic current complicates its weather pattern. The daily temperature range often exceeds thirty to forty degrees in the summer.

While the evening air temperature had dramatically cooled, the intensity of the crowds drifting from bar to bar had not. People congregated in the streets everywhere except adjacent to the Avalon Bay Bar. A short block away, judging from the crowd that mingled in front of it, the Marlin Club was teeming with activity. Bill did not know whether the Marlin Club would reveal anything more about Laura, but he needed to wash away the taste of the atrocious wine served by Christine. Anomalies about Laura, like pieces of a complicated jigsaw puzzle, swirled in Bill's mind as he walked to the Marlin Club. He wondered whether Christine was part of that puzzle. Why would the owners of the Avalon Bay Bar replace Laura with a clone. It certainly did not make business sense, or practical sense either, considering the availability of a large number of experienced bartenders in town. He made a mental note to phone Jenn in the morning and see what she could find out about Laura's replacement.

A thick gray haze of cigarette smoke hung in front of the Marlin Club. California's overarching ban on smoking had supplanted old problems with new. The California laws forbid smoking in public buildings so smokers concentrated outside of buildings. The hazy cigarette smoke made Bill feel nauseous. He fought the feeling as he peered through the front window of the Marlin Club. The Marlin Club, smaller than the Avalon Bay Bar, was jammed to standing room only. Inside at least, he would be away from the nauseating cigarette smoke.

Bill pushed open saloon-like doors similar to the ones you see in old western movies. His concern of being recognized heightened when he remembered that Cynthia and Michelle had told him locals favored the Marlin Club and Locker Room. He quickly rationalized away his concern for the same reason—locals that came to these bars expected to see other locals. Although the bar was packed, Bill spotted two empty stools at the bar and quickly understood why—Deputy Jimenez. The empty stools bracketed Jimenez. *Not surprising,* mused Bill. A thought struck him. Jimenez might be just dumb enough to disclose information concerning the status of the investigation into Laura's murder.

Bill elbowed his way through the crush of bodies, sidestepping couples absorbed in conversational game playing. He moved past men sizing up the *herd* (a term he had recently learned), and restless women wondering why men were hitting on other women but not them. Well, it was *one way* to spend a Monday evening, but he did not envy any of them. Inside to the right of the front door, two Pamela Anderson look-alikes and act-alikes in matching white colored Lycra tank tops contemplated their shots at the Marlin Club's only pool table. One leaned over the table in an exaggerated extended pose lining up her shot. She provided onlookers an ample view of her large, firm, unconstrained breasts. Bill glanced away but the image stayed with him. He was sure she *wasn't* a local.

Bill slid onto a stool next to Jimenez and motioned to the bartender. The Marlin Club's bar is shaped like he prow of a boat with the bow pointing towards the front door. Stools lined both sides of the 'boat.'

"Evening, Deputy."

Startled, Jimenez looked up and hesitantly responded. "Evening, Bill. What brings you to the Marlin?"

"I could ask the same. Are you undercover?"

"Don't be silly. Of course I'm not."

"I'm just making conversation, don't get worked up."

"I'm out for the evening, just relaxing. I'm off duty," said Jimenez.

"Same here . . . went out for a walk after dinner and then decided I'd stop for a drink. How about a drink . . . on me. What's your pleasure?"

"Scotch."

Bill's stomach, still doing battle with cigarette smoke and Christine's wine, twisted as he leaned toward the bartender.

"Two scotches."

"Make mine with soda," added Jimenez.

"Great idea. Mine too," said Bill, somewhat relieved. *Scotch and soda has to be better than Christine's unpalatable version of white wine.* "So . . . anything new on Laura?"

"Not really. Blessinggame's taken over. We're off the case. We're in support—that's what the chief calls it, in support. We're in support."

"Too bad a murder, unfortunately, offers an opportunity to shine—to hone investigative skills, especially on Catalina."

Jimenez had more than a few skills that needed honing. Bill figured feeding him compliments might loosen his lips. If anyone could be duped into being indiscreet, it would be Jimenez.

"Yeah, and our department was first on the crime scene—the chief and I."

It was impossible to miss his air of injury.

"You covered it like a blanket."

"Yeah, more so than you'd think. Those over-town bozos are lousy detectives. They aren't thorough."

"I'd expect local people would have a leg up on those over-town guys. There'd be a sense of ownership and pride in protecting the community . . . know what I mean?"

Jimenez was nodding avidly.

"So, I guess Blessinggame and Co. isn't sharing?"

"Not much."

"I'm kinda surprised somebody called the murder into the police so soon," said Bill. "I mean, Hamilton Cove is out of the way and not many people live there. Someone could be dead out there for days and no one would know."

"It was odd. The station got an anonymous call about six on Saturday. He said he'd heard shots. However, we later learned Laura died between midnight and two. Anyway, we didn't know whether to take the call seriously . . . it being anonymous, you know. We get crank calls all the time. But the morning was quiet so we went out."

"That seems like a long time to wait to make a serious telephone call, I know if I'd heard gun shots, I'd be on it."

"Yeah, you bet, I would too. We broached that with Blessinggame. He just blew us off. He blows everything off."

"Did you trace the caller . . . caller ID?"

"Nope, the number was blocked. I'd thought about that," Jimenez said with satisfaction.

"Maybe the person who called was the killer. He might have waited until to call he was off-island."

"That was my thought also, but Blessinggame wasn't interested in hearing that. He believes it's a drug deal gone bad. The chief and me, we're not so sure . . ."

Jimenez purposely paused.

"Really, a drug deal? Do you have leads?"

"N . . . err . . . I can't say. Confidentiality you know."

Damn, and the conversation had been going so well. "Of course, of course, I can understand that. But Laura didn't strike me as the drug type. She was very reliable paying her rent. Anything surface on her background?"

Jimenez shook his head. "She didn't have many friends or acquaintances. Actually, we couldn't find anyone who really knew her. It's as if she didn't exist. It's weird."

"Have you checked with her bosses at the Conservancy and bar?"

The bartender delivered the drinks and announced stoically, "nineteen bucks."

Bill put down two tens and a few ones hoping the information would be worth the outlay as he was sure the scotch wouldn't be. It smelled worse than Christine's white wine.

"Tomorrow the over-town guys are going to the Conservancy. They learned zip at the Avalon Bay Bar. Blessinggame couldn't find anyone there who knew anything. According to the bartender, the owner wasn't available. He's out of town or out of the country or something like that."

Jenn will not be happy to hear that, thought Bill.

"What about the bartender? Did he know Laura?"

Bill felt pleased with himself about his feigned ignorance of the bartender being female.

"No, and it's a she. She told Blessinggame that she was an emergency replacement."

"How about databases, anything turn up there?" asked Bill, already quite sure of the answer.

"Ours turned up nothing. I don't know about Blessinggame. He's tight-lipped and arrogant. He was here Saturday and Sunday then went back over-town. We haven't heard from him since. Our job is securing the crime scene. We're being treated as bloody security guards."

Jimenez forced a swallow of his drink.

"Secure the crime scene . . . why? Laura's body's been removed hasn't it?"

"Oh yeah, but there's drugs and other clues."

"Drugs?"

"Yeah, we found drugs and needles and stuff like that in her condo . . . and money. Just like with Wanda. Remember Wanda?"

"Kinda." Bill lied.

"You know, the dead woman found at the dump. When we searched her body and then her apartment, we found drugs, paraphernalia, and money . . . hundred dollar bills, mostly counterfeit. Laura's condominium was the same, drugs and counterfeit money everywhere."

Bill shook his head slowly, trying to organize this new information.

"I didn't know Wanda, but Laura didn't seem like a druggie type. Do you think she was using?"

"I don't know. Over-town detectives believe Wanda was a dealer, but if truth be known, there isn't any hard evidence for that . . . drugs didn't show up in Wanda's blood—not that that means anything. Maybe Laura was a dealer or user. There's no toxicology report on her yet."

Bill was feeling hopeful again.

"Have you made a connection between the two murders?"

"Not yet. Over-town is working on it. Maybe there's a connection."

Maybe . . . do these people need a neon sign?

"Any leads on Wanda's murderer?"

"Over-town took that one over also . . . they haven't turned up any leads. No one knows nothing, no one knows nada."

"It seems like the over-town guys aren't on top of things."

"That's for sure, and they missed tons of evidence."

Jimenez was nibbling at the bait again. Bill proceeded carefully.

"No kidding. Like what?"

"The book, for one thing."

"The book?"

"The quorum."

"The quorum?"

"Yeah, the quorum, the Muslim Bible." Jimenez gave Bill a what-are-you-stupid look.

"Oh yes. The Qur'an."

"The quorum, that's what I said."

"What about it?" asked Bill tentatively.

"It was on Laura's nightstand. The book was right there . . . right in plain view and they didn't see it. The idiots didn't see it. It could've bit 'em on their noses. But I saw it."

"And they're running the case? Unbelievable."

Jimenez looked superior.

"They stopped checking into everything after they found the drugs, done deal, fate accomplished as they say."

Jimenez was surpassing himself, obviously quite stoked.

"You believe otherwise."

"Absolutely. This wasn't just a drug deal. Maybe drugs had something to do with it, but there is something else, I feel it in my detective bones. I bet there's a shit more clues at the cove."

"Do you think there's an Islamic connection? I can't think of a single Muslim who lives on island. And Muslims loathe the use of drugs."

"I don't know, but her having that quorum is pretty weird, especially 'cause she's white."

"Mmmm . . . I bet you're right about more clues."

"Sure I'm right, but we'll probably never know because it ain't our case. We're not allowed to look for clues, we're security," he concluded sourly.

"That's really unfortunate because you were onto something."
Possibly, more so than the deputy knew, Bill mused.

The well of information seemed to have run dry when Jimenez blurted, "Sand, that's another thing. There was sand all over the balcony and inside her condominium. Three other units at that level in the building are vacation rentals but were empty. The Association sweeps or washes all the balconies and stairwells every day during summer. The balconies in front of the other units didn't have sand so where did the sand come from? How would it get there? I asked Blessinggame. He looked at me as if I was nuts when I mentioned it. He says sand's all over the place in Avalon, Avalon's just one big beach. Blessinggame hates it here."

This information about the drugs, the Qur'an, sand, and the similarities between Wanda's and Laura's murder sent Bill's mind reeling and the scotch did not help.

"It's getting late I should get home and grab some sleep . . . long day tomorrow. It's been good talking with you, Deputy. Say hello to Dave. I'll pass on Blessinggame."

"Don't blame you. Just watch, in a few weeks he and his buddies will be begging us to take the case back. G'night, Bill. You take care now."

"I will, you too."

Outside, Bill rushed to his office to make notes before the details slipped his memory.

CHAPTER TWENTY-NINE

11:32 PM Monday, August 16, 2010
Khalid's Room, Second Floor of the Avalon Bay Bar
Avalon, Santa Catalina Island, California

"Peace be upon you and the blessing and mercy of Allah," said Khalid.

"And peace be upon you and the blessing and mercy of Allah also," replied Mohamed.

Khalid had summoned Mohamed to town ahead of the other jihadists.

"We have lots to talk about," said Khalid.

"We do?"

"The American converts pollute jihad."

"They more than pollute, they're clueless," said Mohamed. "I pray to Allah, `azza wa jall*, every day that he'll guide us despite the American converts' incompetence. They have put jihad at risk. They aren't committed, not to jihad, not to Islam, not to Allah. They're lip service Muslims. They challenge Islam and the ways of Allah, `azza wa jall*, at every turn. They haven't shed their pathetic Western thinking. They corrupt Islam and don't accept the traditions. They want to modify the ways of Allah, `azza wa jall*. They're impure."

"Yes," said Khalid, his tone ominous, "and worse. We have no choice but to complete this jihad before it is too late. I've determined that a week from Saturday is the day."

Khalid had not determined anything of the sort. The date for jihad had been set by Brooklyn three years ago.

"It is up to us to insure we keep these poor excuses for mujahedeen committed. We must double our effort to keep them in line. I count on you to insure they comply with the desires of Allah, `azza wa jall*. When the time comes, they must detonate the bombs. There can be no discussion, no indecision, and no lack of resolve. We must be sure they act."

"You can count on me."

"We are as one in the work of Allah, `azza wa jall*. Peace be upon you and the blessing and mercy of Allah," said Khalid.

"We are. May the blessing of Allah be upon you."

1:17 AM Tuesday, August 17, 2010
Prayer Room, Second Floor of the Avalon Bay Bar
Avalon, Santa Catalina Island, California

"We don't need this. Why one o'clock in the morning?" complained Abu Tarek.

"I know, we all know," said Saleem-Ali peevishly. "It's disruptive and interferes with everything, it impacts our schedule, and it causes us to violate *salat*. That alone should be enough for Khalid to plan differently."

"He's a control freak," said Abdel el-Shinawy. "We're tired. Our preparation has been long and hard. We are trained we are ready. Brooklyn and Afghanistan should let us do our job."

"You all complain," said Mohamed abruptly. "Complaining isn't part of jihad. Khalid has told us repeatedly this is the best time to meet. The risk is lower, as we're less likely to be noticed. It makes sense."

"It makes no sense. It's only convenient for Khalid. He lives here . . . we have to go back and forth to the compound or find a place to sleep or sleep on this floor. That increases the risk," said Abu Tarek. "Why doesn't Khalid come to the compound?"

". . . and participate in training?" finished Saleem-Ali. "He's part of jihad, I don't get it."

"Watch your tongues! Khalid is Shaykh, the leader. He is in charge. He follows the will of Allah, `azza wa jall. We all do Allah's bidding, `azza wa jall. You must show respect for him."

Mohamed did little to disguise his disgust and anger with the jihadists.

"And where is Fikriyya . . . and Aaliyah?" asked Saleem-Ali. "They should be here. Are they exempt from meetings?"

"Fikriyya hasn't been at the compound either," added Abu Tarek.

"She's with Khalid. They are going over her duties as she has replaced Aaliyah. They're closing the bar for the evening," replied Mohamed snappily.

"Replaced Aaliyah?" Abdel el-Shinawy was unable to keep dismay from his voice. "Before Fikriyya left the compound, she told us she thought that something had happened to Aaliyah. Is Aaliyah dead?"

"Khalid will tell us when it is right," declared Mohamed.

"Was she a target of the Americans? Did they kill her? Are we at risk?" persisted Abu Tarek, pressing the discussion as if Aaliyah were dead while ignoring Mohamed's rhetoric.

"When you need to know, you will be told." Mohamed's voice was rising.

Another non-answer, thought Abu Tarek.

"All of you are undisciplined!" howled Mohamed. "All you ever want to know is why, all the time, why. All you *need to know* is what Allah wants and then do his bidding. Allah knows best, `azza wa jall.*"

"Was she ordered killed?" asked Abdel el-Shinawy, now convinced she was dead.

"Like Faiza?" asked Saleem-Ali and Abu Tarek simultaneously recognizing similarities in an all too familiar scenario.

"Silence! You do what Allah wants, `azza wa jall. Islam is not about democracy!" shouted Mohamed. "The traditions dictate, not your stupid speculation. What the situation is with Aaliyah is none of your business until it is time to be your business. You all behave like infidels, why this . . . why that . . . why, why, why. Behave like believers. Behave like Islamic jihadists."

Mohamed imagined the planning and hard work of the last few years going for naught.

"Peace upon you, and the blessing and mercy of Allah," said Khalid, entering the prayer room. Fikriyya followed.

"And upon you be the peace and Allah's mercy and blessings," responded Abu Tarek, Saleem-Ali, Abdel el-Shinawy, and Mohamed in unison.

"May the blessings of Allah be upon you. There is no power nor strength save by Allah," incanted Khalid. Then, after a pause, he added bluntly, "Aaliyah is dead. She was impure and could not come back to Allah, `azza wa jall.*"

" `*Azza wa jall,*" responded the others in unison.

"She did not choose the straight path, just as Faiza did not choose the straight path. They worked with each other and with an unbeliever, the drug dealer. She had to die. The traditions left no alternative. Allah knows best, `azza wa jall.* I was obligated to kill her. May Allah's mercy be upon her. She will not reside in the garden with flowing streams. The day approaches for what Allah wishes."

"May the blessings of Allah be upon you," echoed a chorus of voices.

"Why did you kill her?" asked Abu Tarek, confused. "Was there no other way?"

"I told you there was no other way, Allah decreed she be killed, `*azza wa jall.* Alive she could compromise us. Aaliyah had become unreliable and untrustworthy. She was a liability."

"Like Faiza?" asked Saleem-Ali.

"Yes, like Faiza."

"Are all of us at risk? Two of our comrades have fallen into the hands of the devil. Are there others?" asked Saleem-Ali.

"No," said Khalid, "we are unified as the time comes upon us. I've scheduled a dry run for this Saturday and in a week the world will feel the full impact of the Avalon Jihad."

"What Allah wishes," chimed the others in unison.

"Abu Tarek and Mohamed are team one, Saleem-Ali and Fikriyya are team two. Inspect your equipment, then double check it, then triple check it. Leave no detail to luck. When the time comes, everything must work. Review your roles. Know the language of the scuba divers. Divers may engage you in conversation on the express boats, so you must know what to say. Leave nothing to chance. Make certain nothing remains in the compound. Destroy or remove anything that links us to Brooklyn or Afghanistan—clothing, equipment, papers. Destroy everything. When you leave on Thursday, presume you will not return. Everything must be as it will be on jihad, may the blessings of Allah be upon you. I will be at the compound to oversee final preparations. Peace be upon you, and the blessings and mercy of Allah."

"And upon you be the peace and Allah's blessings," chanted the Avalon Jihadists as they filed out of the prayer room.

CHAPTER THIRTY

5:55 AM Tuesday, August 17, 2010
Watson Financial Services, Metropole Avenue
Avalon, Santa Catalina Island, California

Forty miles away, across the channel, a blazing summer sun peeked over Camelback Mountain. Sunlight, reflecting off sapphire-tinted San Pedro Channel, bathed Avalon in an eerie white light.

Oblivious to the spectacular morning, Bill mulled over his notes keen for a pattern to emerge. Was this a wild goose chase? *Maybe Blessinggame is right and Aaliyah's murder is drug-related,* he thought. It made sense. Laura could have financed her life style by selling drugs. The bar gig could have been a cover or, more likely, she could have sold from the bar. He was certain that Blessinggame's investigation lacked integrity, discipline, and due diligence and he was sure Blessinggame had charged down the drug trail, eager to ensnare the first suspect that stepped in his way. To be arrested for Laura's murder was illogical but Bill could not risk it.

"Hi, boss."

Bill looked up from the notes spread before him.

"Hi, babe . . . what the hell."

Tiffany stood before him . . . mission-impossible Tiffany in person. Running shoes, jeans (starched, creased, and pressed, but still jeans), and a V-neck, sheer white T over a bright pink sports bra. Her thick brown hair was drawn up in a ponytail perched high on the back of her head, and held in place by sturdy hair elastics. She wore no jewelry save a Swiss Army sports watch with a cloth band.

"It's Tuesday, not casual Friday," said Bill, a smile emerging from one side of his mouth to create a lop-sided grin.

"Very funny, Mr. Boss, but we're dealing with murder. There are clues to discover, motives to unravel, and people to question. *Lackadaisical* doesn't cut it. Who knows what confronts us. We gotta be prepared. All hell could break out at any moment."

Tiffany, hands perched on her curvaceous hips, was not quite Ranger School material, but the thought was amusing to Bill and he continued to smile. "A little over the top, babe . . . that pink sports bra sticks out like a sore thumb. You'd be easy pickings for a sharpshooter. What does your husband think of the new Tiffany?"

"He thinks we're all nuts," said Tiffany, ignoring the pink bra comment.

"Makes sense to me."

"But he knew that about me before we were married. He says there isn't a terrorist within a hundred miles of here, unless they're on vacation."

"Really, isn't he the slightest bit concerned? After all, the Island Company practically runs the town."

"That's the point. He doesn't want bad press, especially during the tourist season. He suggested I stay out of this, as it was going nowhere. He's hopeful I'll convince you and Jenn to back off."

"He really thinks that'll work?"

"Of course not. We're opposites. He's more like you, conservative. I'm sure that was one of the reasons the Island Company hired him. They're the original 'don't rock the boat why change' people—a Wrigley legacy. They loath anything not consistent with pre 1950s."

"It's served them well portraying Catalina as a throwback to the hey-day of the 1930s."

"That scenario is getting a little stale." Tiffany cocked an eyebrow at Bill. "You need to rethink your clothing."

Bill glanced down at himself in puzzlement. "What's wrong?"

"Well for one thing, I doubt you could run down a terrorist in wing tips."

"Give me a break, we're not running down terrorists, we're not running down anyone. We're gathering information, not confronting anyone let alone running anyone down."

"You don't know that. Hey, you snooze, you lose."

She perched on the edge of his desk. "So, how'd it go at the bar? Did you learn anything?"

"I'll share when we conference with Jenn." Dropping to an undertone, he added, "Look who followed you in."

Tiffany turned to see Ken coming through the door. His face bore the unmistakable concentration of someone on a mission.

"Good morning, Ken. A bit early, aren't we?" asked Tiffany.

"Yup, it'll be a long day. I need an early start."

"Why a long day?" asked Bill.

"Vacation, I'm leaving in a couple of days, I'll be gone a few weeks, maybe longer. Gotta get my shit together."

"You hadn't mentioned that before. Where are you going?"

"You men visit, I'll put coffee on," said Tiffany, seizing the opportunity to escape from the usual drivel she knew was coming.

"Coffee, that's a great idea. I'm going to the east coast to see relatives. I'm really excited."

"That's great," said Bill. "Whereabouts?" *Several weeks without Ken would be fantastic and the timing couldn't be better.*

Ken hesitated several moments as if to collect his thoughts and finally said, "North Carolina. It's beautiful there. What's on CNBC? Hey, why isn't the TV on?" asked Ken. Locating the remote on Bill's desk, he picked it up and pointed it at the television.

Bill wondered whether Ken had a television. *Maybe he doesn't and that's why he shows up every morning.* Erin Burnett appeared on the screen.

"Uh-oh, looks like Maria's on special assignment or maybe vacation. Do you think I should spend time in New York and take in Squawk Box? Do you think they have a live audience?"

"I don't know but probably they do," said Bill, although he hadn't a clue.

"What's new on Laura?"

"Let's not do the Laura thing again. I didn't murder her and I don't know anything about the murder that you won't find in the *Islander*."

"I wonder who murdered her, if it wasn't you." Ken smirked. "They say it was drugs. Do you think it was drugs?"

"I don't know. Ask the Sheriff."

Bill was abrupt. Maybe Ken would take the hint.

"How's the coffee coming? I got things to do and people to see."

"Coffee takes time," snapped Tiffany angrily from behind the wall separating her office from Bill's. "It'll be a few . . . remember there's always coffee in the shop across the street."

"Good, that's good. What do you think about Morgan Stanley? Would Morgan Stanley be a good investment? Should I buy it?"

"I don't know. I have no idea about your investment profile, your risk tolerance, or anything about you or your goals. I'm unable to answer your question. Don't ask me that kind of stuff again."

Bill was irritated with himself. He had done it again. *Why do I let him engage me?*

"I wonder how the season's going for Avalon. There're a lot of people in town."

So much for Morgan Stanley.

"This is August. August is always busy."

"Oh yeah, I forgot."

"Coffee's ready," announced Tiffany.

"I forgot my cup. Do you have a paper cup? I gotta go . . . hey, great hairdo, sweetheart."

"Thanks. Paper cups, yeah, we got 'em."

Tiffany went in the back and in a few seconds returned, a paper cup in hand. "Here, be careful, it's hot."

"See you guys."

Ken was out the door.

"What was that all about? I mean . . . thank god, he's gone but what gives? 'Great hairdo, sweetheart.' Is Ken boyfriend material?"

"Give me a break." Tiffany pulled a face, her eyes rolled upward and then closed as she slowly shook her head sideways in an indication of disgust.

"We got him out of here in record time. Good job."

"So what happened last night?"

"Long story, I'll tell you when we get Jenn on the line. Lock the door, I'll call."

6:17 AM Tuesday, August 17, 2010
Watson Financial Services, Metropole Avenue
Avalon, Santa Catalina Island, California

In Tiffany's office, Bill made the call.

He and Tiffany exchanged long-suffering glances as Jenn immediately usurped the conversation. ". . . So this blonde walks into a library, marches up to the librarian, and in a loud voice says, 'I'll have a Big Mac, fries, and a Coke.' The librarian leans forward, her face inches from the blonde's face, and says in a very low voice, 'Honey, this is a library.' The blonde looks around, bends closer to the librarian, and whispers even lower than the librarian did, 'I'm sorry. I'll have a Big Mac, fries, and a Coke.'"

Tiffany groaned as Jenn continued without skipping a beat. "I've been waiting for your call."

"Find anything new?" asked Bill, relieved the blonde stuff was behind them.

"I did. Laura spent a year, maybe two, in Europe in the 1990s—Hamburg and Brussels. Wanda may have been with her, but I'm not certain. If Wanda was with her, they both likely associated with radical Muslim groups. It was there that Laura adopted her alias of Laura Mulholland. I found a reference to an Aaliyah, which may be another alias, but more likely is a different person. I don't know. I've asked another source for information on Aaliyah. Laura and Wanda converted to Islam while in Germany. She and Wanda returned to the States about the same time . . . maybe together. They settled in Brooklyn and remained there for a while. Ultimately, they wound up in Avalon, although they didn't arrive at the same time. Both are dead—murdered and that can't be coincidental."

"Speaking of dead, what about Marilyn Hastings?" asked Tiffany.

"So far there isn't a connection. Marilyn may not be involved in any of this. She may have just left the island, a true coincidence. She moved around a lot: the Midwest, Northern California, and several years in Las Vegas as a blackjack dealer, before settling in Catalina. Nothing indicates she knew Wanda or Laura before Avalon, or that she knew them in any capacity other than as Laura's boss. When she disappeared, she just disappeared. There's no trace of her."

"Do you think she may have been murdered?" asked Bill.

"I don't know. I doubt it . . . that's just my guess. Want to know about other murders?"

"Yes, go on, and thank you for asking our permission," said Bill sarcastically.

"The official records give a different twist to Jim Barber's death, but I think he was murdered. Remember, Barber is the deceased owner of the Avalon Bay Bar. The public records indicate he died in a one-person automobile accident at three in the morning in Norwalk. There wasn't any indication of alcohol, drugs, or foul play. He totaled a rented automobile . . . no one claimed the body. They located his car in the Catalina Landing parking facility several days later. Barber's insurance company paid the claim. Barber was the consummate absentee owner. He hardly ever set foot on Catalina. Within days of Barber's *accident,* his manager for the Avalon Bay Bar, Benjamin Heart, disappeared. No one has seen or heard of him since. He just left the island—sound familiar. Based on what we know about Laura and Wanda, I believe Barber and Heart were murdered. Whoever stepped into Barber's shoes is a key to this whole mess."

"Kaylid."

"Kaylid? Who's that . . . where did that name come from?" asked Jenn.

"Yeah, who's Kaylid?" Tiffany chimed in, looking at Bill curiously.

"Laura told a customer at the Avalon Bay that her boss was Kaylid."

"Holding out on us again, boss," said Tiffany, feigning arrogance and a pout. "Who told you about Kaylid?"

"Joe, a slime bucket . . . a jerk, a real red-neck type, but he had no reason to make up the story. He volunteered the information. It could be correct. Joe's never seen Kaylid, except at the bar, and then only a few times."

"Obviously, finding out about this Kaylid is a priority," said Jenn.

"You're right but we have a name. Blessinggame has nothing. Then there's Deputy Jimenez—according to him, Blessinggame drew a complete blank when he visited the bar. The employees there stonewalled him. They told him the owner was out of town."

"Out of town my ass," said Jenn. "The owner's dead and somebody else is running the joint. Blessinggame is a fool. How did you extract the information from Jimenez?"

"Jimenez was at the Marlin Club last night. He said Blessinggame drew the conclusion that Laura was a loner and that no one really knew her. The same observation we made."

"Avalon Bay Bar, Marlin Club, sounds like bar hopping to me," Jenn quipped.

"Blessinggame's convinced this is a two-bit drug case," continued Bill, ignoring Jenn's remark as well as her tone. "It's believable and purposeful. If he can prove a drug connection to her, the case defaults to low priority and it's shelved. If he cannot find a drug connection to her, the case dies anyway. Drug-murder cases are a dime a dozen, and from law enforcement's perspective, the perpetrators and victims aren't worth the time or resources. For some reason, Blessinggame is hesitant to link the murders of Laura and Wanda, even though the police believe both cases involve drugs, drug paraphernalia, and counterfeit money. Jimenez thinks Blessinggame is wrong and it's not just a drug case. In spite of his lack of professionalism, Jimenez might be right. The Avalon Sheriff's station has been relegated to the sidelines. Blessinggame's in control."

"Anything else, Sherlock?" asked Jenn.

"How come you get the easy stuff . . . Avalon Bay Bar, Marlin Club—that's real tough duty?" Tiffany did not hold back on the sarcasm.

"Thanks. I'll presume that you're in awe of my finely honed detective skills. If you want, though, you can have the bar gig next time. You'd love Christine and Joe."

"Christine?" asked Jenn.

"Oh yes, Christine, but more on her later."

Bill had intentionally yanked Jenn's chain but figured she deserved it because of her bar hopping comment.

"Jimenez told me he found a Qur'an in Laura's bedroom, which the over-town super-sleuths missed. That ties to your finding that she had converted to Islam. He also told me there was sand inside her unit and on the balcony in front of her unit. The other units on that level were vacant and there wasn't any sand." Bill paused to catch his breath. "We've learned a lot that Blessinggame probably doesn't know. Even still, we may be reading too much into this. Maybe this is just a drug case. There are at least two murders, probably more, and they could be linked to drugs. It's common enough."

"But how will we find out?" asked Tiffany. "Nobody really knew either woman."

"You know," Jenn, mused audibly. "Helen thought highly of Laura at least as an employee. She might have additional insight. Or Wanda's boss at the Island Company may be able to shed some light on this."

Bill said, "It's a long shot. Helen did speak highly of Laura, so that's worth looking into. However, I'm *not* going back to the Conservancy."

Tiffany chuckled.

"Okay Miss Wise Ass, you take the run at Helen. I'll check out the Island Company."

"Okay . . . I'll have lunch with her and Melinda. That'll seem normal, just our regular get-together to catch up. Laura's bound to come up, as she's the hot topic in town."

"There's another person," Bill said, relishing the suspense.

"Go on, wise guy, who's the mystery woman?" said Tiffany in verbal retaliation.

"Christine."

"Ah . . . Christine the mysterious Christine," sang Tiffany.

"Christine took over for Laura at the Avalon Bay. Joe said Christine is a clone of Laura. Laura hated working the bar. She barely communicated with anyone and always had her nose in a book. Joe said Christine is worse. I couldn't get Christine's last name. Is it worthwhile to search half names like Christine and Kaylid?"

"Can't hurt," said Jenn. "I'll cross-reference them with Wanda's and Laura's background information. It's a long shot."

"It may be worth trying to trace Laura's trips to the Interior presuming that's where she went. Her jeep trips don't seem to fit with anything else and there were inconsistencies in mileage between actual tours and her training trips. What were the trips about? Do they matter? Are they part of this? All we know is the number of miles she drove . . . there's really no reason to believe she drove to the interior other than that's what she told her bosses. What do you think?" asked Bill.

"That's a great idea. Drive the distance to determine the farthest point she could've gone, that'll limit the search," said Jenn. "You'll need a vehicle permit for the Interior."

"What about Michelle? She has a truck and a permit. I'm sure she'd let Bill borrow it. She likes Bill and always asks if she can help," said Tiffany, with another chuckle.

"Barhopping and now a girlfriend, is there no end to your other life?" said Jenn.

"Very funny. I'll ask her."

"Are you're holding back anything else, boss?"

"Another person," said Bill.

"Another person!" said Tiffany.

"How many people are involved in this?" spoke both women at the same time.

Bill had to hold the phone away from his ear for a moment. "Whoa. I haven't a clue about how many, but there is at least one more—a black man. Joe thought the black man worked at the Avalon Bay. He'd seen him there several times. He said that black man usually came from a room behind the bar, spoke briefly with Laura, and then went back into the room."

"Hmm . . . there aren't many black men on Catalina," observed Tiffany.

"That's right, and Joe's never seen him anywhere else. Unfortunately, I have no name. I'll try to reconnect with Joe this evening."

"You think he'll be there?" asked Jenn.

"Yep, no doubt. It's his hunting space. He starts his prowl at about six."

"Hunting space . . . prowl? What are you talking about now?" asked Jenn.

"Joe's idea of a successful evening is luring an unsuspecting female tourist to his lair. He offered to teach me the ropes."

Bill winked at Tiffany, who rolled her eyes.

"You *have* been busy haven't you? Anything we need to know about this hunt thing or is it a secret?" asked Jenn.

"Top secret."

Bill could feel Jenn's exasperation practically radiating through the phone.

"Ok, seriously, Joe told me that Laura read a lot. I mentioned that already, but get this. She poured over texts on chemistry, physics, and electricity."

"Well, maybe she was taking courses."

"Yeah, my thoughts initially. Apparently she took copious notes."

"You don't sound at all convinced," commented Jenn.

"I'm not. Too many things don't fit and then there's the two men."

"Could they be the same person?" asked Tiffany.

"I don't think so. Joe was specific. He said Kaylid always came in the front door and sat at the bar. The black man always came from a room behind the bar. Kaylid was dark but not black and had a bushy mustache."

"You certainly have been a busy little detective. I'm afraid to ask, is there anything else?" queried Jenn.

"No, that's about it," said Bill, matter-of-factly.

"So," asked Tiffany. "What's next?"

"My opinion is we back off and dump everything in Blessinggame's lap. There have been two, maybe as many as five, murders. Whoever these folks are, they are a nasty bunch. We are in way over our heads. I could meet with Blessinggame and give him what we've found. Jimenez told me he'll be in town tomorrow."

Without hesitation Jenn and Tiffany both roared, "No!"

"Blessinggame's a jerk," continued Jenn. "He wants quick solutions. The information we have could overwhelm him . . . it *would* overwhelm him. He believes this is a drug case. He wouldn't know what to do with what we tell him . . . it runs against his mindset. He might think we are trying to get him off your case by fabricating red herrings. Remember, sweetheart, you are *suspect-one*. We should give this a couple more days. The more corroborating evidence we have, the better. If it looks like terrorism, I'll contact Homeland Security."

Jenn's voice and pace did not invite an opinion from Bill.

"I'll set up lunch with Helen and Melinda," said Tiffany, continuing where Jenn left off.

"I'll work the databases," added Jenn, without hesitation.

"Boss, try to borrow Michelle's truck," continued Tiffany.

Bill sighed . . . resistance was futile and getting a word in edgewise near impossible.

"Okay fine. I'll touch base with Joe at the Island Company and speak with Michelle."

"Behave yourself," said Jenn, with what she hoped was taken as mock sternness.

"You're absolutely no fun at all," said Bill.

CHAPTER THIRTY-ONE

10:37 AM Tuesday, August 17, 2010
Michelle's Dress Shop, Metropole Avenue
Avalon, Santa Catalina Island, California

"Hi Michelle. Any chance I can borrow your truck?"

Michelle looked up from a stack of boxes containing new arrivals of fall dresses. Her dress shop was three doors down from Bill's financial services office.

"Sure, catch." She reached into her shorts pocket and threw Bill the keys. "It's over on Clarissa. When you get back, park it on East Whitley by my house, and leave the keys in the ignition."

"Thanks."

"Where are you going?"

"To the airport. Can I get you anything?"

"I can't think of anything. You will need the gate pass. It's behind the passenger side visor."

Bill pocketed the keys, left Michelle's shop, and walked toward the Island Plaza, the jumping off point for the Island Company's bus tours.

*   *   *

"Good morning, Jeremy."

Surrounded by tottering stacks of schedules and after-action reports, Jeremy looked up from his desk. Initially he appeared confused, but ultimately recognized Bill. "Good to see you, Bill. You don't get over to this part of town often."

Bill smiled and decided against pointing out that "this part of town" was less than two blocks from Bill's office. Outgoing and talkative, Jeremy had spent his whole work life in marketing. "What brings you here?"

"A concern. You got a moment?"

"A concern? Sure what's up?"

Jeremy set a sheaf of papers he was perusing on top of another sheaf of papers and motioned Bill to a chair alongside his desk. Bill was certain he saw a small cloud of dust disperse into the air when Jeremy brought the sheaves of paper together.

"Laura Mulholland was murdered this weekend."

Jeremy looked carefully at Bill and said, "I'd heard a woman was murdered. Out at Hamilton, wasn't it?"

"Worse . . . in my condo."

"Bummer."

"I didn't know her well, actually not at all, but that's not important. It's not every day someone is murdered in Avalon, let alone in my condo. Did you happen to know her?"

"No, why?"

"I've been told she was a friend of Wanda Peabody. I believe Wanda worked for you."

"She did, but not directly."

Jeremy's normally open demeanor turned guarded. His instinct to distant himself from trouble reflected in his normally genial face. "She was a tour bus driver and worked for Joyce, a supervisor of mine. I knew little about her other than what Joyce told me. Joyce said she was a good employee. It's terrible that she was killed and now this Laura person." Then curiosity gained the best of him and he dropped his guard and continued, "Do you think there's a connection?"

"I don't know. The police think both murders were drug-related. If that's correct, I'm not overjoyed that drugs might have been sold from my condo. I'm worried."

"Drugs? Wanda? No. No way. Not Wanda. I don't know about Laura but I'd have a hard time believing Wanda was involved with drugs. According to Joyce, she was a model employee. She never took time off, never was late, always dressed appropriately, and never had friends hanging around while she was working . . ."

"I can appreciate that. Those kinds of problems aren't limited to Catalina."

Jeremy continued. ". . . Wanda didn't drink or smoke. Nope, drugs make no sense at all. It'd be totally out of character."

"That makes me feel better. Do you know if she and Laura were friends?"

"I have no idea. Actually, I can't place Laura. What did she look like?"

"About forty, give or take a couple of years or so either side of that, dark complexion, scraggly dark brown hair, tall, and slim—actually, lean. Apparently she worked out."

"I can't place her. I'd remember a woman like that."

"What about Wanda's supervisor, Joyce? Do your think she might be able to help me?"

"If she were here," said Jeremy, with a scowl and a slight shaking of his head. "She unexpectedly left town just before the season . . ."

God another person who just up and left the island, thought Bill.

". . . That caused me mucho grief. I was pretty pissed off. It was a nightmare to replace her on such short notice. There aren't a whole lot of quality people with supervisory skills in Avalon who aren't already employed. I've been struggling since."

"Do you recall her last name or where she went?"

"Joyce Littleton. I have no idea where she went. She gave short notice . . . seemed like two Nano-seconds. Maybe the Midwest, she once mentioned having family there. Err . . . but that might have been someone else. Sorry . . . can't help you on that."

"Thanks, you've been a real help." Bill stood up. "If you think of anything, let me know. Jenn and I are anxious about the drug thing."

"I can imagine. No problem, I'll let you know if I hear anything. I'll ask around."

Bill raised a hand in farewell.

That didn't turn up anything worthwhile. Mulled Bill as he left Jeremy's office . . . If Laura had been dealing drugs, she could have covered it up, that wouldn't be too hard to hide, but using that's another thing. He speculated that maybe she needed money. Maybe she had a wastrel brother up to his neck in debt, or a sick relative with massive medical bills. Shaking his head in frustration, Bill decided to walk back to his office and check in with Tiffany before getting Michelle's truck.

11:04 AM Tuesday, August 17, 2010
Watson Financial Services, Metropole Avenue
Avalon, Santa Catalina Island, California

Blessinggame was slumped in Bill's chair, feet propped on Bill's desk, with a wad of papers in hand.

Bill's heart raced when he saw him. Blessinggame looked up and acted annoyed as though Bill had walked uninvited into *the* detective's office not vice versa. *Does he have a warrant?* Bill forced a smile and said in mock humor, "Good morning detective and welcome to my humble office . . . the Worldwide Headquarters of Watson Financial Services."

Blessinggame was perplexed by the greeting but charged into the reason he was there.

"Mr. Watson, why do you show up everywhere I look in this investigation? What were you doing at the Conservancy yesterday?"

"That's two questions. Which one do you want me to answer first?"

Playing for time, Bill was not sure how he would answer either question.

"Don't be a smart-ass. I want answers, good answers. I'm suspicious of you turning up everywhere I look. What were you doing at the Conservancy yesterday?"

"Well, I was curious. I mean, c'mon, Laura was murdered in my condo. I need to know what happened."

Not a great answer but it made some sense and bought Bill more time to think.

"Bad answer. You do not have a right to know anything—nothing about Laura, nothing about her death, nothing about my investigation, and nothing about what happened in the condominium. Did you know Wanda Peabody?" shot Blessinggame, clearly trying to catch Bill off guard.

Bill was unfazed. "I answered that question a few days ago and the answer is still, 'No.' Should I be calling my lawyer?"

"As you wish, Mr. Watson, but this'll be easier if it's just you and me."

"How about a reading of rights?" Bill laughed with a sardonic tone.

"Your call," said Blessinggame, who then proceeded to blunder through a chaotic, poorly memorized version of Miranda.

Bill shrugged and shook his head. "So what's your point? What do you want from me?"

"Everywhere I look in this case, you show up."

"It's a small town," said Bill with a straight face.

"You're just too damn involved and interested for me to ignore you. You could be part of a bigger picture. Maybe you're part of a drug ring, maybe Laura gave you more than $1,800 cash every month, maybe your condominium was the ring's headquarters." Blessinggame stared at Bill coldly for several moments. "Any travel plans, Mr. Watson? You do remember you're not to leave the island without my permission."

"How could I forget? My only involvement in this crime is as a victim. This B.S. about me being involved with drugs is whistling in the wind. Obviously, I've an interest in my property and need to know why Laura was murdered there. Her death could affect my property's value and my life. Now you are telling me drugs are involved. If that's correct, I have a right to know if drugs were sold from my property."

"Mr. Watson, I suggest you have a little legal chat with your lawyer. You do not have any of those rights. Stay out of my investigation, stay out of my way, and *do not* interfere with witnesses—*do not interfere, period.* Do I make myself clear?"

"Oh, I think so, detective. Is that all?"

"You think so? You need to do better than just think so. I'll be in Avalon today and tomorrow and I may want to talk with you again, so stay put."

Blessinggame swung his feet from Bill's desk, tossed the papers he had been holding onto Bill's desk, and stomped out of the office.

"Have a nice day," quipped Bill.

Bill looked at the discarded papers . . . Jimmy Goff's tax return. *Where the hell did he get that?* Then he glanced at an open file folder that was in his in box. Bill may have inadvertently violated one of the relatively new over-the-top privacy rules that permeated the financial services industry. He laughed internally. *I thought privacy rules applied to everyone including law enforcement officials.*

Bill swore under his breath

"What a jerk," said Tiffany, coming into Bill's office.

"That's for damn sure. How long has that jackass been here? Did he ask you any questions? How did he get Goff's tax return?"

"Only about ten minutes and he didn't ask me anything except where you were. I told him I didn't know but thought you'd be back soon. Whether you would or not was his problem. Goff's file was in your to-do-pile. He may have rummaged through your inbox and picked it up just to get under your skin . . . You okay?"

"I'm fine, considering Blessinggame's not so veiled threats. We need to step up our efforts. I can almost feel a noose tightening around my neck."

CHAPTER THIRTY-TWO

12:48 PM Tuesday, August 17, 2010
Old Stage Road
The Interior, Santa Catalina Island, California

The access gate to Old Stage Road was annoying and discriminating. It erratically denied or granted access. However, today the gate gods smiled on Bill and the gate easily swung open on the first try. Bill withdrew the deformed plastic access keycard from the gate lock and replaced it in the rusted clip attached to the tattered sun visor. Michelle's 1970s F-Series Ford was mud covered, dented, and rusted—the acknowledged in-town badges of honor that adorned vehicles driven in the Interior. Avalon residents seldom washed vehicles that frequented the Interior.

Bill held his breath, eased off the clutch, and depressed the accelerator. The truck edged forward. He hoped the truck, nothing more than a semi-loose collection of rusted metal, bolts, and balding tires would be up to what might lay ahead. The first two miles of Old Stage Road were a dreadful uphill climb. Rocks, small and large, dislodged from the steep hillsides on the inland side of the road littered the surface of the narrow, pothole-riddled road. Eucalyptus trees lined the opposite side of the road, providing deceptive protection from a series of steep falloffs that paralleled the road. The line of fragrant trees created a final shield, more psychological than actual, for drivers who miscalculated the edges of two-hundred-foot abysses. Curves and soft shoulders lay inches from sheer drop-offs into sage-choked canyons where legend had it vehicles had disappeared forever.

Bill's knees weakened at the thought. His mind flashed to jump school. Training jumps had been from 500 feet and the jumpmaster had had to shove him out the door of the aircraft. There was nobody to help here, though. After two tense miles of ascent, the road topped out at twelve hundred feet and then meandered almost eight additional miles through dusty, parched, rolling hills toward the Airport-in-the-Sky. Maybe the airport had been as far as Laura had gone. That would be understandable. It was conceivable that she wanted to practice driving the daunting road in and out of Avalon. She would continue to the airport, have a cold drink and snack, and then back to Avalon. Bill wondered whether he was wasting his time. This could be a pointless drive, which would add nothing to the investigation.

Bill turned into the almost empty parking lot of the Airport-in-the-Sky and glanced at the odometer. It reported ten and a half miles. That would make for a twenty-one-mile round trip. *Not enough,* thought Bill. Laura's jaunts were at least four to six miles longer. That rules out a quick trip to the airport and back. Then he pondered whether the truck's odometer functioned correctly.

It was hot, dry, and dusty. Bill's head had begun to throb. He decided to see whether the café manager was around. If so, he would get a cold drink and down a couple of pain relievers. Inside, three customers sat at a table and a young woman, whom Bill did not recognize, hovered near the cash register. A low din emanated from the kitchen.

"Is Julie here?" Bill asked the woman at the register.

"Yeah, she's in the back. Do you want her?"

"Yes. Please tell her it's Bill—Bill the planner."

"Bill the planner," repeated the cashier curiously. "I'll check."

Bill gazed around idly at the interior of the 1940s building that more than showed its age. In a recess to the left of the entrance, racks and shelves were crammed with every throwaway souvenir and trinket imaginable, each emblazoned with the words "Catalina,"

"Avalon," or both. T-shirts, miniature replica buffalos (those were a hoot), nature guides, books on Catalina pottery and tile, and bright orange ceramic images of Garibaldi fish were stacked onto the shelves. The inventory could be over thirty years old and no one would be the wiser, except upon closer inspection all bore the identification, "Made in China."

Bill looked out at the east-west oriented airstrip. Both ends of the runway were hidden from his view by undulating dips and rises. *Landing or taking off has to be a nightmare,* he thought. Air traffic control was a joke. The airport manager doubled as an air traffic controller. He depended on an antiquated radio system to communicate with pilots, which was often impractical as Visual Flight Rules governed the airstrip. The Airport-in-the-Sky runway seemed constantly in need of repair and experienced more than its share of fatal accidents.

"Hi, Bill." Julie's voice sang out interrupting his musing. "Want a cold one? It's getting close to Miller time."

Bill had forgotten that Julie tended toward alcoholic. Miller time was an ambiguous concept to her; somewhere in the world, it had to be Miller time, so why not celebrate it here? Bill could not recall seeing Julie without a bottle of beer in one hand, an ashtray in the other, and a cigarette hanging from her lower lip. She was bone-thin. Julie considered laid-back Avalon stressful. Bill laughed silently at the thought that anyone could consider Avalon stressful.

"No thanks. I just drove up from town . . . had to get away from the stress." smiled Bill.

"Yeah, ain't that the truth. Avalon hasn't changed, it's a pressure cooker down there," she said as she twisted the cap off another cold one and swallowed half its contents in a single gulp. "Ah, I needed that. So what's new in town? I haven't been there in ages and it's longer since I've seen you. It's nice to get a bit of eye candy out here now and again." A grin appeared on her weathered face.

"Isn't smoking in a restaurant illegal in California?" asked Bill.

"Probably, but I believe that law's for customers. That's how I see it."

Bill wished he had not raised the matter and changed the topic.

"Not much new in town except there was a murder."

"Yeah, I heard about that, a woman."

"Laura. Thing is, she was killed in my condo."

"Stress! Damn, Avalon's all stress. I bet that's messy for you. Did they catch the son of a bitch?"

"Unfortunately, not yet. Did you know Laura?"

"No, can't say that I did."

"She was a jeep tour guide. She practiced her driving out here."

"Practiced? Hey, you know, there is a woman that drives one of those Conservancy jeeps. She picks up stuff from a plane two or three times a month. She's always here to meet the plane, but she never has tourists with her. She knows one of my employees, Jeff, a black guy."

Bill's attention peaked. *Talk about hitting nine sevens on a slot machine with the first pull.* "Really . . . that's interesting."

"Yeah, actually, now that I think of it, they must work together. Jeff helps her unload the plane and then they load the stuff into the jeep . . . must be Conservancy stuff."

"What does the woman look like?"

"I don't know. Maybe tall, slim, dark hair. She parks far away. I can't really say. I didn't pay much attention."

"How often do you see her out here?"

"Not often, maybe every week or so, maybe less maybe more, I can't help you with that. It's none of my business so I don't care. Jeff always makes up the time he spends with her. Maybe he doesn't know her and just helps. I haven't a clue. It's none of my business."

Julie took a drag on her cigarette.

"Is Jeff around . . . what's his last name?" Bill asked casually.

"Tebbins. It's his day off. Why?"

"Just curious. I don't remember ever seeing him in Avalon. He lives in Avalon, doesn't he?"

"Hardly. He rides a bike."

"He doesn't have a car or truck? Why did Carrie hire him? It's Carrie, isn't it?"

"Yeah, it is, but I haven't seen her in a coon's age either. It's great when your boss hardly shows up. I hired him, not Carrie. I couldn't wait for her. He's a good Catalina employee—fogs a mirror, speaks okay English, and usually shows up sober. Those are primo qualifications. I've had him for almost two years . . . and he has the most important qualification for a Catalina employee: a permanent place to live. That's a major plus in this jerkwater town, especially out here."

"That's for sure. Where does he live?"

"I don't know. Somewhere down the road towards the pony farm, I think."

"There's housing out here?"

"There's not much and it sucks. Jeff never told me exactly where and I don't care. If he's at work when he's supposed to be and sober, I'm a happy camper. Are you sure you don't want a cold one? It's time for another," said Julie, faking a look at her watch and laughing.

Bill shook his head no.

Julie smashed a half-smoked cigarette into her jerry-rigged, omnipresent portable ashtray and headed back into the kitchen.

Bill's thoughts raced. *I have a motive for Laura's trips to the Interior, a lead on a black man, and I have his name. This has to be the man Joe mentioned.*

Julie shuffled from the kitchen, a fresh cigarette hanging from her lip, two Millers in hand.

"Drink up, Bill, it's a long drive back to the pressure cooker."

Julie swigged from her bottle.

"Thanks. I can't, I'm driving."

"More for me."

Bill added. "Seems a little slow today. How's business been?"

"We're between buses. We live and die by the tour bus. Some customers still fly in, but not like in the past. It's a great place to work; hardly anyone around most of the time."

Few customers, unlimited beers, absentee boss, and unregulated smoking . . . that's Julie, thought Bill.

"Well, I gotta be getting back. I needed a break from the stress. Take care, babe."

"You bet . . . sure you don't want this?" said Julie, holding up a bottle of Miller. "You'd finish it before you got to Avalon."

Bill shuddered secretly at the thought of drinking while driving. "No thanks. Cheers. I'll pass this time. When you get to town, stop by."

"I'll try . . . don't hold your breath."

CHAPTER THIRTY-THREE

2:21 PM Tuesday, August 17, 2010
Parking Lot, Airport-in-the-Sky
The Interior, Santa Catalina Island, California

Bill inserted the key into the ignition of the ancient Ford and turned it easily. Surprisingly, the engine turned over on the first try.

A layer of dust covered everything inside the cab. Sweltering midday sun had baked the interior. The hard rubber steering wheel, worn smooth from decades of driving, felt hot, grimy, and sticky to the touch. It reminded Bill of working with double-sided scotch tape . . . you just can't get it off your fingers and onto where you want it. Bill drove along the airport's access road to the intersection with Airport Road and stopped to contemplate alternatives. To the left, Airport Road took him back to Avalon. To the right, Escondido Road took him to god knows where or what. Hands down it had to be Escondido Road.

Airport Road was a freeway compared to the semi-paved hard-packed dirt of Escondido Road. Dust flowed into the cab through the truck's partially shattered passenger-side window, adding to the layers already there. Dust, drawn like a magnet to Bill's sweaty face, turned to grit as it adhered to him. Gratefully, he reached for the canteen lying on the seat next to him. Tiffany had prevailed with her

Boy Scout inspired "be prepared" campaign. She had urged Bill to dress properly and behave accordingly, hammering him with her, *we are on a murder case* message. Although he had grumbled about her over-enthusiasm, which he was convinced was elevated by her addiction to Hollywood thrillers he relented and changed into jeans, a heavy denim shirt, and boots. At her insistence, he had stuffed 7x50 binoculars, a Canon digital single lens reflex camera with a telescopic lens, and a one-quart canteen into a small daypack. She had refused to release him to the Interior until he complied. He would thank her when he got back.

When he added the four to five miles he had driven along Escondido Road to the mileage from Avalon to the airport, the sum approximated Laura's typical training distances. Bill reviewed in his mind his conversation with Julie and wondered what the aircraft delivered. It was not Conservancy stuff, he would bet on that. The plane should be traceable. Did the control tower maintain records on tail numbers? He would stop at the airport on the way back and ask. Jenn would make quick work tracing that kind of information.

Escondido road twisted and curved more than Airport Road whose steep falloffs were a dramatic contrast with the rolling hills and canyons of Escondido Road. He drove slowly. If there was evidence of habitation, he wanted to be sure to see it. Where did Jeff live? The side roads were no more than bullshit-overgrown trails that meandered into impenetrable canyons. Once again, Bill checked the odometer. He had driven almost nine miles—a total of twenty miles from Avalon. Ahead was El Rancho Escondido—Julie's self-described pony farm. Laura had not driven this far on her training trips. Maybe he would see something driving the other way.

He turned the truck around and drove more slowly on the return trip, carefully looking, searching right and left—nothing. Only vegetation-choked paths that trailed into the same monotonous hills he had seen driving the other way. Then a wider path appeared on his right. He wondered how he had missed seeing it earlier.

Bill parked the truck on the shoulder of the road thirty yards beyond the intersection of the path and road and walked back to check it out. Where the path met the road, he saw wide vehicle tire tracks as well as a number of narrow shallow ruts. *The ruts could be bicycle tracks,* he surmised. This might be it. He returned to the truck, collected his backpack, canteen, camera, and binoculars, and set out parallel to the path. He picked his way deliberately over the inhospitable terrain. As he walked, thoughts of the mountain phase of Ranger School crossed his mind. He had vowed never to be in a situation similar to that again. Oh well, shit happens. He grinned—at least it wasn't winter.

He had walked about a thousand yards when he heard faint voices. The voices seemed to come from beyond a ridge. As he neared the crest of the ridge, the voices became louder and more distinct. Bill thought they were chanting. He stopped, crouched, and listened intently. It was chanting. He lowered himself to the ground, crawled to the crest, and peered over it. Beyond the crest, the ground fell sharply away into a narrow, steep sided canyon. The chanters were more than a quarter mile away on a small flat area of the canyon floor. With the sun behind him, he would be silhouetted against the sky, so he flattened himself closer to the ground and hoped the chanters would not see him. He studied the terrain but his attention continually returned to the voices. The group was chanting while exercising with short poles.

He pulled his 7x50 binoculars out of the backpack. Looking through the binos, he used his left hand to shade the lenses so they would not reflect the sunlight. Focusing on the chanters, he discerned there were four, maybe five of them. One was black. Surely, that was Jeff. Suddenly Bill's back stiffened: the poles were not poles, they were rifles. They looked like Vietnam-era AK47s that the "Opp For" used in Ranger School. Bill became aware he was unarmed. *How could I have been so stupid?* he thought. Should he run, just get the hell out of there, or stay the course?

He recalled his military training. He had done well in the Penn State ROTC program, qualified for Infantry, and was granted active duty. The Army offered him Airborne and Ranger School—training that was normally limited to regular Army officers. His ranger buddy was a West Point graduate. Ranger school presented its students with a seemingly unending series of ambiguous complex combat scenarios always crafted in sleep deprived stressful situations. The scenarios lent themselves to options for easy, but not optimal, outcomes and other options with more difficult, but uncertain courses of action, which could lead to outstanding outcome or failure. Inherent in the latter options were opportunities for a superior grade or a failing grade. When there were such options, his ranger buddy inevitably advised, "We choose the harder right over the easier wrong." Then his ranger buddy always added, "This is training. It's best to fuck up now rather than with some fiery-eyed terrorist beating down on your ass." The tough decision making process had served them well. Bill inevitably learned from the process, which applied not only directly to the military scenarios at hand, but indirectly to the real nonmilitary world. Bill and his ranger buddy always received superlative grades. Bill never forgot his ranger buddy's resolute attitude, so he decided to draw on that experience today. Bill reflected that, up to a point, Jenn and Tiffany had intuitively applied a similar approach in their insistence to continue investigating Laura's death.

He needed to get closer, but how?

The terrain was riddled with a series of shallow rock-strewn gullies that channeled water from flash flooding to the canyon floor. Getting to the gullies meant exposing himself to little or no cover but that was the only viable option. Forty yards of open terrain separated Bill from the closest gully. Running would require rapid movement and would silhouette him against the sky. He had to crawl. *This crap was supposed to have ended with discharge papers*, he thought.

Bill checked his equipment, slipped over the top of the crest, and tried not to think about insects, lizards, and rattlesnakes as he began the ordeal. Dust, dirt, gravel, and small sharp stones lodged in his clothes, shoes, hair, and fingernails as he crawled. So far, the discomfort was paying off. The sound of chanting voices was getting louder while the rhythm remained constant. Hopefully, that meant the chanters had not seen him.

A few feet from the gully, he chanced a peek. Bill raised his head, planted his chin in the dirt, and looked at the chanters. Now there were four. Had they clued to his presence and sent reconnaissance? Worried, Bill scrambled to the gully but it was not what he had expected. It provided less than a foot of additional cover and left him dangerously close to being exposed. He lay back down in the dust and then crawled further along the gully. It got rockier and rockier by the inch. Each time Bill moved an arm or leg another scratch opened somewhere on his exhausted body. He contemplated surviving the day only to die of lockjaw. He grimaced. His biggest concern, though, was that his muscles were beginning to burn and threatening to seize up. *I should have gone to the gym with Jenn more often,* he thought. *Hell, who am I kidding, I never ever went to the gym with Jenn.* He grimaced again.

This was not fun anymore. Actually, it had never been fun. He had a vision of Jenn wearing her, "*I told you so look.*" He smiled and pulled himself the final ten feet into a patch of shade. His body was now responding to the familiar rhythm of the chanting, his fingers tapping in unison with the voices. He was close enough to hear distinct words—they weren't English. They had a singsong quality to them. He scrutinized the chanters. They were more than four hundred yards away. The rhythm and rifle movement accelerated. Was drill ending?

Bill risked a longer look to examine the buildings. They were wooden, old, and in abject disrepair. Had it been a farm? Who could farm this land? Maybe it had been a ranch. He saw strange, hauntingly familiar objects in the spaces that separated the buildings. He recognized a pull-up bar. Although in seemingly unsystematic arrangement, the objects somehow fit together. Could it be an obstacle course? A ten foot by twenty-foot trench, partially filled with water and mud, intrigued him. Much stranger, though, was a line of boulders neatly arranged in descending size. He could not figure that out.

Abruptly, the chanting stopped. Bill froze. The chanters secured their rifles in an enclosure that looked like an old metal storage shed and stood talking to one another. It was time for him to take pictures. He, Jenn, and Tiffany could analyze the photos later. If some of the idiots lived in Avalon, maybe, they could identify them. He focused his Canon on the chanters and zoomed in on the leader. The man's features were rugged, dark, and decidedly foreign. Bill snapped the shutter several times. A grinding noise he had never noticed before followed each shot—he held his breath. In the silence, the sound was deafening—and in many respects disconcerting. Miraculously, none of the chanters looked toward him. *They must be far enough away that the couldn't hear the sound.* He decided to take additional shots and then get out of there. He had not yet gotten a clear shot of the black man. Emboldened, Bill decided to crawl closer. A different angle from behind a nearby small bush might yield a better perspective.

When he got there, he steadied himself and snapped several shots in succession. Heads shot up and eyes looked around. This time the grinding sound had not gone unnoticed. When Bill brought the camera to the ground, the lens caught the sun. Several chanters pointed toward Bill's bush.

Bill scrambled backward. Two chanters ran toward him while the other two ran to the shed. Bill evaluated his options. His truck was at least a thousand yards away. The chanters had to run further than he did, and their run began with a steep four hundred yard uphill stretch. He figured he could easily outrun them. He scrambled to his feet, gathered his equipment, and sprinted toward the road, dodging chuckholes that challenged his ankles and footing as he ran. His legs brushed aside prickly bushes whose branches nonetheless caught and ripped his jeans leaving his leg exposed to sharp thorns that inflicted painful lacerations. He judged that running on the path would be easier, less painful, and assuredly would lead to the road and his truck. Since secrecy had become moot, Bill chose the path.

Adrenalin partially masked his pain, but his muscles objected the longer and harder he ran. He felt unstable and had to concentrate to avoid falling. Falling could cost him his life. He forced himself to remain calm and run under control, focus on the ground several feet ahead of him, and run Ranger style. Then he wondered, *would that goddamn rusted collection of nuts and bolts start?* He blocked the thought from his mind. The ground leveled out after nearly a half a mile and finally, gasping for air and struggling to keep from stumbling, he saw the truck in the distance. Bill recalled another Ranger School technique. When under stress, recite in your mind the actions needed to accomplish your goal while envisioning their execution. Bill focused his thoughts while he ran. What did he have to do to get his ass out of this alive? He needed to rid himself of his equipment in order to fit into the truck's seat, he needed the keys, and he needed to start the truck without stalling it.

He recited in his mind as he ran. "Don't panic, toss the equipment into the truck bed, get the keys, open the door and get in, start the truck as if everything's normal. And for god's sake, don't stall the fucking engine." The last bit he added for emphasis. The series of actions repeatedly flashed through his mind like rapid-fire lightning bolts. He visualized approaching the truck, stripping off his backpack and tossing it into the truck bed, grasping the semi-functioning handle to the cab door, twisting *firmly* down and pulling out, getting in, putting the key in the ignition and turning it to the right . . . wait . . . where was the ignition? Oh yeah, in the dashboard on the right side of the instrument panel. God he hoped the truck would start.

He heard a rifle shot, followed by an eruption of dust thirty yards to his left and ahead. The bastards were shooting at him! Bill glanced back and saw a flash followed in a second or two by the sound of a rifle crack—the chanters were now less than three hundred yards behind him. They had made their initial four hundred yard handicap and then some. Another explosion of dust erupted farther from him than before. *Thank god, they are lousy shots,* he thought. Focus. He had to focus. A bullet ricocheted off a rock, bounced off the hood of the truck, and rolled onto the road. *Don't stall the fucking engine.*

He tossed his equipment into the truck bed and scrambled into the cab. *Don't stall the fucking engine.* He took a deep breath and inserted the key. *Don't stall the fucking engine. Don't flood the engine.* He calmly turned the key. *Don't stall the fucking engine.* Just then, the truck took a bullet for democracy. The time between the muzzle flash and sound of the shot was shorter—less than half a second . . . they're closer—a hundred yards or so. He took another deep breath and slowly let it out. *Don't stall the fucking engine.* He turned the key. The engine roared to life.

"Don't stall, don't stall," mumbled Bill repeatedly, as if he could will the engine to respond.

He depressed the clutch, engaged the transmission, and then pressed the accelerator. The truck lurched forward, and then sputtered just as two bullets struck the back of the cab. Bill backed off the accelerator. The chanters' shouting got louder. *They are getting closer. Oh, for a M4 Carbine* . . . I'd take them all out, he thought.

Miraculously, the truck recovered but then sputtered again. Finally, it jerked forward and picked up speed. Bill eased the accelerator to the floor. The decrepit truck responded.

"I'll out-run you, you fucking idiots," he muttered through clenched teeth.

Another rifle shot. Bill held his breath and waited for the hit. Nothing, another lousy shot, soon he would be out of range. Dust billowing from his screeching rear tires obscured his view of the chanters but, thankfully, also concealed him from them. His mind raced. Is it Avalon or the airport? If his pursuers had a vehicle, they could trap him at the airstrip for sure . . . there was only one-way in and one-way out. The sheriff would find his body and probably Julie's. It had to be Avalon. The tail number would have to wait. He braced for the long winding descent into town.

4:37 PM Tuesday, August 17, 2010
Airport Road
The Interior, Santa Catalina Island, California

Bill's mind swirled with unrelated and disconnected thoughts. He frequently checked the rearview mirror. *These idiots are dead serious.* The word *dead* resonated in his brain. Were the chanters terrorists or drug dealers or both? Drug smugglers were a possibility. Fly the drugs to the Airport-in-the-Sky and then transship them cross-channel on the express boat or barge. However, that did not wash with Jenn's research. These jerks were terrorists. But why would Avalon be a terrorist target? Could they identify him . . . the truck? Had he put Michelle in jeopardy? And what about Jenn and Tiffany? This shit was spiraling out of control.

Despite the sweltering heat, shivers ran down his back and chilling goose bumps covered his arms as he held the wheel tightly and sped ahead.

CHAPTER THIRTY-FOUR

5:01 PM Tuesday, August 17, 2010
Watson Financial Services, Metropole Avenue
Avalon, Santa Catalina Island, California

Bill killed the engine, left the keys in the ignition, and slammed the door.

He surveyed the bullet holes. He would figure out what to tell Michelle tomorrow. Walking downhill towards his office, Bill became aware of the pain throughout his body. He ached all over. He ached in places he did not believe could ache—a sad reflection on his fitness. However, for now, personal conditioning was low on his priority list.

*   *   *

"Hi, boss . . . god what the hell happened to you?"

"You don't want to know. There is a shit-load of those idiots out there and whoever they are, they're dead serious . . ."

There was that phrase again.

". . . they're in the Interior."

"You found them?"

"They found me, more or less—my fault. There were four or five of them, maybe more. I'm not sure, I didn't stick around to chat. I watched them doing some kind of training."

"Where exactly?"

"West of the airport, near some dilapidated buildings."

As Bill told Tiffany the story, her jaw sagged and her eyes grew wide. "This is great! We need to tell Jenn. This is so damn exciting."

"Exciting? Give me a fucking break. You weren't shot at."

"I'll lock the door. Dial Jenn," said Tiffany, ignoring Bill's comments.

Jenn answered on the first ring.

"A blonde . . ."

". . . Cool it. Save the blonde stuff for another time. This has turned ugly," said Bill.

"What's happened?"

"Good news or bad?" asked Bill.

"Good news," said Jenn.

"They're lousy shots."

"They're lousy shots? That's good news?"

"From my perspective it's better than they're good shots."

Bill filled Jenn in on the details, Tiffany jumping in at various points with marginally useful insights such as, "Can you believe that," or "This is so awesome," or "Isn't that great."

"So what do we do now?" asked Tiffany.

"We tell the authorities and then get the hell out of the way," responded Bill immediately.

"Tell the authorities—why?" asked Jenn quizzically.

Bill's stomach tightened; he knew it would be two against one again. He tried to sound firm. "We need to turn this over to people trained to deal with this kind of crap. We know of two, three, maybe five . . . god knows how many people they have killed. We're not sure if these jerks are drug dealers, terrorists, or just a group of run-of-the mill crazies out for a little fun. It doesn't matter; we're in over our heads—way over our heads."

"Easy, slow down, catch your breath," cautioned Jenn.

"Slow down? If I'd slowed down earlier, I'd be dead."

An edge of irritation had crept into Bill's voice.

"Okay, okay, I understand. I really don't think these are random acts of a bunch of crazies. While there seems a pattern to their madness, at this point, though, I don't think the police would listen," said Jenn.

"Sure they would, we've done our research. We have evidence. We have photos. We have the connections among Laura, Wanda, and Marilyn. A dead man runs the Avalon Bay Bar. These people have a camp in the Interior and my personal favorite, they're lousy shots. What else do we need, lie detector tests? There are bullet holes in Michelle's truck. Blessinggame would be ecstatic. This would solve several cases . . . Homeland Security would love us," said Bill running out of breath.

"All possibilities. However, Blessinggame would dismiss it," said Jenn, "he wants this done and off his desk with full credit going to him for solving it. If he believed us, he'd have to bring in the feds and he'd be out, poof, gone, off the case. The feds would boot him just like he booted Morales."

"I like the part where Blessinggame gets poofed, but that's only my personal opinion," said Bill. "We must push this to people who are trained to do this kind of stuff. We aren't."

Jenn remained unconvinced. "To Blessinggame, it's a drug case. The issue, as I see it, is Blessinggame's not bright. As far as Homeland Security goes, I doubt they could act fast enough. They get hundreds, probably thousands of leads every week."

Tiffany nodded vigorous approval as Jenn spoke.

Bill glared at Tiffany and silently mouthed, "You don't know if any of that is correct."

His attention returned to Jenn. "You know those guys, you can convince them."

"I don't know them."

"You deal with them at Raytheon."

"At a different level . . . I deal with technical issues, not investigative issues."

"You have credibility. You aren't just someone in off the street. Jenn, we are not equipped to handle this. We're not trained, we're not armed, and we're not the police, the CIA, the FBI, or whatever. We need to move this to a different level . . . a level away from us."

"We're on a roll," interrupted Tiffany. "Look at what we've learned in just a few days. Even if we tell the authorities, they wouldn't believe us. They'd want to validate everything . . . reinvent the wheel. In the meantime, the madmen . . ."

". . . and madwoman," added Jenn.

". . . thank you . . . escape. Worse, they could accelerate their plan whatever it might be. Who knows what might happen? The authorities would want to rehash what has happened so far . . . they'd be far down on the learning curve. We have an obligation to stay engaged."

Tiffany sat back with a smug expression of cautious satisfaction across her face. In her mind, this was *the big one*. The kind of adventure she'd dreamed of, and she was not going to let it slip away.

"We can educate them," said Bill.

"That takes time and remember who we'd be educating—Blessinggame," said Tiffany.

"He's uneducable," snorted Jenn.

"Hey, guys, are you forgetting I was shot at? These lunatics are for real. We can't put more people at risk. I don't know if they can identify me . . . they might be able to. Michelle's truck looks like it's camouflaged with dirt and mud like most trucks on-island, but it has a plate number. They might have the ability to trace it to her and then to us. They might be part of an organization that could track us down and then kill us."

"Slow down, take it easy, let's think this thing through," said Jenn, attempting to get the issues back on track as she saw it. "There has to be some middle ground."

"What middle ground?" asked Bill.

"Do both: tell the police *and* continue our investigation."

"Fat chance," said Tiffany.

"Maybe, but it makes sense," said Jenn.

Bill shook his head. "We can't do both. If we tell Blessinggame and then continue to poke around, he will throw me in jail—he's promised to do that. We need to bring in the experts, the first team, and then bail."

"We are the first team!" said Tiffany in a huff.

"Exactly, we are the first team," agreed Jenn. "Blessinggame would've been cut from the third team, he's such a jerk. If we're in over our heads, he would have already drowned. Telling him could complicate matters and cause more trouble than good. Telling Homeland Security is problematic. While they are well intentioned, they're spread too thin. That is, unless they're already on to these assholes."

"I doubt that. If they were, they would be here and in their faces—and maybe ours. Laura's been murdered and they're not here . . ." Bill sighed. ". . . Okay, I agree, anyone we bring into this would probably be hesitant to believe us and slow to act, and that could complicate things."

"So what do we do?" asked Tiffany, inwardly relieved.

"Both."

"You keep saying that Jenn. Why?" asked Bill.

"It's the only option that allows us to cover all the bases. We tell Blessinggame . . . won't get us anywhere. We tell him what we know and let him make the tough decision. That puts responsibility squarely in his lap. We tell Homeland Security. I'll call them tomorrow. They may not do anything but they'll be on notice. The upside to telling Homeland Security is that having advised them, when we're in a real pinch the situation won't be new to them."

"A real pinch? It doesn't get pinchier than being shot at!"

"And then what do we do?" asked Tiffany, ignoring Bill's comment.

Bill always felt ignored.

"We keep digging around and anything we find, we turn over to Blessinggame," continued Jenn.

"Digging around? We could be digging our graves, or at least mine. If we push Blessinggame too far, he'll throw me in jail that is if the terrorists don't kill me first."

"I like it," said Tiffany.

"The grave part or the jail part?" asked Bill sarcastically.

"The do both part."

"I don't like any part," said Bill, knowing his statement would likely be his parting shot.

"You're voted down boss."

"Yes, you're voted down," added Jenn.

"When did this become a democracy?" Bill knew he was whistling in the wind.

"I don't see a choice. If either or both take our story seriously and act, we'll have accomplished what we set out to do. If neither party buys our story, we're obligated to continue investigating, at least for a few more days."

Tiffany promptly added, "I agree."

"Now there's a surprise, both of you in agreement."

Bill felt fatigued and sore. He rubbed a hand wearily against his eyes and forehead. "Look, there might be some obscure, esoteric reason to continue with this in order to protect people, unknown but we're not obligated. What about protecting the people already at risk: Michelle, Julie, others, and *us*? These idiots have already killed and they weren't firing blanks at me . . . check out the truck."

"We *are* obligated," said Tiffany. "What if more people are killed or there's some kind of major attack, how will we feel then?"

"Okay, okay, but just a few more days. The chanters are likely taking extra target practice as we speak. They'll get me next time. We can't allow them the time to get proficient."

"Chanters?" asked Jenn.

"Yes," said Bill, warily. "The chanters . . . all we know *for sure* are that lunatics are chanters and they are lousy shots."

"Stay away from their hideout. If they don't see you they can't shoot you," said Tiffany.

"Brilliant. You're quite the little strategist, aren't you?"

"Okay you two, enough of that," interjected Jenn. "Let's decide what we do."

"Fine," said Bill. "Do you have anything new?"

"Sort of. There's nothing on Marilyn. I don't think she's involved, at least not as a terrorist. She may have been collateral damage, but I doubt that too. There has been nothing on her since she disappeared. In terms of Laura, I couldn't find any cross-link to a Kaylid. Maybe Laura and Wanda cross-link to Christine. There is mention of a third woman that hung out with them in Europe, but no name. I'll look into that. That's about it on my part. Tiffany, what did Helen and Melinda say about Laura and drugs?"

"Melinda didn't have an opinion but Helen was adamant. Categorically she said, Laura didn't use drugs. The Conservancy trains its managers to recognize substance abuse, especially with employees who could endanger the public. They administer drug tests across the board." Then Tiffany said with a subdued smile, "Helen wondered when you were coming to see her again."

"What!" yelled Bill.

"Just a joke—chill out," said Tiffany.

"Okay," said Bill, with a disgusted expression on his face. "Ditto on Wanda. Jeremy didn't think Wanda was a drug user and he didn't know if Laura and Wanda knew one another. The person who might shed better light on Wanda left the island several months ago on super short notice. Why do so many people leave the island like frightened goats?"

"For the same reason they come to the island . . . to escape," said Tiffany, arching one eyebrow.

Bill exhaled loudly. "When I tell Blessinggame about our terrorist friends, he'll cuff me for sure."

"When are you going to tell him?" asked Tiffany

"Are you hoping for jail? Got plans to take over the vast Watson financial empire?"

"Yeah, right."

"Tomorrow, I'll tell him tomorrow."

"Okay, where do we go from here?" asked Tiffany.

"More research for me," said Jenn. "I'll call Homeland Security first thing in the morning."

"Oh, hey, I almost totally forgot to mention . . . Julie told me the black man's name is Jeffrey Tebbins."

"Fantastic," said Jenn. "I'll get on that."

"And I'll try to track down Joe."

Bill glanced at his watch.

"He should be on his way to the Avalon Bay as we speak. In addition, I'll see if Christine will loosen up; it's doubtful, but trying can't hurt. Tomorrow I'll take another run at Julie. She might remember more about Jeff and Laura. And I'll get the plane's tail number."

"Don't use Michelle's truck," said Tiffany.

"Not a chance. Any ideas for another one?"

"What about Chris? She'd lend her truck. It's another shit box but it runs okay," said Jenn.

"Yeah, and it's red and mud-covered whereas Michelle's is beige and mud-covered. If I run into my friends, they might not make the connection." Bill shrugged hesitantly. "I'll ask her. Right now I need to get cleaned up and over to the Avalon Bay Bar."

Tiffany looked eagerly at Bill. "And what do I do?"

"You're strategic reserve."

"Very funny. First I'm a desk jockey and now I'm strategic reserve."

"Call it a promotion. Remember, you had the Melinda and Helen assignment today."

"Terrific!" said Tiffany.

CHAPTER THIRTY-FIVE

5:32 PM Tuesday, August 17, 2010
Public Telephone, Metropole Avenue
Avalon, Santa Catalina Island, California

"I understand," said Fikriyya emphatically. And not for the first time, wondering why Khalid demanded the use of an open air public telephone across the street from the most trafficked location in all of Avalon—the intersection of Metropole and Crescent to conduct communications. *Everyone who lives in this hellhole of a town passes this location at least once or twice a day.* "Dammit! Are you sure!" Is there anything else?" Fikriyya listened for a few moments more and then slammed the receiver into its cradle and mumbled, "Shit!"

Face flushed, Fikriyya walked briskly to the Avalon Bay Bar and then ran up the stairs to the prayer room. Ignoring protocol, Fikriyya incanted, *"As-salaamu 'alaykum,"* as she raced into the prayer room.

"Wa 'alaykumus salaam," responded Khalid, uncomfortable with Fikriyya's behavior.

"There's trouble."

"What do you mean, trouble?"

"The compound has been compromised. Mohamed reported that a man spied on the compound. They chased him but he got away."

"And what else, what else, Fikriyya?" asked Khalid, shaking his head in disbelief.

"They shot at him. They shot at him several times."

"Damn," said Khalid, lips pursed, a frown deepening on his face. "Did they hit him, wound him, or kill him? Or did he get away?"

"They didn't kill him. They aren't sure if they wounded him, but they don't think so. Like I said, he got away." Fikriyya tried to keep frustration out of her voice.

"With a man running around spreading a story about being shot at in the Interior, the authorities will be on to us for sure." Khalid glanced at her darkly. "Tomorrow I'll go to the compound and oversee preparations for our departure. We must wipe out all evidence of our presence on this miserable island. We can't leave a trail that might lead to Brooklyn or Afghanistan." Khalid paused and said with emphasis, "We are so close, the Avalon Jihad's just a week from Saturday. We must recommit to Allah, *azza wa jall.* Unbelievers will die and the survivors will choose the straight path. The world will rethink Islam. We will be the envy of the Muslim world and martyrdom will be ours."

After Fikriyya left the prayer room, Khalid reflected, once again. *These miserable, undisciplined, wannabe terrorists cannot carry out the simplest of tasks or follow one overriding rule: do not draw attention to yourself. The incompetent idiots are hopeless.* He wondered why Brooklyn had chosen him to test the insane strategy of using homegrown American converts to Islam to perpetrate *hiraba,* terrorism. One-committed Saudi-born Wahhabis was worth a hundred American converts. A Wahhabis did his job or died doing it and never compromised the faith, his comrades, or jihad.

5:59 PM Tuesday, August 17, 2010
Public Telephone, Metropole Avenue
Avalon, Santa Catalina Island, California

Fikriyya paced as she waited for six o'clock.

She wondered why they were even bothering with the stupid practice session. It was unnecessary and could expose everything. We don't need more practice. We're ready. She glanced at her watch . . . seven seconds. Lifting the receiver, Fikriyya dialed the number of the airport pay phone and tapped her foot agitatedly until the call connected.

"Tomorrow."

She hung up.

She needed to hurry back to the bar, but first, she would speak with Khalid. Surely, he would be open to advancing the Avalon Jihad. It made all the sense in the world—especially now. Fikriyya took the stairs to the prayer room two at a time. The room was empty. She turned and knocked on the door to Khalid's room and then entered without waiting for approval. "As-salaamu 'alaykum."

Khalid gave his usual monotone rote response and stared at her inquisitively.

"I need to speak with you about Saturday."

"What now?" he said in disgust.

"Next Saturday makes no sense. This Saturday does," she blurted. "We're all ready, there's nothing left to plan, we're trained, we're prepared to submit to Allah, `azza wa jall,` why compromise the . . ."

"That's out of the question. Saturday is practice. The following Saturday is the day, that's our plan. The week between will allow everyone to make final preparation and reaffirm allegiance to Allah, `azza wa jall.`"

"But . . ."

"No buts. This conversation is over. Brooklyn commanded, Afghanistan commanded, *Allaahu `a lam.* Now get out of here . . . leave my room . . . Wait. Did you discuss your concern with Mohamed? You shou . . ."

"No!" she interrupted—behavior that constituted a major discourtesy to an Islamic male by an Islamic female. "Why would I do that? The compound has been compromised; why compromise communications as well? Why would I compromise the Avalon Jihad? My telephone conversation lasted less than two seconds, no one could trace the call. And even if it were traced, no one could make sense of it."

Enraged, Fikriyya spun and exited the room slamming the door behind her, neglecting all cultural protocol. She realized she had made an inexcusable mistake. She had insulted and demeaned a male. In her adopted faith, that could lead to her death in countries such as Saudi Arabia, but in the U.S. she hoped she would get away with it. For some reason, though, she felt guilty.

Khalid was seething. He mumbled, "The insolent bitch . . . that spawn of Satan. Women are nothing but wells of evil. I will make this mission succeed despite the women and the others. Then after the Avalon Jihad is done, I'll be able to convince Brooklyn of their misdirected experimentation with hypocrisy."

CHAPTER THIRTY-SIX

6:27 PM Tuesday, August 17, 2010
Catalina Avenue, Across from the Avalon Bay Bar
Avalon, Santa Catalina Island, California

Bill stood outside and stared through the grimy windows of the Avalon Bay Bar.

No Joe yet, only bored customers, the same as last night, and of course, Christine perched on her stool. Confident Joe would arrive; Bill crossed the street to wait. True, Mr. Charm could have hit it big and wrangled a second evening with stale, day-old prey, but that seemed unlikely. Joe was not about long-term relationships. A scant couple of minutes proved Bill correct. He waited a few minutes more before following Joe into the bar.

The screeching door again announced Bill. No one cared—and this time, neither did Bill. Predictably, Joe sat on the same stool as last night. Christine did not show a hint of acknowledgement when Bill smiled and nodded hello to her. He shrugged and claimed the stool next to Joe.

"Evening, Joe."

Joe looked up with narrowed eyes and was silent for a few moments. Then he said tentatively, "Welcome back . . . didn't expect to see you again. Figured last night was a one-shot deal."

"Wouldn't miss any of this, it's in my blood. . . . Anyone sitting here?"

"Don't shit with me. Look at this fucking shithole. All the stools are empty. This place is a disaster. I hope we're not in for an extended dry spell."

"So how'd it go last night?"

"Shitty. The prissy bitch seemed interested then dumped me. Can you believe that—*she* dumped *me*. No reason, she just bailed. I came back here, but you'd left. It went downhill after that and it still looks like shit."

Bill stifled a smile.

"You told me six o'clock was good hunting time, the transition from day to evening, that's what you said."

"Good memory. It usually is and maybe it'll pick up, but for now it's still the pits."

Bill sensed movement from the far end of the bar.

"Look, Christine is headed our way, she's alive."

"We can only hope," said Joe. "It would be nice to get a drink. You must be interested in learning the ropes. I bet that's why you came back, you wanna learn the ropes."

Wincing inwardly, Bill summoned what he hoped was a convincing smile and said, "Yeah, it sounds interesting."

Joe perked up. "I'd pleased to teach you the ropes, no consulting fee. I'll be your monitor."

Bill wondered what it felt like to be an ignoramus. He looked up. Christine stood in front of them. She said nothing, just stared.

"The usual for me. No make that two, one for Bill."

"The usual?" asked Christine glassily.

"A Bud, and my friend will have one, too," said Joe irritably.

Christine shuffled away.

"Jesus, I've been here every night since they hired the dumb broad and I order a Bud every friggin' night. What the hell's wrong with her?"

"Actually, I wanted wine."

"Like hell you do. You damn near choked on that crap yesterday. Don't complicate things."

Apparently, Joe was slightly more observant than Bill had assumed. Bill shrugged. "Ok, beer it is. You know, I was wondering about that black man you mentioned last night. Do you remember anything else about him?"

"Why would I? A nigger's a nigger."

Bill had a fleeting fantasy of strangling the bastard on the spot and making the world a better place. "I was in the Interior today and saw a black man."

"So? Why's that supposed to interest me?"

"I got a picture of him."

"So?"

"I'd like to show it to you . . . see if you recognize him."

Joe simply grunted and blankly stared ahead. Bill opened his camera case, took out the Canon, turned it on, and scrolled through the gallery to locate the best shot of Jeff.

"Here, take a look."

He shoved the camera into Joe's face.

"Yep, you're right, it's a nigger. They all look alike."

"Is that so . . . take a closer look. Is this the guy you saw in the bar?"

"Eh . . . could be, they all look the same."

"There are only a few black men on the island. C'mon, take a closer look."

"Alright, alright for god's sake. Why are you so damn pushy?"

Christine headed towards them with the beers. With a pang, Bill realized too late that Joe might show the photo to her.

"Let's ask Christine." Joe grabbed the camera and turned the screen toward Christine.

She plopped two bottles on the bar and walked away.

"Don't show her!"

"Christine, do you know this guy?" yelled Joe after her.

Bill recovered the camera but it wasn't necessary. Christine had already reclaimed her stool.

"Why can't I show the picture to Christine?"

Now Joe was curious.

"She's not interested. Anyway, you said the black man spoke with Laura, not Christine . . . did he also speak with Christine?"

"How do you know Christine isn't interested? Let's ask her."

"Did the black man speak with Christine?" Bill persisted.

"I never saw him with her but maybe she knows him. Maybe he works in the back. He could be here now. You want to know about him maybe she can help. Maybe she can go get him."

"I'll ask her later," said Bill as he returned the camera to the safety of its case. Out of sight out of mind, he hoped. He needed to change the subject . . . pronto.

"Tell me about the hunt. What can you teach me about the hunt?"

"Oh yeah, the hunt. I was ready to go with that but you started on about the nigger. Okay, first, you need a minimum-sized herd. Just a few won't work. So far, the herd tonight is too small—ugly too. Bitches want to be the bitch of choice. They want to feel like they're better than the other bitches. You know what I mean."

Bill nodded, struggling to maintain interest,

"They want studs like us to want them. If there're only a couple of bitches, there's no competition, no game, no reason to show off. So, the more bitches, the better. They have to be tourists though, not local bitches. It don't work with locals. They know me."

I bet, thought Bill, and took a sip of beer to mask his revulsion. He needed to change the subject. "Do you know much about the Interior?"

"The Interior, what the hell does that have to do with the price of coffee in Starbucks or the hunt? You told me you wanted to know about the hunt."

"I do, man, I do, but I have to absorb what you've just told me. I need to talk about other things for a while. Important new information needs to find a place to settle in people's brains. You're the pro. I gotta ease into this hunt thing."

"Yeah, that makes a lot of sense. I'm the expert you're the newbie."

Joe seemed somewhat placated with Bill's senseless explanation.

"Do you go to the Interior often?"

Joe took a swig of Bud.

"Not often. I go there for a job when I have one out there."

"What do you do?"

"I'm in construction."

"Where have you worked in the Interior? I was there today, out past Rancho Escondido. Not much going on out there, it seemed pretty dead."

"Middle Ranch, I've worked there. And I've worked on houses in the coves and on the airport control tower."

"Are there homes on the road to Rancho Escondido?"

"Not really, just some shitty looking old buildings from the thirties and forties. Most are empty and all of 'em are firetraps. Real homes are closer to the water, in the canyons just up from the ocean, or in from the coves."

"Ever work at them . . . the shitty buildings?"

"No why? Jesus, you ask a lot of questions. Are you writing a book or something?"

Bill laughed. "Today I was out there and heard shots. Why would there be shots?"

"Hunters, there're hunters all over the friggin' place. Sometimes they're legal, but mostly they're not. I'm surprised there aren't more people shot with all those bullets flying around. The Interior is like the Wild West. I've hunted there myself, deer mostly . . . I like the taste of deer."

"Yes, venison can be tasty."

"I said deer. That has nothin' to do with Venice."

"Of course. I meant deer."

Bill said a silent prayer that Joe would never breed.

"Doesn't the Conservancy control hunting?"

Before Joe could answer, Christine had planted herself in front of them. "Want another beer?"

"No, thank you, we're still working on these," said Bill.

"Oh . . . Is there anything else?" Her eyes flickered with fleeting signs of life then reverted to her normal glazed expression.

"I don't think so."

"Oh."

She turned and walked away after a brief hesitation.

"That was weird," said Joe. "It was like she wanted something. Maybe it's you. Maybe she's got the hots for you." He looked at Bill expectantly.

"I doubt it," said Bill. "So what about the Conservancy, do they control hunting?"

"Kinda, but they're in the permit business. You know that's how they make money. Want to camp, you need a permit; want to hike, you need a permit; want to pee, you need a permit; want to hunt, you need a permit. It's a big place. The Interior's a big area. The Conservancy can't keep the hikers where they're supposed to hike, they can't keep the campers where they're supposed to camp, and god knows they have absolutely no control over the hunters. The hunters hunt anywhere they damn well please. They shoot at anything that moves—hikers and campers look like deer in disguise, you know, at least hunters think so."

Joe brayed at his feeble display of wit.

A screech erupted as if in response to his joke. A group of women, younger than last night's herd and seemingly unattached, had entered the bar. Joe sized them up as potential prey.

"Heifers . . . they'll do in a pinch; we can't be choosy tonight."

Bill considered quickly. He seemed to have run the table with Joe. Better to take his chances with Christine. He glanced encouragingly at Joe.

"Why don't you work them? I count six and they all seem alone. What do you think?"

"I don't know," Joe glanced at his watch. "Yeah, maybe I'll take a few practice swings. Call it warm up. Kinda like being on-deck."

He grabbed his beer and strode toward the new arrivals, aiming for a stocky brunette.

Bill's thoughts focused on Christine, wondering if Christine was a terrorist also. How does a person safely approach a terrorist? If you provoke a terrorist, you could wind up dead. He decided to fake watching Joe. Maybe Christine would initiate a conversation.

Joe pushed a chair next to the brunette and immediately commenced an animated conversation. Her companions scanned the bar while Joe plied his fiendish trade.

"Ready for another beer?"

Bill turned. Christine's changed behavior from last night was too marked to be anything but some sort of interest.

"I haven't finished this one. Actually, I wanted wine . . . your fine white wine. Can I get a glass of that?"

She moved away, retrieved a bottle, and filled a water glass to overflowing with turbid turpentine-like fluid then set it before Bill.

"How much do I owe? And I don't think Joe paid—I'll pick his tab up also."

"The drinks are on the house."

"Gee, thanks."

He smiled but received only the usual stare in return. After what seemed an eternity, Bill turned away from Christine and watched Joe work his potential prey.

"Joe said you had pictures to show me."

"Uh-oh . . . Um, no . . . it's okay. The batteries in the camera died so I can't show them to you. I didn't want to bother you anyway. Next time I'll show you."

Bill hushed, aware he was acting nervous and probably oddly.

"You wanted Joe to identify someone?"

"I just thought he might know a person I photographed in town today, but he didn't. He thought you might. No big deal."

"What about the shots? You said you heard shots."

Without thinking, Bill took a large sip of wine and then exhaled sharply. He avoided eye contact and strove for a casual tone. He wondered what had piqued Christine's curiosity. "I was at the airport and heard shots. I thought it was odd but other people didn't. Joe said that it was hunters. He's probably right. The people at the airport weren't concerned."

She was silent.

"Do you get to the Interior?" asked Bill.

"No."

Bill waited, and then tried a different tact. "How long have you been on-island?"

"Four months."

"You just started here. Where did you work before?"

"Nowhere."

"Did you know the girl who worked here before you?"

"No."

So far, this was proving as helpful as speaking to a voice-activated telephone system. Then Bill had an inspiration. "It's Christine Rodriguez, isn't it? Your name is Christine Rodriguez."

"I'm Christine Olson."

"Oh. A Swedish gal."

She resumed her stare. Bill felt jubilant. She had fallen for it! He had a last name. Maybe not her true last name but at least an alias.

"So, Christine Olson, where are you from?"

Christine looked past Bill. Just then, Bill felt a tap on his shoulder. Joe's boozy breath wafted past him. "We're in. The brunette and the redhead are ready. They want to move on with us."

Shit, thought Bill.

Bill sensed Christine's imminent departure and silently cursed Joe, the bigoted moron.

"No thanks, I'm making headway with Christine."

"You gotta be kiddin', man. Forget the dumb broad. She's a machine, an ice machine. Maybe she likes you a little, but you'll be collecting Social Security before you get to first base with her. I bet she's gay. The bitches over there are ripe. I can smell it. Let's go."

"No thanks, maybe next time. I'm sticking with Christine."

"It's your loss, more for me. Good luck."

Joe signaled to the two women to meet him at the door. The redhead with the poor dye job stared daggers at Bill. Bill turned to refocus on Christine but she had regained her perch and appeared to have lost interest.

Time to move on.

Outside, Bill collected his thoughts. The Olson information could be helpful. His gut told him he should not wait until tomorrow to share.

"Hi, love," said Jenn on the first ring.

"Hi, babe, I've got new information."

"What's that?"

"Olson. Christine from the bar told me her last name is Olson."

"Cool, I'll get on it, anything else?"

"Yeah. Compared with yesterday, Christine was talkative . . . actually inquisitive. She overheard my conversation with Joe and asked several questions after he left to hit on some poor woman. I sensed Christine knew about the shooting and wanted to know what I knew about it."

"What did you say?"

"I told her that I was at the airport and heard shots, but now I know it was hunters since everyone's been telling me that. I'm not sure she believed me. I was making headway with her when Joe returned and interrupted us. Christine pulled back into her shell."

"And how *is* the beguiling Mr. Joe?"

"A complete asshole, past, present, and future."

"Is that new information?"

"Yeah, right. Do you have anything new?"

"No, but I'll have something on Olson by tomorrow."

"Great, babe. I'm tired, it's been a long day. I haven't been shot at in a while . . . not since Desert Storm."

"I'll let you go, then. Good night, love."

6:48 PM Tuesday, August 17, 2010
Second Floor, the Avalon Bay Bar
Avalon, Santa Catalina Island, California

Fikriyya charged up the stairway, banged on Khalid's door, and entered after a perfunctory greeting.

"Fikriyya . . . again. What do you want now?" said Khalid in utter disgust.

"A man named Bill was downstairs. He said he was at the airport and heard shots. He said other people had told him the shots were from hunters but he seems skeptical. I'm concerned other people may have heard the shots."

"So, what am I supposed to do? The plan is to abandon the compound; this person doesn't change that."

"He had photos."

"Photos?"

"He wouldn't show them to me. He showed them to a customer, who told Bill to show them to me because I might know who was in the photo. But then he wouldn't show me."

"Do you know his name?"

"Only his first name. He's been in the last two nights. I've never seen him before last night."

"What does he look like?"

"Tall, fair, about forty, maybe younger."

"Is he a tourist? That could be why he was at the airport taking photos."

"I don't know, but I don't think so. Do you know anyone named Bill?"

"A few, but I don't think he'd be any of those. They're all businessmen or retired, mostly way over forty. There's the bookkeeper or financial planner or whatever he does, he's about forty or forty-five. He's a fancy pants type of person, though. I can't conceive of him running around the Interior taking pictures." Khalid mused for a moment. "I believe we're alright, we'll stay with the plan."

"Where does the bookkeeper work?"

"His office is on Metropole near Vons."

"I'll look tomorrow and let you know."

"Don't draw attention to yourself. Just take a quick look and come back."

"I'll be careful, *as-salaamu 'alaykum.*"

"*Wa 'alaykumus salaam,*" said Khalid with a dismissive wave of his hand.

Fikriyya sulked out of Khalid's room, her thoughts muddled . . . *Khalid's losing it. This Bill person might be real trouble but Khalid seemed indifferent . . . and why won't Khalid bend on the date for the Avalon Jihad? Is he keeping something from us?*

CHAPTER THIRTY-SEVEN

6:47 AM Wednesday, August 18, 2010
Watson Financial Services, Metropole Avenue
Avalon, Santa Catalina Island, California

Jenn's voice was crisp and exhilarated.

Bill knew he should be paying closer attention. He shook his head to dispel the cobwebs.

"Christine Olson was an associate of Laura and Wanda. They met up in Germany and trained together. They converted to Islam and returned to the States, Brooklyn, to be exact. Christine joined the Al Farouq Mosque. She has no criminal arrests or stuff like that . . . she's under the radar. There isn't a lot of information on her. She went to Avalon directly from Brooklyn. She attended Princeton and a small school named Hathaway College in New Jersey, but didn't graduate from either. After quitting college, she went straight to Germany."

"That's it?" asked Bill.

"So far."

"Anything on . . . oh shit!" said Tiffany.

"Oh shit what?" asked Jenn.

"It's that pain-in-the-ass Ken. We thought he'd left on vacation," said Tiffany softly. "We'll get back to you."

Ken waved at Bill and Tiffany through the locked storefront door.

Bill unlocked the door and ushered Ken in. "I thought you were on vacation."

"I leave Friday or Saturday on the helicopter."

Ken brushed past Bill and plopped into the chair in front of Bill's desk.

Ken seemed agitated, which was usual. Ken always seemed a little high-strung.

"Door's locked, no TV, everyone on the phone, what's going on . . . you out of business?"

"Of course not, we just got off a conference call from back east. They jerk our chain with the three-hour time difference. In the financial services business, everyone runs to East Coast time. Out here we're barely past daybreak when the East Coast is opening for business."

"Oh."

Bill wondered how this could possibly be news to Ken.

"What can we do for you . . . coffee?"

"Yeah, coffee would be fine. I'm just touching base."

"Great," said Bill, hoping his despondency didn't seep through and that Ken's comment meant this would be a short visit.

"You hear about the shooting yesterday at the airport?" asked Ken.

Bill felt a surge of adrenaline. "Shooting? No, I didn't." faked Bill. "What happened? Anyone hurt?"

"Well no, not like the shooting of Laura, but shots . . . people heard shots."

Bill inhaled deeply. "Oh, it could be hunters. I've heard they're out there. Don't worry. So long as you stay clear of them, you won't get shot." Bill fired a knowing glance at Tiffany who was handing a mug of coffee to Ken. The irony of Bill's comment paralleled Tiffany's advice to stay clear of the terrorist camp . . . and hung like an omen.

"Isn't it off season?" asked Ken.

"What are you talking about? Hunting season started nearly a month ago." Bill had no idea about hunting seasons. Ken looked unexpectedly sheepish and tossed back his coffee in an awkward, noisy gulp.

"Well, I guess it's back to vacation preparation. I might see you guys tomorrow."

He charged out the door as if the devil himself were in pursuit.

"Now *that* was odd," said Bill.

"Yeah really odd, we've never been this lucky," said Tiffany. Usually we have to conspire to get him out."

Bill ran his fingers through his hair. "Let's get Jenn on the horn."

*   *   *

"Hi, back already? What'd you do, shoot him?"

"No. It's a thought though. He was preoccupied with yesterday's gunfire in the Interior," said Tiffany. "Then he seemed to get spooked and darted out of the office . . . strange behavior."

"Really," responded Jenn, her voice trailing off into thought.

"Yeah, he left, gone, no hassle, it was weird. He wanted to know what we knew. Ken's usually all about Ken," said Bill. "Today it was all about us."

"I'm on the 1:30 helicopter," said Jenn.

"You're coming over today? That's great honey. How'd you swing that?"

"It's vacation season, no one's here. I talked my boss into letting me work from home, although he doesn't know where home is. All I have is computer work, no meetings, no project sessions for the rest of the week. I should be there about 1:45."

"I'll pick you up," said Tiffany, a smile on her face.

"Anything on Tebbins?" asked Bill.

"Yes, but not much. . . . He's black."

"Not funny—we know that."

"Sorry, I wasn't trying to be funny. I'm reading from my notes. He was born in Ohio and attended community college in Columbus but dropped out. He moved to New York and worked in the restaurant industry as a cook and busboy. That's about it. I'll try to find out more. I'm bringing my laptop so I can do research, if necessary. Anything new there?"

"First thing this morning, I'll find Blessinggame and pitch the terrorist theory. I'll suggest he consider it along with his drug theory. If you hear an explosion, it'll be him. If he doesn't arrest me, I'll be off to the Interior to see Julie."

"Sounds good. Oh, hang on, I forgot. I called Homeland Security earlier. They don't start until nine, East Coast time, and there is no live hotline. I guess they figure terrorists work weekdays, nine to five. I left a message but don't know when I'll hear back from them."

"Keep us in the loop. If we don't speak before you leave, I'll see you this afternoon."

"Bring appropriate clothes; we must be prepared for all contingencies," said Tiffany.

"They're packed. See both of you this afternoon."

"Bye love."

"Bye babe."

"They're packed . . . that doesn't surprise me," muttered Bill.

CHAPTER THIRTY-EIGHT

8:07 AM Wednesday, August 18, 2010
Avalon Sheriff's Station
Avalon, Santa Catalina Island, California

"I need to see Detective Blessinggame. Deputy Jimenez told me he'd be on-island today."

"He is. He just went for coffee. Have a seat."

"You're new, aren't you?

"I am. Got in Sunday. I'm here until October.

"Welcome to Avalon.

Deputies do Avalon, thought Bill. It's like a sitcom or reality show. Bill snickered inwardly as he took a seat. He tried not to stew about what he would tell Tweedle Dee, or was it Tweedle Dumb. Bill decided Blessinggame was Tweedle Dumb and Morales was Tweedle Dee. He gazed idly at the people in the lobby. Tweedle Dumb rolled into the station house ten minutes later, a bag of donuts in one hand, a cup of coffee in the other, and half a donut between his lips.

"Good morning, detective, how are you?"

Blessinggame swallowed the half donut and then asked, "What are you here for Watson? Need permission to leave the island?"

Blessinggame chuckled, and then scowled. "I hope you're here to tell me you've decided to stay out of my investigation."

"I don't need a trip request and I'm off the case, more or less."

"More or less is not an answer I want to hear . . . stay out of my way. So why are you here?" said Blessinggame as he stuffed another half donut into his mouth.

"I need to speak with you—in private," said Bill nodding toward the desk sergeant.

Blessinggame sighed and then slurred, (the half donut interfered with his ability to speak clearly, but he didn't seem to care), "This better be good." Finally, he swallowed and said more clearly, "We'll use Morales's office . . . this way." Blessinggame's pudgy arm flailed in the general direction of a narrow hallway. "Follow me."

Bill followed Blessinggame down the hall to Morales' office, a dingy depressing cubbyhole about ten feet by eight feet with a desk, swivel chair, two grimy looking side chairs, no window, and no wall decoration. *What a miserable work place for the head law-enforcement person in Avalon,* thought Bill choosing the chair that looked the least grimy. Morales's desk chair squeaked and creaked as Blessinggame squeezed his body between its arms. He put the bag of donuts and his cup of coffee on the desk.

Bill wondered what Jenn would think of Blessinggame's diet.

"So, what do you want? And be quick about it. I'm a busy man," said Blessinggame, biting another donut in half.

"Well, it's about Laura. I know you believe this is a drug case, but there are aspects of the case which you may not be aware of."

Bill strove to keep his voice even and polite.

"Such as?" mumbled Blessinggame, while thumbing through papers on the desk after wiping his hand on his trousers.

"Well, err . . . Laura was a terrorist . . . and I think Wanda was also and . . ."

"Terrorists!" Blessinggame looked startled, and then barked out a laugh. "Terrorists . . . Laura and Wanda were terrorists, what an absurd joke . . ."

". . . there's more. I believe their fellow terrorists murdered both of them. There's a bunch of nasty people on island." Bill groaned inwardly. None of his rehearsing had helped prevent him from blurting out random facts and sounding like an idiotic conspiracy theorist.

"And their friends killed them. This isn't a joke, it's fantasy. Watson, you can do better!"

For a few moments, Blessinggame seemed genuinely amused, but then his facial expression changed to anger and his body trembled as he spoke, "Terrorists!"

"Yes, terrorists. They're in the Interior and operate the Avalon Bay Bar. The bar's a cover."

"They operate a bar and live in the Interior. Who told you this crap? Was it Rambo? Or maybe that Bourne gentleman, Gimme a break. Why in god's name would terrorists be in Avalon? Who would they terrorize? Are they going to blow up the glass-bottom boat?" Blessinggame laughed at his joke. "Watson, you've lost your effing mind!"

It was the closest Blessinggame had come to swearing that Bill could recall. Bill took it as a good sign. Bill needed some good signs—as things were, most any sign would be a good sign.

"I don't know why they're here, only that they are."

"The owner of the Avalon Bay has been out of town. I am going to question him when he gets back. His bartender, Christine, said she'd call when he got back."

"Detective, with all due respect, Christine is also a terrorist. The real owner of the Avalon Bay has been dead for over two years."

Blessinggame snorted. "You'd think his employees would know he was dead, especially if it's been that long."

This guy's more naïve than dumb, thought Bill.

"She told me that he's seldom on the island. Right now he's somewhere in Europe, said Blessinggame."

"Hardly. He's dead, killed in a car accident in Norwalk. I'm telling you, all the people who work in that bar are terrorists—every one of them."

"You mean to tell me that sweet young thing is a terrorist."

"Christine is neither sweet nor all that young, and she'd sooner slit your throat or blow your brains out than give you a straight answer."

That is unlikely, laughed Bill inwardly, *since Blessinggame didn't have a brain.* Bill had pissed Blessinggame off. Why was none of this going the way Bill had scripted it?

"Mr. Watson, her answers are straighter than yours. This is utter bullshit. What proof do you have? You do know what proof is, don't you?"

"I do and I have it."

Blessinggame pursed his lips and made a get-on-with-it gesture with his hands.

"I was checking out a building complex off Escondido Road when I stumbled upon their camp. They chased me and shot at me. I got away in a truck. Laura was a Mus . . ."

"They shot at you? Sounds to me like you were trespassing. Why were you there?"

"I was tracking a man, a black man who works at the airport and helped Laura with shipments delivered by plane. I'm sure the black man works at the bar and he's also a terrorist. He has a second job at the airport, and his boss there told me he lived in the Interior so I drove toward El Rancho Escondido, the Arabian horse farm, and dis . . ."

"Hold it! You say a black man, who might work at the bar, helped Laura, who happens to work at the bar, pick up a shipment from an airplane. From *that,* you jump to the conclusion that they are terrorists. Then you go on a wild goose chase, trespass on a horse farm, and the owners retaliate by shooting at you. Did you happen to run into Hopalong Cassidy, or perhaps a dwarf with a limp and a purple eye patch along the way? We're done, Watson. You're delusional. I should arrest you for trespass plus probably a hundred other infractions. Did the thought ever cross that overly imaginative peanut brain of yours that two employees of a bar just might be at the airport taking delivery of supplies for the bar?"

"That's not the point. Laura was a Muslim. She trained as a terrorist in Germany and was a member of a radical mosque in Brooklyn. She . . ."

"Oh for fuck sake. Watson, you have an out of control imagination and watch too many thrillers. This isn't proof, this isn't evidence, this is bullshit. You're wasting my time."

"I have pictures. Here, look." Bill shoved photographs toward Blessinggame. "These are pictures of the terrorists at their camp. They're training . . . see?"

Blessinggame gave the photos a cursory view, and then handed them back to Bill. "Looks like a party to me. This is a drug case. If you have evidence about drugs, let me know. Shove your terrorist theory where the sun doesn't shine and go back to your office and do investments or whatever you do to pass the time of day. Stay out of my case, out of my way, and out of my life."

"But there's more. Laura and Wan . . ."

"Enough! Do you want to cool your heels in the slammer for obstruction of justice? Do you want another rights reading?"

"No, but . . ."

"Get out of my sight or I'll arrest and book you on so many offences it'll make your head spin."

Blessinggame stood up, grabbed the bag of donuts, and maneuvered his way around the desk.

"How can I get hold of you if I have more evidence . . . more proof?" asked Bill.

"More evidence means more meddling and more meddling is exactly what I don't want. Back off, Watson. Stay out of this case and stay out of my way. Good day."

Blessinggame walked to the door of the shabby boxlike office and shook his pudgy outstretched hand toward the front of the station house. "We're done. Find your own way out."

8:26 AM Wednesday, August 18, 2010
Watson Financial Services, Metropole Avenue
Avalon, Santa Catalina Island, California

"How did it go? Yikes, not so good, from the look on your face," said Tiffany.

"Not so good is an understatement."

"Did he listen? Did he hear the evidence or look at the photos?"

"Detective Tweedle Dumb wants no part of the terrorist theory. The good thing is that he didn't arrest me. He gave me the don'tmeddle-in-my-life-or-I'll arrest-you speech, big time. He didn't hear half of what I said and couldn't comprehend, misinterpreted, or ignored the other half. He dismissed the photos out of hand. He's hung up on the drug angle. Let's call Jenn."

Jenn picked up with her usual promptness.

"Hi, guys, how'd it go?" asked Jenn lightheartedly.

"Blessinggame was about as receptive to the terrorist theory as a particularly stupid brick wall. He threw me out of his office, which was a lot better than being arrested," said Bill.

"I'm not surprised. It's kind of what we expected. He's looking for a quick solution that gives him full credit."

"What about Homeland Security. Any hope there?" asked Tiffany.

"They called back and recorded our story. They didn't seem impressed, but they didn't hang up on me, which is better than Blessinggame's response. They gave me a case number and said they would look into it and get back to me. Don't hold your breath. I'll stay close and as we uncover additional information, I'll send it on to them. Gotta run, I've stuff to do before I catch the helicopter. See you about 1:45."

Jenn disconnected.

"What a downer." said Tiffany. "What's next?"

"I'll get Chris's truck and drive to the airport . . . you pick up Jenn. I'll see you back here."

8:41 AM Wednesday, August 18, 2010
The Second Floor, Avalon Bay Bar
Avalon, Santa Catalina Island, California

"It's him, it's the bookkeeper. He was my customer, no doubt about it."

"Damn, why is he involved? Poking around the bar, poking around the airport. Does he suspect something?" ranted Khalid.

"We should move the Avalon Jihad up. We can't risk getting exposed," said Fikriyya, seeing an opportunity to reiterate her plea.

"That's not possible. Why do I have to remind you that that isn't an option," snapped Khalid. "How're preparations going at the compound?"

"Everyone worked through the night. They'll be ready by ten or eleven."

CHAPTER THIRTY-NINE

12:29 PM Wednesday, August 18, 2010
Airport Road
The Interior, Santa Catalina Island, Avalon

Bill had to coax Chris's 1988 Chevy C/K 1500 up Old Stage Road. It didn't appear as reliable as Michelle's truck had been but so far on level ground, it had performed okay. Nevertheless, he hoped he would not have to rely on the truck for a quick getaway.

Bill slowed and pulled as far to the right as the road would allow, to let an oncoming SUV pass. The SUV slowed almost imperceptivity as it approached. Bill moved further on to the shoulder, precariously close to an abyss, to avoid a collision. The dust plume trailing the SUV finally began to diminish as the SUV got within fifty feet of Bill's truck. The inside of the SUV was crammed with people and baggage. Additional baggage, lashed haphazardly to the SUV's roof, swayed from side to side as the vehicle veered along the road. The SUV's door handle nearly brushed the side view mirror of Bill's truck as it passed. Bill caught a glimpse of the driver—it was Jeff—and Ken sat in the rear seat staring down at his lap.

Oh my god it's Ken—a new character in the growing cast of terrorists! Bill's mind swirled. Where is all this headed? Where will this madness end? Bill glanced in the rearview mirror, hoping Ken had not recognized him. Baffled, Bill pulled back onto the road. Ken and Jeff knew each other, the conclusion was irrefutable, they were terrorists. *Who are the others in the car? The chanters, of course, they must to be terrorists also.* Bill realized he should have paid more attention to the vehicle. *Was it dark blue, or black, maybe it was an old Land Rover. It was covered with mud and dust.* Bill had not thought to look at the license plate—why should he have. With a clenched fist, he banged the steering wheel in frustration as he drove.

The miles flew by. Bill was oblivious to the road. He tried to sort out what all this meant. The conclusion was always the same. Unbelievably, Ken was a terrorist. Bill slowed to turn onto the access road to the airport, drove to the parking lot, and parked. He remained seated behind the wheel catching his breath, slowing his heart rate, and thinking.

"Bill, two days in a row, how lucky can I get! Couldn't keep away, could you?" Julie leaned in the doorway of the restaurant and laughed loudly as Bill got out of the truck.

"Hi, Julie, longtime no see."

Julie hustled into the restaurant ahead of him and returned with two cold ones, thrusting one into Bill's hand she raised her cold one above her head and announced, "Bottoms up."

Still distracted by his thoughts on the terrorists, Bill sipped without thinking. "Julie, can you tell me anything else about Jeff?"

"That worthless son-of-a-bitch didn't show up for work today." Swigging from her bottle she added, "I've had to work my ass off. He didn't give me a warning. I couldn't get a replacement. You're not keeping up. Bottoms up good-looking."

"I'm resting. So about Jeff, I think he works in town at the Avalon Bay Bar. Did he ever mention that?"

"Works in town? How the hell would he get there? He rides a fucking bike. He never said anything about town. He kept to himself and was reliable until today. Wait 'til I get hold of that lazy, low-life bastard."

"I think he worked with Laura at the Avalon Bay Bar."

"Laura, she's the dead jeep driver?"

"Yes."

"But that was a Conservancy jeep."

"She had two jobs."

"Really."

"Excuse me, Julie. Is there a pay phone close by?"

"Over there, but use my phone. It's in the office."

"Thanks. I need to call my office, but my cellphone doesn't work out here."

"None do. We're so isolated, we're so lucky—it's so perfect?"

Outwardly Bill smiled at Julie, but inside he was worried, anxious.

In Julie's office, Bill dialed. "Hi Tif, it's me. Have you heard from Jenn?"

"No. I was just going to get her."

"Good, I'm glad I caught you. You won't believe what's happened. On the way to the airport, I passed an SUV with five or six people in it headed toward town. Jeff, the black man, was driving. Guess who was in the back seat—Ken."

"Ken? You mean our Ken . . . Ken Westerly?"

"In person."

"Oh my god Ken's a terrorist! Who else is involved? It seems like every other person in Avalon is a terrorist. The town's crawling with the fucking creeps."

"The car was crammed with baggage. They're up to something. Didn't Ken say he was leaving the island Saturday? And as I recall, he said on the helicopter."

"Yes, Friday or Saturday on the helicopter."

"When you're at the heliport, see if you can find out exactly when he leaves."

"Jimmy will tell me. What about the others?"

"I doubt they're going with him. They'd need a C-17 cargo plane to haul all their crap. Most of it looked like those huge roller duffle bags divers drag around town."

"I'll see what I can find out. When are you coming back?"

"There isn't much more to learn here. I'm going to try to get the tail number of the aircraft and then I'll head back."

"Okay, I'm outta here. See you later. Geez, this is great!"

Bill hung up and thought, *great my ass.* He walked out of Julie's office nearly colliding with her in the doorway. She held two newly opened cold ones.

"Good save on the beers," laughed Bill. "Thanks for letting me use the phone."

"You asked if I knew anything more about Jeff. Well I don't . . . not really, but when you asked about the payphone, something clicked in my head. Jeff hung out by the payphone every afternoon, whether or not he was working . . . 5:30 and 6:00 like clockwork. Each time he either took or made a call. Busy little twit, the fucking lazy-assed bastard."

"Really."

"He never was on the line very long. Sometimes the phone would ring, he'd answer it, and in a second or two, he'd hang up. Bang, bang, thank you ma'am, and just like that it was over."

"Interesting. Anything else?"

"How about another cold one? I'm sure you didn't drive all the way out here just to make time with me . . . or did you?" An alluring smile exposed Julie's uneven teeth, stained the color of weak coffee, with highlights of nicotine.

Bill took possession but did not swallow. "It's always a pleasure to talk with you. I'd hoped I'd get a chance to meet Jeff."

"The little prick. Just wait until I get hold of his black ass. The son-of-a-bitch will turn white before I'm finished with him."

It occurred to Bill that Joe and Julie would have been a match made in heaven.

"I need to get back. Sorry for the brief visit. Tiffany reminded me that I have an afternoon meeting and I'm late as it is. Thanks for the beer," said Bill. He put the full bottle on a table next to the first nearly full bottle. "Oh, is Jerry in? I need to get information for a client."

"He's always in. Good to see you, Bill, make it three in a row and I'll have something really special for you."

Bill did not want to know what really special meant.

1:59 PM Wednesday, August 18, 2010
Airport-in-the-Sky Control Tower
The Interior, Santa Catalina Island, Avalon

Bill climbed the three flights of stairs to the tower wondering, ironically, whether Joe helped build the stairs.

"Hi, Jerry."

Startled, Jerry turned and looked quizzically at Bill.

Bill extended his hand, "How are you today? It's Bill Watson."

"Good, I'm good. Oh Bill, I'm sorry I didn't recognize you. What brings you out here?"

"I was downstairs with Julie and I remembered I have a client who wants a referral to a small airfreight company. Julie said there are a few that fly here on a regular basis. Can you help me out?"

"We have UPS, FedEx, and DHL. They all share the same DC 3 and delivery truck. The 3 is one of the last flying in the States. This airport is suited to those rugged old planes. They can either land on the strip or the dirt alongside it."

"I know about those. My client wants a smaller company, maybe one that flies a Cessna or Beechcraft. Julie said a few of those fly in here. A Conservancy employee meets one of them."

"Oh yeah, that one . . . don't recall the company's name. They fly in, fly out, and never tie down . . . they pay cash."

"Is there any way to identify them?"

"I don't think so."

"How about tail numbers? All aircraft have unique tail numbers, don't they? Do you keep records on that sort of thing? My client would be appreciative for the referral."

"I'm sure they would. Let's see if we can figure this out. I have a cash-receipts log. Maybe that'll work."

"Great, can I help you look?" said Bill, recalling how informative the jeep log had been at the Conservancy.

"Thanks, I can do this."

Jerry pulled a book out of the upper right-hand drawer of his desk and fingered the pages.

"This should be easy because almost everyone pays by check or credit card. Here we are. I only have the tail number, no name."

"Is it the same each time?"

"I don't know."

He ran a finger down some more rows and turned the page.

"Yup, it appears so. N683599, a Cessna Apache. Does that help?"

"It does," said Bill, taking a pen from his pocket and scribbling the information on a scrap of paper.

"Thanks, you've been a real help. My client will really appreciate this."

Bill loped down the stairway. *Once I get this to Jenn, we'll find out exactly who these jackasses are. That might put us over the top with Blessinggame.*

2:29 PM Wednesday, August 18, 2010
Airport Road
The Interior, Santa Catalina Island, Avalon

While he drove to Avalon, Bill's thoughts were focused on terrorists. Connections raced through his head: *Laura to Jeff to Ken and don't forget Christine and then there's Marilyn and Wanda. They're like pieces to a puzzle. We're in over our heads more so than I thought. There's no denying it, these are terrorists, not drug dealers and now they're on the move, but to where and to do what? On the other hand, maybe we've spooked them and they're retreating. Ken had shared his travel plans with me before I disrupted the terrorists so action seems more likely than retreat. How many of the bastards are there, six, seven, ten, or more, and why Avalon? So far, they have killed two, three, and maybe more. We have to turn this over to the police. We have no choice.*

His last thought before he reached town was that he did not want to become part of the growing club of people murdered by the terrorists.

CHAPTER FORTY

3:06 PM Wednesday, August 18, 2010
Watson Financial Services, Metropole Avenue
Avalon, Santa Catalina Island, California

"What's going on out there?" mumbled Jenn as she paced in Tiffany's office.

"Thanks Jimmy, we'll talk later." Tiffany cradled the phone, glanced up from her desk, and smiled at Jenn. "Stop pacing, he'll be okay. He wasn't going to go to their hideout just to the airport."

"Pacing can't hurt."

"Jimmy said Ken's been on the same flight seven times during the last three months and he always returns the same day, often on the next flight. The helicopter people think he's weird. He always wants the same seat on the flight to Long Beach . . . rear left, next to the window. He doesn't care where he sits when he returns. He's on the 2:20 PM this Saturday but it doesn't appear any of his buddies are with him. Jimmy knows most of the islanders on those flights and the people he doesn't know are tourists on round trips. Ken hasn't booked a return flight. Jimmy thinks that's odd, but, then, he thinks Ken is totally odd."

"Ken told us he was going on vacation so why would he book a round trip?"

"You're right. We can't make a case on Ken based on his practicing for a vacation trip," laughed Tiffany trying to ease the tension.

Unsmiling, Jenn just stared ahead. "None of this makes sense. It's becoming bizarre."

Bill entered the office grim faced.

"I'm so happy and relieved to see you love," said Jenn as she rushed to embraced him.

"It's good to be back and alive to boot . . . we have to talk."

"How'd it go at the airport?" asked Tiffany.

"The airport's okay. There's nothing going on there. I got the tail number."

"And what's this about the terrorists?" asked Jenn.

"They were headed to Avalon."

"Did they shoot at you?" asked Tiffany nonchalantly.

"No and thanks for asking. Ken was occupied with something on his lap . . . I'm sure he didn't see me."

"Ken, our Ken, it's hard to believe," mumbled Tiffany, shaking her head.

"Our Ken . . . give me a break. He is not our Ken anymore. He was with a half dozen terrorists."

"If you hadn't happened to be driving to the airport at just that time we wouldn't know Ken was a terrorist," Jenn said.

"I've thought about that. So, what did you guys find out at the heliport?"

"Ken, make that Ken the terrorist, is on the 2:20 PM Saturday. He has been on that flight seven times in the last few months, requesting the same seating arrangement each time," said Tiffany.

"Good work."

"Thanks. After Jenn got off the helicopter, we grilled Jimmy and swore him to secrecy."

"Jimmy likes Tiffany," said Jenn, knowingly.

"Yeah, right," flushed Tiffany.

"Yeah, right yourself. He was eating out of your hand. He couldn't keep his eyes off you—your boobs, actually."

"Alright, alright let's keep focused," said Bill. "These idiots are on the move. I don't think we forced their hand since Ken told us he was leaving the island for vacation before I stumbled onto their camp. I wonder if the others are going off-island also."

"They aren't booked on a helicopter, according to Jimmy."

"Henry told me that Laura told him she was leaving the island soon," said Bill. "I'll call him, maybe he can remember more about that conversation. It fits. Both Ken and Laura told people that they were leaving for a long time or not coming back. I'd bet the others are headed off-island either after they do their nasty work here, or to do it somewhere else. What could be a target on-island?"

"Large numbers of people in a small area." said Tiffany.

"Exactly. Is there a concert or some other event at the Casino or Descanso . . . or a triathlon . . . a marathon?"

"We should look into that," said Jenn. "But first we need to determine if they're leaving the island, and, if so, when and how."

"That means the express boat," said Tiffany.

"We don't have names to check against a passenger list," shrugged Bill. "Except Jeff and Christine's, and we don't know if those are their real names."

"And we don't have a Jimmy to help us, or do we?" asked Jenn with a twinkle in her eye and eyebrows raised expectingly.

"We may, but it'll be trickier," said Tiffany.

"And what might be the name of this young man?"

"Woman," retorted Tiffany.

"Okay, okay ladies, cool it. We can sort out relationships later. I believe that first we have to follow Ken. Is the 2:20 PM flight full?"

"I'll call."

Tiffany pressed the redial button.

"Hi, Tiffany again, is Jimmy there?"

"You can bet the farm he will be," murmured Jenn.

"Hi Jimmy. Yes, it was good seeing you too. About that 2:20 on Saturday afternoon, is it full? . . . Sure, I'll wait."

Tiffany drummed her fingers for several seconds until Jimmy came back on the line.

"Two seats open, great. We may want one. I'll call back in a few minutes. Remember sweetie, no one knows about this, okay? Bye."

"'No one knows about this sweetie.' Don't worry, babe. Jimmy would die before he'd risk getting on your wrong side."

"Geez, Jenn, back off," said Bill.

"Why? If it were me, Tiffany would be all over my case."

"Like a blanket," nodded Tiffany, arms crossed.

"Jenn, have you ever seen or met Ken?" asked Bill.

"Wouldn't know him if he walked in here as we speak."

"Which could happen. Lock the door let's go in the back."

Reassembled in the back room of Watson Financial Services and cradling mugs of coffee, the three resumed their strategizing.

"Okay," said Bill. "I suggest we book Jenn on the 2:20 PM helicopter but under her maiden name. Can Jimmy do that for us?"

"Does a tiger have stripes?" Jenn quipped.

"And we get her the seat next to Ken," said Bill, ignoring Jenn's remark.

"Why?" asked Tiffany.

"Yeah why?" asked Jenn.

"I don't know. It's just a feeling. What he does on the helicopter or when he gets to Long Beach could break this thing open. Maybe he'll meet someone there—perhaps other terrorists or he might pick up or deliver something. That might give us hard evidence for the police."

"Okay, I like flying." Jenn ran her fingers through her hair.

"We also need to check the express boat. Can you handle that, Tiffany?"

"Consider it done."

Tiffany reached for the phone to call Jimmy, but Bill held up a hand signaling her to wait.

"Now for the hard part," Bill exhaled. "We are in over our heads . . . way over our heads. Even you two have to admit that. Everything we know so far points to these bastards being ruthless murderous radical Islamic terrorists. They are single-minded and expect to die for Allah. They get their ticket punched whether or not they're successful. Knocking off a few American infidels along the way is icing on the paradise cake. We're putting ourselves in their crosshairs, if we're not already there. So, do we go forward, and if so, why? I think we turn this over to the police and walk."

"We have to go forward," said Jenn.

"Yeah, of course we have to go forward. What are you thinking? There's no decision point here," added Tiffany.

Tiffany was expert at pushing her agenda. A simple statement to go forward wasn't a consideration.

"That's not a surprise, but . . . why?"

"Because the simple fact is no one else can or will." Jenn had started pacing again. "No one will believe us. Even if we're able to convince the police or Feds we're on to something, they're so bureaucratic and narrow-minded that they couldn't react quickly. *It*, whatever *it* is, would be over before the authorities got started. Moreover, ineffectual, visible actions by police could spook them and they might back off to strike another day. If we don't catch the bastards, they skate. It's as simple as that."

"Jenn's right," said Tiffany. "These assholes aren't organizing a picnic. They are out to destroy our way of life and kill Americans, how, when, or where we don't know—yet. But we're closer to those answers than we were only three hours ago. We are good. We are so damn good! We'll figure it out. The authorities won't *get it* fast enough."

"And when we figure it out, what then?" asked Bill.

"We give Blessinggame another chance," said Jenn.

"To arrest me?"

"No, to make a name for himself . . . Think positive."

"Okay, make the reservation and let's try to find out if the others are going over-town. Maybe they've also booked *vacations*," said Bill sarcastically.

Tiffany was back on the phone.

"Jimmy? Hi, sweetie, it's Tiffany."

This time the two women exchanged conspiratorial winks and smiles. Bill rolled his eyes and shook his head.

"Jenn wants that reservation. Make it under her maiden name. That would be Floyd, Jennifer Floyd. Great, thanks a million!"

Tiffany turned to Jenn. "You're booked, Miss Floyd."

"Okay, next on the list . . . the express boat," said Jenn.

"Alicia works the ticket counter in the morning. I'm sure I'll be able to squeeze the information we need out of her," said Tiffany.

"I'll go with you," said Jenn.

"If they're not on an express boat, we have to find out if there're any large events in the next few days. I'll speak with the Chamber . . . Anything else?" asked Bill.

Jenn looked at him, "I need you to brief me on Ken, love. Let's put on a fresh pot of coffee."

CHAPTER FORTY-ONE

7:23 PM Wednesday, August 18, 2010
Prayer Room, Second Floor, Avalon Bay Bar
Avalon, Santa Catalina Island, California

"Damn it's hot," said Saleem-Ali.

"It's always hot," Fikriyya wrinkled her face, "and the air's always stagnant, always humid, and always stinks like sweat."

"You're all too anxious, relax," said Mohamed. "The last few days have been stressful. We're all on edge, but we're close, we'll get our reward soon."

"Soon? The soon you talk about makes no sense." Fikriyya was frowning deeply. "We're ready now, we're prepared, and we don't need any more practice. We're set to go. Martyrdom is within reach."

"Fikriyya is correct," said Saleem-Ali. "We're ready."

"Maybe we've been discovered," said Abdel el-Shinawy. "Maybe that's what this is about."

"Not a chance. If that were the case, Khalid would already be off island, and we'd be leaderless," said Fikriyya, silently thinking that that might be a good thing.

"Practice could attract attention," said Abu Tarek.

"It won't. Allah, `azza wa jall,` knows best. We cannot afford to have another attack squashed, as so many have been since 9/11. We'd perish, or worse be sent to Guantanamo," said Mohamed.

"That sounds like Khalid," said Saleem-Ali, half turning. "He's always late."

"*As-salaamu `alaykum,*" said Khalid upon entering the room.

"*Wa alakum as-salaam wara h_mantu allaahi wa bara kaa,*" responded the jihadists by rote.

"I overheard your incessant whining and I don't want to hear any more of your gibberish. Your words are inconsistent with steadfast mujahedeen. Allah has commanded, `azza wa jall.` We have learned from the unfortunate failures of our jihadist brothers. Our devout predecessors were inadvertent fools. Planning must be thoughtful, training thorough, and we must practice, practice, and practice. Need I recall the missteps before the Cole attack, the failed attack on the London subway system, the sloppy attempt to slip explosives into LAX, the bumbling in Arkansas? The list of failures is endless. The world has a false sense of security due to the unfortunate ineptness of our jihadist brothers. We will end the string of misfortune and succeed where others have failed. We will be martyred and reside in the garden with cool flowing streams and wide-eyed maidens. Allah, `azza wa jall,` will favor us."

"But Khalid, more practice is unnecess . . ."

"Enough, Fikriyya. Be silent! Always you are complaining. What have I just told you? We proceed with our plan Saturday. Abu Tarek and Mohammed are team one, Fikriyya and Saleem-Ali are team two. Team one leaves Avalon Friday evening on the express boat and returns on the 2:00 PM express boat Saturday. Team two leaves Avalon on the Saturday 2:05 PM express boat. Let's review our plan—our cover. What's our cover, Abu Tarek?"

"We're divers with our equipment—tanks, weights, regulators, wet suits. We tell anyone who asks, that we plan to dive or have just dived at the Avalon Dive Park."

"How do you optimize the effectiveness of the bombs?"

"We stow our equipment on opposite ends of the express boat, in the areas reserved for dive equipment," said Mohamed, pointing to the bow and stern storage areas on a large hand-drawn express boat schematic taped to the prayer room wall. "We sit in the center section but not together."

"Why the center section?"

"So our actuators can activate either bomb. We each have two actuators. We are back-up to each other. One bomb would destroy the boat and kill hundreds. Two bombs obliterate the boat and no one survives."

"What do you do if you're asked to open your dive bags for inspection?"

"That probably won't happen as there are too many divers for each bag to be inspected. Usually all a diver has to do is declare his equipment," said Mohamed.

"But what if they want to see the equipment?" persisted Khalid.

"We show it to them." Mohamed shrugged. "The explosives are in the tanks. They'll never figure it out."

"What about bomb-sniffing dogs?"

"They are of no concern," said Abu Tarek with confidence. "The explosives are packaged in thick vinyl bags inside the tanks. We've sanitized the tanks and their walls are thick . . . there's no residue."

"And the Coast Guard. What if the Coast Guard spot-checks passengers?"

"If they have dogs, they're looking for drugs, not explosives," continued Abu Tarek. "If they don't have dogs, they're looking for illegal immigrants. We have proper identification."

"Abu Tarek, how do you behave on the boat?"

"We remain calm. We don't speak to each another and speak only with other divers or passengers if they engage us in conversation. Ten minutes outside the breakwater on the Long Beach boat or twenty-five minutes from Avalon on the boat out of Avalon, we focus on jihad. When the express boats are about to pass each other we . . ."

"What is the name of the equipment used to haul the tanks?" interrupted Khalid.

"Roller duffel bags . . . mine's an Aeris," said Mohamed. "And the bombs are . . ."

Khalid cut him off. "Fikriyya, where else have you dived?" His eyes were unreadable.

"The wreck of the Rhone in the British Virgin Islands," responded Fikriyya without hesitation.

"What was your experience with that dive?"

"I liked it, but the Avalon Dive Park has been the best. The Rhone did not meet my expectations but it was still worth the trip."

"Saleem-Ali, how did you get to the Rhone?"

"From Los Angeles I flew to Miami and then to St. Thomas and took a ferry to the British Virgin Islands."

"Mohamed, what was the cost?"

"Expensive . . . over $2,500."

"Abu Tarek, what has been your experience with the Manta Bite mouthpiece?"

"I've had trouble with it, it doesn't fit well. I'm considering a Sea Cure."

"Saleem-Ali, when do you leave Avalon?"

"Saturday on the 2:05 PM express boat," answered Fikriyya.

"Fikriyya, I asked Saleem-Ali, not you. You lack discipline. You must pay attention and not always take control. Speak only when spoken to or when it's appropriate. Act your character, act your role, know your place." Khalid hammered his right fist three times into his left palm to emphasize character, role, and place. "Above all, fit in, all of you must fit in. Don't create a disturbance or argue with anyone. You must not draw attention to yourselves."

"Mohamed, how many times have you dived at the Avalon Dive Park?"

"Twice."

"That's not right, it's three times," said Fikriyya.

"Fikriyya, mind your own business!" Khalid scowled. "No one would know the difference. This is just for conversation purposes."

"Mohamed, what is the universal designation for diving and how is it used."

"It is a red flag with a diagonal white stripe. When a boat flies the flag, divers are in the water."

"Fikriyya, in which direction does the stripe go?"

"Upwards, left to right."

"That's wrong . . . come on! That's basic stuff! Every diver knows what the flag looks like. If you don't know basic knowledge you could undermine jihad."

Khalid's questioning continued for nearly two hours.

"Good," said Khalid finally. "Most of you did well, but you all need to work harder to make your story sound credible. Saleem-Ali, what's the difference between this Saturday and next Saturday?"

"We won't use our transmitters this Saturday, next week we'll use them."

"They're called actuators not transmitters," said Fikriyya angrily.

"That is irrelevant," said Khalid with a dismissive wave of his hand. "What are our overriding rules?"

"We behave like divers," Saleem-Ali responded. "Everyone we speak with must believe we're scuba divers. We're either going to Avalon to dive in the dive park or we're returning from Avalon—we always try to fit in."

"Yes! That's the most important rule—we must fit in," grinned Khalid.

"We've rehearsed this diver bullshit every day for hours on end. We know this crap, let's get on with it," protested Fikriyya.

"Silence, Fikriyya, silence! You must believe." He feared Fikriyya would take another run at the need for practice. "I can replace you with Abdel el-Shinawy and you can remain at the bar."

Khalid preferred that Abdel el-Shinawy replace Fikriyya, but he would have to get permission from Brooklyn and that would take time and they probably wouldn't agree.

"I've worked too hard. I'm a bomber. It's just that we should meet Allah this Saturday. Why risk additional exposure and possible failure?"

"I'll have no more of this!"

"Okay, okay. I'm committed. I'm sorry," said Fikriyya.

"Good. This Saturday, Abdel el-Shinawy and I remain at the bar. We will join the rest of you the following week. You'll return here after practice to finalize your personal commitment to Allah, `azza wa jall. One last thing—bring your dive roller bags to my room. The bags will be stored in my room until you leave."

"Why?" asked Saleem-Ali.

"You are undisciplined. Disciplined jihadists do not ask questions or challenge their leaders. Our goal is within our grasp, we cannot leave anything to chance. Your bags will be stored in my room for safekeeping. You have no need for them until you leave."

7:45 PM Wednesday, August 18, 2010
Avalon Sheriff's Station
Avalon, Santa Catalina Island, California

"What's so important to bring me here at this hour?" asked Blessinggame angrily. "This better be good."

"The terrorists are ready to attack."

Bill was determined to remain respectful regardless of Blessinggame's response.

"The terrorists again," moaned Blessinggame, slapping his right hand to his forehead and rolling his eyes, "and now they're ready to attack. Are you nuts? There are no terrorists except in your imagination."

"They're at the Avalon Bay Bar right now. You can go there and see for yourself."

Bill did not know where the terrorists were but it was a reasonable guess.

"Mr. Watson, I've had enough of your drivel. I have told you this is a drug case. Your terrorist fantasy is idiotic, it doesn't hold water, and it won't get you off the suspect list. I've a mind to arrest you for obstruction of justice. If nothing else, you'd be out of my hair. I know I can wrap this up in a few days and not have to return to this god-forsaken island. Do I make myself clear?"

"You do but . . ."

"But what?"

"These people are real. They're here and ready to attack."

"Enough." Blessinggame glowered and stood. "Good night, Mr. Watson. Get out or get cuffed—your choice."

8:07 PM Wednesday, August 18, 2010
Armstrong's Fish Market & Seafood Restaurant
Avalon, Santa Catalina Island, California

"What a heavenly evening. I love balmy weather. It envelops you like a cocoon. There isn't a ripple on the bay except when a fish jumps, a pelican dives, or a sea lion chases a flying fish. It's perfect, just scrumptious," said Tiffany beaming.

At times Jenn wondered what made her friend tick. *"Envelops you like a cocoon?" Give me a break,* she thought.

"Hi, ladies, how are your drinks?" Looking around, Cynthia, their table server, asked, "Where's Bill?"

"I'll have another," said Jenn.

"Me too. He'll be along soon," said Tiffany.

"Back in a flash," said Cynthia, hustling off to the bar.

"I hope he gets here soon," Jenn frowned. "We're draining these Daiquiris like water. Do you think Blessinggame arrested him?"

"Based on what?" said Tiffany.

"He's here," announced Cynthia, returning with Bill in tow. "He was at the hostess stand."

Cynthia placed the drinks on the table but lingered in hopes of overhearing some juicy tidbit. To Cynthia, customers were not just a source of income, but also an inexhaustible reservoir of rumors. Her life was one continuous stream of fresh, juicy rumors.

"How did it go?" asked Jenn.

"Go where, go how?" asked Cynthia, inserting herself into the conversation.

Bill looked at Cynthia and said flatly, "I can't find scotch tape anywhere on this island."

"Did you try Vons?"

"I did but they're out."

"What about the drug store?"

"It's closed."

"What do you need the tape for?"

Bill's contrived need for tape had not achieved its intended purpose. Instead of losing interest, Bill's "scotch tape problem" challenged Cynthia to find a solution.

"Maybe the boss has some, I'll ask."

"No thanks, tape can wait."

"Okay . . . Oh, by the way, have you rented your condo?"

"No, Morales says he still owns it. I'll let you know."

"Great, keep me in mind. Are you sure you don't want me to ask the boss for tape?"

"No, I'll be okay." Bill smiled wanly, silently willing her to leave.

"Great. Are you guys ready to order?"

"I'll have a Kenwood Sauvignon Blanc and a menu," said Bill.

"Good choice and the ladies?"

"We're fine, we just got these," said Tiffany, holding up her daiquiri.

Cynthia scurried off, her resolve to harvest rumors or fix the shortfall in scotch tape truncated by a need to fill a drink order.

"Cynthia . . . a tenant? Are you serious or just plain nuts?" asked Jenn incredulously.

"Of course not, but she thinks she could be."

"She won't be back for a while," said Tiffany.

"So what happened?" asked Jenn.

"Nothing new, Blessinggame wants no part of the terrorist theory. The next time I approach him, I'll bring a toothbrush."

"A toothbrush?" asked Tiffany.

"Bill will need one in the clink. Jails don't supply toothbrushes," said Jenn, laughing.

"He'll arrest me for sure."

Bill lowered his voice as Cynthia approached.

"Here's your wine. Ready to order?" asked Cynthia.

2:09 AM Thursday August 19, 2010
Khalid's Room above the Avalon Bay Bar
Avalon, Santa Catalina Island, California

It had been a long day, all the jihadists slept soundly on the prayer room floor. They had arranged their bags in Khalid's room in a neat row against the wall away from the prayer room. Khalid would easily be able to complete the modifications before morning prayers.

Khalid unlocked his desk and took out an actuator with a preset frequency of 34.97 MHz. He would accomplish everything without jeopardizing control. He would salvage the Avalon Jihad using Aaliyah's ingenuity and knowledge to insure he met the master schedule.

The jihadists had not been instructed in the use of an embedded safety lock in the detonator that blocked frequency changes. They had no need to know about that feature. Khalid planned to permanently set the frequency of each bomb to 34.97 MHz, activate the safety lock, and then reset the frequency on the dial of each detonator to their initial settings. The safety lock would block any frequency indicated set on dial of the detonator. Then only Khalid could detonate the bombs—all of them simultaneously. The destruction of the express boats would coordinate with other attacks around the country. As important, he would have absolute control over the detonation of the bombs thereby eliminating the impact of discretionary decisions by the jihadists. Khalid would be in complete control. If a Jihadist got cold feet, and tried to bail, he could not. More importantly, he'd join the thousand or so tourists along with the destruction of the express boats and then have a painful time explaining to Allah why he should be admitted to paradise and not taste the fire.

Khalid chuckled, "Those fools, they're all fools."

The hardest part of modifying the bombs was to enable the embedded safety lock. Aaliyah had told him exactly what to do. She surely had no idea that sharing such detailed technical information about how the bombs could be manipulated had sealed her fate. She had told Khalid, "Disconnect the red and yellow wires from the rounded connector then solder the red one to the rectangular connector and then coil the yellow wire, as it isn't needed." She had also told him that there were decoy wires in the detonator, mostly red ones. Khalid laughed and thought, *Aaliyah you are the biggest fool of all.*

Khalid paused and stared at the circuit board. "Damn," he mumbled. *What had she said about the rectangular connector—something about markings? Do I use the one with markings or the one without markings?* There were two red wires connected to two rounded connectors and two red wires connected to two rectangular connectors. Khalid, unaccustomed to being unsure or confused, shook his head, made a less than informed decision, and continued. *Infidels always made things so complicated*, he rationalized, *if they believed, jihad would be unnecessary.*

Khalid replicated the modification on the remaining bombs. When done, he was satisfied nothing would go wrong with his plan. It was perfect. The express boats blown up, the unbelievers slaughtered, the jihadists in paradise, and he would be on to bigger and better schemes. Khalid would postpone martyrdom—he had too much to accomplish in this life.

CHAPTER FORTY-TWO

7:13 AM, Thursday August 19, 2010
Catalina Express Ticket Office, the Mole
Avalon, Santa Catalina Island, California

The Catalina Express ticket office is tiny—maybe a hundred square feet. It is located at the base of a one hundred and seventy-five foot rectangular pier called the "Mole." The eastern side of the Mole borders the San Pedro Channel and offers an unobstructed view of the ocean and the mainland beyond. The other side of the Mole faces into Avalon harbor towards the City of Avalon. Moorings, gangplanks, and ramps that channel passengers to and from the express boats connect to the Avalon side of the Mole.

Eight times a day in the summer, passengers form long lines on the Mole while waiting to board an express boat. The far end of the Mole provides a dramatic view of the historic Avalon Casino. Anglers cast lines from the Mole for halibut, white sea bass, striped sea bass, and Catalina Sand Dabs while pelicans and seagulls provided persistent raucous companionship to the anglers, the birds always hopeful for a hand out.

Jenn and Tiffany parked their golf cart in the small parking lot and walked the short distance to the express boat ticket office. The window of the office was large, taking up most of the front of the

252

office, but the opening to pass tickets, credit cards, and money was small, about the size of a small toaster. Jenn and Tiffany leaned against the counter of the ticket office. Tiffany spoke into the speaker above the opening. She greeted Alicia and posed the dilemma of determining whether Christine, Jeff, and others might be on an express boat leaving Avalon.

"I can't do that, that information is private," objected Alicia.

"No, it's not private, passenger lists are public," assured Jenn, edging closer to Tiffany to speak into speaker while cautiously looking around. She added, "can we talk about this away from the passengers?"

"Passenger lists are public? I don't think so . . . are you sure?" asked Alicia, first looking at Jenn and then at Tiffany.

"Yes, absolutely," affirmed Tiffany. "We need to know if any of these people are on an express boat. They could cause trouble."

The woman's eyes grew wide.

"What kind of trouble? Shouldn't we tell the company or the police?"

"We need to talk about this away from passengers. Can we go in the back?" reiterated Jenn.

"Well I don't know . . . you're islanders . . . so I guess so."

Once inside, Jenn and Tiffany continued to plead their case. "If they're on a boat, we'll tell the police. It's better that way. Your company could be in trouble if we alert the police and these people turn out not to be on the boat. It's complicated," emphasized Jenn, silently praying the smoke screen would work.

"Really." Alicia chewed her lower lip. "So, who are you looking for?"

"Christine Olson, Jeffery Tebbins, and maybe others." "Maybe others . . . so just how do I find *maybe others?* I'm not sure about this."

"Okay, okay, only look for Olson and Tebbins," said Jenn, hoping she had pulled their ploy from the jaws of defeat.

"Geez, I could get fired. Are you sure this information isn't private?"

"Absolutely. Don't worry. We'll take full responsibility. No one will know, even if the police get involved."

"Alright, I'll see what I can do . . . are you certain no one will know? I really need my job."

"No one will know . . . trust us," said Jenn, trying to sound convincing without appearing anxious.

In the back room, Alicia entered the names into the reservation system and printed a report.

She walked from the back office. "They're on two boats,"

"Two *different* boats . . . really."

"Yeah, Christine's on the Saturday 2:05 PM Avalon to Long Beach. Jeffery's on the Friday 8:50 PM Avalon to Long Beach."

"When do they return?" asked Tiffany.

"They don't."

Tiffany and Jenn exchanged puzzled looks. Then Tiffany turned to Alicia and asked, "Are you sure they haven't booked returns?"

"Yes."

"Have Christine or Jeffery booked passage in the last few months?" asked Jenn.

"Nope, that would have showed up. I used a criterion of six months before or after today. These are the only boats they're on."

"Thanks a lot, Alicia. We'll let the company know if there's a problem and don't worry, we won't mention your name. They won't know we've talked with you," assured Tiffany.

"That's good," said Alicia, who had resumed chewing her lower lip.

7:21 AM Thursday August 19, 2010
Heliport, Pebbly Beach Road
Avalon, Santa Catalina Island, California

Bill entered the heliport terminal building.

"Hi, Ted. How's the new job?"

Bill knew the heliport manager well. Ted had piloted Apaches during Desert Storm and Bill had served as an Infantry company commander in Barry McCaffery's 24th Mechanized Division—the point unit of the "Hail Mary" flanking maneuver that cut off the

Iraqi escape. Bill and Ted had never met in Kuwait but bonded when each learned the other had served there. As a civilian, Ted had flown French AS350 Eurocopters for Catalina Express Helicopters. Recently he had been promoted to manager of the Pebbly Beach heliport operations.

"It's okay but it can't beat flying. The money's good, though."

"Sorry to get right down to business, Ted, but I'm a bit short on time. I'm interested in someone on one of your flights later this week. Can you help me?"

"Sure, what do you need?"

"Ken Westerly is on your Saturday 2:20 PM flight. Jenn is on the same flight, although she's booked under her maiden name, Jennifer Floyd."

"Floyd? What's all this about . . . sounds mysterious."

"It is or might be. I'm curious why Ken has flown the same flight a half dozen times in the last few months and . . ."

". . . and immediately returned," completed Ted.

"You've noticed?"

"We've all noticed, but it's none of our business. Why are you interested?"

"I'm not sure. I don't know what he's up to, it may be nothing, or it may be something."

"You said Jenn booked under her maiden name."

"Yes."

"Why?"

"Ken doesn't know her but he knows me. She used her maiden name so he wouldn't make a connection."

"But why are you interested in Ken and why all this cloak and dagger stuff?"

"I want to know where he's going and what he's doing. Jenn is sort of following him. Whatever he's up to may not be on the up and up."

"Should I be concerned?"

"No, it's a financial thing . . . turned up in my review of a client file. I'm doing due diligence." Bill felt bad lying to Ted, a fellow comrade in arms. However, he had no choice at this point.

"I don't want to get tangled up in anything, Bill. Keep me outta this."

"I will, don't worry. But please don't use Jenn's married name. Can you do that?"

"Okay, that's simple enough . . . can't harm anyone. That's her business."

"Can I get the same commitment from the pilot?"

"Yeah, I guess so."

"Who is it?"

"I think it's Heather. Let me look . . . yeah, it's Heather."

"She knows Jenn."

"Don't worry, I'll brief her. Heather loves intrigue."

"Thanks, Ted, I really appreciate this. Oh, one more thing, when does he return? As far as I know, he always returns the same day. That's what caught my eye when I reviewed the file."

"Usually he does, but not this time. I'll pull the future bookings to see when he's returning. They're in the back."

"Any chance you can check on baggage, too? Did he have baggage with him each way?"

"Can't help you there. We record the total weight of baggage on a flight, but not who owns it, or even how many pieces. I don't recall exactly, but I don't think he usually had baggage . . . I can't be sure."

Ted disappeared into the back office.

Bill glanced around the terminal. No passengers, it was early. The first flight arrived from over-town at 8:15 AM. He thought about the helicopter service and smiled slightly. He enjoyed the fourteen-minute trip. Certainly, it was not for everybody.

Each chopper seated six, plus a pilot. With seven people, space was restricted, even claustrophobic. Each passenger's hips and thighs fit snugly against at least one other passenger's hips and thighs, which could add unintended excitement to the flight. Passenger's knees were closer to their chins than to the tops of their feet. The cramped cabin made for a cozy or miserable, flying experience, depending on your point of view.

Passengers could easily eavesdrop on radio transmissions and observe the pilot operating the controls. The view from the cabin was spectacular . . . truly awesome . . . more than worth the price of the flight. The wraparound window of the helicopter provided passengers with a panoramic view of the sky, the channel, and sea life. Sometimes the pilot would descend to ocean level and hover the chopper so passengers could watch whales, dolphins, and sea lions cavort. Marlin, ocean sunfish, shark, and swordfish were often seen jumping between waves. Weather permitting; pilots would maneuver the helicopter to optimize photo ops for the passengers.

Ted emerged from the back office area carrying a large loose-leaf binder. Its pages fluttering as he approached the ticket counter.

"As best I can determine, he hasn't booked a return trip."

"That seems odd, doesn't it?"

"Yeah, but that isn't our problem—or is it?" asked Ted, eyeing Bill.

"Not yours, maybe mine."

"Are you sure I shouldn't be concerned?" Ted said with obvious elevated anxiety.

"It's not important for you, don't worry. It's a financial thing. I have a professional due diligence responsibility. You know . . . CFP license obligations and such."

Bill lied. License obligations carried no requirement to conduct investigations to the level Bill pretended he was doing.

"Oh yeah, I fully understand that."

"If the situation changes, you'll be the first to know. Don't worry, you won't be dragged in. Just to be sure, though, don't mention this to anyone."

"I won't."

Bill tried to redirect the conversation.

"So how's business this year?"

"We're doing okay. August has been real good."

"Yeah, pretty much the same all over. Well, thanks again, Ted. I have to get going. I have an 8 AM meeting. I'll let you know if I need anything else. See you soon."

Ted gave Bill a blank look and a wordless wave.

7:53 AM Thursday August 19, 2010
Watson Financial Services, Metropole Avenue
Avalon, Santa Catalina Island, California

Jenn and Tiffany had beat Bill back to the office. Cloistered in Tiffany's office, Jenn sat cross-legged on the floor, intently working her laptop. Tiffany alternated between scrutinizing scraps of paper, scribbling notes on other scraps of paper, and writing furiously in a notebook.

"How did you guys do at the express boat?" asked Bill, now standing in the office doorway and wondering what in hell these two women were up to.

"In a sec. I don't want to lose this thought," said Tiffany without looking up.

Engaged with her computer, Jenn did not acknowledge Bill.

Finally, Tiffany looked up.

"What's with the writing in the notebook?" asked Bill.

"I'm recording the last few days in kinda a diary. If we aren't clear on something, we can rely on the diary to refresh our memories. How'd it go with Ted?'

"Good. He promised not to tip off Ken on Jenn's identity and he confirmed what Jimmy told you . . . Ken hasn't booked a return trip. So what about the express boat folks—did you get what we need?"

"We did, but it was torturous. Christine's on the Saturday 2:05 PM express boat out of Avalon and Jeff is on the Friday 8:50 PM express boat out of Avalon. They didn't book round trips."

"It seems, then, we don't have to be concerned with an incident on island, but I'll check with the Chamber anyway. And the others, what ab . . ."

". . . Don't say it . . . the request for *others* almost got us banished from the express boat ticket office forever. Alicia freaked out at the thought of searching passenger lists for people whose names *we didn't know.* Even if we can determine additional names, asking her to help will likely be fruitless. Alicia is so skittish now I believe she's lost as an informant."

"Frankly, she should be skittish," said Bill.

"You're right," piped up Jenn. "We could go to jail for some of the things we've done the last few days, especially the charade we used to extract confidential information from Alicia. We told her that passenger lists were public."

"And she *believed* you?"

"She did, but not with a lot of conviction."

Bill rubbed his hands over his eyes, shook his head, and sighed. "At least three terrorists are leaving the island, each at a different time and in a different way. What do you make of it?"

Jenn had gone back to her laptop so Tiffany answered.

"Jenn and I figure that maybe they've decided to divide and conquer. If one gets caught, another one follows up to complete the mission. We also believe what they're doing is off-island as they're leaving at different times."

"That makes sense. I've been thinking that we should put a tail on Jeff and Christine also. What do you think?"

"Good idea or at least half of one . . . we've run out of people. I can follow Tebbins as he doesn't know me. Christine might make a connection with me. For sure she would with you. Anyway, you're stuck here since you don't have a room pass from Blessinggame," laughed Tiffany.

"Very funny smart ass."

"You won't believe this!" exclaimed Jenn.

"What now?" asked Bill.

Tiffany added with a chuckle, "Another person?"

"Close but no cigar. Kaylid isn't an Arabic name but Khalid is. There are shit-loads of Khalids. Some have small variations in the spelling of the name, but it's the same name. When transliterating from Arabic, anyone can write a word as they think it looks or sounds. There could be as many different spellings, punctuation marks, upper and lower case representations, and vowel emphases for a word as there are people using the word. The Arabic language can be a nightmare to translate. You have to know intent as well as the actual meaning of a word. I couldn't make a connection between a Khalid with any of the women, so I focused on Khalids who were or are activists and lived in Brooklyn from 1990 until now."

"By activists you mean terrorists?" asked Bill.

"All too often when you're dealing with Islamic fundamentalists, the terms activist and terrorist are synonymous. I found three Khalids that might be our boy. Terrorists love to use aliases so I don't know if these are real people. One Khalid was involved in the Al Farouq Mosque about the same time Laura and Christine were there. He was a recruiter for sleeper cells. There's another Khalid, which might be an alias for someone known as Al-Hussein. He was a mid-to-high-level al-Qaeda operative and set-up man. He plotted, did preliminary organizational work, recruited operatives, and then beat feet. He left the martyrdom bullshit to others. No one has seen or heard from him for over five years. There's speculation he's in Iraq. The third Khalid was a chemical company executive at the company where Laura worked in Brooklyn. Any of these men could have known Laura, Christine, or Wanda or all of them, and could be our man. Now get this . . . N683599."

"The tail number," said Bill.

"Exactly—N683599 is owned by a chemical company in Brooklyn."

"I bet it's the same company where Khalid number three worked," screeched Tiffany.

"Bingo," said Jenn, pointing an index finger at Tiffany. "In addition, one of the owners of the aircraft on the registration records several years ago was an Al-Hussein. Two of the Khalids, and possibly all of them, could be the same person and *may* be our guy."

"This proves our case! Can we print all that?" asked Bill.

"I can, but we're not close to proving anything. Nothing positively links any of the Khalids to Catalina or to any of the women. We need an irrefutable connection between a person on island and a person in Brooklyn . . . That could be Ken or Khalid or whatever his name is. We need, however, to learn more about him to be able to tag him as that person."

"Do you really think we'll see him again? I don't," said Tiffany, disgusted. "From what you just told us, Ken's one-way trip off island on Saturday fits the profile of Khalid the organizer—he beats feet and the others bite the martyrdom bullet."

"You're right, Tiff," sighed Jenn knowingly. "We don't have enough to tie this into a neat package that Tweedle Dumb could understand but we're getting close."

CHAPTER FORTY-THREE

8:31 PM Friday, August 20, 2010
The Mole
Avalon, Santa Catalina Island, California

Departure of the Friday 8:50 PM express boat from Avalon was the ritualized beginning of the weekend for Avalon residents.

The waiting line confirmed the express boat was sold out—it usually was during the summer months. Most passengers were islanders. Islanders who had succumbed to island fever, islanders who could not tolerate tourists, or islanders drained by seventy-plus-hour summer workweeks. The waiting line for the express boat meandered across the Mole. The Mole served a secondary purpose as breakwater, partially protecting Avalon Bay from the unpredictable ravages of the San Pedro Channel. From most anywhere in Avalon, it was easy to determine the condition of the channel by glancing at the flagpole at the north end of the Mole. No red flags—water flat; one red flag—small craft warning; two red flags—gale force winds; three red flags—hurricane force winds. Three red flags were almost unheard of. Two red flags meant, practically speaking, the crossing would be uncomfortable. When two red flags flew, islanders often chose to defer their trip over-town. The Mole provided no protection from the elements for passengers. Passengers waiting to board an express boat were sweaty in the summer months, wet when it rained, or bone chillingly cold in winter months. Tonight there were no red flags.

Tiffany had disguised herself as best she could. A consummate network person and social butterfly, she was on a first-name basis with many islanders. This would be a definite liability tonight when she sought to go unnoticed. Scrubbed of makeup, she wore large dark glasses, worn jeans that she had planned to contribute to goodwill, running shoes, and a bulky faded red University of Pennsylvania sweatshirt that squared her figure. She had twisted her hair into a tight bun and covered it with an oversized headscarf. A small canvas overnight bag hung from her shoulder. She had stuffed the bag with two changes of clothing similar to what she wore.

Arriving minutes before boarding placed her near the end of the queue and minimized her contact with island residents. Coincidently and unintended, it also afforded her an unobstructed view of the passengers in line ahead of her. She looked for Jeff but did not see him. She wondered whether she should board if she did not spot him.

"Hi, Tiffany, going over-town? I'm surprised, you seldom leave the island."

If Patricia only knew, thought Tiffany, *so much for my clever disguise.* "Oh hi Patricia, I could say the same for you . . . going shopping?"

"I'm on my way to San Diego to see my son . . . he's off to college. He'll be a junior this year."

"He's going to Arizona, right?" said Tiffany, somewhat distracted as she looked past Patricia. She focused on a black man midway in line ahead of her. It had to be Jeff.

"He is. And are you going over-town to shop?"

"Yes, shopping, I'm going shopping."

Tiffany made a mental note to remember the lie.

"Nice camera. Do you always take pictures when you shop?" said Patricia, laughing.

"You never know when a photo-op might present itself. I'm a photography nut."

This was categorically nonsense. Tiffany had no idea about photography. A second lie she would have to keep track of. She cursed inwardly for not preparing for such situations.

"Are you in Commodore? I booked late and had no choice."

"No, I'm in steerage," giggled Tiffany, wondering why Patricia had asked, since she was not in the waiting area for Commodore seating.

"The line's moving. I have to get over to the Commodore line. See ya, sweetie."

"Have a good trip. See you on the other side," said Tiffany.

God I hope not, thought Tiffany. She breathed a sigh of relief, hoping no one else recognized her in her ludicrous disguise. She focused on Jeff. This time she noticed the enormous bag he was dragging. Several other passengers also had dive bags. She tried to take note of their faces without staring. If one of those sat with Jeff, it might be a connection. The line began to move quickly toward the ticket taker. As Tiffany moved with the line, she continued to watch Jeff. He had not spoken to anyone. She looked away from him for a moment and handed her commuter book to the ticket taker.

"Hi Tiffany, how're you doing?"

Damn. Even Bobby recognized me. I'm an idiot.

"Hi, Bobby, got ticket duty tonight, huh?"

"Yeah, I volunteered. When I'm done, I'm on the boat. Kinda bundled up for such a warm night, aren't you?"

"I never seem to get the clothing thing right. You said you're getting on the boat?" said Tiffany in an attempt to deflect attention away from herself.

"I'm going to see my girlfriend. She's picking me up in Long Beach."

Bobby ripped a coupon from Tiffany's commuter book and added it to the passenger count.

"Have a good trip. See you on board."

I hope not, thought Tiffany again. *I should have planned this whole thing better.*

Tiffany walked down the ramp to the mooring float, realizing she had lost sight of Jeff. He was not on the ramp ahead of her or on the float leading to the express boat. She hurried onto the boat, hoping he had not bailed. On board, she wandered the decks looking for Jeff. She decided that when she found him, she would try to sit close but behind him. She wondered if FBI or CIA people got training on how to follow suspects.

Aha! There he is she thought. Tiffany settled in. Before boarding, she had glanced at the weatherboard at the ticket counter. It indicated a one-foot swell and winds at 1 to 5 knots. She anticipated a smooth trip.

9:51 PM Friday, August 20, 2010
Long Beach Harbor, Nearing Catalina Landing
Long Beach, California

As the express boat approached Catalina Landing, a voice blared over the PA system jarring several passengers from an early snooze. "Attention passengers. We will be dockside at Long Beach in a few minutes. Please check around your seat for your belongings. Passengers with stored baggage should line up on the starboard side, that's the right-hand side of the ship, claim your baggage, and disembark through the rear door. Passengers without stored baggage may disembark through the door in the middle of the ship."

Tiffany had silently mouthed the words as the PA announcement droned on, wondering idly why they could not be more creative or occasionally change the script. Jeff had not spoken with anyone. He sat quietly staring straight ahead in total concentration. He seemed to be alone. Tiffany wondered what he would do when he disembarked. Willing herself not to stare, she would stay close. Apprehension washed over her and she grimaced involuntarily. Who was she kidding? She had no idea what to do. Following someone through the Catalina Landing terminal without being conspicuous wouldn't be exactly easy . . . that also had not dawned on her. Tiffany's eyes darted around nervously, questions raced through her mind. What should she do when Jeff left the terminal? Would he leave? Of course he would, there wasn't any point in staying there. He had to leave the terminal. Did he have a car? Would he take a cab? Would someone pick him up? Walking was unlikely. There was no place within easy walking distance of the terminal, and hauling his dive bag would make walking difficult. What would she do if she lost him after he left the terminal? She felt like crawling into a hole in the ground and cursed her confusion. *Bill and her husband, Tom, were right—this is insane. This is a job for trained people.*

The throng of passengers around her was thinning out. Tiffany realized she did not have stowed baggage—so why was she standing in the baggage line. Idiot! She desperately hoped Jeff did not turn around. He got up and walked toward the baggage line without looking back. Tiffany felt her breath catch in her throat. This would be as close as she would get to him. What would she say if he talked to her? Her heart was racing. Jeff walked past her and headed to the stern area where the divers stowed their gear. She exhaled. Now she could go through the regular baggage area and get off the boat before he did.

Tiffany walked, in what she hoped was a casual manner, up the ramp then toward a low concrete garden wall that marked the perimeter of the terminal area. There she sat on the wall in the shadows and hoped desperately to remain unnoticed. She watched for Jeff. Finally, she saw him. Burdened by his oversized duffel bag, he struggled up the ramp. Tiffany then noticed a passenger who had gotten off ahead of her and had remained lingering near the gate. The man seemed to have no intention of going into the terminal, and since there were no more express boats tonight, he could not be waiting for the next one. He was waiting for some other reason. Could this be another terrorist? His bag was identical to Jeff's.

Jeff shuffled toward the terminal building towing his duffle bag. The lingering passenger waited a few moments, then followed him. Tiffany thought he looked foreign, maybe Hispanic, or Middle Eastern. Terrorists generally were Middle Easterners. Her stomach knotted with the thought but then she recalled that she had endorsed this plan. Without thinking, she followed the two into the nearly vacant terminal. She realized too late that she stuck out like a sore thumb in the cavernous terminal. It was she, the terrorists, a dozen or so passengers, and a few uninterested employees anxious to go home. She stopped, looked around, and glanced at her watch as if she were expecting someone to meet her. She anguished that there could not be a worst-case scenario than this.

Fortunately, Jeff and his shadow were not paying attention and certainly were not looking at Tiffany. Instead, they walked toward the reservation counter. How could she remain in the terminal and not be conspicuous? Tiffany drifted toward the reservation counter, fidgeting as if distressed (which she was but for a different reason). She looked fervently at her watch, and then scanned the terminal in contrived disgust. After about ten seconds of this charade, she dramatically flipped open her cellphone and faked a call. "Where the hell are you?" she shouted into the inactive phone. "You need to get your dead ass over here . . . I've been here more than fifteen minutes!" While talking she drifted towards the reservation counter.

"I want to go to Avalon at 2:00 PM tomorrow," said Jeff.

"How many travelers?" asked the reservation clerk.

"Two."

"I'll need identification . . . is he the second person?" said the clerk, pointing to the person standing near Jeff.

Jeff said weakly, "No, err . . . just make the reservation. We'll pick up the tickets tomorrow."

"What names?"

"Tebbins, Jeffery Tebbins, and Mohamed Aliz."

"That'll be sixty-one dollars. Pay tomorrow when you pick up the tickets. Be here at least fifteen minutes before departure. There's no boarding after five minutes prior to departure. And don't forget your IDs."

"Thank you, we'll be here."

Jeff turned and walked away. The second man waited a few seconds then followed. As far as Tiffany could tell, these men were together but were doing a shit job disguising it.

Jeff and Mohamed exited the building.

Tiffany waited a few moments before setting out after them, not sure how she would follow unnoticed. When she reached the curb, she saw them. They were about forty to fifty yards ahead of her walking toward downtown Long Beach.

I'll be damned. They're walking!

Tebbins and Mohamed had closed ranks and commenced an animated hand-waving discussion. Tiffany followed. After a few minutes, Mohamed looked back at her. Tiffany's stomach clenched but she continued to walk normally, hoping not to attract attention.

He looked at Tiffany for several moments, then turned away and resumed conversation with Tebbins. Had she dodged another bullet?

Damn this is gut wrenching.

The terrorists walked to Ocean Boulevard, turned right, walked a few more blocks, and then headed inland. At that point, although Tiffany wanted to follow, her trailing was over. Parts of the neighborhood inland from Ocean Boulevard was not considered safe, even in daylight.

11:41 PM Friday, August 20, 2010
Rock Bottom Café, Ocean Boulevard
Long Beach, California

"They're going back to Avalon tomorrow on the 2:00 PM express boat."

"What? They're coming back? How do you know that?" asked Jenn.

"When they got off the boat, Jeff went into the terminal and made reservations. Both are coming back. Both Jeff and a foreign looking guy named Mohamed something or other, maybe Mohamed Ali, or something like that."

"Where are they now?"

"I don't know. They walked into the neighborhood east of Ocean Boulevard and I didn't follow them. I waited for a few minutes, but they didn't return. Hopefully I'll catch up with them tomorrow at the terminal."

"Good thinking. I wouldn't go there either."

"Bullshit. You'd go there. I know you would . . . I don't have your guts."

"Where are you?"

"At the Rock Bottom Café, up close and personal with a margarita."

"There's a surprise. Stay away from the singles' bars."

"Don't worry. When I'm finished here, I'll get my car from the landing parking garage, and go to my condo."

Many Catalina Island residents maintained apartments or condominiums in Long Beach near the Catalina Landing terminal in order to accommodate the need for frequent overnight trips over-town.

"Do you have the Long Beach Police number in your cell?"

"Of course."

"Good, set it. When you're in your car, call me okay?"

"Wilco . . . god, this is exciting."

CHAPTER FORTY-FOUR

1:22 PM Saturday, August 21, 2010
Khalid's Room, Upstairs from the Avalon Bay Bar
Avalon, Santa Catalina Island, California

Seated behind his desk, Khalid proclaimed, "We're on our way. Our mujahedeen are practicing as we speak. The Avalon Jihad will make its mark next week and we'll be martyred. We will receive our reward."

"God is great," said Abdel el-Shinawy, "*Allaahu a `lam, `azza wa jall.*"

"You have worked hard, Abdel el-Shinawy. We have all worked hard and overcome many obstacles, *Allaahu a `lam, `azza wa jall.* Soon, we'll walk in the garden with cool flowing streams and sit in rows with wide-eyed houris."

"What Allah wishes, *`azza wa jall,*" said Abdel el-Shinawy confidently.

"Next Saturday we will all be martyred, if Allah wishes, *`azza wa jall.* 'We are all from Allah, *`azza wa jall,* and to him we shall return.' For now, though, you must go downstairs and ready the bar. I'm sorry you have to endure the unbelievers, but we must maintain our cover."

"I'm not looking forward to working the bar. I'd rather be with the others."

"I know, I know, so would I. Don't worry, martyrdom will be ours, if Allah wishes, *`azza wa jall.* We'll join the ranks of al-Qaeda immortals. Go, Allah knows best, *`azza wa jall.* May the blessings of Allah be upon you, *azza wa jall.*"

"And upon you be the peace, Allah's mercy and blessings."

Abdel el-Shinawy stood and walked to the door that opened to the prayer room. He did not hear the shot that sent a hollow-nosed lead slug into the back of his head. No one heard it. Another Evolution silencer had done its job. Abdel el-Shinawy's body fell into the doorway, his blood and brains splattered on the prayer room walls and floor.

Khalid rose from his desk, walked to the doorway, and stepped over Abdel el-Shinawy's still twitching body. *One more loose end eliminated and one less connection to al-Qaeda removed.* Khalid was determined to finish the Avalon Jihad fiasco despite the idiots that burdened him. He yearned to end this troublesome plot so he could plead his case to Brooklyn and Afghanistan. No more homegrown terrorists, no more American converts masquerading as mujahedeen, and certainly no more women . . . *especially no more women.* Jihad was not their place. The Qur'an was clear on that. Americans were weak, not worth the trouble. He grimaced and then smiled ever so faintly at the thought of al-Qaeda rewarding him with a more significant assignment for his great work in Avalon.

Khalid took four bottles of gasoline and four igniters from a storage cabinet in the prayer room. Dispassionately, he doused Abdel el-Shinawy's body with gasoline and set the half-full bottle and one of the igniters next to his body. Khalid set the timer on the igniter for three o'clock. He repeated the process in the prayer room, the downstairs back room, and the bar drenching furniture and rugs with gasoline. Returning upstairs, he withdrew a small canvas sports bag from the storage cabinet. He searched the room for any items that might not be destroyed in the fire . . . he found none. Confident in his plan, Khalid descended the rickety stairs to the bar for the last time.

Sitting at the bar, he poured a glass of Jack Daniels, admired the pale yellow liquid in the hazy sunlight streaming through a grimy window, and mused. *Thankfully there is no religious police in the United States.* He sipped the smoky liquid and smiled. *It's a shame that all this liquor will be destroyed along with this wretched building.* Khalid eased the remainder of his drink down his throat, contemplating the completion of the detested assignment and getting back to reality. The alcohol calmed his excitement as it worked its way to his stomach. He would wait in the bar until it was time to walk to the cab shack for a cab to the heliport. The Avalon Jihad would be history within an hour.

All was going as he had planned.

CHAPTER FORTY-FIVE

1:38 PM Saturday, August 21, 2010
The Mole
Avalon, Santa Catalina Island, California

The taxi eased into one of the parking spaces at the foot of the Mole reserved for taxis and hotel shuttles. Bill walked with Jenn to the taxi. "Good-bye, love. Don't take unnecessary chances, okay? Play it safe, just observe, got it?"

"I got it, babe, I won't take chances. Talk to you soon," said Jenn getting into the cab.

Bill watched the taxi pull away and turn south onto Pebbly Beach Road toward the heliport. Pebbly Beach Road separated Lover's Cove and San Pedro Bay from sheer hillside as it wound its way out of Avalon to the heliport. Bill wondered why he had agreed to allow two women follow violent terrorists. He should have been more adamant about his opposition, however, he knew there was no way he could have talked them out of it. The police should be doing this, not civilians. As far as he was concerned, the U.S. was too lax with suspected violent criminals and terrorists. In other countries, such menaces would be in the slammer minus their fingernails—that is if they were still alive.

He sighed and turned to walk toward the waiting line for the 2:05 PM express boat. During the tourist season, the 2:05 PM inevitably sold out. The waiting line meandered across the mole among children casting their lines into the channel, people searching for friends who had just arrived on the previous express boat from Long Beach, and tourists—hordes of tourists taking pictures of their companions with the town of Avalon or the Casino in the background. Bill stood thirty yards from the gate and ticket taker and studied the passengers as they marched down the ramp, across the float, and up the gangway onto the catamaran express boat.

Christine stopped at the gate to surrender her ticket. In stark contrast to other women attired in brilliantly colored blouses and short shorts or skimpy bathing suits, Christine was clothed in a grayish, granny-type dress that covered her from her neck to her toes. She towed a diver duffle bag behind her. Bill deduced the bag was similar to the ones Tiffany had described last night. Whatever the bag contained, it was all Christine took onto the boat.

Bill wondered how Tiffany was doing at the Catalina Landing terminal in Long Beach. Keeping an eye on Christine, Bill punched five on his cellphone.

"Hi, boss," was the immediate response.

"Have you seen them?"

"They're in line ahead of me. It's the same as I described last night. They're acting as if they aren't together. Both are towing those diver duffel bags. Today Mohamed has the weight belt cinched around his waist."

"Do they suspect you? Don't do anything risky. Workers' comp won't cover this."

"Workers' comp? Give me a break. Don't worry, I'll be cautious."

"Since when?" quipped Bill.

"They're oblivious to what's going on around them. They don't know I'm watching them. They glanced at me only once and that was last night from a distance. They weren't concerned about me then and aren't now. I'll be okay."

"Right, so what's the reason I should believe you won't take chances?"

"Have you seen Christine?" Tiffany deflected.

"She's boarding now. She hasn't talked with anyone and doesn't seem to have a companion. There are six or seven other passengers with diver bags. One might be with Christine. Diver bags seem to be the terrorist uniform-of-the-day," chuckled Bill. "I'll call when the express boat leaves."

"Call quickly, by then I'll be underway and cellphones crap out the farther you go into the channel."

"I'll get back to you in a few minutes," said Bill and disconnected.

Bill watched Christine struggle with her diver bag up the steep gangway and onto the boat.

CHAPTER FORTY-SIX

The Long Beach/Los Angeles port complex has long been considered a prime terrorist target, yet nothing substantial has ever been done to mitigate the threat.

At five knots per hour, the maximum allowable speed in the harbor, it takes almost fifteen minutes for express boats to travel the distance between the Long Beach breakwater and Catalina Landing. Sixteen times a day during the peak tourist season, the express boats ply the distance past thousands of containers staked on congested wharves, dozens of container ships, a cruise ship or two, and the 1930s luxury liner Queen Mary tourist attraction.

The express boat company prides itself on emulating the timeworn legacy of yesteryear's cross-country trains. Mid-channel or weather emergencies aside, you could set your watch by the arrival or departure of the cross channel express boats.

Jeff and Mohammed had already boarded the express boat. Once Tiffany was on board she took an aisle seat on the right side of the boat two rows behind Jeff, the same relative position she had had the evening before. Jeff sat in the middle of the fourth row. Mohamed was in the second row, two seats in from the left aisle.

Tiffany's cellphone vibrated against her hip.

"Hi, boss," she said, speaking in an undertone, "we're underway."

"The express boat is buttoning up here. Any idea what's going on?" asked Bill.

"Not a clue. This could be an exercise in futility just like last night. These pigs look like they slept in their clothes. They're unshaven and I bet they stink."

"Be careful."

"I will. Is Jenn on the helicopter?"

"Soon, she'll call before the helicopter takes off. As you know, it's a death wish to use a cellphone on the helicopter. As it is, she'll have to call from a pay phone since there's no cell coverage at Pebbly Beach."

"I'm outta here. Talk in an hour or so," said Tiffany.

"Good luck," said Bill as he disconnected.

CHAPTER FORTY-SEVEN

1:46 PM Saturday, August 21, 2010
Heliport, Pebbly Beach Road, Pebbly Beach
Avalon, Santa Catalina Island, California

Jenn leaned forward from the back seat and said to the cabbie, "Please stop behind the Nickel . . . don't enter the parking lot."

The Buffalo Nickel Mexican restaurant shared a parking lot with the heliport. Jenn had decided to wait in the restaurant to avoid unnecessary contact with Ken. She handed the driver a twenty, got out of the cab, walked around the building, and entered the front door of the restaurant.

"Can I get you a drink?" the bartender asked.

"An iced tea . . . I'll take it on the patio."

"No problem."

The patio was a perfect location. She could observe the parking lot, the front door to the terminal, and the gate to the helipad. The only problem was her disguise. Jenn slowly shook her head with lips pursed and sighed. *Why did I allow Tiffany to convince me? Anyone who knows me will recognize me and wonder what the hell I'm doing.*

Jenn's get-up was more a potential magnet than a disguise as far as she was concerned. When she flew on the helicopter, she never wore her hair in a ponytail, she never dressed in jeans and a sweatshirt, and she *never ever* wore a headscarf anywhere. Large lensed sunglasses were a ridiculous final touch, making her look like a blonde Audrey Hepburn. All she needed was a Vespa.

The passengers were beginning to line up at the gate—but so far, no Ken. Everything Jenn had with her was crammed into an oversized shoulder purse. Since FAA regulations prohibit carry-ons on commuter helicopters, she hoped Heather would not ask her to stow the purse. Jenn was pleased Heather was the pilot. Heather was a brilliant pilot, although first-time flyers or persons with weak stomachs often had a different opinion. The helicopter responded to Heather's commands as if it were an extension of her body. Frequent flyers appreciated her skill. The inexperienced believed her flying was more luck than proficiency until they flew with her a second or third time. They then realized how good she was. A favorite technique of hers was to put the helicopter into a "death spiral" during a flight when an interesting sight appeared on the surface of the ocean. Within seconds from five hundred feet up, passengers came face-to-face with a sea lion, dolphin, or whale at sea level. Flying with Heather was like an E-ride at Disneyland. Jenn liked it.

As far as the helicopter company was concerned, Heather was a godsend. She weighed less than a hundred and ten pounds, far lighter than her male colleagues, which translated to lower fuel consumption. Not surprisingly, Heather logged more than her fair share of flight time.

Jenn still had not seen Ken. Maybe he was already inside the terminal. She decided to remain on the restaurant patio until the aircraft arrived and then check in at the terminal counter for the weigh-in ritual. She had flown two days ago but she knew the fiends would weigh her. How much weight could a person gain in two days. But wait, today, she was not Jenn Watson she was Jenn Floyd. She resigned herself to the weigh in—it was a tradeoff.

A cab pulled up to the terminal and a middle-aged, dark-skinned man emerged. He carried a small canvas bag. Jenn decided to call Bill. She walked to the pay phone outside the restaurant.

"Hi, babe," said Jenn.

"How's it going?"

"He's here, I think. He has a small bag. He travels light for an extended vacation."

"The vacation thing has to be a ruse. Just be careful. Call if you have any trouble."

"I will. I'm waiting at the Buffalo Nickel until the helicopter is on the ground, then I'll go into the terminal. Any last-minute advice?"

"Only what I've already told you . . . be careful and don't take chances . . . I love you."

"I love you, too. Take care.

Jenn hung up the pay phone, turned toward the channel, and strained to see the distant helicopter. She had heard the sound of the Doppler-enhanced whine of rotary wings. The sound intensified as the helicopter drew nearer. Then the whine changed abruptly to the familiar chop, chop, chop that accompanies rapid deceleration, transition to hover, and set down. Deceleration from over one hundred knots to motionless hover in seconds was another Heather trademark.

Jenn sipped the remnants of her iced tea, took a deep breath, stood, and walked confidently out of the restaurant toward the terminal. The Pebbly Beach terminal accommodated seating for fifteen passengers, a ticket counter, and a television that mercilessly cycled a video that touted the safety features of the aircraft and reiterated fiendish rules for passengers. The universally feared scale was center stage—directly in front of the counter. It was the first thing seen by hapless passengers when they entered the terminal.

Express helicopters are smallish Huey look-alike aircraft. Limited capacity dictates strict adherence to takeoff weight and load distribution. The loadmaster weighs each passenger as well as his or her luggage at the terminal counter. Self-reported weight has no standing. Most women regard the scales with utter fear. Some shed their coats, removed their purses, removed their shoes, and then piled them with their luggage before stepping onto the truth-telling torture machine. They cautiously glanced over their shoulders when the scale registered their weight to insure that other passengers do not notice the outcome. No passenger ever did; no one cared. The agent did not announce a person's weight; he simply noted it on the flight log.

"Miss Floyd?" asked Jimmy.

Jenn had known Jimmy for more than four years. He saw her often—the last time just three days ago. His greeting assured her that he had bought into the deception.

"Yes."

"You're just in time, we're loading." Pointing, he said, "Go through that door and then to your right."

"Thank you," said Jenn, falling into character.

She had avoided the scale. She contemplated the benefits of arriving for future flights closer to take off time.

The loadmaster waved the passengers to the helicopter. He motioned an older woman to the left front seat and then two twenty-somethings to seats in the right rear of the cabin, the man next to the window and the woman beside him. Jenn was next. The loadmaster indicated the seat next to the twenty-something woman was hers. Ken was the last to board. He sat between the left-rear window and Jenn. Anxious about sitting close to a woman, he pressed tightly against the window in an attempt to put additional space between himself and Jenn. It did not work. Jenn took advantage of the new found space.

Looking over her shoulder from the right front seat, Heather asked, "Does anyone need a cab on the other side?"

No one responded. Then Ken slowly raised his arm to signal his request.

"It'll be waiting for you on the other side . . . Everyone buckled up? Great. Thanks for flying Island Express Helicopters."

Jenn made a mental note that Ken needed a taxi.

Satisfied her passengers were secure and the helicopter buttoned up, Heather signaled to the loadmaster she was ready for lift-off. Now positioned fifty feet in front of the helicopter, the loadmaster searched the sky for aircraft that might interfere with lift off and determined there was none. He signaled thumbs up. Heather acknowledged his signal. She transitioned the aircraft to hover, pointed it toward the mainland, and tipped the nose down. With a deafening roar, the aircraft surged up and out over the channel. Heather leveled the aircraft off at five hundred feet within seconds. The G-level returned to normal.

Jenn noticed the skyline of the mainland twenty-six miles to the east was partially concealed in orange-brown smog.

CHAPTER FORTY-EIGHT

2:22 PM Saturday, August 21, 2010
Aboard Tail TWO SEVEN ONE ECHO
The San Pedro Channel En Route to Long Beach,
California

The two twenty-somethings peered over Heather's shoulders.

"Look at that," said the man, "we're at 500 feet . . . wow!"

"And we're flying at 110 miles an hour," exclaimed his girlfriend.

"That's not miles per hour, that's knots," he chided.

"Knots, what are knots? Knots are in ropes."

"It's like miles per hour, but faster. It's a nautical term."

"This is a helicopter; we're flying, not sailing."

"I'll explain later. Enjoy the view."

"You always blow me off. Why do you always blow me off?"

The older woman in the front seat searched for photo op targets of opportunity—her camera at the ready.

"Base, TWO SEVEN ONE ECHO out of Pebbly at 500 feet, zero zero three degrees. Over."

Squinting at the horizon, Ken was oblivious to anything going on in the cabin.

To Jenn, he seemed uneasy. He shifted in his seat as if to get a better view of the channel, his right hand stuffed deep into a pocket of his jeans. He had scarcely blinked since liftoff, pressing even closer to the window in order to move away from Jenn. It had not worked the first time and it did not this time. Jenn further optimized her space.

His intensity made Jenn anxious. What would happen next, a repeat of what Tiffany had experienced last night—which was basically nothing? She fleetingly wished Bill had convinced the police to take the case, a belated and rather useless concession at this point. Looking toward Long Beach, Jenn saw two white specks on the horizon—two catamaran express boats. Tiffany was trailing Jeff on the one headed to Catalina, the other was headed to Long Beach. The helicopter would pass over them in minutes.

*   *   *

Fifteen seconds from the two express boats, Ken began to mutter words that were not in English. Ten seconds from the express boats, he removed his hand from the pocket of his jeans. Clutched in his hand was a small rectangular object that resembled a TV remote only, thicker and shorter.

Jenn recognized the object immediately: an actuator. It was similar to some of the ones Baghdad had recently sent her. *What the hell is he doing with an actuator?* She felt a surge of adrenalin. Was he going to blow up the helicopter? Jenn's arm was a blur. The forward edge of her right hand crashed into Ken's right wrist. The sound of shattering bones and pained screams competed briefly with the roar of the helicopter. The actuator flew into the front of the cabin and bounced off the left side of the windshield landing in front of the older woman. She looked down at the strange object at her feet, then at Heather, and then behind her. A terrified feeling surged over her when she saw Ken in anguish.

"Don't touch it, no one touch it!" screamed Jenn. "Heather, I need Long Beach!"

Heather calmly responded, "Got 'em."

In agony, Ken bent forward, holding his shattered wrist. He had failed. The Avalon Jihad had been compromised . . . another defeat for Islamic jihad. He had no idea who the blond woman was, but decided to make the best of a deteriorating situation. He incanted in Arabic, "All praises due Allah, we are all from Allah and to Him we shall return, praise be to Allah." He withdrew a Glock 17 from another pocket and raised it level with the top of the back of the seat occupied by the older woman.

His left wrist and the Glock met the same fate as his right wrist and the actuator had moments before. The pistol rocketed to the front of the cabin and rattled around Heather's foot controls.

The older woman focused on this second object flung from the back. "Oh my god, a gun!" she screamed, "I'm trapped in a helicopter with a bunch of crazy people." The woman's eyes followed the gun from the cabin floor to Heather's hand to Jenn's hand. She made eye contact with the twenty-something man and woman—they were frozen in fear. What would the crazy lady do with the gun?

Jenn pressed the pistol into Ken's gut. Looking directly into his eyes, she demanded, "Put your hands under your ass you bastard . . . now!"

Ken did not respond.

"I said hands under your ass or you're dead . . . now!"

Ken struggled to move his nonfunctioning hands to his seat and then stopped.

"Under your ass!" hissed Jenn, cocking the pistol. She moved the gun from his gut to inches from his nose.

He complied.

"Heather, do you still have Long Beach?"

"I do."

"I want a SWAT team at the helipad when we get to Long Beach. Have them notify the FBI and Homeland Security that we've captured a real live terrorist."

The word terrorist resonated like a death knell among the other passengers. The twenty-something woman mouthed the word while her mind filled with visions of a suicide bomber destroying the helicopter and killing everyone on board. The older woman's hands flew to her face and covered her eyes, as though she would be safe if she could not see what was happening. The twenty-something man remained rigid as if he saw and heard nothing.

"Base, this is TWO SEVEN ONE ECHO. Request a SWAT team meet me at Long Beach. Over."

"What?"

"This is TWO SEVEN ONE ECHO. You heard me. Over."

"What's going on?"

"This is TWO SEVEN ONE ECHO. We have a small problem. We've captured a terrorist and we'll need assistance when we land. We're four out. Over."

"Are you crazy?"

"This is TWO SEVEN ONE ECHO. No. Do it goddamn it or I'll kick your dead asses to San Pedro and back when I get there. Out."

"Wilco."

"This is TWO SEVEN ONE ECHO. Further to my last. Notify the FBI and Homeland Security. Out . . . Jenn, we're less than four out," said Heather over her left shoulder.

Ken observed the interaction between the woman pilot and the blonde woman and concluded the two spawns of the devil knew each other. He had been had.

"They'll have to hurry," said Jenn. Then turning to Ken, she said, "Okay, asshole, talk. What's all this about? What did you plan to blow up with your little toy?"

Ken smiled smugly.

Jenn shoved the pistol against his teeth. "Talk or your tonsils will have powder burn."

Only the twenty-something woman realized what Jenn was doing. She grasped her seat, shut her eyes, and her body became rigid. This had to be the end. At this point, Ken could not answer even if he had wanted to. Jenn withdrew the pistol a couple of inches.

"Are you ready to talk?"

Ken nodded.

"Then talk. What the fuck is this all about?"

"I need a doctor. My hands are broken."

"You'll need a mortician unless you start talking. Doctors come later—if you're alive."

"I need a doctor," protested Ken.

"Gee, I'm sorry. We don't have one on board . . . so fucking talk. What's with the express boats and this helicopter?"

"Crossing the breakwater, less than two out," said Heather.

"How are we doing for ground support?" asked Jenn.

"On the way but we'll beat them by at least five minutes for sure."

"Put us down close to the water and as far away from the passenger terminal as possible."

"Base, this is TWO SEVEN ONE ECHO. In-bound to the Queen Mary. I'm one out. How are we doing with the SWAT team? Over."

Turning to Jenn, Heather said, "Base said the SWAT team is on the way and they want to know what's going on."

Jenn pursed her lips and shrugged her shoulders sending the classic body language message: "Damned if I know."

"This is TWO SEVEN ONE ECHO. We'll talk later on that. Out."

"You'd better pray, asshole, that the police are there when we land, or you get more of me and I've lost all patience with you."

Ken had become convinced this situation had not happened by chance. This blonde bitch had planned it. She knew who he was and so did the pilot bitch.

"Talk, you sorry-ass coward, or you won't see the Queen Mary much less Guantanamo."

Ken remained silent, smiling.

Jenn would have finished him right there but as far as she knew, he was the only source of information about the express boats and her only chance to learn what was happening. She pursed her lips and bit her tongue.

"On final, twelve seconds to touch down," announced Heather.

The roar of the turbine increased and then was replaced by the distinctive chop, chop, chop as the rotary wings reversed to break the helicopter's descent. Heather nosed the aircraft up, oriented it toward the landing pad, omitted the hover phase, and settled the aircraft onto the tarmac without a bounce. "On the ground."

The twenty-something man lost his lunch. His girlfriend breathed for the first time in what seemed like minutes but maintained a death grip on her seat. Caught between a woman who repeatedly threatened a man with his own gun and her green-faced boyfriend soaked in puke, she wondered whether the two days in paradise had been worth it.

"Can I get out?" asked the older woman in the front left seat, already grasping the door release.

"Please don't touch the door handle ma'am. I'll tell you when you can get out," said Heather firmly, calmly, and politely.

"Where's the ground support?" asked Jenn.

"On final, I saw flashing red lights about five miles north on the 710."

"Tell the ground crew to stay away until support arrives."

"Too late, here they come."

"Wave them off!"

Heather waved them off and then radioed. "Base, this is TWO SEVEN ONE ECHO. Please keep away from my aircraft until the SWAT team arrives. Over."

"You said you needed help."

"This is TWO SEVEN ONE ECHO. Back off and I fuckin' mean back off. Out."

The ground crew stumbled backward to the terminal building and gawked at TWO SEVEN ONE ECHO.

Turning to Ken, Jenn shouted, "You thought I'd lost interest in you, didn't you, you sorry excuse for a human being. I want answers. Are those boats at risk? I know that several of your deranged friends are on the express boats. Can they blow up the boats . . . What are their orders?"

Ken smirked.

Jenn pressed the gun into his cheek—still no response.

"Heather, radio the terminal and have them contact the Catalina Express boat company. The express boats must not enter the harbors. Have them diverted in a way that doesn't alert the terrorists on board that something is wrong. We do not know if they can or will blow up the boats."

"Base, this is TWO SEVEN ONE ECHO. Please contact the Catalina Express boat company and advise them that their express boats approaching Avalon and Long Beach harbors are not to enter. Over."

"Why?"

"This is TWO SEVEN ONE ECHO. Because terrorists might blow them up. Insure they are stopped but without panicking the terrorists. Over."

"Terrorists, there are terrorists on the express boats?"

"This is TWO SEVEN ONE ECHO. Yes—So stop jaw jacking and get cracking. Out.

Here come the cowboys," said Heather glancing over her shoulder at Jenn.

The SWAT team formed a skirmish line, M-4s at the shoulder, and commenced a measured advance toward the helicopter.

"Heather, radio the terminal and have the SWAT team stop. We have the situation under control. We need to evacuate the helicopter before we deal with the asshole."

"This is TWO SEVEN ONE ECHO. Please tell the SWAT team to stop their advance toward my aircraft. Everything is cool here. Wait on my command. Out."

"TWO SEVEN ONE ECHO. The SWAT team commander wants to know what's going on and who's in control. He wants to talk to the person in control. Over."

"Did you hear that?" asked Heather.

"Screw 'em, I can't do that right now."

"Base, this is TWO SEVEN ONE ECHO. Roger. wait."

"Base to TWO SEVEN ONE ECHO. The SWAT team leader demands to talk with the person in control. Over."

"They don't like your response. They want to talk to the person in control," relayed Heather.

"I can't do that right now," barked Jenn. "This shit-head demands my undivided attention. Tell them to send a few men forward so we can unload in a controlled manner. Front left seat first."

"I'm ready," announced older the woman, her voice cracking.

"Cork it, ma'am," responded Heather brusquely.

"This is TWO SEVEN ONE ECHO. Send two or three men forward so we can unload the aircraft in an orderly manner. Out."

The team commander and two of his team, M-4s at the ready, approached to within ten feet of the helicopter. The team commander then moved to the helicopter and opened its left door. The other team members continued to aim their carbines at the helicopter's passenger compartment.

The older woman went rigid. "Don't shoot!" she screamed.

Heather flashed a nasty glance at her and snapped, "I told you to cork it, lady."

The twenty-something woman reached for her boyfriend's hand then quickly withdrew it when she remembered the pungent vomit. The thought caused her to gag.

"Afternoon, folks," said the team commander cheerfully. "Who's first? My choice is the man sitting on his hands with the gun in his face. We can handle him."

"The woman in the front seat and then the two next to me," directed Jenn.

"Okay by me. It's my policy to always follow instructions from a woman holding a gun."

"I want a doctor," Ken piped up.

"Is he injured or sick?" asked the commander.

"Not your problem," shrugged Jenn.

After evacuating the three, the team commander returned to the left side of the helicopter.

"Okay, who's next?"

"The shit-head. He has two broken wrists but he's still a threat. He's pissed. We've just ruined his day. Take him to the side room in the terminal and keep him there. I'll follow. He has information needed to understand what's going on."

"I've been tortured. I want a doctor. I am injured and in need of immediate medical attention," bleated Ken.

"He's fine," scowled Jenn.

"You're right, ma'am. He looks just great. Okay dipstick, get your dead ass out of the chopper. I'm not as nice as your gun totin' girlfriend," said the SWAT team leader. Then turning to Jenn, added, "We can interrogate him. We're trained to do that."

"I'm sure you are," said Jenn. "But you don't know the background and there isn't time to bring you up to speed. You're welcome to observe. No medical attention until we have what we need. At least 800 lives hang in the balance."

Ken winced as he edged out of the chopper. When he was clear of the door, two SWAT team members grabbed him by his arms and manhandled him into the terminal building.

Jenn dropped her newly acquired pistol into her purse and hopped out of the chopper. She reached back into the front of the cabin to retrieve the actuator and dumped it into her purse. Then she pointed her right index finger toward Heather and wisecracked, "Later."

Heather did not stray from her post-flight checklist. She responded by waving a finger on her left hand vaguely in the direction of Jenn and mumbled, "Later."

"Any status on the express boats?" asked Jenn turning to the commander.

"I don't know what you mean."

"Two express boats approaching Avalon and Long Beach shouldn't be allowed into either harbor. They may have bombs on them."

"I wasn't aware . . . we should get on it."

"That's an understatement."

CHAPTER FORTY-NINE

2:43 PM Saturday, August 21, 2010
Island Express Helicopter Terminal
Long Beach, California

"Stop those boats!" screamed the reservation desk clerk into the mouthpiece of a telephone handset he held in his right hand while holding a second handset to his left ear.

"I'm sorry we can't do that, we have schedules," replied Frank Douglas, Executive Vice president of the Catalina Express. He was speaking from the company's headquarters in Long Beach.

"Fuck your on-time record. Do you want to bury 800 people or get the ferry-boat-company-of-the-year award for the best on-time record?" snarled the reservation clerk. He was doing the best he could. After all, he was just a reservation clerk. There is little love lost between the helicopter company and the express boat company.

"Hand me those phones son, I'll deal with this."

The reservation clerk eagerly complied.

"This is Lieutenant Collins, LA SWAT Team Four Commander. We have a critical emergency. I order you to halt the express boats heading toward Avalon and Long Beach harbors immediately. The lives of all on board are at risk. Do you understand? With whom am I speaking?"

Lieutenant Collins paused to listen.

"Thank you, Mr. Douglas. We will keep this line open to update you. Please stay on the line. Do you understand? Good . . . Sergeant Williams will be on this end."

"How did it go?" asked Jenn.

"They're stopped. One of the express boats was moments from entering Long Beach harbor. Now can you update me? I've let you take control, the shit-head is yours to interrogate, and the express boats are stopped. Things are calmer and we're in control. How about some reciprocation? First off, who the hell are you?"

"Name's Jenn and we are not in control, not by a long shot. You can learn as we go. Where's shit-head?"

"In the side room. He wants a doctor and an attorney."

"Fat chance," Jenn smiled.

2:48 PM Saturday, August 21, 2010
Side Room, Island Express Helicopter Terminal
Long Beach, California

Jenn made immediate eye contact with Ken when she and Lieutenant Collins entered the room. He drew straight up in the stiff-backed wooden chair when he saw the nut-case blonde bitch. Lieutenant Collins rejoined his SWAT team, which had surrounded Ken. They stood with their backs against the walls and their carbines pointed at him. Jenn positioned herself five feet in front of Ken. Eight feet separated him from anything else in the room except her.

"Well, dick-head, we meet again . . . so soon."

"I need a doctor. My arms are broken and I am in pain."

"No doctors. Not until you tell me what I need."

"This is torture. I want an attorney."

"Torture, don't make me laugh. You don't know what torture is—*yet.* Let me put this in perspective, as your demands for a doctor and an attorney are quite bizarre. We have five rifles in the hands of trigger-happy LA police officers pointed at your head, and a very angry woman who broke both your wrists and who controls your continued existence on this planet standing in front of you. No doctor. No attorney. Start talking."

Ken smiled.

"Look, Mr. Allah-is-great . . ."

A startled expression replaced Ken's smile.

". . . There are 800 innocent people on two express boats bobbing around in the channel and only you can tell us what we're up against."

A smile returned to Ken's face.

"Enough."

Jenn removed her newly acquired pistol from her purse.

Ken's smile evaporated.

Two SWAT team members moved toward Jenn. Lieutenant Collins waved his men off.

"But lieutenant, this *is* torture. We can't permit this," said a team member.

Ken's smile retuned.

"I know, corporal, but 800 lives hang in the balance."

Lieutenant Collins knew his team member was correct. Jenn's actions constituted torture and it was wrong. The only thing he could hang his hat on was Miss I'm-in-Charge's emphatic statements about the potential for massive loss of lives. Lieutenant Collins recalled that Machiavelli's *The Prince* explored the use of cruelty, fear, and coercion as legitimate tools for a ruler to establish and maintain stability and provide security for his citizens. Those tools were good, in Machiavelli's view, if used to achieve a desirable outcome. Machiavelli and Miss I'm-in-Charge seemed to share the same understanding of the use of those tools irrespective of civil rights.

Jenn faked admiring Ken's gun for several moments and then pointed it at Ken's head and said, "Nice weapon, now tell me what's going on. Can your asshole buddies blow up the express boats?"

Confirmed, thought Lieutenant Collins. *Miss I'm-in-Charge has no hesitancy to use fear and coercion to accomplish her goals.*

Ken remained silent.

"Answer me what's going on? I'm a poor shot but I know how to pull a trigger. Start talking."

Ken's smile transformed to a sneer.

Jenn pulled the trigger.

Confirmed, thought Lieutenant Collins. *Miss I'm-in-Charge has no hesitancy to use cruelty to accomplish her goal.*

The bullet grazed the inside of Ken's thigh, shattered the seat of the wooden chair, and tumbled onto the floor. Ken shrieked and his eyes flew wide. He felt a sharp, burning sensation on the inside of his right thigh. Two SWAT team members stepped toward Jenn. Again, Lieutenant Collins raised his hand and again they retreated—this time hesitantly.

The LA Police Department has been under federal scrutiny for its long history of alleged infringement on civil rights. Each of Lieutenant Collins' SWAT team members wondered what to do. Jenn's style of interrogation was an over the top violation of civil rights. Should they comply with what might be an illegal order from their commander or take matters into their own hands?

"Not a bad weapon," said Jenn nonchalantly. She inspected the pistol again and then blew smoke from its barrel. "Now that I got the hang of this, start talking or your pecker meets Allah before you do."

Jenn aimed at Ken's balls. "That's about right. What do you think, dick-head?"

Ken looked at the blood seeping into his pant leg, then at Jenn. His fear had changed to disbelief.

"Don't worry, it's a flesh wound . . . just a scrape. Look at it this way, dick-head. I've broken both your wrists, missed your pecker by inches with an errant shot from what used to be your weapon, and now I have your balls in sight. Do you think for half a heartbeat that I won't do what I say?"

Jenn cocked the pistol, held it at arm's length in both hands, and glared into Ken's eyes over the barrel of the pistol.

Ken rose from the chair, then dropped to his knees.

"Please don't shoot, please don't shoot. I'll tell you, I'll tell you. What do you want to know?"

"Everything."

3:13 PM Saturday, August 21, 2010
Main Terminal, Catalina Island Express Helicopter Heliport
Long Beach, California

"Sargent Williams, what's the situation with the boats?" asked Lieutenant Collins.

"They're still stopped. The Catalina Express boat company made up a story that the intake for the water jet turbines sucked up floating debris and they had to shut down the engines. So far, so good. The passengers believe the story, but the natives are becoming restless."

"Hand me the phone," said Lieutenant Collins, clearing his throat first.

"Mr. Douglas, this is Lieutenant Collins. We have more information so please listen carefully. There are at least two terrorists on each one of your express boats. We believe the terrorists have placed bombs on each boat. We do not know if they can or will detonate the bombs. According to an unreliable source, this was a practice run, a rehearsal of sorts for the real thing. Radical Islamic jihadist terrorists control the bombs and expect to die for Allah. We can't profile them, as several are Caucasian Americans and at least one of them is a woman. They're dangerous and have already killed many times. We know the names of three of them and we have a contact on the boat out of Long Beach. Her name is Tiffany Castilingo. Find her without tipping off the terrorists that we're on to them. She should be able to fill in some of the blanks in your situation."

CHAPTER FIFTY

3:17 PM Saturday, August 21, 2010
Pilothouse on the Express Boat out of Long Beach
Outside Avalon Harbor, San Pedro Channel

"Captain Daniels, this is Douglas," crackled the radio. "A woman named Tiffany Castilingo is on your boat—a brunette, an islander. Find her and bring her to the Pilothouse. We need to speak with her; she has information about the current situation. *But by all means, do not alarm anyone.* This is very important. Oh, arm yourselves."

"What?" gasped Captain Daniels.

"This could get ugly. Find Tiffany; she'll know what we're up against," directed Douglas.

Captain Daniels turned to First Mate Donnelly and Deckhand Sinclair. "We got big trouble."

"You mean deep shit," said First Mate Donnelly. "I never thought we'd need the pistols."

"We have to find a woman named Tiffany. I don't know how. Do either of you know her?

"She's an islander, Betty, the cabin attendant, should know her," said Deckhand Sinclair.

"Great, get her on the intercom."

Within ten seconds, Betty was cooing over the intercom, "Hi, Mr. Captain, sir, and what can little 'ole me do for a big boy captain like you? Want me to come fix your motor, sweetie?"

"No, we're working on that, but thanks. Have you seen Tiffany Castilingo?"

"She's in the back section, but why her? She's cute, but not that cute."

"We need to speak with her. Ask her to come to the pilothouse, but be discreet. I know that will be hard for you, but it's important that you don't alarm anyone. Got it?"

"Yes sir, Mr. Captain, sir. Is she going to drive your boat? Remember, when you showed me how to do that."

"Just get her here and quickly. And for god's sake, be discreet."

"Kinda grouchy today, aren't we?"

3:20 PM Saturday, August 21, 2010
Main Cabin on the Express Boat out of Long Beach
Just Outside Avalon Harbor, San Pedro Channel

Tebbins and Mohamed had not reacted to the debris stoppage announcement. They just sat in their seats and swapped occasional glances. Tiffany watched them while she wondered whether the announcement about the debris stoppage was real. She doubted it because she knew clearing a debris stoppage was usually a fifteen-minute operation. If this went on much longer, Jeff and Mohamed might become suspicious. Out of the corner of her eye, she spotted Betty, also affectionately known as Miss Airhead, heading towards her. Looking surprisingly focused, Miss Airhead appeared to be on a mission.

Miss Airhead leaned over and whispered into Tiffany's ear, "Hi, please don't look surprised or concerned. The captain wants to see you in the pilothouse. Could you follow me?"

"Okay," said Tiffany softly.

Tiffany hoped her face did not betray her feelings. She shot quick looks at Tebbins and Mohamed. They seemed unsuspecting. But what could she do if they became anxious, or suspecting, and started to do something? Tiffany followed Miss Airhead toward the front of the express boat, then up the stairs through the windowed door that led to the commodore class seating area. Once in commodore class, they walked along the left aisle toward the pilothouse door.

Before they reached the pilothouse door, Miss Airhead looked back over her shoulder at Tiffany and asked, "What's up?"

"How should I know? You're the cabin attendant and you asked me to follow you."

"Captain Daniels called and asked me to find you. He sounded worried. Does this have something to do with the debris stoppage?"

"I don't know," said Tiffany matter-of-factly.

They reached the pilothouse door, which was always locked. *Thank you Patriot Act,* thought Tiffany.

Miss Airhead knocked, then said "It's Betty. I have Tiffany." She turned the doorknob and pushed. It did not budge. "That's odd," said Miss Airhead. "They always unlock the door when I identify myself."

She tried again but it still did not move. After a click that seemed to resonate throughout the express boat, the door opened. Deckhand Sinclair motioned them in. When Miss Airhead and Tiffany were inside, he re-locked the door. Both Miss Airhead and Tiffany noticed Captain Daniels and First Mate Donnelly had shoulder holsters strapped to the left side of their chests.

"Oh my god, what is going . . ."

Before Miss airhead completed her thought, Tiffany offered, "It's the terrorists, isn't it?"

"Ter . . . ter . . . terrorists," stammered Miss Airhead. "What terrorists. Where are they?"

"In time, Betty, be quiet . . . stand over there." Captain Daniels pointed to a corner of the pilothouse and then turned to Tiffany. "Do you know what's going on? Can you help?"

"I hope so. There're at least two terrorists aboard; there could more, but probably only two."

"Headquarters believes there are two and said that they may have bombs."

"If they do, I'd guess they're in the roller duffle dive bags."

"Bombs!" yelped Betty holding both her hands over her mouth, muffling a scream.

Tiffany rolled her eyes.

"Easy, Betty, everything will be okay," said Captain Daniels. He keyed the radio, "Tiffany's here."

"Great, put her on."

"Who am I speaking with?" asked Tiffany.

"Jenn . . . They patched me in. I'm at the heliport in Long Beach. What's going on there?"

"Tebbins and Mohamed are in the rear of the main cabin. They seem okay for now. The debris thing's a charade, right?"

"Yes."

"Nice work."

"Not my idea, but it's worked so far. It's given us a small amount of breathing room. Lieutenant Collins just advised me that the Coast Guard is headed your way. Do you have any idea where the bombs are?"

"They have to be in the dive bags . . . Lieutenant Collins, err . . . who's he?" asked Tiffany.

"An LA SWAT team leader. I believe Ken was trying to detonate bombs on both express boats from the helicopter when I stopped him."

"Oh my god, I owe you my life!"

"So far we've prevented a nightmare . . . a catastrophe."

"What about Ken?"

"Unfortunately, that sorry sack of shit will survive to see Guantanamo."

"Do we know if Tebbins or Mohamed can set off the bombs?" asked Tiffany.

"We're not sure if they can or will. Ken told us he disabled the terrorist's remotes so he would have complete control over the bombs. We can't count on that because he isn't sure he was successful. We have to assume the terrorists on the express boats can detonate the bombs. According to Ken, they think this is a practice run. They don't know that he planned to blow up both express boats from the helicopter."

"He would have killed us all . . . what a shit-box," said Tiffany.

"My sentiments precisely. We have to come up with a plan. I have a SWAT team here. We've notified the FBI and Homeland Security. However, neither of those options are a consideration, there's not enough time. It's up to us. There's no way we can keep these idiots at bay for much longer. Hold on there's another call coming in."

CHAPTER FIFTY-ONE

3:42 PM Saturday, August 21, 2010
Main Terminal, Catalina Island Express Helicopter Heliport
Long Beach, California

"Jenn?" This is Bill.

"I'm here . . . how's it going on Catalina?"

"I'm fine, how are you?"

"It's been hectic but we've regained a small semblance of control and a little breathing room."

"Where's here? And what's this about control?"

"Long Beach, the helicopter terminal. The police have Ken in custody and we're trying to figure out how to deal with terrorists on the two Express boats."

Bill was silent for a few moments, and then said, "The express boat from Long Beach is drifting a mile outside Avalon harbor, off Hamilton. They say it's debris in the intake but that's a ten—to fifteen-minute deal. It's been over half an hour. Tiffany's on that boat. I hope she's okay."

"It's a scam. The Express Boat Company made it up to keep the express boat from entering Avalon harbor. The same reason is being used to keep another express boat out of Long Beach harbor."

"What about Tiffany?"

"She's okay."

"And what's this about Ken?"

"I believe he was trying to blow up both express boats from the helicopter. I stopped him. The LA Police have him."

"And what about the express boats?"

"Terrorists . . . terrorists are on both express boats. We don't know what to do about them. So far they seem to be unknowing that we're on to them."

"My god you've been busy," said Bill.

"Tell me about it—it isn't over yet."

"Jenn, the Avalon Bay Bar is toast."

"What!"

"According to the fire department, at about three o'clock the building burst into flames and within minutes was totally engulfed. People around here are speculating. The rumors are running wild."

"Is the fire out?"

"It's under control, but there won't be anything left of the building. What about the terrorists?"

Jenn paused for a moment. "We don't know what they can or will do. That's our problem in a nut shell . . . it's bad. The good thing is we believe they haven't communicated with each other, so they are unaware of each other's' situation."

"So what's the plan . . . is there a plan?"

"Not really. It's too involved to talk about it on this call, though. Get on a landline and call the heliport in Long Beach. I'll tell them to expect your call. You can help us come up with a plan. I gotta run. I'll talk to you in a few, bye love."

Bill's parting words to Jenn were becoming all too typical: "Be careful."

Lieutenant Collins was puzzled. He looked at Jenn and asked, "*Bye, love?* Who *are* you? Who *is* Tiffany? And now who *is* this Bill?"

"Later." Jenn tried to blow him off.

"Later hell! I've relinquished all control and deferred to your every wish. I could lose my job. LAPD would fire me on the spot if they knew what was going on . . . and then maybe press charges. I don't even know who you are. I haven't a clue."

"I told you, I'm Jenn. Don't worry, everything will be okay. Have I led you astray?"

"Who would know whether you've lied to me or led me astray, or anything else for that matter? I have no reason to believe you. For all I know, you're in cahoots with dick-head."

"Yeah, right. How's he doing?"

"He's in agony."

"Good."

"He'll survive. He keeps asking for an attorney. It seems his legal status is more of a concern to him than his medical situation."

"He'll need all the lefties on the Supreme Court to get his sorry ass off the hook when this hits the streets."

"Medical help is on the way."

"Cancel it."

"Cancel it . . . why? The man has two broken wrists, a gunshot wound, and god knows what else you might've overlooked telling me about."

"None of it's life threatening. Cancel 911."

"Why?"

"We need to question the prick again, maybe several times, and I can't have some bleeding heart paramedic interfering. They're trained to take control and we don't need that. Cancel the call. I'll take responsibility."

Lieutenant Collins shook his head in exasperation.

"Cancel the paramedics, Sergeant Williams. I'll . . . no, Jenn will take responsibility."

"I will, don't worry."

"So where did you learn your interrogation skills . . . the al-Qaeda School for little girls?"

"It's intuitive."

Before Lieutenant Collins could continue, Jenn looked directly into his eyes and said, "Look, we have to act fast, we can't waste valuable time on twenty questions. Eight hundred lives hang in the balance. Your job is to keep anyone headed here from getting here—no more people, no more helpers. We have more than enough people to handle this . . . presuming it can be handled."

"How am I going to do that? I'm just a lowly SWAT team leader."

"Figure it out. You're an adult and we pay you a lot of money to handle these kinds of things. Declare a state of *critical emergency* or whatever you called it. Make something up. I know you can do it."

Jenn heard Sergeant Williams' hollering, "Hey Jenn, a Bill is on the phone. He says you're expecting the call."

"Good, set up a conference call. Me, Bill, the Captain on the express boat outside the Long Beach harbor, and the Express Boat headquarters. Tiffany's already on hold."

"I'll try."

Jenn turned toward Sergeant Williams, shot him a wicked scowl, and said, "You'll try . . . you'll try? Eight hundred lives are at sta . . ."

". . . I'm on it."

Unsuccessful at hiding a faint smile, Jenn turned to Lieutenant Collins and asked, "Good, now where's dick-head? He's our only hope and that's not a pretty thought."

"He's still in the side room."

"Let's go see how he's holding up. Wait a second . . . have Sergeant Williams call Homeland Security, have him reference case number 27A4419, and tell him to bring them up to speed on what's happening. We will need them, but it'll take hours or days for them to respond and this will be over long before then. Is the Coast Guard deployed? While I was in the chopper, I asked someone to contact the FBI, has that been done?"

"So you're with Homeland Security? I'd forgotten about them. The Coast Guard has dispatched two cutters to the express boats and the FBI's been notified."

Jenn did not respond. *Unintended but brilliant,* she thought. *I created instant credibility with my presumed connection to Homeland Security.* That should keep Lieutenant Collins off my case long enough for us to finish this. Her smile broadened. She and Lieutenant Collins picked up the pace as they walked to the side room.

"Any feedback from the FBI?" asked Jenn over her shoulder.

"No."

"Have Sergeant Williams include the Coast Guard captains on the conference call as well."

"Sergeant Williams . . ."

". . . On it."

Jenn smiled again.

3:51 PM Saturday, August 21, 2010
Side Room, Catalina Island Express Helicopter Heliport
Long Beach, California

Ken's pulse rate doubled when he saw the crazy blonde bitch enter the room.

"I demand an attorney. You're trampling on my rights."

"Fuck off, asshole . . . we've been over that crap. You have no rights. The only rights I'm concerned with are the rights of eight hundred people *you've* put at risk."

"I need a doctor. I'm dying."

"You don't know what it feels like to die . . . yet. All the doctors are busy right now, but if you continue to be a good boy and provide accurate information, you just might live to see a doctor."

"I'm dying."

"Quit whining and shut up! You told us three of your cronies were on each express boat. What do they look like?"

"There are only two. I didn't say three. There are only two on each boat. I said two."

"Okay two . . . men or women?"

"Two men on one boat and a man and woman on the other boat."

"Are you sure?"

Ken's eyes widened at the sight of the pistol Jenn had slipped from her purse.

"I'm sure! I'm sure!"

"Okay, one more time. Which express boat has which terrorists?"

"The boat from Long Beach to Catalina has two men. The other one, the one coming to Long Beach, has a man and a woman."

"Good, we knew that. Keep telling the truth and a doctor could be in your future. Lie and I blow your balls to kingdom come. Alright one more question. Can your cronies detonate the bombs?"

"Yes . . . maybe . . . I don't know."

"Yes, maybe, I don't know. That's three bullshit answers. You're falling into old patterns dick-head. You only get *one* answer per question. You're losing credibility. More importantly, I'm losing patience and my trigger finger is getting itchy."

"I don't know! I told you I deactivated the detonators, at least, I tried to. I don't know if I was successful. There were too many red wires. I told you that." Ken gasped to catch his breath.

"Too many red wires?" Jenn glanced at her pistol and then back at Ken. She waved the gun in his direction. "What the hell are you talking about?"

"I don't know, I don't know, I'm telling the truth, I think they're deactivated. The bombers were not to use the activators this time. They don't know anything about my deactivating the activators."

"Okay then, if they didn't like what was going down, what would they do?"

"On jihad, if anything went wrong they were instructed to detonate the bombs. They'd detonate the bombs immediately."

"Would they do that this time?"

"I don't know. I think they would, I think they'd try. If they thought they were about to be captured or killed, they'd try to detonate the bombs."

"Is there anything else, anything at all? Are there other terrorists: on the docks, in the harbors, in Avalon, anywhere?"

"No."

"Very good, dick-head. You're doing well."

"Do I get a doctor? I'm in pain." Tears swelled in Ken's eyes.

"Not that well . . . no doctor. Maybe later when I'm sure the passengers are safe. Which reminds me—if one passenger gets so much as a scratch, I'll blow your fucking balls off; if two passengers get hurt, I'll blast your sorry ass through this back wall?" Jenn flicked the barrel of the pistol at the wall. "Have I communicated?" Jenn paused for a moment. "So, if you remember anything, anything at all, let the nice policemen with the rifles know. Do you understand?'

"Yes."

"Why has the Avalon Bay Bar burnt to the ground?"

"Uhh."

"Uhh? Uhh is bullshit. Uhh is not an answer. Why'd it burn?"

"To destroy evidence. I need an attorney. What about the Fifth Amendment?"

"It doesn't apply to assholes."

Jenn turned and walked out the room and into the main terminal. There she asked Sergeant Williams. "How are we doing with the conference call?"

"Got `em all except the Coast Guard."

"Okay, let's get started. Lieutenant Collins, please get on the extension. I'll use Sergeant Williams's phone. Sergeant, find another line and run down the sailor boys."

"On it!"

Jenn smiled as she picked up the phone. "This is Jenn, who's on?"

"Tiffany and Daniels on the express boat near Catalina."

"Bill at the Catalina Express Boat ticket booth on the Mole."

"Captain Gaspar on the express boat near Long Beach harbor. What the hell's going on?"

"In time," responded Jenn. "Anyone else?"

"Douglas at Catalina Express Boat headquarters in Long Beach."

Satisfied that everyone who could be was on the line, Jenn started, "We have a mess on our hands. I'm sure that's no surprise to anyone. There are two terrorists with bombs on each of two express boats. Why two boats and why two terrorists we don't know, but we believe that's the situation. The leader of this nightmare assured me those facts are correct and since he's developed a real concern about his body parts, I believe him. Is there any reason not to believe him?"

"I can identify two, Tebbins and Mohamed. And I'm convinced that's all there are," said Tiffany.

"Do you know where they are?"

"Yes," said Tiffany.

Jenn began again, "Captain Gaspar?"

"Yes."

"Your situation is a little different. One terrorist is a woman and we know what she looks like. We have no idea about the other person. The woman is a brunette, tall, about 35 to 40, looks unkempt. She is dressed in a gray granny gown type dress that covers her body from her neck to just above her ankles."

Captain Gaspar said angrily, "Why didn't you put one of your agents on my ship? It would have made things much easier."

"I don't have agents and don't waste time second-guessing. Our immediate concern is passenger safety. Captain Gaspar, are you armed?"

"No, but I can be."

"Do it," ordered Douglas.

"Does anyone have an idea how to get the passengers off the boats? Docking's not an option," asked Jenn.

"We could tell the passengers that we can't fix the damage and that we'll have to shuttle them to the dock," said Douglas.

"That could alarm the terrorists especially if they were told they couldn't take their dive bags with them," said Jenn, "and we believe if they become alarmed, they'll try to detonate the bombs. We must avoid that at all cost. We don't want to do anything that'll push them to take action. They believe this is a practice run. The bombs are real but their leader deactivated their activators, or at least he tried to, without their knowledge. He's not sure if he was successful so we have to assume he was not. I believe the fucking coward planned to blow up both express boats from the helicopter in order to destroy all evidence, including his fellow terrorists, and then beat feet."

"We could take out the two on our boat," said Tiffany. "Put a gun to their heads and if they don't comply, blow their brains out. I know it would work. Then we evacuate the boat and turn it over to the bomb squad."

Jenn thought, *classic Tiffany.* She silently shook her head, and asked, "What do y . . ."

". . . Commander White here on the Coast Guard cutter Timothy Strong, we're twenty-five minutes from Avalon. The Samuel Adams is ten minutes from the Long Beach breakwater."

"Welcome, Commander. I'm Jenn. We're trying to develop a plan to get the passengers off the express boats without agitating the terrorists. Commander, I suggest you keep your ships away from the express boats until we have a plan. A Coast Guard cutter would put the terrorists on alert and they might blow up the express boats."

"Okay, I'll get approval . . . god, what a mess."

"I have another suggestion," said Douglas. "We could announce that we can't fix the engines and the Coast Guard will take the passengers off the express boats. On the express boat near Catalina, the backup could be to take out the terrorists if they don't comply or if they act strange."

"Okay. Are there any suggestions around that course of action? It could be also be disastrous. Are there any other suggestions ?"

Jenn paused for comments.

"Why tell them anything like that? Tell them something that would put them at ease." suggested Tiffany. "We could tell them the engines are fixed, but for safety purposes everyone must be in their seats before the engines restart. When everyone is seated, we confront the terrorists. If they don't comply, we kill them."

Jenn had known that last part would be in Tiffany's plan.

"That sounds like a better plan. It's simple and easy to execute," said Bill.

"What about the other boat?" asked Douglas.

"Maybe we have to go with the first idea on that one as we have no other choice," said Jenn.

"Okay, but keep a watch for unusual behavior," said Douglas. "Captain Gaspar, how many crew do you have?"

"Nine . . . eleven, counting the cabin attendants . . . and two pistols."

"It's a crap shoot, but I don't see any other way," said Jenn.

"Commander White here. We have approval to stand by and wait for your order. Who would give the order?"

Jenn glanced at Lieutenant Collins.

"I'll give the command . . . Lieutenant Collins, LAPD SWAT team leader."

"Okay, let's do the express boat near Catalina first," said Jenn. "Maybe we'll learn something we can use with the other boat. When done, we'll come back on conference and decide what to do about the boat near Long Beach."

CHAPTER FIFTY-TWO

4:01 PM Saturday, August 21, 2010
The Pilothouse of the Express Boat near Avalon Harbor
San Pedro Channel

"It's show time," proclaimed Tiffany.

"Cute . . . real cute. Were you a drama major?" asked Captain Daniels, with an appalled expression.

Tiffany brought her shoulders back, thrust her boobs up under her hoodie, and said, "*Hello*, can't you read?"

"I don't get it," said Captain Daniels, trying to avoid looking at Tiffany's chest.

"If you can read, the words say . . . *University of Pennsylvania Wharton School of Business*. My degree is in finance. We're doing serious stuff here . . . don't you know levity eases tension?"

"Nothing can ease this tension."

Captain Daniels thought acerbically, *Good grief I have a finance major calling the shots in a terrorist situation.*

"Okay, okay, whatever," said Tiffany.

Captain Daniels turned to his First Mate Donnelly and ordered, "Get Deckhands Tim, Andrew, and Chaney up here. They will organize containment and panic control. Donnelly, when we take down the terrorists, the black man is mine, the other one's yours. Tiffany will point him out."

Donnelly's face turned white. "I can't do this."

"What can't you do?"

"I . . . I can't do this . . . I can't use the gun. I might have to kill someone."

"My god," said Captain Daniels. "We have two maniacs capable of destroying the ship and killing all of us and yo . . ."

". . . Give me the gun," hissed Tiffany, as she moved between Daniels and Donnelly. "Donnelly, you the Tim, Andrew, and Chaney people go do containment and panic control. The goal is to keep everyone in their seats. Passengers in the forward cabin are to stay there—no one moves to the rear cabin."

Tiffany slid the gun into her purse.

"I understand," said Donnelly sheepishly. He removed his empty shoulder holster and offered it to Tiffany.

"I don't need that," said Tiffany arrogantly with a wave of her hand.

"Our concern is the rear cabin. Betty and the other cabin attendant can handle the upper deck," said Captain Daniels.

Betty nodded. "I can do that. I'll brief Sandy. You can count on us."

"Okay, Donnelly, you and Betty have three minutes. Brief the crew and get them in place. Tiffany and I'll be down in four minutes, and remember, do not create anxiety. Be calm . . . act as if everything is normal. There'll be more anxiety than we can handle when we take down the terrorists. Donnelly, once you have the crew in place, come back here. Are there any questions?" Captain Daniels looked at each person in turn. "I assume silence means no . . . okay . . . go!"

Shrugging out of his shoulder holster Captain Daniels turned to Tiffany after the others were gone and asked, "What do you think?"

Tiffany looked directly at him. "It's a crapshoot. Somebody trained in this shit should be running the show."

Tiffany half-assed believed what she had just said. She would not trade this real live situation for anything in the world.

"Aren't you with the FBI or CIA or somebody like that?" asked Daniels.

"Well . . . not exactly."

"Not exactly . . . just what does that mean? What about the woman in charge . . . the woman on the radio? Do you work with her? Is she FBI or CIA?"

"Well . . . not exactly."

"Well not exactly. Don't you know other words to describe who you are, who you're with, or what you do? Are you with anyone?"

"Well . . . not exactly, but I'm all you got and the plan will work. Remember, do not hesitate to pull the trigger if there is the slightest indication Tebbins is not doing what you ask. Kill him."

Daniels decided it wouldn't be wise to cross this woman, and for sure, he would never consider asking her for a date.

"Then who are you and who is this other woman?" persisted Daniels.

"I'm Tiffany. The *other woman* is Jenn."

"So, you're just two women in off the street with time on your hands."

"Kinda . . . wrong time, wrong place, wrong situation. We weren't lucky this time around."

First Mate Donnelly burst through the door, gasping for breath.

"Everything's in place, everyone's in place."

"Donnelly, catch your breath . . . take deep breaths, and breathe out slowly. Take the bridge. We're going to the main deck."

Tiffany was out the door. *Thank god, Donnelly came back,* thought Tiffany. *I couldn't have strung Daniels along much longer. He might have fucked up the whole deal.*

4:04 PM Saturday, August 21, 2010
Main Deck on the Express Boat near Catalina Harbor
San Pedro Channel

Captain Daniels followed Tiffany down to the main deck and then they walked into the rear cabin.

Two crewmembers stood near the refreshment area, laughing and faking an animated conversation. Several crew members, including, Tim and Chaney were in the rear of the cabin near a door that led to the baggage area where an intercom handset was located. A few passengers remained standing. Both terrorists had remained seated in the center seating section. Daniels recognized Tebbins exactly where Tiffany had said he'd be.

Captain Daniels glanced fleetingly at Tebbins then back at Tiffany.

She gave him a slight nod.

Captain Daniels continued to walk down the aisle on the left side of the boat and around the back of the center seating section. He then walked up the aisle on the right side of the boat and stopped a few rows behind Tebbins.

Tiffany positioned herself in the aisle on the left side of the center seating section several rows behind Mohamed.

Captain Daniels took a deep breath, looked at Tim, and nodded.

"It's a go," whispered Tim into the intercom. "Make the announcement."

The PA system crackled to life with a voice of a male crewmember. "Please give us your attention . . . your attention please. We have repaired the engines, and in about five minutes, we will proceed to Avalon. There is a slight chance when we restart the engines that the dislodged debris could cause erratic vibration. This is normal. For your safety, all passengers please return to your seats now and remain seated until we are underway. We will tell you when it is safe to move around the cabin. Additional instructions will follow in a few minutes. Everyone please take their seats now. We're very sorry for the inconvenience."

While the announcement was being made, the crew fanned out, ostensibly to usher passengers still standing back to their seats. Tiffany and Captain Daniels used the distraction of the announcement to improve their positions with respect to the two terrorists. Tiffany's position was better in terms of controlling Mohamed, since he sat near the front of the center seating section one seat off the aisle, on the left side of the boat. She stood less than five feet behind him. She pointed the gun, concealed under a wrap borrowed from Betty, at the back of Mohamed's head.

Captain Daniels was less well position. Tebbins was in the center seating section but three seats in from the aisle on the right side of the boat. Daniels needed to be closer to Tebbins and he did not want any passengers between him and Tebbins. Calmly, in a low voice, he asked, "Excuse me, could you please move to another seat? There are several in the back. I need to be here when the engines are restarted." The passengers, although puzzled, moved without objection.

Captain Daniels now stood in the row directly behind Tebbins in an advantageous position to control him. The announcement, the activity of the crew, and the movement of the passengers, heightened Tebbins's and Mohamed's anxiety. Bewildered, they glanced at one another. A glance that ominously implied, *what do we do now.*

Daniels and Tiffany exchanged nods.

As soon as the aisles were clear, Daniels pulled his gun from his pocket and pressed it to the rear of Tebbins's head. Tiffany stepped closer to Mohamed, dropped Betty's wrap, and pressed her gun to his head.

"Mr. Tebbins, do not move," said Captain Daniels. "Please place your hands over your head and then bring them down slowly to the top of your head."

Tebbins did not move.

Pressing his gun harder, Captain Daniels said, "Do it. This is a gun and I'll use it."

Nearby passengers gasped.

When Tebbins sensed two crewmembers edging toward him he raised his arms over his and eased them down onto the top of his head.

Captain Daniels's eyes remained riveted on Tebbins's hands. "Good decision, now stand up . . . stand up real slow."

A deafening pistol shot resonated throughout the ship. Mohamed's actuators flew into the air, and tumbled to the carpeted deck in front of the refreshment stand. Screams reverberated throughout the boat. Mohamed's body jerked forward and then slumped onto the back of a seat occupied by a woman in the row in front of him. Blood had splattered onto the woman's head and back. She fainted.

"Don't worry," shouted Captain Daniels. "Everything's under control. I need you folks next to this man to move to the rear of the cabin—now!"

When the row was clear, crewmembers grabbed Tebbins and dragged him into the aisle.

Crewmembers swarmed into the cabin, shouting, "Return to your seats, return to your seats. Remain calm and return to your seats. Everything's under control."

A few passengers complied but most did not. The crush of passengers rushing into the forward cabin spread panic before them like a wave. Passengers in the front cabin jumped to their feet frantically looking for a place to run or hide. Then as quick as it had begun, it ended—there wasn't a whole lot of room to run and certainly no place to hide. Passengers who had rushed into the forward cabin anxiously remained standing in the aisles. Passengers who had stayed in the rear cabin nervously returned to their seats.

"Lie down," barked Captain Daniels. "I said lie down . . . face down . . . spread your legs. Do it or you're dead." Daniels thrust his pistol into the rear of Tebbins's head to assure compliance. Tim cuffed Tebbins. "Remember my friend," said Captain Daniels evenly, "this is a gun. How many of your asshole friends are on this ship? Answer me?"

"One," sputtered Tebbins.

"We don't have to worry about him," said Captain Daniels.

Tiffany raced up to Captain Daniels.

Grinning she said, "I have Mohamed's remotes."

She flashed them to Daniels and then tucked them and the gun into her purse. She pointed at Tebbins, "I want his also."

CHAPTER FIFTY-THREE

4:19 PM Saturday, August 21, 2010
Island Express Helicopter Terminal
Long Beach, California

"We're back on conference," said Jenn. "How'd it go?"

"I've had less exciting days, actually every day before this has been less exciting," said Tiffany.

"Are the passengers okay?" asked Douglas hesitantly.

"They're fine. Worried, anxious, but fine. We've just advised them about the evacuation plan a few minutes ago and we're in contact with the Coast Guard and the shore boats," said Captain Daniels.

"The passengers are calm all things considered," said Tiffany.

"All things considered, just what happened?" Jenn's voice tightened.

"Mohamed didn't do what I told him to do. He stood up, reached into his pocket, and pulled out what looked like TV remotes. He raised them over his head and started punching buttons. Well we . . . err . . . I didn't wait for the explosion. I shot him."

"You did what?"

"I wasted him. No one else was hurt. The cabin and a few passengers got a little messed up with blood and such, but no one was hurt. I have the actuators."

"You wasted him. My god, what went wrong?"

"Jenn, nothing went wrong," said Tiffany, sharply. "There wasn't any option. I followed the plan. Almost anything we did could've gone wrong. C'mon, Jenn, we knew that, this shouldn't be a surprise."

"What about Tebbins?"

"He's hog-tied and cuffed. One of the crew has a gun pressed against his head." Tiffany chortled. "His face is buried into the carpet on the deck."

"I'm afraid to ask . . . anything else?"

"No, we had it easy. We knew who the terrorists were. The situation on the other boat won't be easy."

"I know, I know. I've been thinking the same thing. We know what Christine looks like but no one on the express boat does. The other terrorist's a complete mystery . . . any ideas?"

"Based on what Mohamed did," Bill chimed in for the first time, "they'll try to detonate the bombs if something seems wrong. We should expect the same on the other boat and plan for that."

"Makes sense," added Douglas.

"The tall, unkempt, brunette—is there a better way to identify her?" asked Captain Gaspar. "She could be one of twenty or thirty women on board. Some tourists think the slob look is cool when they go to Catalina."

"She's covered head to toe in a gray granny dress," said Bill.

"We don't know what the man looks like, but we're pretty sure both are posing as divers," said Tiffany. "They've hidden the bombs in scuba tanks."

"Posing as scuba divers?" asked Captain Gaspar.

"Yeah, they have those huge bags that divers lug around," said Tiffany.

"That's helpful," said Captain Gaspar, "that's very helpful. I doubt we have more than five or six onboard. Divers typically don't use this crossing. They favor earlier or later boats. I'll have my first mate ask the crew."

"How will we know what equipment belongs to who?" asked Tiffany.

"We won't for sure," said Captain Gaspar. "Divers stow their equipment on the bow or stern so it's out of the way of the regular passenger baggage. Maybe one of the crew will remember who owns what."

"It's a long shot," said Douglas, "but it's something. Every little bit of information helps."

"Any other ideas?" asked Bill.

"I just had a thought," said Jenn. "Why do we want to match divers with their equipment?"

"Well, it would limit the people who we'd need to watch," said Tiffany.

"Yes, I understand that, but who cares about matching equipment with people. Why not first deal with the bombs and then deal with the terrorists?" said Jenn.

"I don't follow," said Gaspar.

"Me neither," added Tiffany.

"Jettison all the dive crap, all the dive bags. Deep-six it all," said Jenn. "Right now we're more interested in saving lives than capturing terrorists."

"I understand that, but we still won't know who the terrorists are," said Bill. "Matching diving equipment to a person would at least limit our search to six people or so instead of all the passengers. Oh wait, I get it. Dumping the bags in the ocean is easier than trying to match terrorists with equipment, which doesn't help us much anyway as we could easily match the diving equipment with the wrong person. If we dump *all* the dive stuff in the ocean, the divers will be angry, but who cares. And dumping the diving equipment might panic the terrorists and they might expose themselves. At worst, we can sort the terrorists from the other passengers later. Can we dump all the diving equipment before the terrorists detonate the bombs?"

"We should be able to," said Captain Gaspar. "If we chuck it all overboard before the terrorists recognize what we've done and they try to explode the bombs it won't matter. Even if we don't get the bombs into the ocean and they reveal themselves, we may have a chance to take them out before they can detonate the bombs."

". . . and we'll be in no worse position." said Jenn. "Captain, how much dive equipment is onboard?"

"I'd estimate less than twenty pieces. I'll get an accurate count."

His muffled voice could be heard giving instructions.

"Good, but don't do anything until we work out the details," said Jenn.

"There are eleven pieces," reported Captain Gaspar several moments later.

"That's not a lot," said Bill. "Assign a person to each piece and then on signal have them toss all of it overboard as fast as possible."

"Make the roller bags a priority and then get the rest," added Jenn.

"You must distract the terrorists. That is crucial," said Tiffany. "The signal to dump the scuba equipment can be an announcement to update the passengers about the engine trouble or something that will distract them for a few moments."

"Ditching won't take more than five or six seconds, we should be able to ditch the equipment during the announcement . . ." said Captain Gaspar. "Any chance the bombs could be somewhere else?"

"Not likely," said Tiffany. "The terrorists only took the dive bags on board, nothing else."

"Christine only had a roller duffle dive bag," added Bill.

"That's why the diver bags are priority," reiterated Jenn.

"How do we deal with the terrorists?" asked Gaspar.

"You have guns, don't you?" asked Tiffany.

"Two."

"The terrorists on this boat were in the rear cabin of the main deck in the center seating section. I'd think the terrorists on your boat would be sitting in similar locations. Have the crewmen with the guns in that area and tell them to kill anyone who acts suspicious or becomes aggressive."

"Kill anyone . . . are you serious?" gasped Captain Gaspar.

"She is, trust me," interjected Captain Daniels somberly.

"We could kill innocent people," said Gaspar.

"Shit happens," said Jenn. "When you're in the business of saving lives, collateral damage is expected and acceptable. Make an announcement for passengers to take their seats, no exceptions. That will limit the potential for misidentification. As Bill said when the announcement begins, start dumping the dive stuff into the ocean. Hopefully, we'll get lucky."

"Do it," said Douglas.

4:32 PM Saturday, August 21, 2010
The Express Boat outside the Long Beach Harbor
Breakwater
San Pedro Channel

"Please give us your attention . . . your attention please. We need everyone to take their seats while we restart the engines, no exceptions. Everyone please take your seats now. We will let you know when we are about to restart the engines. Thank you for your patience."

Passengers grumbled as the announcement ended but they begrudgingly started moving toward their seats. Deckhands reported the progress to the first mate.

"Is everyone seated?" asked Captain Gaspar.

"Yes," said the first mate.

"Okay, let's do it. You take the front part of the rear cabin, I'll take the back."

Captain Gaspar spoke into the intercom to order the announcement."

Four seconds later, a voice boomed over the Public Address system. "Attention . . . attention everyone. Please remain seated, we're about to restart the engines." Simultaneously with the announcement, the turbines sputtered and kicked in, and the ship shuddered briefly. The passengers cheered loudly.

No one noticed the crew jettisoning the diving equipment, or if they did, they did not seem to care. That is, no one except Boris Massouli, who saw dive bags splashing into the ocean. Massouli leaped to his feet waving his actuators above his head and shouted in Arabic, "There is no power or strength save by Allah. Die infidels, die unbelievers!"

He poked at one of his actuators twice in succession and then again. Nothing happened . . . there was no explosion. Then he repeatedly poked at the other one—still no explosion. He could not comprehend why Allah had failed him. "There is no power or strength save by Allah!" he shouted again.

"What's with that jerk?"

"What's he doing? What's he saying?"

"That sounds like Arabic."

"He's a terrorist! He's a terrorist! He's going to kill us!"

"What's that in his hand?"

"A bomb . . ."

". . . A bomb!"

"Get him! Get him! Remember flight 93 . . . get him, *let's roll!*"

Several of the passengers in their twenties and thirties bolted from their seats and descended on Massouli. *Let's roll* were the last words Massouli ever heard. Within moments, he disappeared under a pile of humanity resembling football players scrambling to retrieve a fumble. Feet and fists pummeled Massouli. His muffled cries changed to muted grunts. Then silence. His body sank to the deck under the pile of twenty- and thirty-something year olds.

"There is no power or strength save by Allah," screamed Christine in Arabic. She had recognized something had gone terribly wrong. She leaped to her feet repeating in Arabic, "There is no power or strength save by Allah!" She repeatedly poked at one of her actuators but with results similar to Massouli's. Her eyes flashed in disbelief. "Allah has failed me," she murmured.

The twenty- and thirty-something year old passengers stopped pummeling Massouli and glanced at this new lunatic. They quickly recognized they needed to deal with her. The twenty- and thirty-somethings abandoned Massouli's lifeless body and piled on the female terrorist. Christine disappeared beneath them. No one heard her final pleas.

Captain Gaspar had no target. Actually, he had too many targets—the pile of twenty- and thirty-somethings writhing on the carpeted deck. By the time he figured out what had happened, it was over. The twenty- and thirty-somethings calmly returned to their seats seemingly disengaged and disinterested with what had just occurred. Christine and Boris lie dead sprawled in pools of their own blood.

"It's over. Please remain calm," the announced Captain Gaspar over the Public Address system.

The passengers that witnessed the incident did not require reassurance. Inwardly, they prized the outcome. Outwardly, they remained indifferent—apathetic.

4:39 PM Saturday, August 21, 2010
The Pilothouse on the Express Boat outside the Long Beach Harbor Breakwater San Pedro Channel

The Coast Guard cutter Samuel Adams pulled alongside the express boat outside the Long Beach Harbor breakwater.

"I'm off the conference call, I have to deal with the Coast Guard," said Captain Gaspar. "Thanks to all of you, we'll talk later."

"Wait," shouted Douglas, "What's that din?"

"That din *is* the passengers. They're singing God Bless America."

CHAPTER FIFTY-FOUR

10:26 PM Saturday, August 21, 2010
The Mole
Avalon, Santa Catalina Island, California

"Bye, love," said Bill. "Talk to you soon. Let me know how tomorrow unfolds."

Bill ended the call and closed his cellphone. He turned to Tiffany's husband, Tom. "The FBI's still grilling Jenn."

"Grilling her? Why?"

"According to Jenn, she's the only game in town. The FBI read Ken his rights and he clammed up so they shipped him off to the hospital. Jenn says the FBI is trying to insert themselves into the final picture," said Bill, scrutinizing the passengers disembarking the most recent arrival of a shore boat. "Any sign of Tiffany? How many trips are those boats going to make?"

"Tiffany told me the Coast Guard is screening each passenger and their luggage before releasing them."

"You'd think Tiffany would have some priority and get released early," said Bill.

"Get released early—come on, Bill, give me a break. Do you think for a moment, she would leave that boat as long as there was a remote chance she could get herself into the middle of something else? You know her as well as I do."

"You're right. They'd have to stuff her into a life jacket and throw her overboard before she'd volunteer to leave."

"She told me the Coast Guard spent about an hour with her and didn't seem overly troubled that she'd killed a terrorist. They told her they'd contact her later on that . . . What about Jenn?"

"She said when the FBI finally showed up, the LA SWAT team had already arrested Ken. She thinks the FBI's trying to figure out a way to get credit for the whole shebang."

"It looks like the entire town of Avalon is still awake," said Tom. "Have you heard some of the stories? People have wild imaginations. My favorite is that the Coast Guard removed Bin Laden from the express boat and has him in custody in the Casino."

10:59 PM Saturday, August 21, 2010
The Mole
Avalon, Santa Catalina Island, California

"Tiffany called and said she's on this shore boat," said Tom pointing at the boat tied up at the mooring. "Do you see her?"

"Not yet. Oh there she is! Boy, does she look happy," snickered Bill.

"Like the cat that ate the canary," added Tom, laughing.

Tiffany trudged up the gangway, engaged in an intense one-way conversation with a woman who looked frazzled, disheveled, and unmistakably not interested in anything Tiffany had to say.

"Over here, honey," shouted Tom, waving his arms.

Tiffany searched for Tom's voice and when she spotted him, a Cheshire cat grin crossed her face. She waved, deserted her uninterested fellow passenger, and raced up the gangway into Tom's arms.

"Thank god you're safe and back home, honey."

"It was great," she said. Then she turned to Bill. "See, I told you . . . Jenn and I both told you, we could do it—and we did!"

"Good job . . . but you're both lucky to be alive."

"What's luck got to do with it? We're good . . . we're all so damn good! We're better at this crap than the whole kit and caboodle of Homeland Security, FBI, LA Sheriffs, and all their dead-ass affiliates rolled into one . . . I need a drink."

"We have reservations at Steve's Steak House."

"Steve's? Steve's is closed. It's after eleven. He's in bed."

"Guess again, Miss Rambo. He's been feeding your boat friends gratis since eight earlier this evening. As has Russ, at Armstrong's," said Bill.

"Then why are we waiting around here?"

11:41 PM Saturday, August 21, 2010
Steve's Steakhouse
Avalon, Santa Catalina Island, California

"Geez, there are a lot of people still in the streets," said Tiffany, "and Steve saved us a great window table. That was nice of him."

"You're a hero," said Bill.

"I know. Isn't it great!"

Tom glanced at Bill, "How're we going to live with this and we haven't heard from Jenn yet."

"I told you it'd be tough," said Bill.

"Only a joke, it's only a joke," said Tiffany, laughing at her own sarcasm.

Their table server, Ann, had waited patiently for a break in the conversation. "So, what can I get for the hero?" she said grinning.

"Oh terrific," said Bill, covering his eyes and shaking his head.

"I'll have a daiquiri, a double," said Tiffany.

"And you guys?"

"Doubles all around and bring the cold shakers," said Tom.

"Yeah, we're going to need them," said Bill resolutely.

"Anything to eat?"

"Not for me," said Tiffany.

"And you guys?"

"I'll have a T-bone, medium rare," said Bill.

"Me too, but make mine well done," Said Tom. "Aren't you hungry, honey?"

"Should I be?"

12:33 PM Sunday August 22, 2010
Villa Portofino Ristorante
Avalon, Santa Catalina Island, California

The conversation among Bill, Tom, and Tiffany paused for a few moments. Tiffany took her cellphone out of her purse and declared, "Let's call Jenn."

"It's almost one, honey, you'll wake her up," said Tom.

"No I won't. I spoke to her just before I got off the shore boat. I bet she's still working over the FBI."

Tiffany punched the speed dial.

"Hey Jenn, it's me, Tiffany."

"I know, sweetie, you're in my cell."

"When are you coming home?"

"Don't know. The FBI showed up at eight-thirty and they haven't quit yet. I'm bushed. Where are you?"

"At Steve's with Tom and Bill."

"Shouldn't you be at home, asleep?"

"Why?"

"It's almost one and it's been a long day. If I were home, I'd be in bed, asleep. Look, I'll see you tomorrow. Get some sleep. Bye."

"Bye," said Tiffany.

"How's Jenn?" asked Tom.

"She's a wimp."

"She's a wimp? Why do you say that? She's one of your best friends," said Tom.

"*She is my best friend.* She told me to go home and get some sleep."

"She's right," said Bill.

"You're all wimps."

6:34 PM Sunday August 22, 2010
Sidewalk Patio at the Ristorante Villa Portofino
Avalon, Santa Catalina Island, California

Tiffany and Tom sat at an outside table overlooking Avalon Bay sipping cocktails.

"I can't wait to see Jenn . . . it's been two days, for god's sake! We need to compare notes," said Tiffany. "She's spent more time with the FBI than she spent catching Ken. I wonder what gives."

"She's dealing with the FBI. You only had the Coast Guard," said Tom.

Tiffany arched an eyebrow but decided to ignore her husband's comment.

"Isn't this the best place for supper on a splendid balmy evening? We're outside with the bay across the street . . . isn't it great?" She sipped at her drink. "It was nice of them to give us such a great table. I wonder when Jenn will get here. Can you believe that SWAT team dude got her a flight back on an LA Police helicopter . . . isn't that great?"

"They'll be along soon," said Tom.

"I hope so. Another daiquiri is in order," said Tiffany.

Tom motioned to Tina, their table server, and then said to Tiffany, "Oh by the way, what did the Sheriff call about before we left the house?"

"He wanted to know what happened to the gun."

"The gun . . . what happen to it?"

"I have it."

"You what—you kept a gun involved in a killing? It never belonged to you in the first place, it's express boat property. They just lent it to you. Where is it?"

"They didn't lend it to me. I took it from that dumb ass First Mate Donnelly who didn't have the balls to use it. It's in my purse. Want to see it?"

"No . . . you have to give it back."

"Yeah, that's what the Sheriff said. I told him I'd bring it to the station on Monday."

"What possessed you to keep it?"

"It's a souvenir. No one asked for it so I kept it. Weren't you going to get me another drink?"

6:47 PM Sunday August 22, 2010
Sidewalk Patio at the Ristorante Villa Portofino
Avalon, Santa Catalina Island, California

Tom put his cellphone on the table. "That was Bill. Jenn just got off the helicopter, they'll be here soon. He wants us to order a bottle of Sauvignon Blanc . . . Nobilo."

*   *   *

Tiffany nursed her drink while keeping an eye on Crescent Avenue.

"There they are . . . there's Jenn!"

Tiffany darted from her seat and raced down Crescent toward Jenn and Bill. "We did it! We did it!" shouting as she ran up to Jenn. They hugged each other.

"We did," said Jenn.

"We all did it!" said Tiffany.

Tiffany turned and simultaneously embraced Jenn and Bill.

"You did. Thank god both of you are alive," said Bill.

"We're damn good. We are so damn good!"

"Where's that wine?" asked Jenn.

"We got it. We're on the patio," said Tiffany, pointing. "Wine's on the patio."

Tiffany grabbed Bill's and Jenn's arm and dragged them to the restaurant. Tom handed Bill and Jenn each a glass of wine and then greeted Jenn warmly.

7:09 PM Sunday August 22, 2010
Sidewalk Patio at the Ristorante Villa Portofino
Avalon, Santa Catalina Island, California

"So, how did you finally handle the FBI? Those guys sound like a nightmare," asked Tom.

"For sure. They were angling to dismiss out of hand what we'd done and take credit for everything. The questions kept coming and coming, the same ones over and over. They wouldn't go away. I didn't get to sleep until after three o'clock."

"I can relate to that on two counts. Endless repeated questions from law enforcement and not getting to sleep until early morning . . . thank you, Blessinggame and Morales, and thank you Tiffany," said Bill wryly, looking at her.

"Amen," said Tom

"They criticized me for what I did. Can you believe that?"

"What the hell else could you have done? You had a lunatic with a bomb transmitter trying to kill eight hundred people. What were you supposed to do, negotiate? Radical extremists don't negotiate. The FBI knows that—the FBI never negotiates," said Tom, shaking his head incredulously.

"One of them actually accused me of using excessive force. He questioned why I had to break both Ken's wrists. He said one would have more than done the job."

"How the hell would he know?" asked Bill.

"One hand held the transmitter, the other a gun, that's two wrists by my count," said Tiffany.

"Later, he said I shouldn't have shot Ken because it will compromise their case against him.

"Their case! They wouldn't have a case without you . . . or any of us, for that matter. They'd have eight hundred people dead and a terrorist on the loose. How could that compromise their case?" asked Tiffany.

"Something about abusive interrogation . . . god knows what that's about. I got the information I needed to save eight hundred people. I guess they considered that abusive," said Jenn sarcastically.

"What were those guys smoking? What did you tell them? I would have told them to go fuck themselves," said Tiffany.

"We all know what you would have told them, honey," said Tom, dryly.

"I told them I should've blown Ken's balls off and then blasted his dead ass through the terminal wall after I got the information I needed. That would've put all of us out of the anguish of dealing with the aftermath and a trial."

"Seems logical. Did they understand why you didn't kill him?" asked Tiffany.

"Don't you wonder? Good thing Lieutenant Collins stayed around. The FBI tried to get him to leave, but he wouldn't. He told them jurisdiction wasn't determined so he was hanging out to hear the evidence."

"Good for him," said Tom.

"Did he help?" asked Tiffany.

"Boy did he. He didn't give an inch. Eventually, he backed those FBI bozos into a corner. I don't think they like each other."

"How did he do that?" asked Bill.

"He told them Ken was a threat and my actions had prevented him from becoming more aggressive. He told them I probably saved Ken's life as his team would have killed him for sure."

"Really!"

"Yeah, and then he told them he condoned everything I'd done. He said that he was there . . . he was a *witness*. The FBI shuddered at the 'w' word. Lieutenant Collins used the 'w' word frequently. He said I had prevented a catastrophe, captured two terrorists, and the FBI hadn't done a damn thing except show up after the party was over. They pretty much gave up after that."

"That's great. He did good," said Tiffany.

"Yeah he did, he lied."

CHAPTER FIFTY-FIVE

(Thirteen Months Later) 11:35 AM Monday, September 19, 2011
Watson Financial Services, Metropole Avenue
Avalon, Santa Catalina Island, California

"Can I help you?" Tiffany scrutinized the man. *He's dressed too normal to be an islander. I hope he isn't an IRS auditor or such. Probably not, they always call for an appointment.*

"I'm looking for Mr. and Mrs. Watson."

"They're not here. I'm Mr. Watson's assistant. Can I help? I'm Tiffany." *Definitely not an islander. No one here uses terms like Mr. or Mrs.* She became wary.

"Tiffany, yes, you're in the file. Great work on the Catalina case. You saved the government a lot of money. Off the record, and just between you and me, I believe judge, jury, and executioner has its place. I'm pleased to meet you. My name is Terry Harrington. I'm with Homeland Security."

"May I see your identification folio, Mr. Harrington?"

"Of course . . . yes, of course. That question should not surprise me, should it? If memory serves, you are Miss Action-oriented. You're not going to shoot me are you?" Harrington laughed at his joke while handing his folio to Tiffany.

"Depends," said Tiffany not looking away from Harrington's folio.

"Err . . . thanks. Do you . . . err . . . do you have a gun?"

"Want to see it?"

Without waiting for an answer, Tiffany grabbed the hemline of her summer weight white cotton sundress and raised the skirt to her chest. Her action invited Harrington's attention more to her sheer panties than to the Beretta strapped to her thigh.

"Very nice . . . err . . . a leg holster . . . I mean the holster and the pistol of course . . . I mean the gun err the holster. It's all nice, very nice."

"You like my gun? It's a Beretta Brigadier .40 caliber. It packs quite a wallop. The Brigadier was designed for the INS. Want to see more?"

"Err . . . no, it's all very pretty . . . the gun that is. No thank you, I've seen enough."

Tiffany released her hem and smiled at his discomfort. *At least he knows I'm a natural brunette.* "I have a bigger gun, a Beretta Vertec. Want to see it?"

"No, thank you."

Tiffany memorized the ID, R845902. She would check it out later.

"Why do you have a gun—do you handle large amounts of cash?"

"Checks only and not as many as we'd like."

"So why the gu . . ."

"The fatwa."

"The fatwa?"

"The fatwa. Come now, Mr. Harrington, your file must contain that." Tiffany narrowed her eyes, cocked an eyebrow, and glared at Harrington. "Half the nut-case Islamic fundamentalists in the world consider Bill, Jenn, and I their first-class ticket to martyrdom and paradise. Whether they kill us or we kill them, their ticket is punched and they're on their way. Wheeee . . . an E-ride to Allah! They kill us or we kill them . . . low risk for them, high risk for us. Thank you, Mr. Harrington," said Tiffany handing Harrington his folio. "Now, what can I do for you?"

"I would like to speak with Mr. and Mrs. Watson . . . err . . . The fatwa thing—that isn't in the file, as I recall."

"Tsk tsk, sloppy record-keeping, Mr. Harrington. The FBI believed we had a need to protect ourselves after that half-wit moronic lowlife Islamic cleric decreed a fatwa. So they authorized us to carry concealed weapons. Evans occasionally looks in on us to see if a terrorist is lurking nearby or to check our pulses." She smiled sarcastically. "We have a 24/7 hotline of our very own—straight to the FBI, straight to Evans. You want to talk with Bill and Jenn . . . about what?"

"To debrief the Watsons. They did an outstanding job and we want to let them know that we, and the nation, appreciate what they did . . . and, oh yes, of course you, you did a great job too."

"Thank you, we're always happy to help out. So what has happened with those jackasses? Have they been executed?"

"Well . . . err . . . we believe they'll be tried soon, hopefully very soon, and we also hope to try some of their associates along with them. We're working toward capturing the associates. Execution may take a while longer. You know appeals and stuff like that. If anybody deserves the death penalty, these men do. I'm here to bring the Watsons up to date . . . and you also."

"Does Homeland Security have telephones?"

"I should've called ahead," said Harrington sheepishly.

"Something like that would've been nice. They're at Jenn's jewelry shop. Give me a second, I'll close down here and take you there."

"Oh please don't do that on my behalf. I know you're running a business and need to be here. I can find them . . . you said a jewelry shop?"

"Not a problem. Have a seat. I'll be back in a few. I have to turn off some equipment in the back. Here's the remote you can surf the channels . . . cartoons are on thirteen."

Cartoons? Why would I be interested in cartoons? wondered Harrington.

"Not a problem," mumbled Tiffany to herself as she walked into the back room. *I hate that phrase. It makes me sound like a twenty-something airhead.* She hit two on her cellphone.

"Boss, a man from Homeland Security is here . . ."

After a few minutes, Tiffany returned to the front office. "We're good to go. Come with me, it's only a few blocks."

"Mrs. Watson has a jewelry business? Hmm . . . that wasn't in the report."

Tiffany shook her head in disbelief. "It seems your file is mostly holes. Jenn expanded her Internet jewelry business after she left Raytheon and moved to the island. I help her with it."

"She left Raytheon?"

"Yes, the capturing the terrorists' thing gave us a lot of visibility and publicity. Bill was able to expand his business significantly and that allowed Jenn to quit Raytheon and move to the island permanently—seems like another hole in your file. Your file is looking more and more like Swiss cheese the more we talk."

Harrington looked away.

"That's when she opened the jewelry store," said Tiffany.

"What kind of jewelry?"

"Basic stuff now, we're just getting started. Our goal is to sell limited lines from around the world. Jewelry you can't buy in a mall."

"Sounds great. Any lines yet?"

"Only one, art pins, but we have a super lead on a unique gemstone, Gold-in-Quartz, mined in Northern California. Jenn plans to go there in a few months on a buying trip." Tiffany pointed, "There's the shop, over there on the corner, next to the Villa Portofino."

"I see it. The Jewelry Hunter," said Harrington.

12:23 PM Monday, September 19, 2011
The Jewelry Hunter Store, Crescent Avenue
Avalon, Santa Catalina Island, California

"Good afternoon. Mr. and Mrs. Watson, I presume. No pun intended," laughed Harrington a tad nervously.

"I'm Bill; this is my wife, Jenn."

"It's a pleasure and an honor to meet both of you. I'm Terry Harrington, Homeland Security," said Harrington handing business cards around.

"Thank you, Terry, welcome to Catalina. You caught us a little by surprise."

"Sorry about that." Harrington glanced at Tiffany.

She glared.

"What can we do for you?" asked Jenn.

"No, it's what the Secretary and I want to do for you. We'd like to give you an update on where we are on the case and what we expect as it goes forward. Do you have a few minutes?"

"Of course," said Bill. "But as you can see this shop is super tiny and there isn't room for chairs. Should we do this somewhere else?"

"Absolutely not a problem, here is fine. First, I want to thank all of you for your effort in stopping those maniacs."

Harrington glanced again at Tiffany, who this time, smiled back.

"How is Khalid, or Ken, or whatever his name is?" asked Jenn.

"It's Al-Hussein, that's his real name. He's a Saudi national associated with al-Qaeda. He's fine. His thigh wound healed nicely and he has almost full use of his left hand. The right one is still in bad shape. It's been an issue."

"An issue?" asked Bill.

"Yes, it's slowed down bringing him to trial. His attorneys raised allegations of excessive force. In a separate action, they requested damages from the government for injuries. The judge threw out their damage claim against Mrs. Watson. However, the court is considering the excessive force issue. We should hear in a few months or so."

"That was so kind of the judge to drop the action against me . . . I should've killed that son-of-a-bitch Al-Hussein or whatever his name is when I had the chance and saved all of us from this bullshit," said Jenn evenly, ending with an exaggerated demure smile.

Harrington remembered Tiffany's holster and the contents of her panties. He blushed and continued hurriedly. "Err . . . well, that might have prompted a wrongful death suit."

"Has our whole goddamned legal system gone to hell in a hand basket?" asked Bill.

Harrington noted that Tiffany had moved her right hand to her skirt waist. This time he didn't remember her panties.

"Ahh . . . and then there is the county," said Harrington, looking at the front door then at Tiffany, and then at Bill.

"The county?" asked Jenn.

"Yes LA County. They want jurisdiction. They want to try Al-Hussein on multiple murder counts."

"Now there's a novel idea . . ." said Jenn sarcastically.

". . . especially since the county refused to acknowledge Al-Hussein's existence until Jenn handed him over to the SWAT team," added Bill tightly.

"Hey . . . give those guys a break! At least they were trying," giggled Tiffany.

Harrington was visibly squirming by this point. He had never dealt with over-the-top vigilantes before and as far as he was concerned, that's what these people were. Harrington continued, "Al-Hussein is in Guantanamo and Tebbins is in Leavenworth. We expect both will be tried . . . hopefully soon."

"So, what was all this about? What did they want to do?" asked Bill.

"Pretty much all the terrorists except Al-Hussein were to be sacrificed. He'd killed or planned to kill all his accomplices. Tiffany, and we believe some passengers on the express boat, took care of a fair share of his plan. The FBI interviewed the passengers on the express boat but none recalled how Olson or Massouli died. They didn't remember seeing anything. Same with the crew. It was odd. The crew said that they had pressing matters at the time. I guess it was hectic.

"Al-Hussein also killed the owner of the Avalon Bay Bar and his manager and he burned, or had someone burn, the bar to the ground. The FBI found a body in the rubble. When the FBI searched the terrorists' compound, they found a shallow grave containing the body of a woman. You guys disrupted Al-Hussein's plans. He was going to detonate bombs on the express boats from the helicopter and kill the last four people who could identify him along with 857 passengers and crew. He had tickets to Afghanistan via seven countries and six fraudulent passports when the FBI apprehended him . . ."

"What!" shouted Tiffany. "What do you mean when the FBI apprehended him! The FBI didn't apprehend him, Jenn did. She turned the prick over to them."

Both Tiffany's hands went to her waist.

Harrington's eyes flashed to Tiffany's hands. "Why yes, yes of course . . . Jenn apprehended him. What I said was a manner of speaking . . . a technicality." Harrington wished Tiffany would move her hands from her waist. "Catalina was part of a larger plan. There were eight other targets. Seven targets, including Catalina, failed. They were marginally successful in Schaumburg and Detroit. I'm sure you remember those; they were in the newspapers. Except for Catalina, the failed attacks didn't make the papers. Catalina made the papers because of you folks. The government compromised the other attacks long before they were to happen. They classified them as secret . . . and the decision to classify them secret was classified secret."

"How come?" asked Bill.

"National security. As a policy, the government doesn't want potential terrorists' activities known to the public . . . that's also secret."

"Oh isn't this wonderful . . . a secret-secret-secret!" laughed Tiffany as she placed her right index finger in front of pursed lips. "Shhhh, don't worry, we won't tell."

At least she moved her hand away from her waist. I hope she's right handed, thought Harrington.

"Well, you should know that we're indebted to all of you for your consistently indifferent response to our fervent pleas for help while all this was going on," said Bill sarcastically. "The FBI didn't even assign a case number until it was over. The county wanted to turn it into a drug case, and all you Homeland Security guys did was assign a case number."

"Well yes, we recognized the severity of the situation and assigned a case number . . . ," said Harrington, proudly, smiling from ear to ear. ". . . and . . . we opened a file."

"A case number and an open file—that and five-fifty-five gets you a cappuccino at Starbucks," said Jenn in obvious disgust.

"And . . . your file is like a piece of Swiss cheese—full of holes," added Tiffany knowingly.

Harrington stood up anxiously and prepared to leave, wishing nothing more than to put as much distance between himself and these over-the-top vigilantes as quickly as he could. "I know it appeared that we weren't all that interested at first, but we're a very busy organization. We try our best."

"Whatever. Anything else you want to share about these creeps?" asked Bill.

"Yes. Thanks to our investigation, we linked Al-Hussein to terrorist organizations in Brooklyn and overseas . . ."

"And?" asked Jenn, her head cocked to the left.

". . . We're watching them."

"Terrific, that's really terrific. It has been over a year and no one has been tried, much less executed, the government is considering excessive force charges in a situation that saved almost nine hundred lives, and the FBI is watching known terrorists run around doing their thing. Has it occurred to you, they just might be watching back?" asked Jenn shaking her head in disgust.

"We believe we are close to making arrests," said Harrington, purposefully.

Tiffany brightened, "Want help?"

WHAT'S REAL AND WHAT'S NOT REAL

Avalon Bay, a Jewelry Hunter Thriller is a work of fiction. The characters depicted are fictional and do not represent any person living or dead. That said, the novel is set in the real town of Avalon on the real island of Catalina; the story describes real issues, albeit in a fictional setting, present in today's world. While the general descriptions of the localities, business establishments, and residential communities are real with some minor alteration to fit the story, the characters that inhabit those locations are not real.

The Catalina Island Conservancy is real. It was established as a 501(c)(3) nonprofit organization with the responsibility to conserve and preserve the 88% (42,135 acres) of the island under its stewardship by eliminating selective invasive plant and animal species, protecting and fostering naturally occurring species, and overseeing other ecological matters. Scenes in the book depicting Conservancy activities, its employees, and opinions of the book's fictional characters are not real. The characters depicted in the book that inhabit the Catalina Island Conservancy are not real. The employees and the situations associated with the story are fictional and do not in any way indicate the manner in which the Santa Catalina Island Conservancy normally operates.

The Santa Catalina Island Company (commonly referred to as the Island Company) is real. Scenes in the book depicting Island Company activities, its employees, and opinions of the book's fictional characters are not real. The characters depicted in the book that inhabit the Island Company are not real. The employees and the situations associated with the story are fictional and do not in any way indicate the manner in which the company normally operates.

The Island Express Helicopters and The Catalina Island Express boat company are real. The physical descriptions of their facilities, the helicopters, and the express boats are accurate to the best of my abilities. The employees and the situations associated with story as depicted in the book are fictional and do not in any way indicate the manner in which those companies normally operate.

Hamilton Cove is real; the actual units described in the story do not exist. The description of the community is correct to the best of my ability.

The Interior described in the book (42,135 acres comprising 88% of the island of Catalina) is primarily the responsibility of the Catalina Island Conservancy. Within the Interior are the Airport-in-the-Sky and the airport café; they are real. The employees of the Airport-in-the-Sky and the airport café are not real.

Locations of the scenes in the city of Avalon are generally real. The restaurants (Armstrong's Fish Market & Seafood Restaurant, Steve's Steak House, and the Villa Portofino) are real, Vons is real, the mole is real, the Casino is real, the Descanso Beach Club is real, the Marlin Club is real, and the city streets described in the story are real. The characters depicted in these locations are not real. The public phones were real but have since been removed. The Avalon Bay Bar, the Jewelry Hunter store, and Watson Financial Services do not exist.

References to the US Army Ranger School, West Point, and Desert Storm are accurate.

Quotations from the Qur'an are compiled from several translations of the Qur'an and are accurate to the extent the translations are correct. The participants in the Avalon Jihad are fictional. Many parts of the sermons and speeches of Khalid are from actual Islamic fundamentalist clerics opined in actual Friday Prayers (*jum'ah*).

BIBLIOGRAPHY

Ali, Arooj Ahmed. *Al-Qur'ān*. Princeton, New Jersey.: Princeton University Press. 1994.

Fadl, Khaled Abou El. *The Great Theft*. New York, New York.: Harper Collins. 2005.

Gaafar, Fethi & Jane Wightwick. *Arabic*. New York, New York.: Hippocrene Books, Inc. 2007.

Haleem, Abdel. *Qur'an*. trans. MAS Abdel Haleem. Oxford, England.: Oxford University Press. 2008.

Irving, Washington. *Life of Mohammed*. Ipswich, Massachusetts.: The Ipswich Press. 1989. (originally published December 1849 by Putnam, New York, New York).

Lawrence, Bruce. *The Qur'an*. New York, New York.: Grove Press. 2007.

Machiavelli, Niccolò. *The Prince*. trans. Peter Bondanella. Oxford, England.: Oxford University Press. 2005.

—. *Discourses on Livy.* Trans. Julia Bondanella and Peter Bondanella. Oxford, England.: Oxford University Press. 1997.

Monsouri, Fethi. *Instant Arabic.* North Clarendon, Vermont. Tuttle Publishing. 2007.

Smith, Huston. *The Illustrated World Religions.* New York, new York.: Harper San Francisco. 1995.

BIOGRAPHY

 Ron von Freymann earned a BS degree from the United States Military Academy at West Point and was then appointed an officer in the United States Army. Upon graduating from the Army Ranger School Ron was assigned to the 25th Infantry Division. Returning to the states after a combat command tour of duty, Ron was assigned to the United States Army's Behavioral Research Laboratory; while there Ron earned a master's degree from the George Washington University, attending courses at night. As a seasoned combat commander augmented with experience gained at the United States Army's Behavioral Research Laboratory, Ron possesses unique insight into the mind-set of terrorists, their motivation, and their tactics. Ron appreciates the difficulty to discover and defeat terrorist activity before they can complete their objective. Ron resides with his wife, Janet, in Avalon, Catalina; on California's Central Coast; and in San Francisco.

CPSIA information can be obtained at www.ICGtesting.com
Printed in the USA
BVOW011625100113

309423BV00001B/1/P

9 781477 220214